What Happened
After Mr Jones Died

Paul Wreyford

O&U
Onwards & Upwards

Onwards and Upwards Publishers

3 Radfords Turf
Cranbrook
Exeter
EX5 7DX
United Kingdom.

www.onwardsandupwards.org

First edition, published in the United Kingdom by Onwards and Upwards Publishers Ltd. (2019).

ISBN: 978-1-78815-731-5
Typeface: Sabon LT
Graphic design: LM Graphic Design

Printed in the United Kingdom.

This book is dedicated to:

Daphne and Dennis Wreyford

"And if by grace, then it cannot be based on works; if it were, grace would no longer be grace."

Romans 11:6

1

"Time for him had merged itself in Eternity; he was, as we say, no more."

Characteristics
Thomas Carlyle

IF GORDON HAD KNOWN THAT HE HAD ONLY A FEW minutes to live, he would have probably spent them eating chocolate. Of course, that was the problem... Gordon *didn't* know that he had only a few minutes to live. However, he should perhaps have realised it was too early in the evening to be suffering from 'cabin fever' – that being what he put his malaise down to at first. He had been feeling restless and a little queasy even before Bill had suggested that they should play charades.

"It is Christmas, after all," Bill justified. There could be no other reason, of course.

Gordon's rotund housemate grabbed a handful of peanuts from a bowl on the coffee table and bundled them into his mouth, before leaping from his chair and positioning himself in the centre of the living room.

"Right, I've got one," he declared, hitching up his jeans excitedly. "You'll never get it."

Gordon groaned and sank into his armchair.

"Turn that TV off, Clare!" Bill demanded, lobbing a peanut in the direction of his inattentive friend. "You've been watching it *all* night."

"It's only half past seven," Clare pleaded, flicking away the said peanut that had landed on the open copy of her *Radio Times*. "You're not going to prevent me from watching *Coronation Street* like you did last year."

"Right, where's the remote?" Bill responded, knocking a bowl of crisps on to the carpet as he began his search. No one made any attempt to clear up the mess. "It doesn't matter," Bill continued, deliberately adopting a new position in front of the television screen. "I'm starting anyway. Ready?"

Gordon groaned again and sank *further* into his armchair.

It had been like any other Christmas Day, which might explain the lack of enthusiasm that greeted Bill's suggestion – or perhaps we should say *decision* – that it was time to play party games. The housemates did so, under duress, every year.

It was normal for Gordon to develop 'cabin fever', as he called it. He only needed to get out of the house for a couple of hours a day to keep it at bay. And, of course, he *had* left the 'cabin' to attend the Christmas morning service at church. On a normal day, that would suffice. However, Christmas Day was no normal day. The 'fever' could grip much earlier. Gordon put it down to the fact that he felt obliged to socialise: to sit in front of the television or play charades. Do not get me wrong, Gordon was not an unsociable fellow, but he was a creature of habit. Christmas Day was different from other days and that irked him. He did not like the fact that you were expected to do something different on Christmas Day, even if you preferred to do what you would normally do on all the other days of the year. Gordon knew he had to make an effort and it was an unwritten rule that those left in the house at Christmas should spend the big day together. You could hardly retreat to your room. And this year all five housemates had declined various family invitations and were present, the first time ever. However, the novelty of that – if there could be such a thing among five people who also share a house for the other 364 days of the year – had worn off even before the Queen's speech.

And so, yes, Gordon could have perhaps been forgiven for initially assuming that 'cabin fever' had struck, though his agitation eventually gave way to a feeling of drowsiness and lethargy. Yes, he was feeling very sleepy. However, he could hardly retire for the night... just after 7:30pm... and on Christmas Day! The fact he was a few years older than his housemates and affectionately mocked for the 'privilege' would have also had much to do with his decision to stay put. Our noble hero should have just confessed he was not feeling well, but Gordon did not want to spoil the party.

"Is it a film?" Veronica inquired, all eyes now focused on the gesticulating Bill.

"How many words did you say it was?" Alex added.

"Sorry, have you started?" Clare chipped in, with a hint of sarcasm in her voice.

Gordon tried to focus on the animated figure of Bill, but chose not to partake in the proceedings. And he soon found himself looking beyond the large frame of his friend to one of the fairy lights on the Christmas tree. He was trying to work out if the magenta-coloured bulb was flickering slightly. Yes, it was. He would have to do something about that. And on any other day, he probably would have got up there and then to sort it out. That should have been another clue to the fact it was *not* 'cabin fever'. Gordon really wasn't himself tonight.

The voices of his friends became more distant and his eyes started to close. Sleep was only prevented when he heard his name being called.

"Gordon!"

Bill had finally spotted that his housemate had not been giving him his full attention.

"Gordon!" he barked again. "You're not dropping off to sleep, are you?"

Gordon rubbed his eyes and stretched.

"No. I'm listening. You carry on."

"You're looking a bit pale," Clare suggested. "Are you feeling all right?"

"I'm just a bit tired," Gordon responded, contriving a yawn.

"That will teach you to get up at the crack of dawn to open your presents," Alex quipped.

Gordon shifted uncomfortably. He did not like people staring at him.

"Are you sure you're all right?" Veronica persevered. "Not had too much wine, have you?"

"Stop fussing," Gordon snapped. "I'm absolutely fine. You just carry on and put Bill out of his misery."

His friends obliged – or attempted to. When all eyes were back on Bill, Gordon hauled his lethargic body into an upright position in an attempt to rouse himself, even going as far as to find the most uncomfortable position he could in a bid to stay awake, still determined not to spoil the fun. However, it was not long before he found himself slipping back into the armchair, as though it were sucking him in. His bid to stay awake was doomed and he soon got to that wonderful point when you no longer have the desire to resist impending sleep. Gordon's eyes began to close once more, the magenta-coloured fairy light that had attracted his gaze becoming blurred, before darkness and unconsciousness freed him from reality. He could no longer hear the protestations of Bill, who was becoming increasingly frustrated over his friends' inability to 'put him out of his misery'.

And so that was it; Gordon had spent the final few minutes of his life playing charades… and *not* eating chocolate.

He did not know how long he had been asleep and, at first, was not sure what had caused the noise that woke him from his slumber. However, he could not have failed to hear the clapping hands. When he opened his eyes, the first thing he saw was a man standing over him, his face almost pressed against his. The stranger clapped his hands again, though it was unnecessary this time.

"Wakey, wakey," he commanded.

Gordon rubbed his eyes and, as he came to his senses, quickly realised that the man had not been part of the scene he had drifted away from only moments earlier.

"Mr Jones?" the intruder inquired politely. "It is Mr Jones, isn't it?"

"What's going on?" Gordon muttered. "Who are you?"

The man never answered, but continued to lean over the dazed occupant of the armchair. He watched as Gordon, still in a slumped position, moved his head to one side in order to look beyond the intruder in a bid to cast an eye around the room. The man was standing so close to him, Gordon could not see much, though the Christmas tree, its lights still shining brightly in the relative darkness, assured him he was still in his own living room. He could also see the silhouetted figures of his friends, though they made no sound and were now motionless.

"They're not playing musical statues now, are they?" he joked.

The fact Gordon, despite being confused and disorientated, was still able to make a sarcastic comment highlighted the perhaps bizarre fact that he was not filled with terror. Of course, he should have been. An uninvited stranger was standing before him, well within his personal zone, one also has to add.

The stranger at last stood back, allowing Gordon a clearer view of his friends. They were either seated or standing, but all quite still, like waxworks; unflattering, gormless expressions on their faces, though, in the dim light, Gordon could not at first pick out such detail. Bill was standing with one arm on his head and with a leg suspended in mid-air. Despite the unnatural position, he never wavered, and that was odd for someone as clumsy as Bill. Anyone – as Gordon did now – would have soon come to the conclusion that the partygoers were frozen in time. And, of course, that was exactly the case.

Gordon looked back at the man, unable to comprehend the surreal situation he now found himself in. "What's going on?" he demanded. "Who let you in?" The second point had only just dawned on him.

The stranger did not answer and looked to a clipboard he was holding. He began thumbing through some papers attached to it, giving Gordon time to study him. He was smartly dressed, in a suit, but the fact every article of clothing he wore was black persuaded Gordon that he was a rather dreary individual. Everything was black: his trousers, shirt and jacket, all black – even his tie. Needless to say, his shoes were also black, but for a thin white stripe on the well-polished toe caps, though he was standing too close to Gordon for the latter to be able to see his feet. Even if he could, the dim lighting would have again prevented him from picking out that detail. Most people that dared wear an all-black outfit might be described as slick or trendy, but these were words Gordon would not have pinned on the stranger. Strangely, Gordon found it difficult to focus on the man's face. It appeared almost featureless to him, so uninteresting did he perceive it to be. In fact, it is a good job the man meant no harm, because if the police had later asked Gordon to describe the appearance of the intruder, he would have been unable to do so. He would not have been able to give them even the height or age of the man – those details also bizarrely not registering in Gordon's mind. Fortunately, as I have stated, the man had not come to do any harm and Gordon somehow sensed that.

"What's going on?" he asked calmly, sure that this time the man would answer his question.

The stranger rested the papers back on the clipboard and stared into Gordon's eyes.

"You are Mr Jones?" he asked again.

Gordon nodded dumbly. Still Gordon found it difficult to focus on the man's face.

"Good," the intruder declared. "You know, for one moment I thought I had gone to the wrong house again. You wouldn't believe how many Joneses there are."

The intruder spoke clearly. He had no accent, but had a slight speech impediment, which meant he was unable to correctly pronounce 'th' – the word 'thought' sounding like 'fought'.

"Look, I don't know who you are," Gordon said a little more forcefully, "or who let you in, but can you kindly tell me what's going on?"

The man smiled and lifted a single peanut from the bowl on the coffee table, two long fingers delicately popping it into his mouth. He chewed it for a few seconds before swallowing, dabbing his lip, as though it was a sign of approval.

"I'm awfully sorry, Mr Jones. You must think me very rude, but I had to make sure I'd got the right house this time. I wouldn't want to make a mistake."

He stopped and looked at Gordon, who had at last risen from his armchair.

"You'd better sit down," the man instructed. "This might come as a shock."

"I'm perfectly fine where I am," a defiant Gordon insisted.

"Very well." The stranger glanced at his clipboard and cleared his throat. His voice became officious in tone. "Mr Jones," he began, "I am sorry to inform you that your life on planet earth was terminated exactly 84.34 seconds ago."

"What?"

"I am sorry to inform you that your life on planet earth was terminated exactly 93.58 seconds ago."

"What the..."

"I am sorry to inform..."

"No, stop!" Gordon interrupted. "I heard you the first time. I just don't have a clue what you're going on about. Are you trying to tell me I'm dead or something? Are you crazy?"

"No, Mr Jones. I am Death."

"What?"

"I said, I am Death."

"Oh! I'm sorry," Gordon replied, raising his voice. "I SAID, ARE YOU CRAZY?"

The man contrived a smile. "Not deaf, Mr Jones... Death," he said, sticking his tongue between his teeth in a bid to emphasise the correct pronunciation. He declared once again, this time raising his *own* voice: "I AM DEATH."

Now it was Gordon who was forced to put his hand to his ear. "I hear you! No need to shout... just because *you're* a little bit deaf."

The stranger lifted a bony finger to his forehead and scratched it thoughtfully. He turned his back on Gordon, walking towards the centre of the room.

"My name is Death, Mr Jones," he said theatrically, adjusting the shirt collar of the static Bill. "Surely you have heard of me? I am *Dear, beauteous Death,* as the poet Henry Vaughan rightly remarked, *the jewel of the just.*"

He turned around sharply to see if Gordon had reacted in any way. He had. The bemused host had sat down again. He said nothing, now vigorously rubbing his hand through his hair, as though the explanation to the mystery would fall out on to his lap. Clare was the nearest to him, sitting on the sofa just a few yards away. He looked at her figure, silhouetted against the lights of the Christmas tree. Gordon did not need to check if she was playing a joke on him. Even in the semi-darkness, he could sense she was not making any effort to remain still and silent. It came naturally. She was oblivious to what was going on around her.

"Death?" Gordon mused, running his eye up and down the figure before him. "So there really is a person called Death? I didn't think you'd look like this, though," Gordon added suspiciously. "In the films you're usually wearing a hood of some sort... and carrying a scythe or something. With due respect, you're even drearier than I imagined you'd be, though I guessed you'd be in black – they always dress you in black, don't they."

Death had stopped listening. "Writers have never got me quite right," he sighed. "Not one has quite captured the essence of me. Of course, you can't blame them. No one has met me and when they do, well, it's too late then."

Death walked purposefully towards the bookshelf. He tilted his head so that his eyes were only a few inches from the books. The only light in the room was from the Christmas tree and the television, the picture, like everything else, frozen in time, as though someone had pressed the pause button. Death rubbed his index finger along some of the spines of the books, blowing the dust off when he had finished. He turned to Gordon, shaking his head, not because no one had bothered to dust in more than a year, but because he clearly did not share Gordon's taste in literature.

"Have you no poetry, Mr Jones?"

"I've got a Pam Ayres book somewhere."

Death sniffed and moved towards the dining table. He lifted up a half-full bottle of wine and put it towards his nose, before reeling back in horror, as though he had snorted a powerful chemical.

"You clearly have no taste for good wine either, Mr Jones."

Gordon got up and began pacing the room, a few crisps on the carpet breaking under his slippers.

"I must be dreaming. This isn't real," he muttered. "I must be going mad. How can I be dead? I feel fine. In fact, I feel better than I did earlier tonight, I can tell you."

"Well of course you do," Death interrupted. "As Sir Thomas Browne correctly identified: *Death is the cure of all diseases.* I am the great healer, Mr Jones. You were ill and I cured you. Perhaps a little thank you would not go amiss."

"What?" a dumbfounded Gordon responded. "You want me to *thank* you? You didn't exactly bring tidings of great joy! What do you expect me to do: to throw my arms around you and give you a great big hug?"

"No need for that," Death replied, stepping back as though he feared his host should do exactly that.

"What am I supposed to have died of?" Gordon inquired. "I thought I was pretty healthy."

Death began thumbing through the papers on his clipboard, but quickly gave up the search. "Oh, you don't want to know," he concluded. "Best not to reveal the gory details."

Gordon sighed. "I must admit I was getting a few headaches lately, but Bill is kind of partial to heavy metal... and he does like it loud. He likes the old stuff: Black Sabbath... Megadeth..."

"Mega... death?" Death mused. "I feel I should know him."

Gordon almost raised a smile.

"I don't believe this," he grumbled, running his hand through his hair once again. "What on earth have I got to laugh about? A complete stranger has just come into my house and told me I've kicked the bucket!"

"That's not strictly true, Mr Jones."

"You mean I'm not dead?" Gordon inquired hopefully.

"Oh, you're dead, but I'm not exactly a stranger. You're no stranger to me anyway. I thought I recognised the face when I arrived. I came to you once before, you see. Do you remember when that lorry came towards you on the wrong side of the road? We almost met then. You don't know how close I was to introducing myself to you. It wasn't your turn, of course. I was convinced it was. It was an easy mistake to make. That's why I carry this now," he continued, nodding towards his clipboard. "I don't try to guess who's next. I just go by the official list these days. It's so much easier – if only it weren't for the fact there are so many Joneses!"

Gordon turned up his nose. "I thought that lorry was a lucky escape, but it might as well have hit me!"

"Don't be like that," Death replied, shaking his head disapprovingly. "You got an extra seven months, didn't you? In fact," Death whispered, coming closer to Gordon, "you actually gained a fraction of a second tonight."

"What?"

"Well, don't tell anyone, but I was a bit late. I was due at 19:34.28," Death said, looking to a piece of paper on his clipboard for confirmation.

Gordon glanced at the carriage clock on the mantelpiece, screwing up his eyes to make out the time.

"It's no good looking at that," Death continued. "Don't you know time stops when someone dies? *Stop all the clocks,* as W.H. Auden declared, but there's no need to, of course. It happens naturally. You are outside time now, Mr Jones."

"If there's no time, how can you be late?"

Death smiled. "I don't think you're quite ready for me to answer that yet. It's kind of complicated."

"Just tell me why *you* were late, then," Gordon inquired suspiciously.

"So many Joneses," Death admitted, lifting his arms in the air. "I went to number five by mistake at first."

"That must be old Mr Jones?" Gordon pondered. "He must be in his late nineties by now. It's not fair. Can't you go back there?"

"You'd better take that up with someone else. I'm just doing my job. I just cross off the next name on my list and it happened to be yours."

"Can't you just rub my name out and go to the next one?" Gordon pleaded. "Can't you come back another day, in about forty years? I've got so much I wanted to do."

"Yes, everyone I meet says that. You all have so much to do, but never get around to doing it. I just don't know why you just don't do it. You knew I'd be coming someday."

"Just not today," Gordon moaned.

"If not today, then tomorrow. I come in the end."

Gordon gingerly seated himself on the sofa, in the space between Clare and Veronica. He looked at both, before shaking his head sorrowfully.

"It's not fair. I don't want to die."

"That's another thing they all say."

"Well, what do you expect us to say?" Gordon responded testily.

"All right," Death replied, placing his hand on Gordon's shoulder. "Don't take it out on me. As I told you, I'm just doing my job. I don't deliberately target an individual just because they've got bad breath or support Arsenal. Your name just came up. That's the roll of the dice. What more can I say?"

Gordon did not respond and Death had plenty more to say.

"Do you think I enjoy this job?" he continued. "It's not easy, you know, being the one to break the bad news. People hardly welcome me with open arms. In fact, they spend all their lives trying to avoid me. I mean, they're not exactly dying to meet me… though that's not exactly true," he laughed.

Gordon tutted. He did not appreciate the joke.

"You should hear some of the things people say about me," Death continued. "You don't know how many names I've got… and the Grim Reaper is nowhere near the worst. Even the bard himself – whom I admire much – didn't always exactly shower me with compliments. Do you know what Claudio called me in *Measure for Measure?* A *fearful thing.* That's right; he called me a *fearful thing!*"

Gordon shook his head, not through sympathy, but bewilderment.

"But that's not all," Death went on. "It's not just about my job. I can perhaps understand people feeling a little aggrieved when I meet them, but some have the audacity to mock my personal appearance. Do you know what Thomas Lovell Beddoes said about my ears?"

"Who?"

"Poet or no poet… he said I had the ears of an ass!"

Gordon could not help glancing at Death's ears, even though he tried to resist the temptation.

At last Death paused for breath and began to examine some of the half-unwrapped Christmas presents that lay strewn across the floor. He lifted a pair of socks emblazoned with cartoon pigs and shook his head in astonishment.

"Anyway," Gordon started, "if I'm dead – and I still don't believe it – what exactly happens now?"

Death smiled. "I was wondering when you were going to ask me that... even though the answer should be obvious."

Gordon moved to the edge of his seat and lifted his head towards Death's face. He still did not take in the features of the presence before him – though he had concluded that his ears were nothing out of the ordinary.

"So, what happens now?" Gordon persisted.

Death returned a smile, but did not respond immediately. It was almost as if he was pausing for effect. Gordon fidgeted nervously.

At last Death spoke, turning his back on his host.

"You will be taken to a place where you will reside forever," he pronounced, his voice resembling that of a sentencing judge.

"What do you mean?" Gordon asked, even though he had a good idea what he meant.

"Eternity, Mr Jones; you will be taken to a place where you will spend the rest of your life, or should I say existence."

Gordon rolled his tongue around his mouth. He was fishing for the only answer he wanted to hear. In the end, he lost patience and asked directly: "And where is that place?"

Death turned around abruptly and stared at Gordon. He may have said that he did not enjoy his job, but he was relishing the power he seemed to now hold over the twitching man that sat before him.

"Where am I going?" Gordon asked again.

"Well, that depends, Mr Jones," Death replied mischievously. "That depends on you."

Gordon could sense that Death was still staring at him, even though he had deliberately turned his head away from the uninvited guest, his thoughtful gaze now resting upon the magenta-coloured fairy light on the Christmas tree. It was no longer flickering, but he never noticed.

2

"In heaven an angel is nobody in particular."

Maxims for Revolutionists
George Bernard Shaw

GORDON DID NOT AT FIRST NOTICE THAT AN ANGEL HAD arrived on the scene. Of course, he had no idea the man was an angel. He looked more like an insurance clerk.

"You're a what?" Gordon repeated, after the latest intruder had introduced himself. "An angel? I don't believe this. What next?"

The man, or should we say angel, smiled, almost apologetically.

Gordon was now pacing the room, his hand rummaging through his hair. Somehow the arrival of yet another immortal had caused him to lose the composure he had started to regain. He was trying to convince himself that he was the victim of some elaborate – very elaborate – hoax, but the sight of his static friends was a constant reminder this was reality.

The angel produced a business card from the breast pocket of his brown suit and offered it to Gordon.

"I am Angel Gilmore," he repeated. "It is nice to finally meet you in the flesh, Mr Jones."

"An angel?" Gordon continued to mumble, almost in a bid to convince himself. "This is ridiculous. I can't take much more of this."

He stopped and stared at the little figure before him. "You don't *look* much like an angel. What did you say your name was?"

"Angel Gilmore, but you can drop the former bit. Most people just call me Mr Gilmore. That will do if it's easier for you to get your head around."

"Gilmore? That doesn't sound very angelic either."

Mr Gilmore was about to place the business card back in his pocket, but Gordon at last reached for it. He perhaps should not have been surprised to discover it was not a lot different to one that an insurance clerk might possess, though it read very differently. In typed letters were the words: *Angel John Gilmore, messenger of God, guardian, etc.* Gordon handed it back and sat down. Neither Mr Gilmore nor Death, who was flicking through the pages of a newspaper, spoke; both content to let Gordon come to terms with his predicament in his own time, and, of course, he had plenty of that now. He leant back, his eyes studying the large lenses of the burgundy-framed spectacles that dominated the face of Mr Gilmore. Clearly, the glasses were from a different era. The lenses were so thick, they distorted the angel's eyes when you looked at him from a certain angle, momentarily giving the impression that he was boss-eyed.

Mr Gilmore was below average height, a good few inches smaller than Gordon. He was completely bald on top, his only hair just above his ears and at the back of his head, once brown but now white. He was not exactly plump, but rounded. He had a pleasant face. Like Death, he had appeared in the room in an instant, and it was no surprise that Gordon had not noticed his arrival.

"An angel?" the stupefied Gordon inquired once more, eyeing Mr Gilmore suspiciously. "Shouldn't you be wearing all white? And where are your wings… and what about your halo? All angels have a halo, don't they?"

Mr Gilmore smiled. He never attempted to answer, and Gordon did not really need him to. Although he had difficulty imagining the figure before him possessed celestial powers, a lot had already happened to convince him that anything was now possible.

"So, you *really* are an angel and you *really* are… Death," a melancholy Gordon uttered, looking in turn at the intruders. Both nodded in reply, the glasses slipping from the bridge of Mr Gilmore's nose as he did so. He readjusted them.

"And I *really* am dead," Gordon continued, scratching his head. "So, this is it? It's all over."

"All over?" an incredulous Mr Gilmore chirped. "All over? It's just beginning, Mr Jones."

Death tossed his head back. "As T.S. Eliot will agree: *In my beginning is my end… in my end is my beginning.*"

Gordon nodded thoughtfully and then smiled. "You mean heaven," he said quietly.

"I thought you would be a bit more excited about it than that!" Death exclaimed.

"I'm sorry. I just can't seem to get my head around anything at the moment."

"That's understandable," Mr Gilmore assured Gordon, placing his hand upon his shoulder. "Death does not bring the end, Mr Jones. That is why I am here." He paused. "Yes, today is the first day of the rest of your existence."

"He's right, Mr Jones," Death interrupted. "I do not bring the end. I think it was John Masefield who remarked on my service to mankind." Both Gordon and Mr Gilmore waited for Death to toss his head back. He obliged: "*Death opens unknown doors. It is most grand to die.*"

Mr Gilmore continued: "That's correct, Mr Jones. Another door, though it shouldn't be an unknown one, is about to open for you, one that leads to paradise, I should add. You are going to heaven to meet your maker, Mr Jones. I am here to take you to heaven!" He paused, himself almost in awe of the thought, even though we can perhaps safely assume from his glasses and attire that he had resided there for some time. "Take it in, Mr Jones," he drooled. "That's heaven with a capital 'H'. Yes, it's a *real* place. And it's where you're going."

He said the last few words slowly and deliberately, as though he wanted them to sink in. They did. After a few moments, Gordon sat back and shook his head in wonder.

"I'd forgotten all about heaven – and then when he reminded me," Gordon added, nodding at Death, "I was beginning to think that I might not be going there anyway."

He stopped. "Heaven," he repeated, this time with a sense of awe in his own voice. Mr Gilmore was smiling profusely, as though he were a parent who had just handed his son a Christmas present.

"When do we go?" Gordon asked.

"When you are ready, Mr Jones."

"I suppose I'm ready now."

Gordon rose from his chair and looked at his friends. "I wish I could let them know that there really is a heaven. Of course, I've always believed in heaven, but... well, it *really* is true."

Death came to Gordon and stood in front of him, placing both hands on his shoulders.

"I told you dying wasn't all that bad, Mr Jones. Perhaps now you'd like to thank me for my part in it."

Gordon smiled and offered his hand, which Death took and shook, the latter's grasp surprisingly limp and, dare Gordon think it, almost effeminate.

"No hard feelings," Gordon declared. "I'm sorry if I was rude to you in any way. I know you're only doing your job."

Gordon sat himself between Clare and Veronica, stretching his arms to rest on both of their shoulders. They never flinched.

"They are going to be pretty shocked when they find me curled up in the armchair... dead." Gordon stopped. He still found it difficult to use that word. "Hold on a minute," he started to question. "How come I can't see myself?" He stared at the vacant armchair he had been sitting on and instinctively put his hand to his chest. "Is this my soul or still my body? Shouldn't my body remain where I die? It does in the films."

"So many questions, Mr Jones," the angel smiled. "Don't worry, you've plenty of time to find the answers."

Gordon shook his head and looked at Bill. One leg was still off the ground and he wore an expression of anguish on his contorted face. He did not look like a man enjoying Christmas. "I wonder what his charade was?" Gordon muttered. "Don't suppose I'll ever find out." He stopped and turned to Alex. "Sorry, chaps, I didn't plan to leave you. I imagine that will be Christmas over for this year!"

"They'll soon get over it," Death assured him. "People do."

Mr Gilmore flashed Death a disapproving look.

"Sorry," Death checked. "That must have sounded pretty insensitive. I'm sure they'll all be devastated for many weeks."

Gordon grinned. "It might sound morbid, but I'd love to see their faces when they wake up and discover I'm... dead."

Mr Gilmore looked shocked by the comment, but Death stared mischievously at Gordon. "You know you can," he said simply.

The angel returned a look of horror. "Don't encourage him."

It was too late. Gordon had already seized upon the remark.

"What do you mean? Encourage me to do what? Do you mean I *can* see into the future?"

"You are outside time now, Mr Jones," Death explained. "You can go anywhere... at any time, because there is no time. Time no longer exists for you. There is no future or even a past. We don't expect you to be able to get your head around that just yet, of course."

"It's not a good idea, though," Mr Gilmore interrupted. "Sometimes you see things that you wish you hadn't. The future does not always hold what you want it to. It can be quite painful."

"But I thought there was no more pain and suffering in heaven," Gordon pointed out.

"You are not *yet* in heaven," the angel replied, taking off his glasses and wiping them with his handkerchief. "Of course, when you are in heaven, earthly problems and tribulations will become insignificant to you. Forget about your old life, Mr Jones. It is over. Look to eternity; that's all that matters now."

Gordon was deep in thought. However, he was not pondering Mr Gilmore's words of wisdom.

"Can I see my funeral?" he asked suddenly.

Mr Gilmore looked horrified, while Death just laughed. "I knew that was coming," the latter chuckled. "Why do people always want to see their funeral?"

Gordon shook his head. "I'm just curious," he said. "I'd just like to see what people are saying about me. Let's face it, it's got to be the only time when no one has a bad word for you."

"Don't bet on it!" Death interrupted.

"Perhaps you would like to see something else?" Mr Gilmore suggested. "What about Fulham winning the FA Cup? That's your favourite team, isn't it?"

"You mean they *do* win it?"

"I think so," Mr Gilmore reflected, "though we may have to fast forward a few centuries."

Gordon smiled. "No, really, I would like to see what people are saying about me. Besides, if it's something not very nice, it doesn't really matter. As you said yourself, my life on earth will pale into insignificance once I'm in heaven, and I will have forgotten about it, true? It's not going to matter, is it? No one can hurt me now. Please. It'll be fun, I'm sure."

Mr Gilmore shrugged his shoulders. "I don't suppose it will do any harm," he said. "OK. Let's get it over with. Ready?"

Gordon nodded.

The angel straightened his glasses and clicked his fingers.

It all happened so quickly; Gordon did not have time to inquire as to how time travel worked in eternity. Before he even had the chance to open his mouth, he found himself somewhere else. He expected to be standing in a churchyard over an open grave and was slightly disappointed to find himself in his own kitchen, which he recognised immediately.

People were chatting, holding paper plates that were bending under the weight of food upon them. It has to be said, there was not a lot of solemnity.

"I thought we were going to see my funeral?" Gordon whispered to Mr Gilmore. "This looks like a party!"

The angel smiled.

Of course, one must explain at this point – though I'm sure there is little need to – that the partygoers (if that is the right word to use for guests at a wake) did not notice the arrival of Gordon and Mr Gilmore. They were oblivious to their presence. However, the angel still needed to explain the fact to Gordon.

"No need to whisper, Mr Jones," he said. "They can't hear you, or see you," now aware that Gordon had unconsciously edged closer to him. "I'm sure you've seen *A Christmas Carol*, Mr Jones? You must know how it works. Think of yourself as Ebenezer Scrooge at this particular moment... only I hope people are a little bit more complimentary in your case."

"I just thought everyone would be standing around my grave, like they do in the films, throwing flowers and dirt on to the coffin."

"Perhaps you were cremated?"

"Oh."

"It's the wake that's the interesting bit anyway," Mr Gilmore continued. "That's when the guests start to let their hair down and... it looks like a good turnout, doesn't it?" he added, thinking it better to change the drift of the conversation.

Veronica and Alex were among the mourners in the kitchen. The latter wore a black suit but had a blue and white scarf draped over his shoulders.

"He's still wearing his Chelsea scarf!" Gordon complained, throwing his arms into the air. "What a cheek. Has he no respect? He could have put a black and white one on in my honour."

There were a lot of individual conversations in full flow and Gordon had to move closer to hear what Veronica and Alex were saying. He listened for a few moments, before stepping back disappointed.

"They're talking about last night's TV!" he whined.

"What did you expect them to be talking about?"

"Me! It's meant to be *my* day."

Mr Gilmore smiled and reached for a ham sandwich.

Gordon looked horrified. "Are you allowed to do that? Won't people notice?"

The angel nodded. His mouth was so full, he had to pause before answering the question. "Some do, but they just put it down to it being one of life's little unexplained mysteries," he started to explain, halting again to take another bite. "Haven't you ever wondered how something you were looking for somehow turns up somewhere else, even though you're convinced you'd never put it there, or why there appears to be less of something than you first thought? People at first try to come up with an explanation and can't, but because it's something pretty insignificant, like a ham sandwich, it doesn't trouble them for too long and they soon forget about it."

Gordon scratched his head. "Now that you mention it, every time I go to the biscuit tin, there always seems to be fewer than when I last looked. I used to always blame Bill. Was that you?"

Mr Gilmore laughed, some of the contents of the sandwich slipping from his mouth.

"Only if they were custard creams. I do like custard creams," he said. "I wonder if there are any here?"

Gordon was about to point to the tin on a shelf, but realised the angel was not giving him his full attention. Mr Gilmore was casting his eye around the table, an assortment of dishes laid out upon a scarlet tablecloth.

"Nice to see they've at least got the posh cutlery out in my honour," Gordon declared, "though they could have used those expensive napkins we'd been saving for a rainy day. I mean, this has got to be classed as a rainy day, hasn't it? I told Bill to put them somewhere where we could all find them."

"Don't be hard on him. He probably has a lot on his mind," Mr Gilmore suggested.

"Suppose so," Gordon shrugged, about to pick up a paper serviette. He stopped and then turned sharply towards Mr Gilmore with a puzzled look on his face.

The angel smiled. "You're wondering whether they'd see it rising in mid-air," Mr Gilmore anticipated, nodding at the serviette, but making no attempt to give an answer, his attention now drawn to a plate of sausage rolls.

Gordon shook his head perplexed and reached for a jam tart, watching to see if anyone noticed the said object rising apparently unaided in the air. They didn't. He was careful not to touch an old lady who was sitting upright in a chair beside the table. He assumed that she would still be able to feel him if he had brushed against her, even though she could not see him. He took it for granted he was still a physical presence in the room and, perhaps strangely, it never occurred to him that he *might* be able to walk through people. When he returned to the side of Mr Gilmore and started to nibble at his jam tart, he had a good look at the woman.

"Strange," he piped, still nibbling. "I have absolutely no idea who that woman is. Must be some long-lost aunt or something?"

In fact, there were quite a few people whom Gordon could not put a name to.

"I should have kept in touch with more of the family," he said. "Still, it's good of them to make the effort to attend, whoever they are. I'm not bothered if they all come out of the woodwork now; it can't be for my money – didn't leave an awful lot. Oh no! I hadn't even made a will!"

Mr Gilmore now had a plate of chicken legs in his hand. He offered it to Gordon, who wondered if the diminutive angel was taking things a little bit too far.

"No, thank you, but please don't let me stop you."

Before he had finished the sentence, Mr Gilmore was already chewing one of the legs, the skin of the chicken hanging off, his lips smeared with grease. Gordon again began to question whether he *really* was an angel.

"Shall we make our way into the living room?" Mr Gilmore inquired. "Although that's not the best name for it on a day like this, is it?" The angel chuckled at his own joke. "Is there anyone else you would like to see, Mr Jones?"

Gordon shook his head. "Hold on! Where's Bill? I hope he hasn't sneaked off to his room to play on his computer?" Gordon stopped and lifted his head to the ceiling. "I can hear someone in my room. I hope that's not Bill messing up my stuff. Can we go up?"

Mr Gilmore seemed reluctant to do so and, in order to divert Gordon, nudged him in the ribs, a cheeky grin on his face, as he nodded in the direction of a man asleep on the sofa – another person Gordon did not recognise, it should be noted.

Gordon groaned. "I'm sorry my death has kept you up, sir." He shook his head, turning towards another small group of mourners. "This isn't as exciting as I thought it would be," Gordon continued. "I think Clare's talking about a blister on her foot now! I'm not surprised with those heels," he added, nodding his head in the direction of her shoes. "It's all a bit disappointing – and I still don't know half of these people."

"Very well," Mr Gilmore replied hurriedly, pleased that Gordon had had enough, as though he was fearful his charge might do something out of turn if they stayed any longer. "It's probably time to go back now."

"I thought we were outside time?"

"Just a figure of speech, Mr Jones," the angel smiled.

Within an instant (though of course it was really in no time at all, as they were outside time) both were back in the living room of Gordon's house; the living room of the time that the housemates had been playing charades in, one should clarify, to avoid any confusion.

Mr Gilmore was still holding the plate of chicken legs. Gordon had not failed to notice, and the angel acknowledged his mistake, though Gordon did wonder if he had deliberately brought it back with him. He did seem to like his food and that fact prompted Gordon to question in his mind whether one ate in heaven. He was about to inquire, when something caught his eye in the far corner of the room. It was Death. He had discovered one of Veronica's Christmas presents – a set of juggling balls. Gordon shook his head bemused, as he watched Death grow increasingly frustrated at his failure to keep the balls airborne for more than a few seconds. One of the balls fell to the carpet and rolled under the dining table. "What a stupid game," Death snorted, tossing the other two over his shoulder. He walked towards Mr Gilmore and delicately lifted a chicken leg, but immediately replaced it on the plate, rubbing his hands together to wipe the grease from his fingers, a look of disdain on his face.

"I know it wasn't exactly a celebration, but I don't suppose there was any Dom Pérignon 1966 there?" he inquired.

"No," replied Gordon. "I don't know anyone by that name."

Mr Gilmore grinned and placed the plate of chicken legs on the dining table. The room was just as Gordon had left it, but somehow he now found it more difficult to look at his motionless friends. He wanted them to be talking and laughing, as he remembered them. Clare could complain about her feet as much as she wished. Gordon found the solitude unnerving. He looked around him, almost for something of comfort, his eyes being drawn to the only sources of light: the shining Christmas tree and the television screen, though the statuesque Bill, having deliberately positioned himself in front of the latter, blocked out most of that, he being of generous proportions.

"Well, I suppose I'd better go," Death suddenly declared. "I've done my job, and another one awaits. He looked at his clipboard. "I have a rendezvous with Dwight Morelli of Chicago, Illinois. I'd better go – he's been at my door for a long time."

He adjusted the knot of his tie and smiled at Gordon, who looked into his face, but it still appeared as a blur to him.

"Goodbye, Mr Jones. I don't suppose we will meet again. I only have to come to you once, you will be pleased to know. Now, who said that? Someone must have said that?"

Gordon grinned. He was almost sorry to see him go. "You're not such a bad guy, after all," Gordon offered.

"Of course I'm not," Death replied. "As John Donne famously said of me: *Death, be not proud, though some have called thee mighty and dreadful, for thou art not so.*"

He glanced down at his clipboard and – at the exact moment Gordon blinked – disappeared. When Gordon reopened his eyes, Death was no longer there.

Mr Gilmore turned to Gordon. "Are you ready now?"

"I suppose so."

Gordon had forgotten about paradise and was feeling low again. It was finally time to leave his friends and he felt some pangs of sorrow. He studied each in turn.

"I'd better say goodbye now," he said. "I'll see you all whenever."

He walked up to Alex and removed the familiar blue and white scarf from his shoulders.

"I won't be a minute," he said, turning to Mr Gilmore, Gordon's eyes momentarily lighting up, "but you did say we had all the time in the world."

The angel smiled politely, but it was obvious that he was becoming a little restless. Gordon disappeared into the hallway and reappeared after a few moments with a black and white scarf in his hand. He placed it on to the shoulders of Alex and wrapped it around his neck, as though he were dressing a snowman.

"It will be like one of those little unexplained mysteries in life," he suggested, a mischievous grin on his face. Mr Gilmore made no attempt to stop him.

"He'll be more horrified to wake up to find this around his neck than to find me dead in the chair," Gordon continued. "I think I'm ready now," he added, turning to Mr Gilmore.

The angel frowned, but did not comment.

"I almost feel like I should say some last words," Gordon added suddenly, his spirits seemingly on the rise once again. "Trouble is, I don't really know what to say. Funny, isn't it, I've had a lifetime to think of something good, a profound final declaration, but when it comes to the time, I'm lost for words."

"How about goodbye?" Mr Gilmore suggested, now showing more overt signs that he was losing patience.

"Sorry, I'm ready now," Gordon said. "Well, adiós, everyone." He gave each of his friends one final look. "See you in heaven!"

He turned sharply towards Mr Gilmore. "So, how do we get up there then?"

"We fly, Mr Jones. You wanted me to be like a proper angel, one with wings, didn't you?"

Gordon almost expected him to produce some wings, the sort you would get from a fancy dress shop.

"Fly?" Gordon inquired. "Can we go through walls?"

He did not know whether the angel was serious or not.

Mr Gilmore locked his own arm through Gordon's and lifted his head towards the ceiling. "Ready?"

3

"The devil hath power to assume a pleasing shape."

Hamlet
William Shakespeare

"HEY! HOLD ON A MINUTE."

Gordon was surprised to hear another voice. He had closed his eyes, expecting to begin the ascent at any moment. When he opened them, he was not floating through the clouds, but still standing in the living room of his own house.

Another stranger had appeared.

"Stop right where you are, Mr Gilmore," the man continued. "You're not going anywhere."

Mr Gilmore sighed and released Gordon's arm. He eyed the latest intruder with contempt. It was clear from his look that the two were known to each other and had met on more than one occasion previously.

"What are *you* doing here?" the angel inquired suspiciously. "What are you after?"

"Him," the man replied coolly, nodding in Gordon's direction, his arms folded.

Mr Gilmore instinctively pulled Gordon away from the stranger. He readjusted his glasses, which had again slipped from the bridge of his nose.

"Well, you can't have him, Dumas," the angel declared. "He doesn't belong to you... it's as simple as that."

Dumas, as we should now call the latest intruder, was a dominating figure. He was more than a foot taller than Mr Gilmore, but his height was not what drew attention. His attire was responsible for that. He wore a maroon tunic of velvet that almost met his knee-high leather boots, his baggy brown trousers remaining virtually hidden from view. A crimson sash was tied around the shoulder and descended diagonally across the chest towards his waist, where it supported a scabbard. Gordon immediately looked for a sword, but the scabbard was empty. As Gordon continued to study him closely, the man obligingly removed his wide-brimmed hat, his dark, flowing hair in ringlets falling on to the white lace ruffle that covered his neck. Dumas stroked his thin moustache with one of his gloved fingers and began pacing the room, as though it was to allow Gordon a closer inspection. He strutted about like a king. Gordon had never been particularly good at history, but he immediately associated the figure with the English Civil War. He tried to remember which side were which, and it bothered him that he could not.

"You look perplexed, Mr Jones," the man said, turning around sharply and placing his hat against his mouth, before lightly blowing the blue plume that adorned it.

"I was just..." Gordon stuttered. "I was just..."

"It's the Cavaliers," Dumas assisted.

"Sorry?"

"The Cavaliers or Royalists. That's what you were trying to think of, wasn't it?"

Gordon looked horrified. "Can you read my mind?"

The man did not answer, which was good enough to convince Gordon that he could.

Mr Gilmore was less impressed. "No, he can't," the angel explained. "Don't listen to him. You are not the first, and will not be the last, to think he's off to a fancy dress party. He has heard it all before... over many of your centuries. It's not difficult to guess what you and many others in your position are thinking. He's a sly old fox. You be careful of him." He stopped and looked at Gordon. "Not even us angels know what is on your mind, or your heart, Mr Jones. Only the Master has that privilege, if it is one."

Dumas smiled at the angel and gave a condescending bow. He reached inside a pocket on his tunic and pulled out a scroll. Although he wore black leather gloves, he unfurled it without any problem.

"Mr Jones... let's see now," he cogitated, casting his eyes on the crisp sheet of paper before him. "As I thought, you *do* belong to me."

"Let me see that!" Mr Gilmore interrupted, snatching the scroll from his hands. "I can't see his name," he concluded after a brief moment, the scroll snapping back into its original cylindrical state. The angel took off his glasses and began wiping them with his handkerchief, now supporting the scroll under his armpit as he did so.

"Sadly, Mr Gilmore can see very little," Dumas quipped, snatching back the scroll, before returning it to his pocket.

The angel stepped back and ushered Gordon towards the sofa. "I'll be with you in a moment, Mr Jones," Mr Gilmore assured his host. "This won't take long. Dumas has made a simple mistake, that's all."

Gordon sat down between Clare and Veronica without complaint. He believed he had no right to interfere in what he thought, even now, was not his business. In fact, if he was honest, he was relieved that he was not required to partake in the ensuing conversation. His eyes were drawn to the page of the *Radio Times* that lay open in Clare's lap. "I don't suppose I'll be watching *The Wizard of Oz* tomorrow," he mumbled under his breath.

Curious as it may seem, Gordon found the sudden urge to find out what else was on television tomorrow. It is wrong to say he had forgotten that he would not exactly be in a position to watch the television tomorrow, but he drew some comfort in being in a position to at least know what he might be *missing* on television tomorrow! Indeed, Gordon was still finding it difficult to detach himself from normality, as ridiculous as that may seem when two uninvited immortals were at this very moment, just a few feet away, arguing over his soul, though Gordon had not exactly cottoned on to the fact that this was indeed what they were doing.

Mr Gilmore and Dumas had made a point of positioning themselves away from Gordon, but they did not bother to lower their voices.

"You know the deal, Dumas," Mr Gilmore continued. "We get the Christians and you get the rest."

"You don't have to remind me of that fact, Mr Gilmore. I know what I'm entitled to."

"So why are you here?"

"Because he belongs to me. He's on my list. I've already told you that. Your ears are not going the way of your eyes, are they?"

Mr Gilmore scratched his head.

"Now stand aside," Dumas ordered. "Not even your boss can deprive me of those that do not belong to him. Are you ready, Mr Jones?" the demon asked, turning abruptly in the direction of the sofa.

Gordon did not hear the man. He was busy trying to turn a page of the magazine that still held his attention, he being prevented by the fact that Clare's fingers were still clasped on to it. The page eventually ripped free, leaving Clare holding a tiny piece of the corner, like a corpse in a thriller that refuses to relinquish a vital piece of evidence.

"Mr Jones!" Dumas repeated, this time a little more forcefully.

Gordon looked up. "Sorry, are we going now?"

"Yes," Dumas responded defiantly. "We are."

"No, we are not," Mr Gilmore replied, staring accusingly at Dumas. "What I mean to say is that you're not going – just Mr Jones and I."

"Oh, yes I am."

"Oh, no you're not."

"Oh, yes I am." Dumas laughed. "I have no intention of recreating a scene from a pantomime," he said, even though that is exactly what he was trying to do, much to his own amusement. And Gordon thought that Dumas would make a perfect pantomime hero, thanks to his attire and theatrical mannerisms. It has to be noted that Gordon, even at this point, still depicted Dumas as a 'hero' and not a 'villain'. That would change within the next few moments, however.

"I'm ready if you two are," Gordon said, rising from the sofa.

"Mr Gilmore will not be escorting you, after all," Dumas continued politely, giving a little bow. "That pleasure belongs to me."

Gordon shrugged his shoulders nonchalantly. "That's fine by me."

Mr Gilmore did not protest. He had produced an electronic personal organiser and was pressing some buttons. He looked ruffled and it was clear he did not really know how to work it.

Dumas glanced at the angel and laughed, placing his gloved hand on Gordon's shoulder, before replacing his hat on his head.

"It's all right, Mr Gilmore," Gordon intervened, the angel still frantically pressing some buttons. "He can take me if you like, so long as he's going to the same place."

No sooner had he finished the sentence, Gordon stopped, the thought suddenly dawning on him. There was a moment's silence.

"Hold on a minute!" he said, momentarily looking into Dumas's gleaming sapphire eyes. "You are taking me to *heaven,* aren't you?"

"Only as far as the gates. I wouldn't dare go any further – and wouldn't want to, I must add."

"He's not allowed any further in anyway," Mr Gilmore added, now shaking his electronic personal organiser, the battery falling on to the carpet as he did so.

"I'm sure that will be fine," Gordon replied, his confidence restored. "No doubt I'll be able to find my own way from there."

He stopped and continued to focus on Dumas. "How come you have a different master? And why aren't you allowed in? I thought all angels lived in heaven."

Mr Gilmore was now on his knees, searching for the battery. His nose was almost touching the carpet when he stated, almost apathetically, and without looking up, "He's *not* an angel, not as you know them anyway."

Dumas simultaneously produced a business card. It was not too dissimilar to the one that Mr Gilmore possessed, other than for a few key words, of course.

"You're a *demon!*" Gordon shrieked, as he held the card aloft.

The demon, as we can also now call Dumas, smiled. He never tired of the reaction the revelation of his identity created.

Mr Gilmore finally found the battery and attempted to replace it.

"I couldn't have made a mistake," he continued to mumble, now sitting cross-legged on the floor. "He's definitely on my list. It's here somewhere," he added, pressing more buttons. "Why are there so many Joneses?"

Gordon walked to the table and poured himself a glass of wine. He did not know why. In his life he had certainly never turned to drink to calm his nerves. Perhaps he had just watched too many films and thought it was the thing to do at this particular moment. It was an unconscious move and one he soon regretted, as it only highlighted the fact that his hand was shaking and he had difficulty holding the glass without spilling the contents.

"A demon?"

"That's right, Mr Jones."

Gordon looked at the card that was still in his other trembling hand and read the words aloud, again in a bid to convince himself: "*Demon Raphael Albertine Dumas.*"

"Come, Mr Jones," Dumas said, studying his gormless expression. "You didn't think I would have little red horns and a tail, did you? And I'm sorry that I've left my trident at home."

He threw his head back and laughed; a fitting, devilish cackle. Gordon let the business card slip from his fingers, as if it had suddenly caught fire. He walked towards the comfort of his armchair and sat down, taking a sip of his drink, a dazed expression on his face. If Mr Gilmore had not been so preoccupied, he might have pointed out the fact that people always found the existence of demons even more difficult to comprehend than the existence of angels. Of course, that shouldn't be the case, but it was.

"Found it!" Mr Gilmore suddenly declared, jumping to his feet in a way that was not befitting of someone of his advanced years. "I knew I was right."

He took the electronic personal organiser to Dumas and shoved it under his nose. The demon never even looked at it and turned his head away with disdain, before gracefully stooping to retrieve his business card from the carpet.

"I knew he was a Christian," Mr Gilmore declared. "It says he officially became one at the age of fifteen, on February 12, in the year…"

"I could have told you that," Gordon interrupted. "If you had asked me."

Dumas was not convinced and remained calm. "He has not been deleted from my list, so as far as I'm concerned, he belongs to me."

Gordon rose and moved towards the demon.

"If you're a demon, how come you said you were still taking me to the gates of heaven? Shouldn't you be taking me somewhere else?"

Mr Gilmore intervened. "Because everyone must face their creator. Sadly, not everyone gets to stay with him. Dumas can only wait outside the gates for those that the Master has to turn away."

"And then he takes them to…"

"That's right, Mr Jones," Dumas answered. "I then take them to *my* master. You've heard of my master, haven't you?" He began pacing the room, lifting his hat from his head and stroking the feather upon his cheek. "Of course you have. Everyone has heard of him, but few really believe in his existence, even Christians. That is to his advantage, of course. Humans see him as some sort of comic figure. Who would possibly believe in the existence of something like that? The fact you view us demons in that way would be somewhat amusing if it were not so serious. It is, of course, imperative that we keep Christians like you in ignorance of our existence. If you really believed in us – I mean *really* believed – you might make more of an effort to flee from us and that, of course, would make our job that little bit more difficult."

Dumas suddenly stopped. He noticed Mr Gilmore had a smug smile on his face. "I'm surprised you would take so lightly a subject like that, Mr Gilmore."

The angel did not need to answer. Dumas now realised his mistake.

"I see," the demon attempted to clarify. "When I said, 'Christians like you', Mr Jones, I used the term loosely. Of course, I could have said Christians or non-Christians."

"But I *am* a Christian," Gordon insisted. "Mr Gilmore is right... and I can prove it." An agitated Gordon was oblivious to the fact that some of his wine was now spilling from his glass on to the carpet. "I don't suppose your records show that I went to church every Sunday," Gordon addressed the demon defiantly, nodding towards the pocket that contained the scroll.

"Of course they do," Dumas replied nonchalantly. "What proof is that? Thousands of people go to church every week. Thousands go to university too, but you don't have to be a genius to go there."

"This is going nowhere," Mr Gilmore interrupted.

"But *I* am," Dumas responded, grabbing hold of Gordon's arm.

Mr Gilmore retaliated by clutching Gordon's other one.

Gordon looked at his wine glass, Mr Gilmore unaware that it was he who was this time responsible for the latest splash of red wine on the beige carpet. Gordon freed himself from the grasp of both immortals and bent down to carefully place the glass on the coffee table. As soon as he straightened his body once more, both Mr Gilmore and Dumas took hold of him again. It was Dumas who finally released his grip to end the stalemate. Mr Gilmore followed suit, taking the chance to pull out his handkerchief to blow his nose.

"This is not going to resolve anything," Dumas announced, stroking his chin thoughtfully. "We will have to take it up with our superiors."

Mr Gilmore agreed. "I will take him to Archangel Clifford. He'll know what to do."

"No, no, no," Dumas protested, wagging a finger disapprovingly in the air. "I don't think so. You're not going anywhere with him, Mr Gilmore. How do I know you'll come back?"

The angel looked at the demon in amazement, astounded that his integrity had been questioned. "You judge others by your own book. We do not all operate in such devious ways," he said.

Mr Gilmore stopped. He suddenly noticed that the demon had retaken hold of Gordon's arm. The angel did likewise. "I told you he's a sly old fox. You won't catch me off guard again, Dumas," he insisted.

Mr Gilmore could sense that the demon was trying to pull Gordon closer to himself. He retaliated. Dumas tugged again. Mr Gilmore took the bait and pulled even harder, so hard, in fact, that as he did – Dumas having let go – it resulted in Gordon and the angel losing their balance and falling to the ground. The demon grinned.

"You did that on purpose," a red-faced Mr Gilmore complained, replacing his glasses and dusting himself down, his brown suit now adorned with tiny pieces of broken crisps. He tightened the knot in his tie and stroked his head, as though he were straightening strands of hair that he did not possess.

Dumas turned his back on the angel and started to tap his empty scabbard. "I've got a better idea," he started, turning abruptly to face his adversary. "I'll take him to Demon Moulski. He will…"

A loud bang stopped him in mid-sentence.

Gordon was now sitting on the floor. He had found a stray Christmas cracker and had pulled it himself, no easy exercise if you have ever tried. The two immortals stared at him, Gordon's hands still holding the two ends of the torn cracker.

"Sorry," he said meekly.

Two tiny dice slipped from a now open end of the cracker, and Gordon lifted one up from the carpet, examining it closely. "We could roll it – odds I'm yours, even I'm yours," he suggested dryly, nodding his head in turn in the direction of Mr Gilmore and Dumas. He stopped, spotting a tiny piece of paper in the remains of the cracker.

"Shall I read the joke?" he offered. He never waited for an answer. "What do you do if an angel and a demon are fighting over your soul?"

Mr Gilmore and Dumas remained silent, almost expecting Gordon to come up with the answer to the riddle.

"I made it up," Gordon continued sheepishly. "But I do have a suggestion. You could leave me here."

To his surprise, neither Mr Gilmore nor Dumas dismissed the idea.

"He's right, you know. There's nothing else we can do," the angel conceded. "That way neither takes him. It shouldn't take long to clear up this mess and then we can return together."

"No," Gordon replied hopefully. "I meant that you could come back *much* later, say in about forty years or so?"

Dumas pulled his gloves tighter.

"Very well," he said, turning to Mr Gilmore. "We'll leave him and seek counsel. There is nothing else we can do, and I have had enough of your childish games."

"*My* childish games?" the angel protested. "You started it!"

"Oh no I didn't."

"Oh yes you…"

The angel stopped, fully aware he had again fallen into the trap, Dumas flashing him a mischievous glance. "Are you ready?" the demon mocked.

Mr Gilmore put his hand upon Gordon's arm, but it was to reassure him this time. "Don't worry, Mr Jones. We won't be long."

"Take your time," Gordon sighed. "You said that there wasn't any, after all!"

The angel and demon stared at each other. Both raised one of their hands and simultaneously clicked their fingers, but only Mr Gilmore disappeared. Within an instant, he reappeared and stared accusingly at the demon.

"Just my little joke, Mr Gilmore," Dumas explained, a smug grin on his face. "You didn't think I would sneak off with him, did you?"

"This time we go together," the angel instructed. "After three. One… two… three."

Mr Gilmore did not take his eyes off the demon. They vanished in unison on this occasion. Gordon shivered. He felt uncomfortable without them and actually missed their banter, if you could call it that. In the silence, the room felt strangely oppressive… one might even say eerie. It had been the first time Gordon had been left alone with his statuesque friends and he deliberately avoided looking into their eyes. Somehow, he could not face doing that at this particular moment. His housemates remained transfixed in their same positions, a constant reminder that he was not dreaming. Now that Mr Gilmore and Dumas had gone, you could have forgiven Gordon if he had questioned, yes, even now, whether this was reality and not a nightmare.

Gordon did not know what to do. He was lost in his own house. As he glanced around the room, he noticed that Death had taken some of his books off the shelves. He started to replace them, glad that he had found a constructive way to pass the time. It was as though he were the host clearing up after a party, and this party was definitely over. Strangely, his own fate was not what occupied his thoughts at this moment. Mr Gilmore and Dumas might have been fighting over his soul, but Gordon was instead contemplating a world without him. Who would replace him at work? Would his replacement be better at the job? Would his friends advertise his room? What about his stuff? And what about Blubber? What will happen to Blubber? He wandered to the far side of the room and sprinkled some goldfish food into the glass bowl.

"Here you go, Blubber. You'd better have a bit more than normal, as people are going to be a bit tied up over the next few days."

Blubber was motionless, suspended in what could have been mistaken for ice. The flakes of fish food merely rested on top of the static water.

Gordon moved towards the window and pulled back the heavy, scarlet curtain. All was still outside, but that was not unusual. He lived in a quiet road. And, of course, it was Christmas Day – most people would be sprawled out on their sofas in front of their televisions, their stomachs full. He doubted if anyone would be playing charades.

Gordon, the tube of fish food still in one hand, gazed at the Christmas lights in some of the windows. At first glance, nothing outside gave any indication that time had stopped. Gordon was only reminded of the fact when he looked at the street lamps. He could make out the rain within the light they emitted, the thin streaks of water suspended in the air, motionless. He noticed the distant light of an aeroplane high in the sky. He thought at first, rather hopefully, that the red light was moving, and stared intensely at it, not budging an inch, having set a static raindrop on the window as a marker. However, the light never got any closer to the raindrop. Gordon sighed and momentarily closed his eyes. He felt like he was in a world in which he no longer belonged. Familiar things – outside and within his home – now felt strangely alien to him.

Gordon was relieved to hear the voice of Mr Gilmore and turned around, closing the curtain neatly behind him.

"There you are, Mr Jones," the angel said, walking towards his charge. "I hope you didn't get up to any mischief."

Dumas stood in the shadow of Mr Gilmore, his arms folded, his hat covering most of his dark locks.

"So, who won?" Gordon inquired. "Have you decided who has the pleasure of taking me to heaven? I don't see that it really matters. As you said, everyone has to face the judgement of God. I'm ready for that... so long as Mr Dumas understands that he won't see me again once he drops me off at the gates." He looked towards the demon. "Mr Gilmore is right. I am a Christian. That is the end of the story. I know I belong in heaven."

"Brave words, Mr Jones," Dumas sniffed. "Let's hope, for your sake, you are right."

Gordon looked at Mr Gilmore nervously. "I *am* a Christian," he pleaded, his voice showing signs of desperation. "You know that, and so does God, doesn't he?"

"Then you will be fine," Mr Gilmore assured him. "Don't worry. Now, are you ready, Mr Jones?"

Gordon nodded dumbly.

This time there was no hesitation. Both Mr Gilmore and Dumas had clicked their fingers. Gordon was not even sure whether he had closed his eyes or merely blinked, but when he opened them again, he realised he was no longer in Buckinghamshire.

4

"And yonder all before us lie
Deserts of vast eternity."

To His Coy Mistress
Andrew Marvell

IF YOU WERE TO ASK A CHILD – OR AN ADULT, FOR THAT
matter – what their favourite colour was, few, if any, would choose
white. The colour (some might even debate whether it is a colour at all)
had never done much for Gordon either. He would never choose to paint
a wall in his house white. Of course, it has to be said, decorating was not
an occupation Gordon had much experience in, and the fact there were
indeed no plain white walls in his house was because of the efforts of past
occupants rather than through his own labours with a paintbrush.

The fact that everything in front of Gordon was now white meant
that our hero could be under no illusion that he might still be in his own
house. In fact, as far as he could see, *everything* in front of him was white.
There was no horizon, so it was impossible to ascertain just how far the
whiteness extended. If he had not been able to see his own body, he might
have been fooled into thinking a white screen had been placed a few
inches in front of his face.

The bemused Gordon sat transfixed, afraid to move his head even an
inch. If he had done so, he would have noticed four orange chairs, exactly
the same as the one he now sat on, laid out to his right, in line with his
own. They were not particularly special chairs – the sort you would
probably find in a school classroom. What was more interesting was the
fact that one person sat on each. The occupants, like Gordon, were sitting
upright, staring directly ahead into the distance – if there was a distance
– their eyes adjusting to the brightness. Was this heaven... or maybe hell?
All was quiet; no sound of an angel playing a harp, or of crackling flames.

Gordon soon became aware of the fact he was holding something in
his hand. It was the tube of fish food from his living room. As he looked

38

down to examine it, he at last realised he was not alone. He momentarily turned his head to his right and, at the exact same time, the occupants of the other chairs also chose that moment to survey their surroundings, their nervous glances meeting simultaneously for a fraction of a second. That their glances met at that exact moment, if only for an instant, was uncanny. It was almost as if someone had pressed a button to command them to turn in unison. However, the five people quickly reverted their gazes and were soon again staring blankly ahead at nothing in particular. Indeed, it has to be reiterated, there was nothing for them to stare at.

All seemed reluctant to be the one to break the silence, unsure whether it was permitted or even safe to do so. They might have been animated characters drawn on a piece of white paper by a cartoonist who had yet to put in the background or to formulate a script.

Gordon fidgeted. He glanced down at his feet. There was just more whiteness, and no indication of where the ground began or finished, other than that the legs of the chairs all seemed to be standing in a line together, at the exact same height, seemingly suspended in mid-air. Gordon wriggled his dangling feet. There was nothing solid he could rest them on, even though his legs stretched below the base of the legs of the chairs. It did not take a genius to conclude that there was indeed no ground, but, of course, Gordon could not explain how the chairs appeared to be standing on at least something firm. In a bid to test his theory, he shifted closer to the edge of his chair and stretched one of his legs, pointing his toes in the hope that there may yet be something solid to stand upon, but that was not the case and he soon gave up for fear of one of his slippers – they were not a good fit – slipping off his foot into the abyss.

A man in dark green sat next to him. Gordon had gathered that fact when he had turned his head. It is surprising just how much you can take in of a scene even in a mere fraction of a second. He had even ascertained that a woman in white was sitting to the right of the man. He only sensed that there were another two people farther along the line, but had not been able to glean any information about them.

Gordon straightened himself in his chair, still not tempted to move his head to his right for another peep at the people next to him, preferring to procure further information by moving his eyeball as far as he could to the right, though the exercise proved unsuccessful and a little bit painful.

It seemed an eternity before the silence was finally broken and it was perhaps no surprise who should be the one to do so. A man at the very far end of the row, farthest away from Gordon, had been fidgeting more than the rest. He was clearly very agitated.

"What a time to die!" he exclaimed. "It's just typical, isn't it? I was five-three up, you know... set point as well!"

His outburst was the invitation the others needed to move their heads. They all shifted forward slightly in order to focus on the rotund pensioner. He was leaning back in his chair, tapping his knee with a tennis racquet. He was muttering what appeared to be some expletives under his breath. Gordon was immediately drawn to the natty, matching blue tracksuit top and bottoms the man was wearing, clothes more suited to someone of less advanced years, Gordon thought. It was perhaps strange Gordon should focus on his clothes before being drawn to the red sweatband positioned around the man's head, which looked even more ludicrous.

"I was actually going to beat the rascal," the man continued, still staring ahead and not in the slightest bit tempted to look at those who were now focused on him. "We've been playing all day and he'd beaten me every game. Finally, when I'm about to wipe the smug smile off his face, I go and die. Oh, the timing!"

He stopped and shook his head, his face adorned with balls of sweat, the band seemingly having failed to do its job.

"Christmas Day! Yes, it is pretty rotten luck, I suppose." It was the woman in the middle of the row who had responded. "I never thought I'd go on Christmas Day," she continued. "It might have been a bit easier to swallow if it had been on a Monday morning!"

"I was in the middle of an emergency cholecystectomy," the man next to Gordon chipped in. The green blur Gordon had earlier not failed to notice when he had turned his head was, in fact, the colour of the surgical scrubs that the man was wearing. He still sported his scrub cap, but his gauze mouth mask was now pulled below his chin and was resting around his neck. "It's quite ironic," he continued, slowly removing the disposable rubber gloves that were still on his hands. "It's usually the patient that dies... not the surgeon."

Being on the end of the row, Gordon only had to turn his head one way. The surgeon was sitting so close to him, Gordon felt it not appropriate to look at his face when he spoke. He actually had a better view of the woman, she being positioned just that little bit further away.

She wore a white bathrobe and her hair was wrapped in a white towel. She was the youngest of the five and must have only been in her early twenties, Gordon reflected.

"It's a good job I didn't actually die *in* the shower," she joked. "Glad I had the chance to put my robe on. Didn't know I'd have four blokes leering at me."

The men instinctively reverted their gazes from the young woman.

"It just happened so quickly," the tennis player added. "I was just about to return his serve, when some literary buffoon arrives to tell me that I've been terminated or something to that effect."

Gordon chuckled under his breath. His own meeting with Death already seemed a long time ago now. He thought of Mr Gilmore and Dumas, and wondered what had happened to them. They were nowhere to be seen.

"What were *you* doing?" the surgeon asked, swivelling in his chair to face Gordon, the medical man not bothered by their proximity, his probing eyes momentarily meeting Gordon's, before the latter deliberately turned his head away from them.

"Playing charades," Gordon replied. "A fate even worse than death! Can you believe it? I don't even like the game. Of all the things I could have been doing in my final moments."

"That's right," the woman interrupted. "If I knew I was going to die, I wouldn't have saved my chocolate cake for Boxing Day. It's still in the fridge!"

"It's an inconvenience, that's what it is," the tennis player complained. "One would like to have had a bit of notice, that's all. I wasn't prepared to go tonight. There was absolutely no warning. I was feeling fine. It's just not cricket!"

"Or tennis," the woman quipped.

"I don't suppose there's ever a good time to die," Gordon reflected. "But you're right; I wish now I was a bit more prepared for it. It's come as quite a shock."

"How long have you all been sitting here anyway?" the surgeon inquired. A few mumbled responses followed, and they came to the conclusion that they had all arrived at exactly the same time, simply because none of the party had been sitting alone at any point or had even noticed anyone else arrive.

"Where are we anyway?" the woman asked, her head turning in every direction as though she expected to see something other than the colour white.

"Where do you *think* we are?" the tennis player responded in an incredulous tone. "It must be heaven, of course."

"Heaven?" the woman reflected. "Well, if this is heaven, I don't think much of it. It's not exactly paradise, is it?"

They again reverted their gazes to the whiteness ahead of them. It was the surgeon who did what everyone else had wanted to do from the moment they had arrived. He stretched out his hands, his rubber gloves now resting on his lap, as if he was expecting to touch a wall.

"Bizarre, isn't it?" he said. "There's nothing. You don't think we're in a great big cloud or something?"

"I'm sorry to put a spanner in the works," the tennis player suddenly announced, "but I might have been mistaken. I've got a funny feeling this is probably *not* heaven."

As he finished his sentence, he nodded his head in the direction of the man next to him, who had so far refrained from taking part in the conversation, hence the fact he had not yet attracted any attention. Gordon shifted forward a little in order to get a better look. He gripped the back of his chair with one hand, for fear he might get too near the edge. Of course, there was little chance of falling off his chair. How often do people fall off a normal chair (and, as we have said, this was just a normal chair)? However, put that chair on a precipice and somehow the very normal act of sitting down becomes more difficult, at least in the mind, with the individual now believing that falling off a chair is something that happens every day.

Gordon focused his eyes on the occupant of the fourth chair. The man sat motionless and still chose to remain silent. Of course, Gordon assumed it was a man, from his figure, but he could not immediately ascertain that fact from the face; the man wore a black balaclava and only his eyes were visible. The rest of his attire was also black. He held a torch in his gloved hands and had a tatty black rucksack resting on his lap. He must have known all eyes were centred on him, but he did not respond, remaining transfixed in his chair, his gaze focused on the nothingness ahead of him.

"Good grief!" exclaimed the surgeon, a look of disdain and bewilderment suddenly appearing on his face. "What's *he* doing with us?"

"What do you mean?" the woman asked.

The surgeon scoffed, "Well, it doesn't take a brain surgeon – not that that's my particular field – to come to the conclusion that he wasn't up to much good this evening, does it? Good heavens... I didn't think they'd let all the riff-raff in."

"As I said," the tennis player attempted to explain. "This obviously *can't* be heaven."

"He's right," said the woman. "You'd expect there to be more than five people up here."

"Then it can't be the other place either," the surgeon responded. "You'd expect even more to be there!"

Gordon pictured Mr Gilmore and Dumas fighting over the right to take him to the gates of heaven. He wondered whether he should share his own experience with the others, but decided to remain silent. Besides, he was not exactly sure where he was, or where those two particular immortals had disappeared to.

"Well, if this is heaven," the woman announced, "I don't exactly think much of it. You would have thought there'd at least be a couple of angels playing some harps or something."

Gordon smiled. The image of heaven that was portrayed in cartoons and books had almost become reality in the minds of many. Instead of letting the imagination run riot, thinking of the most wonderful things that they could, the best image of heaven they could come up with involved clouds and harps.

"How come you were playing tennis on Christmas night?" the woman asked suspiciously, turning suddenly to face the tennis player, as though she were accusing him of some hideous crime. "Who plays tennis on Christmas Day? Besides, it must have been dark. You could have hurt yourself..."

She stopped and grinned when she realised that what she had said may have hit the nail on the head.

"Have you not heard of floodlights?" the surgeon suggested. "There were some big houses in my neighbourhood. Most people had a floodlit court or a swimming pool."

"They didn't in my street," the woman mused.

"As a matter of fact," the tennis player continued, "I do have a tennis court... and a swimming pool, though it's not lit; I mean, the tennis court isn't lit. Of course, this wasn't real tennis I was playing."

"Real tennis?" the woman interrupted. "I've seen that before. It's what all the posh people used to play in their big houses a long time ago. Not like the US Open."

"No, I meant I wasn't playing *real* tennis, or even lawn tennis," the tennis player attempted to explain. "It was tennis on a computer – it was a virtual computer game, only you use a real racquet, instead of a control or a joystick, whatever they call it these days, and you hit thin air instead of a real ball. It's very clever," he added doubtfully, almost trying to convince himself, his explanation sounding as ridiculous to him as it did to the others.

Gordon smiled. He knew the others were thinking the same thing as him: why exactly the man had felt the need to don a tracksuit – not to mention the ridiculous headband – to play a computer game? No one asked, of course. It was clear he was the sort of person that took things very seriously – that also being evident by the perspiration on his face.

"It was Godfrey's Christmas present – he's my grandson," continued the tennis player, as we shall still continue to call him. He stopped and reflected on his final game. "As I said, I was beating the rascal when it happened. Just my luck!"

"Need we inquire as to how old your grandson is?" the woman grinned.

"Six," was the somewhat rather muffled reply.

"I had bought myself a new car for Christmas," the surgeon announced suddenly, as though he felt it was a good time to inform people of the fact. "I was going to pick it up on Tuesday. Typical!"

"Oh dear!" the tennis player yelled. "I forgot about the Rolls! I left it parked on the drive. I hope Rogers will garage it tonight."

"Who's Rogers?" the woman inquired.

"His manservant, probably!" the surgeon retorted.

The tennis player did not argue and seemed almost pleased someone else had made the remark.

"Wow! Fancy having a servant," the woman drooled. "Did he dress you... and cut your toenails? I've always wondered whether the Royal Family cut their own toenails?"

No one felt the urge to respond.

"Anyway," the woman continued, "we're all equal now. Death said something about being the great leveller. We'll all be the same in heaven."

The surgeon looked rather disturbed at the thought. It had seemingly never crossed his mind up to now.

"But this can't be heaven?" the tennis player harped on. "What about him?" There was no subtle nod in the direction of the man in black on this occasion. His tennis racquet was now pointing in the direction of the hunched figure next to him, almost touching his face. It caused the man to turn in his direction.

The first movement the man had made since the five had found themselves sitting together had a big effect. Immediately, the tennis player removed the offending object and turned his head. The eyes of the man may have been all that was visible on his face, and Gordon did not see the look he flashed the tennis player, but he felt relieved he was not on the receiving end of it. At last the man in black pulled off his balaclava. He made no attempt to brush down the hairs on his head that 'stood to attention' as he did so. The man was of middle age, his grey stubble the greatest indicator that he had seen more years than one might have at first guessed. Everyone waited for him to speak, but he did not oblige, returning his gaze to the nothingness in front of him.

"Did anyone see the first part of *Coronation Street* tonight?" the woman asked suddenly. "I hate it when an episode ends on a cliffhanger. I always somehow end up missing the next one – you know, the one when everything's revealed. Still, I've got a good excuse this time."

Her attempt to make polite conversation in a bid to remove the tension created by the man in black did not help. Another awkward silence merely followed. Gordon was not used to solitude. He had rarely experienced total silence. There was always a car engine, the jets of a distant aeroplane or merely the sound of his creaking house. He found the new experience disturbing. No one seemed to know what to say. There was no obvious explanation for the situation they now found themselves in and that is what was really on their minds, of course. No one had much desire to make polite conversation, but, as is so often the case, felt compelled to do so.

Inevitably, it was the tennis player who broke the latest silence.

"What if this is it?" he declared with a shudder.

The others looked at him confused.

"What if we are destined to sit here forever?" he continued. "We might have to spend eternity sitting on these chairs. Perhaps that is our fate?"

The thought had not previously occurred to anyone. They had all assumed they were waiting for someone, or something to happen. It was a sobering moment.

"This can't be it," the surgeon said hopefully. "We can't just sit here forever. That would be..."

He stopped. The others knew instantly what his next word would have been. It was the man in black that finished the sentence.

"Hell," he calmly said.

The man did not elaborate, and the very fact he had at last chosen to speak startled the rest of the group. It was Gordon who responded this time.

"I remember a story my headmaster told me during an assembly. It was about some people who thought they were in heaven when they saw a great feast laid out in front of them, the most sumptuous you could ever imagine. Only it wasn't heaven. The guests were allowed to sit at the table, but chains prevented them from reaching any of the food."

"Damn it!" the tennis player roared. "This can't be hell. What have I done to deserve this? I've been a law-abiding citizen all my life, which is more than I can say for at least one of us sitting here."

He did not look at the man next to him, but the others did.

The tennis player continued. "Of course, he might have a perfectly good explanation as to why he's dressed all in black and wearing a balaclava on Christmas night?"

"It was quite cold," the woman responded.

"Or why there's a silver candlestick poking out of his bag?" the tennis player went on suspiciously. All eyes focused on the said object.

"Perhaps he's an actor and was on stage playing the part of a criminal," the woman suggested, keen to protect the man, more in fear he might lose his temper to their cost.

The man pushed the protruding candlestick further into the rucksack, before using the zip to secure it safely inside.

"That looked a nice piece," the surgeon smiled. "I'm into antiques *myself.* What else did you get?"

The burglar, as we should perhaps now call him, became interested at last, presumably because the conversation had switched to his newly acquired possessions rather than the method used to obtain them. He felt into his coat pocket and removed a gold chain and locket.

"They left this on the dressing table. Honestly, some people," he said, shaking his head. "They almost ask you to take it, don't they? How much do you reckon it's worth?"

The surgeon moved to the edge of his chair and stretched over the woman next to him in order to take the item from the gloved hands of the burglar.

"Yes, it is nice. I've got one exactly like this," he stated. "They're worth a few bob, you know. Mine's got my initials engraved on the..." He stopped and stared accusingly at the burglar. "This is mine! You were robbing *my* house!"

"Sorry, mate. I didn't choose your house on purpose. Everyone else was in. It was Christmas evening, remember."

The burglar turned his head away from the surgeon, removing the black leather gloves from his hands and placing them on top of the rucksack, which still rested on his lap. "Anyway, you can keep it if it's yours," he added nonchalantly, returning his gaze to the nothingness in front of him.

The surgeon returned a look of incredulity. He ignored the sniggers coming from the tennis player at the far end of the row.

"If it's any consolation," continued the burglar, "I won't sue you."

"Pardon?"

"It's because of you I'm sitting here. I took the liberty of using your ladder to reach your bedroom window. That ladder's a death trap!"

The burglar rubbed his head, as though he still felt the full force of his fall. Gordon wondered how he had managed to keep hold of the bag when he fell, but judging the way he still, even now, held on to the fruit of his labours, he could see that it would take more than a fatal fall to prise it from his hands.

"What happened to you?" the woman asked, turning towards the tennis player.

The portly pensioner shook his head. "I've no idea. It all happened so quickly. That literary imbecile didn't reveal the details."

"I just came over all faint," the woman said. "I just thought it was all the hot steam from the bathroom. Obviously not."

"I must admit I was feeling lousy," the surgeon contributed, having regained his composure, "but I just thought I'd drunk too much sherry."

The woman looked horrified. "I thought you said you were carrying out an operation?"

"Oh, come on, dear. Even surgeons are allowed a drink now and again. It was Christmas, after all. What about you?" the surgeon asked, turning quickly to Gordon.

"I've no idea. I just felt tired and drifted off to sleep. I suppose that's the best way to go."

Another brief period of silence ensued. The occupants were all becoming restless, fidgeting much more now.

"These chairs are not very comfortable," said the woman. "They remind me of the chairs at my local health centre. Thought we might get something better than this in heaven."

"How many times must I tell you?" the tennis player groaned. "This is *not* heaven. It can't be. There is no way someone like him would get to heaven. He's a criminal."

The burglar did not protest.

"And yet," said the surgeon, "we've already established that this can't be hell... it can't be," he tried to reassure himself. "Do you really think someone like myself, who works day and night for the good health of others – even on Christmas Day – would be condemned to eternal damnation? I think I deserve a better fate than that."

"Me too," added the woman. "I do a lot of charity work."

"And I..." the tennis player began, "I... well... well, I'm just a damn decent chap. Never broken the law in my life."

"Probably because you never had to," the burglar suggested. "You might have forsaken your principles if you hadn't been born with a silver spoon in your mouth... if you'd needed a few pennies to buy a loaf of bread."

"Is that why you turned to crime?" the woman asked sensitively.

"No."

They waited for the burglar to elaborate, but, not for the first time, he did not oblige.

The surgeon scowled at the burglar, placing his gold locket in the pocket of his surgical gown.

Gordon did not feel the time was right to explain that salvation did not depend on good works. If they were destined to sit together for eternity, he would have plenty of time for theological debates. He still could not understand why he was sitting with these people. He was the only Christian among them. That was becoming obvious. Where was Mr Gilmore? What was keeping him?

"This is ridiculous," the tennis player said suddenly. "We've got to do something. I'm not just going to sit here and stand for this."

"What exactly do you suggest we do?" the surgeon asked, looking all around at the nothingness in order to emphasise his point.

The tennis player took off his headband, wiping the perspiration from his forehead with it. The said object must have been on so tight, it left a white mark on his skin, as though all the blood had been prevented from reaching his brain, which the others might have used as an excuse for his childish demeanour. "I don't know, but I can't stand much more of this," he moaned. "It's not knowing what's going on that's so frustrating. I don't like waiting."

"We don't even know what we're waiting for," the woman said. "There might not be *anything* to wait for. As we said… this could be it."

Every trivial conversation always seemed to lead to a discussion on their fate. Of course, that was perhaps hardly surprising. However, it did not stop them from at least trying to talk about the mundane.

It was Gordon who suggested that they should play a game to pass the time, which was rather surprising, as he, as it has already been established, did not like games. The idea only received a few groans, and Gordon thought of Bill, when he had jumped to the centre of the room not so long ago with a similar proposal. Gordon smiled ruefully and added, "Anything but charades, though."

The burglar was first to respond. "I spy with my little eye something beginning with…" He looked around him and smiled. "W."

No one bothered to answer.

"That's it!" the tennis player declared, thumping the racquet against his leg, so hard that it must have hurt. "This really is it. If they think I'm spending the rest of my existence sitting in a chair playing 'I spy', they are sadly mistaken. I'm not going to stand for this any longer."

The others all turned to face him, waiting in anticipation, wondering exactly what he proposed to do. The tennis player was pink in the face, the veins in his head protruding and vibrating.

"This is an utter disgrace," he continued, shifting in his chair, looking for someone to release his venom on. "No one has the right to treat me like this. I demand an explanation. I say…"

He had now begun to shout for attention, waving his headband in the air. "I say…"

The rest of the party were now silent, staring at him in astonishment.

"There's got to be someone around," he continued. "There's got to be… I say…"

Still the others remained silent. However, they were no longer looking at the headband or even listening to his pleas for help. The tennis player suddenly realised they were now looking towards his feet. In the commotion, he had risen from his chair and was now standing up... but on thin air, or so it seemed. It was like something from a cartoon. No sooner did he look down and notice there was seemingly nothing solid to hold him than he fell from view, his cries fading into the distance.

The others did not say a word and just stared at his empty chair.

5

"They are not long, the days of wine and roses."

Vitae Summa Brevis
Ernest Dowson

"THIS IS OUTRAGEOUS. I COULD HAVE BEEN KILLED!" THE tennis player screamed, as he was carried back to his chair. His rescuer, if you can call them that, placed him down gently and handed him his tennis racquet.

Gordon and the others did not feel it was up to them to speak, choosing to remain silent. The tennis player had only been gone a few moments, but when he had reappeared, he was in the arms of a tiny but plump woman of an advanced age. They dared not ask how she had managed to carry him with so little effort, though, strangely, that was the only thing on their minds at this particular moment. That a woman of her size or age could carry a man, as though he were a baby in her arms, was of more concern than discovering as to exactly who she was or where she had come from. Perhaps they subconsciously believed an answer to the latter question would be beyond the limit of their understanding. They could comprehend the physical world, but the spiritual still left them completely at a lost and was a world which they preferred to put to the back of their minds.

The tennis player, now seated back in his chair, replaced his headband, his barrage of complaints eventually subsiding. He attempted to compose himself by blowing air out of his mouth, his cheeks inflating as he did so. It was his way of trying to restore his dignity. It didn't work. He looked like an embarrassed schoolboy and, mindful that all eyes were still upon him, he eventually zipped up his tracksuit top, positioning his chin within it, as if to hide his face, before sinking lower into his seat.

The eyes of the rest of the party eventually settled on the old woman.

"So, who might you be?" the surgeon sneered. "You don't look much like St Peter..."

The woman had a sweet face and her warm smile instantly put Gordon at ease. She did not need to say anything. If you had to pick your grandmother from a face alone, she would have been first choice. She wore a simple dark cotton dress that extended all the way to the ground, if there had been a ground, of course. A white apron covered most of her dress and her short, curly hair was stuffed into a white cap that was too small to hold all of it. Apart from some frills on the cap, her clothes were conservative and practical. It was clear she was, or had been, a domestic worker of some sort.

"Are you an angel?" Gordon asked bluntly.

The woman nodded.

"So, this is heaven!" the surgeon gasped.

The angel continued to smile, but made no attempt to speak. After a while, she opened a blue folder – the sort a college student might have in their possession – and started to thumb through the pages within it, occasionally putting her finger to her mouth to aid the turning of any page that might be difficult to separate from the next. However, that was more through habit than to actually obtain any saliva on her finger. Without looking up, she at last spoke, but it was to herself.

"Now then," she mumbled, "what have we got here? Yes, I see… you're the 19:34s."

"Why don't you fall?" the woman alongside Gordon suddenly asked, pointing her finger towards the angel's feet. "Like he did," she continued, nodding in the direction of the tennis player. "Aren't you standing on thin air?"

The angel looked down. Her shoes were not actually visible, her long dress hiding them from view, though it was probably safe to assume her footwear was functional rather than flattering.

"Don't you know that angels can fly, my dear?" she replied smiling.

Her voice was not patronising, even though the answer was. She had a country accent, as Gordon imagined all servants to have, but she spoke well, almost too well for a humble domestic worker. Her rounded figure also suggested she may have had a taste for the sweeter things in life and, even if she had spent her days serving others, she clearly never went without herself.

"Do you have a name?" Gordon inquired.

"I beg your pardon, young man," the woman apologised. "How rude of me not to introduce myself. I am Angel Harriet."

"Hi! I'm…"

She did not wait for him to finish.

"I know who you are, Mr Jones. You're on my list."

It did not take the tennis player long to put his embarrassing episode behind him. "We're not pleased, you know," he began, waving his tennis racquet. "We thought heaven would be better managed than this."

The angel chuckled. "Heaven? Oh dear, you still think this is *heaven?* How amusing."

"So, this *isn't* heaven?" the young woman inquired.

"Of course not," said the angel. "Whatever gave you that idea? Does it look like heaven?"

"As a matter of fact, we didn't know what it would be like," the surgeon interrupted. "It's funny, everyone wants to go there, but no one has the foggiest what's there." He stopped and raised his finger. "One can assume that we are also not in... well, you know?"

"Hell?" the angel calmly answered. "No, of course not."

"So, where are we?" the tennis player demanded. "On some cloud or something?"

"You are nowhere."

"Nowhere?" said at least three of the party in unison.

"That's right," Angel Harriet replied. "I don't expect you to understand. On earth you would perhaps call it 'no man's land'. That's the nearest thing to it, I suppose, but it's not really the same thing."

"I'm afraid I don't understand," the surgeon admitted. "How can we be nowhere? I'm an educated man, Miss Harriet. There is no such place as nowhere."

The angel tapped two of her plump fingers on the folder she was holding, tossing her head back thoughtfully. It was as though she was a teacher trying to think of a new way to explain a theory to her confused pupils.

"You must remember that you are now outside time," she persevered, "which means you don't have to be somewhere all of the time. Think of this as being a waiting room." She looked at their blank faces. "Oh dear, I'm not explaining this very well, am I? Never mind, in time – and we have plenty of that because there isn't any – you will understand."

The angel returned her glance to her folder and began muttering to herself once more.

"It's still not good enough," the tennis player complained. "What are we waiting for anyway? We've just been dumped here. It's not on. I'll be taking it up with your superiors, of course."

The angel looked up sharply. "Oh dear, is that so? That's interesting. Of course, there might also be one or two things my superior will be taking up with you."

It was no joke. Her face was solemn and regretful, and it stopped the tennis player in his tracks, even though he did not understand the meaning of her words.

"Anyway," he said, swiftly changing the subject, "when are we actually going up to heaven?"

Angel Harriet smiled. "I'm sorry. I do apologise for the delay. We've been very busy."

"Don't tell us," the burglar interrupted. "Everyone's dying to get in."

He nudged the tennis player in the ribs with his elbow, though the latter did not appreciate his humour and only returned a snarl, rubbing his side at the same time.

The angel's apology had gone down well among the party. They felt as though their impatience had been justified.

"Let me explain what's happening," the angel continued. "You are the 19:34s from Buckinghamshire. Death came to you at exactly the same time."

"He gets about a bit, doesn't he!" the young woman chipped in. She stopped. "But how can he be in five different places at exactly the same time?"

The angel smiled. "You forget..."

"We know," the surgeon interrupted. "There is no time. He's outside it; that's right, isn't it?"

"Very good, doctor. You're starting to understand. Anyway, on normal occasions, Death goes through the formalities and then waits for your allotted angel to appear."

Gordon thought of Mr Gilmore.

The woman was more sceptical.

"*Allotted* angel?" she responded suspiciously. "Do you mean a guardian angel? Did we really have one – someone who watched over us throughout our life?"

"More than one," Angel Harriet smiled. "The Master's children have many angels looking out for them. It's no secret. Did you not read Psalm 91 in the great book?"

"That's the Bible," the woman whispered to the surgeon. "Psalms is a book in the Bible. I learned to say them all in the right order when I was at school."

The burglar sighed. "A lot of good the angels did us! What's the point of having guardian angels if they fail to guard us? Mine could have warned me about *that* ladder."

"I'm sure the Master himself did," Angel Harriet responded, shaking her head sorrowfully. "He would have done his utmost to prevent you from going to that house. Who do you think put those doubts into your head? The Master can do much – but, of course, he will not interfere with free will."

There was a moment's silence, as all the party sat thoughtfully, presumably trying to recollect times in their lives in which an angel may have been watching over them. Gordon remembered Death's reference to that approaching juggernaut. He tried to picture Mr Gilmore sitting in the back seat of his car, leaning over and turning the steering wheel as the lorry came dangerously close.

"As I was saying," Angel Harriet continued, "once Death has done his bit, your allotted angel is meant to take you to the gates of heaven."

"Never a demon?" Gordon inquired, thinking of Dumas.

Angel Harriet smiled sympathetically. "Sadly, it is too often a demon, though demons are angels anyway, but I won't get started on that subject just now."

Gordon was beginning to understand. He thought of Mr Gilmore and Dumas bickering over the privilege of taking him to the gates of heaven. "*We get the Christians,*" Gordon muttered under his breath, repeating Mr Gilmore's words. "*You know the deal.*" He paused and looked wistfully into the whiteness ahead of him. It was obvious to Gordon that the others in the party were still oblivious to what was going on. They were not Christians and, even though they had probably been visited by demons, rather than angels, they had clearly not comprehended the fact or, if they had, its significance.

"The angel, or demon," Angel Harriet stressed, "takes what belongs to them, but only as far as the gates of heaven. The demons are not allowed in and have to wait outside until the Master has finished with their subject. Everyone has to face the Master, regardless of where they go from there."

"So what are we doing here?" the young woman inquired. "Why are we 'nowhere', as you put it?"

It appeared she was the only one, apart from Gordon, who had not given up trying to make sense of it. The tennis player and burglar were at this moment sneering at each other, while the surgeon had taken out his mobile phone and was pressing the buttons. "I wonder if I can still get a signal?" he mumbled. "Don't suppose they'll be able to get hold of me when I'm up there."

Angel Harriet reopened her folder.

"To answer your question, young lady," she said, without looking up, "to put it bluntly, I regret to inform you that we had a little discrepancy over the 19:34s from Buckinghamshire."

She ran her eyes along a page in the folder. "There was a bit of confusion over one of you and so I'm afraid all of the 19:34s from Buckinghamshire were held up until the problem had been resolved. It doesn't happen often. As I said, please accept my apologies."

Gordon gulped. He knew she was referring to him when she mentioned the word 'problem'.

"Anyway," she added, "we're ready now. I've got your tickets."

"Tickets?" at least three of the party uttered in unison, the angel at last regaining the full attention of all those seated before her.

"That's right. Everyone is allocated a ticket. To be honest, we don't usually distribute them, but because there was a bit of confusion this time, we've dug out yours."

She took an envelope from a pocket in her apron and waved it in the air. "Your angel (she deliberately chose not to also use the word 'demon' on this occasion) will be back shortly to take you up, once I give you your ticket."

Gordon sat back. He tried to convince himself that the 'confusion' had now been cleared up and that the victorious Mr Gilmore would be returning at any moment to escort him to paradise.

"There are just a few formalities to sort out," said Angel Harriet. "If you would bear with me, I've just got to run through a few details."

"No problem," the surgeon mocked. "We weren't planning on going anywhere."

She buried her head in her folder again. "Let me see, the 19:34s from Buckinghamshire. It's surprising how many people die on Christmas Day," she mused.

"I blame *The Sound of Music*," the burglar joked.

The angel did not respond and only the surgeon laughed, more through politeness, his spirits lifted by the appearance of this latest immortal, she being a sign that he would soon be winging his way to a better place... presumably.

The angel did not lift her head from the folder and continued to talk to herself. "It's quite unusual for *five* people from one area to all go at the exact same time. It's no wonder there was a bit of confusion."

Gordon wondered how many people normally died in a day. He could not even begin to guess.

Angel Harriet looked up. "I just need to check you're all present and correct, and to establish who is who."

Gordon thought that odd. She had obviously known who *he* was, and he was convinced she knew the identity of the others too. He wondered why she was pretending to be a dithering pensioner when, really, she was sharper than any of those that occupied the chairs in front of her. Gordon might have thought it odd, but she was so sweet and gentle that it was merely odd and not sinister.

"We must make sure you get the *right* ticket now," she continued smiling.

"Does that mean we won't all be going to the same place?" the young woman asked.

The angel pretended she did not hear the question and turned to Gordon.

"Let's start on the end with you, Mr Jones, shall we? It says here you died of... oh dear, very sad. Who's next? Miss Davies... I presume that must be you, madam?" she inquired, swivelling her body to face the young woman.

"I think you could be right, honey," the solitary female replied sarcastically, but still pulling the towel from her head, so that her long hair fell to her shoulders, as if to prove her point. Her hair was still wet, Gordon noted.

"Of course that's you, dear. I'm sorry," the angel apologised, "but you can't always tell these days. You died of... oh dear, not another one, and so young as well."

Neither Gordon nor the woman felt it their place to ask the angel to elaborate and, if truth be told, they would rather remain oblivious to the full details of their demise. Gordon had always been a bit squeamish when it came to medical matters.

The angel paused and turned another page in her folder. "Is this right? *Fingers* Maloney?" she inquired innocently.

"That will be me," the burglar explained. "It was a sort of nickname. And you don't need to tell everyone what killed me. It was *his* dodgy ladder!"

The surgeon turned his head with disdain, preferring not to set eyes on the villain.

"And you must be Dr Marsden?" the angel continued.

"Good guess," he replied dryly, looking down at his own attire. "Don't tell me... I died of a..."

He rattled off two words that Gordon had never heard spoken in his lifetime or had even known existed. The angel looked at the surgeon surprised.

"I am a doctor," he explained smugly.

"Exactly," Angel Harriet replied. "That's what worries me. You're way off the mark, Dr Marsden. Still, you won't be able to do any more harm where you're going."

The comment was not a sneer and apparently said in all innocence, though Gordon could not be sure.

The angel moved towards the other end of the line. "So you must be Edward Ponce-Foot Jones? Not another Jones! How many of you are there?"

"It's *Paunce,* madam! Edward *Paunce*-Foot Jones, if you don't mind," the tennis player corrected her.

The angel continued unperturbed. "Death occurred via a blow to the head caused by a..." She halted and smiled. "Tennis ball?" she added doubtfully.

"And it was going out!" the tennis player responded.

Gordon looked at the tennis player in astonishment.

"How can a tennis ball kill you?" the burglar inquired.

"Especially a virtual one!" Gordon laughed.

The others had forgotten that fact and stared at the tennis player. He merely turned up his nose and started plucking at the strings of his racquet.

Angel Harriet closed her folder abruptly, so that it made some of the party shudder, even though there was no noise. She reached inside her apron pocket and pulled out a white envelope. All eyes immediately focused on it. It was not a particularly impressive envelope, the sort you would find in a stationery cupboard in any office. The angel looked inside but did not remove the contents. She looked up embarrassed.

"Oh dear... I don't know what to say," she fidgeted.

"What is it?" the surgeon inquired.

"There's only four tickets."

"I don't believe this," the tennis player reacted angrily. "This is a complete shambles. I'm going to…"

He stopped in mid-sentence. Angel Harriet had vanished before their eyes.

"Now what do we do?" the surgeon sighed, picking up his mobile phone once more. "Shall we call a cab?"

"It's no joke," the tennis player raged. "You can't mess with people's lives like this… or deaths. It's outrageous. We've been treated abominably from the moment we popped our clogs. It seems nothing, even dying, is sacred anymore…"

The tennis player continued to mumble a few expletives, but the others were not listening. They had become silent.

Gordon lowered his head and momentarily closed his eyes. It had been a long day, or so he presumed.

"I wonder what it's really like up there," said the burglar dreamily, tilting his head upwards. "Do you think it really is paradise?"

"What's it to you?" snapped the tennis player. "You don't really think you'll be getting a ticket to heaven, do you? It's no doubt because of you that we've been held up. Angel Harry, or whatever her name is, said that there had been some confusion over one of us. It's not that confusing to me. You're obviously going to the other place. You're not going to be coming with us, are you?"

The burglar shrugged his shoulders and started to play with the switch on his torch. He had a look of resignation on his face and Gordon almost felt sorry for him.

"Where's she gone now anyway?" the surgeon groaned. "Why does it take them so long to do things? I thought there wasn't any time up here? Why don't things just happen straight away? I don't like waiting."

The woman sneered at him, drying her still wet hair with the towel she had earlier removed from her head. "It's a good job you were the surgeon and not the patient. I had to wait about seven months for my knee operation. It'll do you good to wait for a change. We all have to have some patience now and again."

The surgeon looked at her. "I think I've had more than my fair share of *them* over the years, don't you?"

"What's the hurry anyway?" the burglar insisted, shrugging his shoulders. "Wherever we're going, we're going to be spending eternity there, so a few hours sitting on a chair is not going to make a huge amount of difference, is it?"

Of course, it was perhaps no surprise that the five should be impatient to reach their destination. People are still anxious to board a long-haul flight as quickly as possible and will queue to get onboard. They know they might have fourteen hours to sit on the plane, but they still can't wait to get to their seat.

"I wonder how big heaven is?" the woman reflected. "There must be billions of people up there already. Hope there's room for us all."

The surgeon shook his head despondently. He was not willing to partake in any more surmising. "I can't stand much more of this," he said softly. "I don't want to die. I really don't."

It was the most human thing he had said since their arrival.

Gordon instinctively put his hand on the shoulder of the surgeon.

"*Everybody wants to go to heaven, but nobody wants to die,*" Gordon sang. "It's a song. My grandfather used to play the record to me." He stopped and offered a warm smile. "Don't worry. I'm sure everything will be all right," he added, doing well to sound convincing.

"Isn't he the one who's meant to tell us that?" the unsympathetic tennis player tutted.

"It's just not fair," the surgeon sighed, his eyes tearful. "I had so much to live for. I spent years getting to the top, years of blood, sweat and tears. I was looking forward to my retirement, putting my feet up, spending time with the grandchildren, playing a round of golf now and then. It's not fair."

"At least you had a decent innings. Look at her," the burglar nodded in the direction of the woman.

No one looked. They did not need to. However, they all fell silent, almost as a mark of respect, a visible act of compassion towards her. The woman *did* seem very young, Gordon thought.

"Don't worry about me," she said, tossing her head back defiantly. "Life was overrated, if you want my opinion. There wasn't a lot of point to it all. We got up, went to work, went to bed…"

She stopped suddenly, noticing a knot in her hair, which she endeavoured to detangle.

Gordon looked at her with sadness, the surgeon with surprise.

"How can you say that?" the latter challenged. "Life was wonderful. The miracle of birth…"

"And death," the burglar interrupted, preventing him from waxing lyrical. "She's right. What was the point of it all?"

"And it was all over in the blink of an eye," the tennis player added. "She does have a point, you know."

Gordon did not know what to say. He had enjoyed life, and he had not expected it to be over so quickly. He remembered Death telling him that everyone regretted not having done what they had intended to do during their lives. Gordon had, like so many, put things off. The thought that he would not get around to doing all those things he had meant to do had never occurred to him. Boldly in life he had declared that he would never have any regrets when it was over. Now that it was over, he had many.

Gordon was momentarily lost in his own thoughts. He did not notice that the tennis player had now climbed on to his chair. He was standing up, but in a bent position, so that he could still hold on to the back of it.

"What are you doing now?" the burglar asked.

"It worked last time," the tennis player replied coolly. "I say," he began shouting, trying to raise his racquet in the air, but failing to lift it even a few inches, being so preoccupied with his attempt not to lose his balance, fully aware of what had happened the last time he inadvertently vacated his chair. "I say... can we have a little service over here?"

"A little service," the burglar smiled, giving the woman a friendly nudge in the ribs, his head pointing in the direction of the tennis racquet.

The tennis player had settled into a crouched position, still facing in the opposite direction, which meant he did not see Angel Harriet return. He was still shouting, trying in vain to attract the attention of perhaps a passing flying angel. She stood watching him for a few moments, a curious expression on her face, before putting him out of his misery.

"Is there something wrong, Mr Ponce-Foot?"

He turned around sharply, almost falling off his chair. "It's *Paunce*," he roared, gingerly attempting to resume a sitting position. Of course, she knew *that* already, Gordon surmised.

The angel apologised as the tennis player adjusted his tracksuit top, a look of contempt in his eyes.

"Anyway," the angel began, "you will be pleased to know that I now have your tickets, all of them." She retrieved what looked like the same envelope from her apron pocket, slowly and deliberately, as though she were about to announce the winners of an award.

"Come on, get on with it," the surgeon demanded impatiently. "Hand them out."

Angel Harriet had no intention of being rushed. Gordon smiled as she struggled to open the envelope. She then pretended that she had forgotten the names of the recipients, as she slowly, one by one, handed out four tiny green cards. The surgeon received the fifth one, but not before the angel had gone back to the envelope to produce it, finally handing it over with a cheeky grin on her face. The surgeon had snatched it out of her hand when it was finally within reach.

The cards were all identical and blank. Gordon wondered why they were green. Why not blue, red or purple? It seemed a strange point to reflect on. That there was nothing printed on the card did not bother him at all.

The others were less than impressed.

"Is this it?" they muttered, or words to that effect. "I thought they'd be gold and shiny," the woman suggested, "like a golden ticket in *Charlie and the Chocolate Factory*."

"I don't suppose it matters," the surgeon declared, putting his card to his mouth and kissing it, his recent bout of melancholia instantly cured by the appearance of his ticket. "This is it! A ticket to heaven! Can you believe it? We've got a ticket to heaven in our hands. We're going to paradise!"

"But they all look the same," the tennis player suddenly pointed out, raising his card in front of his face, as though it might reveal some kind of watermark. He looked at the card in the gloved hands of the burglar. "He's got a green one as well."

"Does that mean he's going to heaven with us?" the woman asked bluntly.

Angel Harriet hesitated. "Don't worry, they might not look much, but each has been personally assigned to you."

"Heaven!" the surgeon continued excitedly. "We're going to heaven!" he repeated.

"You didn't answer my question," the woman persevered, staring intently at the angel. "I asked if he was coming to heaven as well?"

The burglar appeared to be disinterested, but Gordon was sure that that was not the case.

Angel Harriet knew she could not pretend she had not heard the question for a second time. She twitched nervously.

"Oh dear," she said. "I don't really know how to put this. This never gets any easier."

"What's wrong?" the surgeon asked, suddenly jolted out of his own personal ecstasy. "What's the matter now? Just tell us, woman... I mean, angel."

Angel Harriet opened her blue folder and turned a few pages. She was not actually looking for anything in particular. She merely wanted to avoid looking at the people in front of her. She never looked up as she spoke.

"I'm afraid there's something you should perhaps know... You are not *all* going to the same place."

"Is that it?" the tennis player exclaimed, a look of relief on his face. "I would have thought that was obvious. We know that already. I'm sure even he..." The tennis player stopped and nodded unashamedly towards the burglar. "I'm sure even he knew he wouldn't be going to heaven."

The angel now looked up. She paused and scratched her wrinkled cheek.

"Oh dear," she stuttered. "I don't think you understand. What I'm trying to say is..."

"What?" the surgeon demanded.

"Just spit it out," the tennis player added.

They waited, all eyes focused on the angel. She cleared her throat. Only Gordon anticipated what she was going to say. Her voice was barely above a whisper.

"I might be wrong, as I'm only a mere angel, and it's not really my place to say this, but I do believe... I do believe only *one* of those tickets is for heaven."

6

"The free and unmerited favour of God shown towards man."

Definition of 'grace'
Collins Pocket Dictionary of the English Language

GORDON DID NOT FLINCH. HE SAT QUITE STILL IN HIS CHAIR and never uttered a word. Of course, the same cannot be said of at least some of those sitting alongside him. One or two of the party preferred not to lose themselves in their own thoughts. Instead of digesting the latest revelation in silence, they immediately chose to voice their concern in the strongest possible terms. Needless to say, the tennis player was among the more vocal of the protestors.

"Is this some kind of joke?" he roared.

"Only one of us is going to heaven?" the surgeon added in an incredulous tone. "Surely there's been a dreadful mistake?"

"There's no mistake, doctor," Angel Harriet said sadly. "I'm sorry. Now, if you will excuse me, I do have other business to attend to."

The angel started to finger through a thick bundle of green cards, which she had removed from her apron pocket. The elastic band that had held them together was now hanging between her lips. She looked like a child about to swap picture cards in the playground.

"Perhaps you've given us the wrong ones?" the young woman suggested hopefully, still vigorously rubbing her hair with her towel, pointing her head in the direction of the tickets. "I assume those in your hands are all blank as well. It would be an easy mistake to make."

The angel removed the elastic band from her lips. She placed it around the cards, before slipping them back into her apron pocket. "Angels don't make mistakes, my dear," she smiled sympathetically. "Not often anyway."

The protests continued, but the angel did not hear them. She had vanished in an instant, though no one actually saw her disappear. When they realised there was no one standing in front of them, the protestations gradually came to a halt.

Gordon, the tube of fish food in one hand and his ticket in the other, looked at it thoughtfully – the ticket, that is. Of course, he knew it was he who had the ticket for heaven. He was a Christian, after all. The despairing figures beside him had probably not even set foot in a church before. He felt like the only child in the class to have passed an examination. He wanted to cheer, but felt he could not, out of respect for those that had been less successful than him.

The surgeon held his ticket aloft, searching for any clue that might reveal a destination on it. He flashed an occasional glance towards the other tickets, hoping his own might be different in some minute detail. He even put it to his ear at one point in the hope it might make a sound.

It was the woman who finally asked the question that most of them wanted answered.

"So, how do we know which one of us has got it?" she inquired bluntly.

The tennis player tossed his head back. "My dear," he scoffed, "I don't want to be the harbinger of doom, but I think that should be obvious."

The surgeon, less convinced he was himself bound for paradise, was uttering some obscenities under his breath. The woman sitting to his right heard him and tutted. "Language, doctor. Remember where you are."

He glared at her. He did not appreciate her remark and was genuinely shocked by her apparent nonchalance.

"It's a mystery, isn't it?" she continued, almost deliberately baiting the surgeon. "Whodunit? I mean, whodunit as in lived a good life? You almost expect Hercule Poirot to come along at any minute… Mes amis, the one with the ticket to heaven is…"

Her woeful Belgian accent only seemed to irritate the surgeon further. He crossed his legs and turned his back on her, so that he was now almost facing Gordon.

The burglar was the only one, with the exception of Gordon, who had not spoken since the angel had disappeared. He stared blankly ahead, resigned to his fate, as he had seemingly been all the time.

The woman continued to dab her hair with her towel. It was still wet and Gordon wondered if it would ever dry. However, she seemed oblivious to the fact that her efforts were seemingly in vain.

"I suppose *one* is better than none," she said. "At least one of us has won the raffle."

Even though the surgeon had his back to the tennis player, one might have been forgiven for thinking that he had noticed the smug smile on the face of the man farthest from him. He turned around sharply.

"Don't think it's you," he exclaimed, staring intently at the tennis player. "I don't doubt I have *the* ticket. I was just expressing my concern for your sakes."

He did not sound convincing, but the woman could not resist winding up his spring even further.

"And what makes you think it's you, Dr Marsden? Why should you have the golden ticket?"

"Of course it's me. I'm a top surgeon, one of the best in the country."

The others eyed him doubtfully.

"Is that it?" the tennis player sneered. "What's that got to do with it?"

"I've devoted my life to the well-being of others," the surgeon explained. "It's not a job; it's a vocation. I've saved many lives. I only suggest that it's payback time. It's time for me to inherit my reward."

The woman shook her head. "You had your reward on earth. You earned enough money to buy a big house and a flashy car. I don't doubt what you did was honourable, but it doesn't make you any better than the rest of us."

"And what was your contribution to society?" the surgeon inquired.

"Now that you mention it, I did help out at an old folks' home twice a week. It was voluntary work as well. That's right, doctor. I didn't get paid anything. I did it out of the kindness of my heart. What do you say to that?"

"I helped someone the other day," the burglar suddenly announced. "I helped this old girl carry her shopping to her car."

"I'm surprised you never ran off with it," the tennis player quipped.

"I don't understand it," the surgeon mused. "We're obviously all good people... so why aren't we *all* going to heaven?"

"Well, we've obviously done something wrong," the woman suggested. "Everyone has a skeleton hanging in their cupboard."

"The only skeleton I have is the one in my consulting room," the surgeon scoffed.

"He's right," the tennis player nodded. "It doesn't make sense. We're not criminals like *him*." This time he did not even feel the need to make any gesture towards the burglar. "We might not be angels, but we're good people, I'm sure of that. There are more good bones in our bodies than bad ones, isn't that right?"

"What about you, Mr Jones?" the woman said suddenly, aware that Gordon had not chosen to partake in the conversation. "Have you got any skeletons hanging in your cupboard?"

Gordon shifted uncomfortably. All eyes were now upon him. He knew he had to reveal exactly what was on his mind.

"I don't know how to put this," he hesitated, "but I think... I think it's... *me.*"

"What's *you?*" the tennis player snapped.

"The one that's going to..."

"I see," the surgeon interrupted. "He reckons he's got the golden ticket to heaven! What makes you think that, Mr Charlie Bucket?" he mocked.

Gordon could hardly say the words. He let out a cough of embarrassment before almost whispering, "I'm a... I'm a Christian."

The others did not respond in the way he was expecting. Clearly, they had been bracing themselves for an earth-shattering revelation, confirmation that he was the chosen one and that they were doomed. However, as far as they were concerned, they had not received that and there was relief in their voices.

"Is that it?"

"So what?"

"I'm a Christian as well."

"It's a Christian country."

"Look, I wear a cross."

Gordon scratched his head. He was speechless, knocked back by their reaction. It was the woman who came to his rescue. She was fingering the aforementioned gold cross that hung on a chain around her neck.

"Oh, I get it," she said. "I know what he's trying to say. He *really* is a Christian."

"What do you mean?" the tennis player continued to argue. "We all are, aren't we?"

"Mr Jones is talking about church and all that stuff," the woman continued. "Is that not right, Mr Jones?"

"Church?" the burglar uttered, as though he was referring to a distant planet.

"Is that all?" the surgeon piped. "We've all been to church, haven't we?"

"Yes, I was christened in one," the tennis player pointed out.

Gordon stuttered. "It's not just about going to church. It's more than that."

"More?" the tennis player questioned. "What do you mean?"

"You know what he means," the woman interrupted. "He doesn't just *go* to church. He's what we call a Bible-basher. That's right, isn't it, Mr Jones?"

Gordon had a sheepish grin on his face. "Being a Christian is not just about going to church," he explained. "It's about..." He paused and subconsciously put his hand over his mouth before mumbling. "It's about... Jesus."

Strangely, he found the name difficult to say. He need not have concerned himself. They all looked at him with incredulity. He might as well have been referring to Mickey Mouse.

"Is that all?" the tennis player continued. "We know who Jesus is. Who doesn't?"

Gordon coughed again. "It's not just about knowing who he is, it's about knowing him personally, having a relationship with him... and serving him."

The woman turned to Gordon. There was now a serious look on her face.

"He died for our sins, didn't he? He was nailed to a cross to save us. That's what it was all about, wasn't it?"

She looked down at the cross hanging around her neck. It was now resting in the palm of her hand. She studied it closely. It was obvious that she had never really looked at it in this way before, let alone questioned its relevance.

"We all know the story," the surgeon interrupted. "He was raised from death after three days. But it's just a story!"

Incredible as it may seem, despite having been in the presence of angels, even now, those alongside Gordon still had difficulty comprehending the existence of God. The fact God apparently was indeed real had seemingly, for the first time, suddenly dawned on the surgeon and those beside him.

"So it *was* true?" the woman reflected. "It wasn't just a story."

"But that's good then, isn't it?" the burglar suggested hopefully. "You said this Jesus died for our sins. We only have to thank him and everything will be all right, won't it?"

"But it's too late now," the woman sighed. "You're meant to have thanked him when you were alive. We've left it *too* late!"

There was an air of desperation in her voice. She let go of her cross and sat back, now anxiously chewing its gold chain between her teeth. Her face was pale and, for the first time, she looked genuinely concerned.

The surgeon shook his head. "But the whole thing wasn't fair. I'm an educated man. You can't expect me to believe in something like that. The Bible's just full of fairy tales, men parting the Red Sea and big fish swallowing people. God can't blame us for not becoming Christians. The whole thing was so unbelievable."

They all looked at Gordon for an explanation. He shrugged his shoulders. "I'm sorry. I don't have all the answers."

"I'm not convinced he's right," the tennis player scoffed, pointing his racquet accusingly at Gordon. "Christians are no better than the rest of us. The churchgoers I know are all hypocrites. There are far better men in the world that do not go to church every Sunday."

Gordon did not attempt to argue. He had to agree. However, he knew the others were looking at him for further explanation.

"Being a Christian doesn't automatically mean you're a good person," Gordon added. "I'm no better than the rest of you, I'm sure."

"But *I am*," the surgeon insisted. "So why should you go to heaven instead of me?"

Gordon twitched.

"It's not about how good we are. It's about grace," he attempted to explain.

"Grace?"

"Who's Grace?"

"I don't remember there being a Grace in the Bible..."

"I have a cousin called Grace."

Gordon puffed out his cheeks as he listened to their responses. This was going to be difficult.

"It's by grace that we're saved, not by good works," he started. "It doesn't matter how many good deeds you do... you can't earn salvation. It's a gift from God. God sent his only son to die for us, for our sins. We're all *sinners,* you see." He paused. He always felt uncomfortable using *that* word. He believed it to be old-fashioned. However, he did not know what other word he could use. "We've done nothing to earn that grace," he continued nervously. "It's a gift and all we have to do is to accept it. It's amazing, really."

Gordon stopped. "I'm sorry. I'm not very good at this. It's difficult to explain."

The woman intervened. "*Amazing grace,*" she said thoughtfully. "I used to sing the hymn at school: *Amazing grace, how sweet the sound, that saved a wretch like me.* That's right, isn't it?"

Gordon smiled. It was his favourite hymn.

"Yes, it is amazing," he reflected. "We don't deserve his grace, but there it is. And because of it, all the things that we have done wrong do not matter anymore. He wiped the slate clean."

"But that's not fair," the surgeon argued. "That means even criminals can go to heaven…"

The burglar looked towards Gordon for ratification.

"*I tell you the truth, today you will be with me in paradise.*"

It was not Gordon who had uttered the words. Angel Harriet had returned.

"The Master said those very words on the cross, to a repentant robber," she said. "That is the grace of God, my friends." She smiled in wonder.

"Look here," the tennis player declared, pointing a finger accusingly at the angel. "We want some answers. He reckons he's got the ticket to heaven…"

He stared menacingly at Gordon, as though the latter had suddenly become his bitter rival.

"Is he right?" the young woman asked nervously, instinctively grabbing hold of her cross, as though it would bring her luck. "Please tell us… is Mr Jones the only one going to heaven?"

The angel shook her head sorrowfully. "That's not for me to say, my dear. As I said, I'm just an angel."

Her response was greeted with groans. She smiled. In normal circumstances that compassionate smile would have brought comfort to anyone that had been looking her way. However, these were not, as you are probably aware, normal circumstances.

The angel tapped her folder and adjusted the tone of her voice, it becoming cheerier.

"I must first apologise to you all," she started, "but I forgot to complete some of the formalities. I had to come back in order to… now

70

then, what was it I came back for? What did I forget to do? Oh dear, I seem to have forgotten what I forgot in the first place," she continued to mutter.

Gordon smiled. He knew the angel had not forgotten anything.

She paused and glanced at the rucksack the burglar was carrying on his lap. "Of course, that's it," she announced. "Baggage! I notice some of you have some possessions. Who has some baggage to declare?"

"Baggage?" the tennis player cried. "If I had known I was going away this evening, I might have packed my bucket and spade!"

"What about that tennis racquet? That looks like baggage to me."

"Don't worry, I can carry it."

The angel put a wrinkled finger to her lips.

"I don't think you understand, Mr Ponce-Foot..." She stopped, almost as if she was waiting for a response. She was not disappointed.

"Paunce-Foot!" the tennis player yelled. "It's *Paunce!*"

"Yes, quite. Anyway, I'm afraid to inform you that there isn't actually a baggage allowance on this particular flight."

Instinctively, the burglar pulled his rucksack closer to his midriff in a futile bid to conceal it.

"Fingers!" Angel Harriet said softly. "You don't mind me calling you that, do you?"

He shook his head dumbly.

"It doesn't belong to him anyway," the surgeon offered. "Most of the stuff in there's probably mine!"

The angel stretched out her arm, the palm of her hand facing upwards. "Hand it over, please."

The burglar slowly began to unzip the rucksack, first pulling out the silver candlestick.

"You might as well just give me the bag," the angel responded impatiently.

He reluctantly obeyed.

Angel Harriet lifted the rucksack as though there were nothing inside, even though the burglar had struggled to even raise it off his lap, such was the weight of the contents. She did not bother to examine the fruit of the burglar's labours, but let go, the rucksack immediately falling from view.

The surgeon glanced down and shrieked, "That was my stuff! Some of that was probably fragile!"

"It's not fair," the tennis player wailed. "Why can't we take anything with us? This racquet isn't valuable, but it's got sentimental value. It's signed by Björn Borg. Can't I keep it?"

The angel shook her head. "I don't make up the rules. I'm just doing my job. I refer you to the first book of Timothy, chapter six, verse seven: *for we brought nothing into the world, and we can take nothing out of it.*"

The tennis player adopted a position of defence, holding his racquet as though he were about to receive a serve.

"Either it comes with me, or I'm not going," he vowed.

The angel looked only mildly surprised by his defiance. "This is your final chance, Mr Ponce-Foot. Will you please pass me the racquet?"

He shook his head, waving it defiantly in the air, almost in an attempt to fend off the angel, as though it had now become a weapon.

"Very well," she said. The others braced themselves. They expected the angel to begin wrestling it from his hand. They should have known better. She merely smiled and the racquet disappeared. "Who's next?" she inquired calmly.

The surgeon began to empty his pockets and placed various items into the cupped hands of the angel. They included his surgical gloves, mobile phone, a packet of chewing gum and a tiny figure of a black cat, the sort of toy you might find in a Christmas cracker. "It was my lucky charm," he explained. "I don't know about my patients, but it didn't bring me much luck."

The angel struggled to keep hold of the objects and, as soon as the last one was in her possession, wasted no time in uncupping her hands, the contents simply disappearing from view.

"You forgot something," she added, smiling at the surgeon. He reluctantly handed over the gold locket and closed his eyes, almost as though he did not want to witness its fate.

The young woman was still holding her towel and she quickly began wrapping it around her head, aware that the angel was now looking at her.

"Do I really have to give this up? It's part of my attire, not really baggage, is it?"

The angel paused. "To be quite honest... I'm not totally sure, my dear," she admitted, opening the blue folder in hope of finding the answer.

"My hair's still wet," the woman complained. "I'll need it. I don't suppose there are hairdryers where we're going?"

"It'll dry in no time once the flames start licking it," the burglar grinned mischievously.

"You can keep it for now," the angel concluded, closing the folder. "I'll have to consult my superiors on that one. What about you, Mr Jones?"

Angel Harriet turned to Gordon and he suddenly realised he was still nervously fingering the tube of fish food. He had unconsciously placed his ticket to heaven in his shirt pocket in order that he could continue rolling the tube through the fingers of both hands. He smiled. "Can you believe it? Of all the things I've acquired throughout my life over the years, the only thing I have on me now is a tube of fish food!"

He tossed it over his shoulder, the angel flashing him a disapproving glance.

"It's not fair," the surgeon reflected. "Why can't we bring our possessions with us? It took a lifetime to acquire some of them. It seems like we were wasting our time."

The angel nodded in agreement. "Yes, you *were* wasting your time."

"What else should we have been doing with our time?" the young woman asked.

"Preparing the one thing everyone takes with them to eternity, my dear."

"What's that?"

"Yourself."

No one responded and even Gordon bowed his head.

"This grace thing," the surgeon reflected, "it all sounds very good – and you say it was available to anyone – but it wasn't really fair, was it? I mean, a place in heaven *should* be decided by how good a person you were... how you lived your life. That would be fairer."

The angel did not disagree. She nodded. "But that's why his grace is so amazing. And what you forget, doctor, is that everyone would fall well short of his standard if it were based on good works. No, this way – by his grace – all have access to him. Don't you think that is even more incredible? Anyone – yes anyone – can have a relationship with the creator of the universe. I just find it incredible that so many choose not to."

The tennis player shifted uncomfortably. "How are you supposed to have a relationship with someone you've never seen?" he inquired in a mocking tone. "He didn't exactly reveal himself very often."

"He revealed himself all the time."

"When?"

"You only had to look around you to see his presence," Angel Harriet replied dreamily. "In a sunset, in a raging sea, in a newborn baby's cry…"

"I appreciated those things more than the next man," the surgeon argued, "but that's not the same as intimately getting to know the creator of them. I can't say I ever knew him personally."

"I know," the angel said sadly. "I think we've established that fact."

"But how were we supposed to get to know him?" the tennis player chipped in. "You couldn't exactly invite him over for a cup of tea."

The angel sighed. "You could. He wanted to be invited into your whole life; to share everything with you. He was waiting for your invitation. You could have spoken to him at any time."

"You mean pray to him?" the surgeon groaned. "Oh, come on! Why would you do that, if you didn't even believe in his existence? He should have revealed himself personally, not just through waterfalls and apple blossom, as you put it."

"He did."

"When?"

"When he came to earth and died on a cross."

"That was two thousand years ago!" the exasperated surgeon complained. "I know I'm knocking on a bit, but I wasn't actually alive then. I might have believed if I'd seen it all for myself. Show me the proof that Jesus even existed."

Angel Harriet removed a somewhat battered copy of the Bible from her apron pocket. "Here's your proof," she said.

The surgeon immediately comprehended what was now in her hand. "Oh, come on!" he sneered. "What evidence is that?"

"The Bible is a history book as well as many other things," the angel returned, lovingly caressing the cover with her hand. "Even most scholars accept that fact. The discoveries of archaeologists in recent years have only verified its historical accuracy, never disproved it. The places in it are real – and so were the people." She paused. "You believe in the existence of Alexander the Great and Julius Caesar, don't you?"

"I suppose so."

"There is more evidence to prove that Jesus existed."

The surgeon did not argue. "All right," he admitted, holding up his hands. "Perhaps I can accept that he was a real person, but the rest is fiction. How can a man walk on water or come back from the dead? There's only one explanation for all those so-called miracles: they didn't happen, and someone made them up to create a good story. You can't blame a right-minded individual from thinking it was all nonsense... or the work of some con-artist out to dupe the world."

Angel Harriet smiled before responding. "There were witnesses, of course," she said. "I need not tell an educated man like yourself that if the only witness to an event does not spread the word then no one will hear about it. Your history books would not have been written if there had been no witnesses. And yet that means we have to rely on their accounts or those that penned them on their behalf. Yes, perhaps on occasions, some historians did make it all up... Perhaps King Harold never got hit in the eye with an arrow, or perhaps Sir Walter Raleigh never laid his cloak on a puddle to prevent the Queen from getting her feet wet..."

The surgeon looked at the angel intently, wondering where she was leading him.

"Let me remind you," she continued, lifting up her Bible, "that the followers of Jesus who took up their pens to write these stories did not stop there. They didn't just put down their pens at the end of it and hope that the world would believe them. No, they went further... a lot further. Indeed, they must have been pretty certain it was the truth that they wrote about or they would not have also gone on to die for the cause. Peter – the most famous disciple – was himself crucified. Would someone who had written a story of fiction fool himself into thinking it was really true to the point he was willing to die to prove to others that it was?"

The surgeon took a moment to digest the question. Angel Harriet looked at him with sympathy.

"But if you are right, doctor, and it *had* been the intention to dupe people, don't you think the writer or writers might have helped their cause if they had not made it so unbelievable, as you put it. After all, they didn't dupe you, Dr Marsden. You never believed it to be the truth."

The surgeon shook his head, not regretfully, but even now seemingly proud of the fact that he had not succumbed. "Of course not," he replied defiantly. "Who would believe in something so *unbelievable?*"

Angel Harriet smiled. "I don't know the exact figure. You see, it rises every second of every day. Yes, people from all nations, from all walks

of life, are still being 'duped' by the most influential book ever written."
She patted the Bible in her hand and gently replaced it into her apron
pocket.

Gordon studied the angel closely. She could no longer hide the smile
on her face. She may have been attempting to do so, for the sake of the
surgeon, but she was quivering with excitement at the very thought of
what she had just said. She did not portray a dithering old woman now.
She was more like a gleeful child. Despite her humble clothes, for one
moment, she appeared almost ethereal to Gordon.

"Yes," the angel continued in awe, "it is so unbelievable: the son of
God being born as a human and then voluntarily choosing to go to the
most awful and humiliating death in order to save the people that rejected
him. What god would choose that way to reveal his love? Amazing, isn't
it?" She paused. "So you see, doctor, does it not become believable
because it is so *unbelievable?*"

The obstinate surgeon continued to shake his head. "This is
nonsense," he declared. "We're not getting anywhere."

"No," the angel reflected, a genuine look of pity returning to her face,
that heavenly aura that Gordon had sensed evaporating at the same time.

"So it is him going to heaven?" the woman asked suddenly, pointing
her body towards Gordon, the towel around her head unfurling and
dropping in front of her face.

Angel Harriet never answered. She attempted to return a reassuring
smile but did not succeed. The angel had had no intention of answering
the question, of course. It was as though she knew something would
prevent her from doing so. It did. It was the arrival of four figures that
had appeared in front of the four people sitting beside Gordon. They
were an assortment of immortals, decked in various clothes from
different periods of history. Gordon wished he had longer to study them,
but Angel Harriet immediately, and regretfully, gave the order: "They've
got their tickets. You can take them now."

The four frightened occupants of the chairs alongside Gordon
recognised their own particular immortal, the one that had taken them
thus far. If they had earlier mistaken them to be angels, they were now
clearly no longer under any illusion that they were, of course, demons.

"No..." the desperate surgeon screamed, gripping hold of his chair
with both hands. "I don't want you to take me. There's been a dreadful
mistake. I'm not a bad man."

"Please, I don't deserve this," the young woman wailed. "I really don't."

"This is outrageous," the disgruntled tennis player added. "Absolutely outrageous!"

Only the burglar, as he had been all along, was resigned to his fate. He made no sound.

It was a disturbing moment and Gordon closed his eyes. He should have felt sorry for the individuals next to him, but – like any human – he could only think about himself and the fact that everything was going to be all right, for him at least. Yes, of course it was. He wondered why he had ever doubted it would be. He was a Christian, after all. Any moment, Mr Gilmore would reappear to take him to paradise.

The cries from the others became more distant.

"Please. I haven't done anything to deserve this."

"I don't belong in hell... I really don't."

"Look! I wear a cross."

"I'll get to know the Master now."

"There must be some mistake."

"You can't do this. I'm a top surgeon."

"And I'm Edward Paunce-Foot..."

Abruptly the cries ceased. Gordon opened his eyes. He did not need to look at the chairs next to him. He knew they were vacant now.

Only Angel Harriet was present. "Well then, Mr Jones. It's your turn. Have you got your ticket?"

Gordon smiled and pulled his green card from his shirt pocket. He did not feel the need to say anything. He closed his eyes again. Mr Gilmore would probably be standing next to him when he reopened them. Heaven! Yes, he was going to heaven! Gordon did not notice that he was trembling in anticipation, but his moment of exultation was brought to a sudden halt.

"Hey! Hold on a minute."

Gordon sighed. He had heard that voice before.

7

"Then I saw that there was a way to hell even from the gates of heaven."

The Pilgrim's Progress
John Bunyan

WHEN GORDON OPENED HIS EYES, DUMAS WAS LEANING over him, a smug grin on his face.

"Hello, Mr Jones," he teased. "You weren't planning to go off without me, were you?"

Gordon turned his head to escape the demon's mocking eyes. "Where's Mr Gilmore?" he asked. "I thought *he* was going to be taking me up?"

Angel Harriet cast a suspicious eye over the demon. "I didn't think you looked much like Angel Gilmore," she said. "Mr Jones is not your property. He's got a ticket to heaven. You've no right to be here. Where's Angel Gilmore?"

The demon smiled and strutted towards the confused angel. "Don't worry that lovely face of yours, my dear," he said patronisingly. She reeled back in horror as he attempted to gently caress her cheek with a gloved finger. "You've done nothing wrong," he went on, turning his back on her. "How were you to know that Mr Jones is the subject of an appeal?"

"An appeal?" Gordon protested.

"That's right," Dumas responded, now turning to face Gordon. He held his hat against his chest, in such a way that the feather upon it stood upright and reached as far as his mouth. It failed to hide the smirk on his face, however.

"Who's appealing?" Angel Harriet inquired.

"Me," Dumas said calmly, blowing the plume away from his mouth.

"What are you appealing?"

"I am of the opinion that Mr Jones is not the rightful property of Angel Gilmore," Dumas said smiling, still focused on Gordon. "Looks like you are bound for warmer climes, Mr Jones, if you know what I mean."

"Don't get ahead of yourself, Dumas," another voice uttered. It was Mr Gilmore. He looked flustered, almost breathless, though Gordon did not know why, for he was sure angels had no need to run.

"What's going on, Angel Gilmore?" Angel Harriet asked. "Why is *he* here?" she continued, nodding her head in the direction of the demon. "I had orders to issue Mr Jones with a ticket to heaven. He's a Christian, isn't he?"

"Of course I am," Gordon snapped.

"There," said Angel Harriet. "I knew I hadn't made a mistake. I only had one ticket for heaven and I knew the other four never knew the Master."

Mr Gilmore removed his handkerchief and started to wipe his forehead with it. "We don't exactly know who's taking him at the moment," he attempted to explain. "You and I know that Mr Jones is a Christian, of course, but Demon Dumas has put in an appeal. He's convinced he isn't a Christian. He's wasting his time, of course."

"An appeal?" Angel Harriet cogitated. "I haven't heard of one of them taking place since Angel Angelo had his wings clipped. I hope you know what you're doing, Demon Dumas. They won't be pleased if you're wasting everyone's time."

Gordon wondered why everyone still spoke as though time could be wasted, when there was supposed to be an infinite amount of it. He looked at the ticket in his hand and sighed, leaning back in his chair.

"I'll take that," said Dumas, snatching the green card from Gordon's grasp. "You take *this* in return." He let a scroll drop into Gordon's lap. "It's what you might call a summons, Mr Jones."

"A what?" Gordon gasped, looking to Mr Gilmore in search of an explanation. "What have I done?"

"Or haven't done," the demon smiled mischievously.

"Don't worry," assured Mr Gilmore. "It's just a formality – nothing to concern you. There will be a preliminary hearing, that's all. It won't go further than that. Dumas has the right to appeal, but the court will throw it out immediately. I'm sure it won't go to a trial."

"A trial?" Gordon shrieked, Mr Gilmore's intention to reassure having the opposite effect. "I don't understand. I haven't done anything wrong. I'm a Christian."

"And that is what the preliminary hearing will confirm," Mr Gilmore added. "Then I will take you to meet your master. It's just an inconvenience, that's all. It'll be sorted out soon."

Dumas wiped an errant piece of fluff from his tunic. "Well, I'll be off now, Mr Jones," he said, placing his hat on his head, and flicking back his long hair. "See you in court," he grinned.

The demon vanished, but Gordon was convinced he could still hear him laughing. He nervously fingered the scroll, not daring to unfurl it.

Mr Gilmore sat on the seat next to Gordon, the one previously occupied by the surgeon. "Cheer up, Mr Jones," he smiled. "Don't let him get you down – if you excuse the pun. He's just doing his job. He's been at it all your life: deceiving you. He can't stop you taking your rightful place in paradise. Let me assure you, demons have absolutely no power in heaven."

"If I'm going there," Gordon sighed.

Mr Gilmore looked at him horrified. "Don't say things like that. If you say that in court, they might start to believe Dumas is right. Faith, Mr Jones – you have got to have faith."

The angel rose from his chair and moved towards his contemporary.

"Thank you, Angel Harriet. I'll take it from here. No doubt, I'll see you at Angel Meredith's ball... if you're going, of course."

"I wouldn't miss it for all the trumpets in heaven," she responded excitedly. "Although no one... well... no one has actually asked me to be their..."

Mr Gilmore smiled. He straightened his tie and stood tall, or as tall as his diminutive figure would stretch to. "I would be delighted if you would do me the honour..."

"Why, of course, Angel Gilmore, that would be simply divine..."

Gordon coughed and the two angels, both a little crimson in the face, turned to look at him.

"Goodbye, Mr Jones," Angel Harriet announced. "It has been a pleasure meeting you. I wish it had been under better circumstances."

Gordon did not respond. He was shaking his head and rubbing his weary eyes. He did not even see the angel disappear.

"I don't believe this is happening," he groaned. "Why me? I thought death was supposed to bring an end to all your problems, not start them. It's not fair."

Mr Gilmore allowed Gordon to continue to wallow in self-pity, preferring to offer a sympathetic ear – his good one, we should add.

"Angels and demons?" Gordon went on, a look of exasperation on his face. "I just can't get my head around all of this. It's crazy. It has *got* to be a dream."

"Are you ready, Mr Jones?"

Not only had Gordon still failed to notice the departure of Angel Harriet, he was oblivious to the fact that Mr Gilmore had helped him to his feet. He was now standing on thin air, if that was the correct term. The angel, fearful that Gordon would soon notice the fact himself, seemed anxious to move on. "I think we should go," he suggested politely.

"Where?"

"Court number one, if I'm not mistaken."

"Already? Don't I get time to prepare my case?"

"There's no need to. As I said, it's just a preliminary hearing: a *prima facie*."

"A what?"

"Did you not study Latin, Mr Jones? A *prima facie* case is one in which the plaintiff must produce sufficient evidence to prove he can win... I think," the angel added doubtfully. "In short: Dumas has got to convince everyone that he has a case against you. He's got to persuade the archangels that he has some proof that there's been a mistake and that you belong to him. If he can't even do that – and he can't – there won't be a trial. I told you there was nothing to worry about."

"But what if he *has* got a *prima donna* case?" an anxious Gordon asked.

"But he hasn't. You and I know that more than anyone, don't we, Mr Jones?"

"Yes, I suppose so," Gordon replied dumbly.

"You're a Christian, Mr Jones," the angel stated defiantly. "Dumas hasn't got a case and that's the end of it. It's as simple as that."

Still Gordon was not aware of the fact he was apparently not standing on anything solid, and Mr Gilmore clearly did not want him to. The angel was keen not to give Gordon the chance to look down at his feet and yet he was subconsciously doing all he could to encourage his charge to do just that. He found it difficult to keep his eyes away from Gordon's slippers. It was as though he were an excited child who had hidden something and could not resist the temptation to glance at the hiding place, thus giving the game away.

"If you're ready then, Mr Jones," he announced, deliberately raising his head upwards, in the hope that Gordon would do likewise. He didn't. Instead, Gordon bowed his head sorrowfully. Surely now he would notice that there was apparently no solid ground to support his weight?

"I like your slippers," Mr Gilmore observed, in one final attempt to prevent Gordon from doing just that.

"They were a Christmas present," Gordon explained. "There's a cartoon eye on each one and if you stand with your feet together..."

"Ready?" Mr Gilmore interrupted forcefully.

"I suppose so. Is it a big court?" Gordon probed, at last looking heavenwards, if that term is appropriate in the circumstances. "I bet it's ever so grand... solid gold benches and marble floors," he went on dreamily. "Where did you say it was?"

"Next to the old gasworks at the bottom of your high street," replied Mr Gilmore. "Ready?"

This time the impatient angel did not wait for Gordon to answer. He clicked his fingers and brightness was replaced by darkness. It could not have been a bigger contrast: from white to black in an instant. Gordon at first thought he had closed his eyes. He could not see *anything*.

"Mr Gilmore?" he asked nervously. "Are you still there?" He sensed the angel was no longer close to him. "Mr Gilmore?"

Gordon twitched, not daring to take even one step in the darkness. He knew he was inside a building, that fact he could establish by the overbearing smell of newly laid carpet. Aware he was still holding the scroll Dumas had given him, he fumbled for the pocket of his shirt and attempted to place it in it, oblivious to the fact it was too long. The scroll merely fell to the floor and came to rest from view under a chair – if Gordon had been able to see *that* chair, of course.

Suddenly, fluorescent lighting high above Gordon began to flicker into life. It took a few seconds before it seemingly won the battle with the darkness, at last illuminating the courthouse foyer, for that is where they were. Mr Gilmore was standing by the main entrance, his hand still hovering over the light switch. He was wiping his feet on the chunky doormat. Now Gordon could *see* that the carpet was brand new, a plush royal blue. He instinctively checked the soles of his slippers to see if they had any mud on them, but all he could find were the fragments of a few crisps. The darkness of the outside world, illuminated by a solitary street lamp and a couple of shop facias in the distance, could be made out through the large glass doors through which Mr Gilmore was giving the impression he had entered. The glass itself was peppered with raindrops, but, of course, none would finish their journey to the bottom of the window panes. Everything outside was still.

"Won't there be anyone here?" Gordon inquired, gazing up at the vast ceiling. "Are you allowed to commandeer a court?"

"It's Christmas Day," Mr Gilmore grinned. "Everyone's watching *Coronation Street*, don't forget… or playing charades."

Gordon returned a look of bemusement, not in response to the quip, but because Mr Gilmore was now putting down a red umbrella, shaking drops of water from it as he did so. He cut a bedraggled figure, as though he had spent the last few minutes running to take shelter from the rain. When he had placed the folded umbrella in what looked like a paper bin that was conveniently situated beside him, he proceeded to turn down the collar of his suit jacket, presumably it having been purposely turned up to keep the cold from his neck in the absence of a scarf. Gordon was not aware they had been out in the rain and he himself showed no signs that they had. He was dry and, come to that, so was Mr Gilmore!

Gordon did not attempt to seek an explanation, now drawn to the large reception desk.

"I keep forgetting it's Christmas," he sighed, spotting a small Christmas tree, no bigger than an outstretched arm, on the counter. He fingered a piece of tinsel that was wrapped around its branches, knocking one of the baubles on to the ground in the process. It rolled along the wooden floor, for the carpet was only reserved for what looked like a waiting area. He gave chase and gathered the stray bauble, before looking to Mr Gilmore apologetically, though the angel chose not to pass comment on his clumsiness. In fact, the celestial being was already making his way to one of three huge doors that lay farther down a corridor just beyond the waiting area. Gordon hurriedly replaced the bauble on the counter next to the Christmas tree, making no attempt to hang it on one of the branches for fear of causing further destruction. He turned and went in pursuit of his guardian. Mr Gilmore was now looking at a piece of paper attached to the wall beside the door, his glasses almost touching it. It was a court list.

"I've never been to court in my life," Gordon explained. "Will my name be on there?"

"Of course not, Mr Jones. This will be next week's list."

"Hold on!" Gordon announced, peering around the head of the angel. "I recognise that name... Maloney! Do you think its Fingers? Well, if it is, I don't think he'll be turning up on Monday morning."

Suddenly, the door farthest from them opened and a bald, spectacled man popped his head out.

"Mr Jones?" he shouted. "Court number one, please... Mr Jones to court number one."

There was no one else in the foyer, but the man did not personally address Gordon. His announcement might have been made to a packed courthouse.

"That's me," Gordon gulped, instinctively grabbing Mr Gilmore's arm. "I didn't think it would be starting so quickly. We've only just got here."

Mr Gilmore, his arm still linked to Gordon's, headed towards the man, who now held the door open for them. The angel had difficulty walking with the added burden of pulling Gordon along and stopped so that his client could remove his arm.

"Just relax, Mr Jones," Mr Gilmore whispered to his charge. "Just relax."

The man at the door eyed Gordon suspiciously.

"I'm sorry, your lordship... your majesty," Gordon stuttered. "I've never been to court before."

"I can see that," the man tutted, making a point of nodding down at the black gown that he wore. "I'm the court usher. No need to address me with that title. Save it for the archangels."

The usher beckoned them to enter. Gordon took a deep breath. He did not know what to expect behind the door. The courtroom would be packed, he surmised, and there would be lots of individual conversations taking place. And, of course, the chattering would instantly come to a halt when Gordon emerged into the room. Accusing eyes would fall upon him and he would feel inclined to bow his head in shame. He hoped he did not trip over his own slippers. As it has already been established, they did not fit him properly and, it should also be noted, those said slippers had earlier today been the cause of him almost falling to the bottom of his stairs. He had just managed to save himself on that occasion – or perhaps one of his guardian angels should be credited for that...

To Gordon's surprise, the courtroom was not at all like he had imagined, or feared. The first thing he noticed was that it was virtually empty. The second thing he noticed was that it was so very brightly lit. The third thing he noticed was that it was a large but uninspiring room: modern and functional. The fourth thing he noticed (though it might have really been the first, second or third thing) were the walls – white again. However, Gordon could have been forgiven for noticing the pine-coloured varnish that adorned the array of matching benches and chairs even before taking in the colour of the walls. The varnish was so shiny; the fluorescent lights high on the ceiling above were reflected off it to often dazzling effect.

Of course, Gordon had perceived much about the courtroom without actually looking at it. He had dared not look up when he followed the usher up the aisle, his head lowered, his eyes preferring to focus on the cartoon eyes on his slippers. He need not have feared meeting any condemning stares. As has been mentioned, there were very few people present and no one took much interest as he was being directed to a long bench at which Dumas was already positioned. Gordon immediately recognised the distinctive demon, his dark locks resting on the back of his tunic, his hat still upon his head. The demon never turned around as Gordon was told to take the seat at the opposite end from the one that Dumas occupied. Mr Gilmore sat next to his client, in between Gordon and the demon, though a fair distance from his adversary. Gordon knew Dumas was aware of his entrance. Even though he could not see the face of the demon, his twinkling eyes immediately came to mind and Gordon almost imagined that they were fixed upon him. He was just as sure that the demon also had a smug smile on his face.

In front of their bench was a lone table at which the clerk of the court sat facing them, though Mr Gilmore had to again explain that this particular individual was not an archangel. Behind the clerk was a raised bench, with three dominant chairs, which could have been mistaken for thrones if they had been a bit more majestic. The only other sign of any sort of opulence was a huge coat of arms situated on the wall high above the middle chair. Even someone who had never set foot in a court of law, such as Gordon, would have immediately concluded these were the chairs reserved for the magistrates or judges, or perhaps we should say archangels in this case. All three 'thrones' were at this moment in time vacant.

Mr Gilmore took some papers from a briefcase and placed them on the desk in front of him. Gordon wondered where the briefcase had come from, as the angel had certainly not been carrying it when they had entered the building.

Gordon could not see Dumas without physically turning his head (and then he would have needed to lean forward or raise his head to peer over the frame of Mr Gilmore), all three now finding themselves positioned on the same bench facing the clerk of the court. Mr Gilmore and Dumas made no attempt to acknowledge the other.

The usher had retreated to the back of the courtroom.

"Court rise," he suddenly bellowed, as a door in the wall behind the raised bench opened slowly. Two individuals, a man and a woman, entered purposefully, before pulling two of the three vacant 'thrones' from under the bench in order to sit on them.

"Are they the archangels?" Gordon whispered, turning to Mr Gilmore, both now on their feet. The angel nodded and put his finger to his mouth to silence his client.

Gordon sat down, in unison with everyone else, and continued to study the two immortals. The female archangel, as we should now call her, was wearing a pale blue summer dress. Her golden hair was just about visible under an enormous hat, one that women only dare wear to a wedding. In the hat was arranged a small bouquet of flowers, looking as fresh as the day they had been picked. She poured herself a glass of water from a decanter positioned on the desk in front of her and made a comment to her companion. The male archangel appeared to be also from the same era, though his clothes were more casual: beige slacks, a blue shirt – his tie barely visible under a woolly jumper adorned with a maze-like pattern. Both were of middle age… if archangels have an age. There was no particular aura surrounding them. You could not find two more ordinary-looking people, or should we say archangels. There was nothing remarkable or memorable about them. Indeed, there was nothing to even hint that they were celestial beings.

It was the clerk, sitting below the archangels and positioned at his table facing Gordon, who spoke first. He was a young man, attired in a crisp white shirt and burgundy tie. He had a huge red nose. Gordon stood up again, this time under direction from Mr Gilmore, trying in vain to shift his gaze from *that* nose.

"Mr Jones," the clerk began. "You are he, of Buckinghamshire, deceased 19:34, approximately?"

Gordon nodded, after first looking to Mr Gilmore for permission to do so.

"Please listen carefully," the young man continued hurriedly, almost as if he were already bored by the proceedings. "I am sure Angel Gilmore has explained why you are here. There is no need for you to do anything at this stage. Angel Gilmore will speak on your behalf. Do you understand?"

Gordon nodded meekly. The clerk forced a smile and nodded in the direction of Dumas, the signal for him to begin.

The demon rose from his chair and grinned. He was not going to hurry, deliberately shuffling some papers laid out neatly on the bench in front of him. The archangels stared at him in a way that did not portray any of their inner feelings. As we have noted, Gordon could not see Dumas without shifting his body and instead took the chance to further survey his surroundings. There were no windows in the courtroom; that made him feel uncomfortable, as though reality was hidden from him. One of the fluorescent lights was making a buzzing noise and flickering at the same time, reminding Gordon of the magenta-coloured fairy light on his Christmas tree. There was the occasional sound of the shifting of wood from behind Gordon, someone of a great weight presumably adjusting his or her position on one of the benches. There was also a lot of coughing for so few people.

"I do not need much of your time," Dumas announced suddenly, looking up but purposely avoiding the stare of the archangels. "My allegation is a simple one: I have reason to believe that the deceased who stands before us now is the rightful property of my master."

"Reason to believe, Demon Dumas?" the male archangel responded. "Have you not something more substantial? You will need more than that."

"Forgive me," Dumas bowed. "I should perhaps say 'evidence'. Yes, I have evidence to confirm that the deceased's rightful resting place is with my master and not with... your master."

The female archangel frowned, not impressed with the disdain in his voice.

Dumas continued unfalteringly. "I don't question the pact that your master made at Calvary. I know my master has no right to those that belong to your master, but I do know that my master is entitled to those that don't. That's the deal, isn't it? I am only claiming for him those that belong to him."

Mr Gilmore was shaking his head.

"And why do you think the deceased belongs to *him?*" the male archangel inquired.

"Because he's not a Christian," Dumas replied.

"I am!" Gordon pleaded, leaping from his chair. "How many more times do I have to say it?"

Dumas smiled. "It's a pity he never said it a few more times when he was alive!"

"Silence," the clerk ordered. "Please sit down, Mr Jones. You will have your say later."

Dumas nodded at the clerk and grinned; buoyed by the fact Gordon had been roused.

"Of course," the demon continued, "Mr Jones claims to be a Christian and he has even fooled my learned friend, Angel Gilmore, into thinking that is the case... but let's take this orange."

Dumas stretched out his arm and the fruit appeared in his gloved hand, like a magician would produce a handkerchief. He threw it a couple of inches into the air, catching it each time. "It looks to be a perfectly good orange. It even smells quite nice, but open it up..."

He did not bother to peel the skin, but crushed the fruit. Inside were maggots, and they crawled on to his glove, some falling to the ground. "Inside is a different story," he continued. "When you open it up and have a good look around, all is not as it seems."

Mr Gilmore deliberately folded his arms and shook his head, as if to make it quite clear he was not impressed by the theatrical show. Dumas rubbed his gloved hands together and the soggy remains of the fruit disappeared. Only Gordon stood watching in awe, hypnotised by his magic. The archangels looked as bored and as unimpressed as Mr Gilmore.

"All I ask," Dumas continued, "is to allow me to open Mr Jones up and to take a good look inside. I will prove he is not what he says he is."

"Angel Gilmore?" the male archangel responded. "What have you to say to the allegation?"

The angel sprung from his chair.

"Your honours... worships." He looked to the archangels in the hope that they would inform him as to how he was supposed to address them, but it was clear that even they were not familiar with court etiquette. "Your worships." He stuck with that. "Your worships, Mr Jones was one of many I was personally given responsibility to assist during his earthly life. I have no doubt he is a Christian and that his place is with the Master in heaven, a place which no one, not even your worships, can deny him."

The male archangel nodded in agreement.

"And you, Mr Jones? What have you to say to the allegation that you are not a Christian?"

Mr Gilmore sat down and nudged Gordon in the leg.

"Well... I *am,*" Gordon responded defiantly. "I became one on February 12th... 19... What year is it now? I'm not good with years. I know it was February 12th, though, because that's also the date I passed my driving test. Anyway, you can ask God if you like. I'm sure he'll remember."

Someone at the back of the courtroom started to giggle. The male archangel smiled.

"I'm sure he will, rest assured of that, Mr Jones, but the reason we are sitting here is on behalf of the Master. Yes, everyone must face him; be it the sheep or the goats. We are just rounding them up for the shepherd – putting them in the appropriate pens, if you know what I mean."

Gordon didn't, but smiled politely.

The two archangels put their heads together in a bid to confer, the female archangel having already removed her hat, in fear of it preventing them from doing so. They kept their conversation to a whisper, but the courtroom was so quiet; their private debate was almost audible to everyone.

"Very well, Demon Dumas," the male archangel finally declared, turning to face him. "You *shall* have your say. Your evidence will be heard, but be it on your head. It had better be substantial. This is a very serious allegation. If you are wasting the court's time, there may be consequences. Do you understand?"

Dumas bowed, looking towards the archangel for the first time.

Gordon felt as though he was going to be sick, or at best faint. He did not hear the archangel address him.

"Mr Jones," the male archangel began, "I commit you to stand trial at the court known as the Old Bailey before a jury of twelve dead men and women. You are remanded on unconditional bail."

"Court rise," the usher declared, prompting the two archangels to stand themselves and head for the door from which they had previously emerged.

Mr Gilmore had risen in haste, gathering his papers as he did so, and was now stuffing them into his briefcase. It was clear he was keen to leave as quickly as possible. He nudged a bemused Gordon to the aisle and the pair started to head for the door. Gordon did not have time to look at Dumas, not that he had the inclination to do so. The demon was now seated; his long legs stretched out on the table, his boots twitching, as though in time to the beat of some imaginary music. There was a look of contentment on his face, but, of course, Gordon never saw it – and would not have wanted to.

As Gordon and Mr Gilmore neared the exit at the back of the courtroom, a young man overtook them. The individual stopped as he reached the door, turning to face Gordon. His sole intention was to steal a closer look at the defendant, but he hid that fact by opening the door and holding it open for the departing duo. The man wore a tie, but the knot in his tie was well below the open top button of his shirt, and that shirt was not very successfully tucked into his trousers, hanging down his rear like a cloak. Gordon politely thanked the man as they exited, failing to notice the notebook in his hand.

When they were in the foyer, Mr Gilmore directed Gordon to a chair in the carpeted waiting area and looked his despondent client in the eyes, his glasses slipping off his nose.

"Now look here, Mr Jones," he said authoritatively, readjusting those spectacles. "I must admit I wasn't expecting this, but I want you to know there's absolutely nothing to worry about. I suppose the archangels didn't feel they had a choice. They're just erring on the side of caution. Do you understand?"

Gordon stared at the angel and sighed. "Why me? Couldn't he have picked on someone else?"

Mr Gilmore put his arm on Gordon's shoulder. "I know, he's a rotten devil, but don't worry, the Master will never turn away those that belong to him. Cheer up, Mr Jones. The truth will be established. It'll be over before you know it."

Gordon looked to the closed courtroom door. No one had followed them out and it was all quiet in the foyer, the scruffy young man nowhere to be seen. For a moment Gordon wondered whether the courtroom was real and whether there really had been anyone behind that door.

"What now?" Gordon asked, looking wearily to Mr Gilmore. "I suppose we do have to go and prepare my case, after all?"

"Nonsense," the angel responded, shaking his head. "There's infinite time for that, besides that's *my* job, not yours. There was one good thing to come out of the hearing..."

"Was there? I didn't notice."

"They gave you unconditional bail."

Gordon looked up confused.

"That's right," Mr Gilmore continued. "You're free to do as you please until the trial."

He waited for a reaction, but it was not the one he had expected. Gordon merely tutted. "But I'm dead! What's a dead man supposed to do?"

Mr Gilmore removed his glasses and began to wipe them with his handkerchief. "Mr Jones," he said, shaking his head, "that's like the Invisible Man saying he doesn't know where to go. Where's your imagination? As Death would perhaps say, the world is a stage and we've got all the time in it." He stopped. "No, that's not right. The world's a stage... no, the world's your oyster... oh, it doesn't matter. You know what I mean."

Gordon sighed again. He thought back to his own wake. That experience had had a sobering effect on him and he did not have much desire to repeat it at this particular moment.

"Come on, Mr Jones," the angel smiled. "Lighten up. Don't look so glum." There was an uncharacteristic glint in Mr Gilmore's eye, one that was now clearly visible without the ludicrous thick lens of his spectacles to distort it. The angel rose and slapped Gordon on the back. "We can go anywhere, Mr Jones, anywhere we please."

Gordon looked up and caught Mr Gilmore grinning, now a mischievous and far-from-angelic look in his eyes. The angel replaced his glasses. "It is Christmas, remember, Mr Jones – a time to party!" He paused. "Fancy a nightclub?"

8

"Why should the devil have all the good music?"

Popular saying

GORDON HAD NEVER LIKED NIGHTCLUBS, BUT HE DID NOT have the chance to respond to Mr Gilmore's suggestion. Before any protestations could come from his mouth, the angel had clicked his fingers. Of course, it should be immediately noted that even if Gordon had managed to utter those protestations, he himself would probably not have even heard them. The music was deafening.

Mr Gilmore was clapping his hands and nodding his head, but it seemed to be in time to the flashing lights, rather than to the beat of the music. The angel did not have a musical ear and, if Gordon had asked (and Mr Gilmore was somewhat surprised that he hadn't yet done so), he would have told him that he was not the only angel that *couldn't* play the harp.

Flashing lights made it difficult for Gordon to survey his new surroundings. They were in the middle of the packed dance floor, surrounded by shadowy figures, most of whom were so lost in their own movements, they were oblivious to the arrival of two more revellers. One dancer persistently brushed against the static Gordon, but never seemed to notice or care, though Gordon, who might have under normal circumstances taken issue with anyone who infringed upon his own personal space, found it more than irritating.

Gordon did not like crowds and remained rooted to the spot, only occasionally inclining a mere inch this way and that to prevent someone knocking against him, though, as we have ascertained, he did not have much success.

Mr Gilmore had started to dance, but clearly he was not gifted in that department either. To be fair to the angel, the music was not of his era, whatever era he was from, Gordon not yet having established when he had roamed the earth. In truth, the music was probably not from the era of anyone on that dance floor. If Gordon had at this initial stage been able to distinguish the faces of his fellow partygoers, or make out their attire, he would have immediately comprehended that fact. However, his eyes were still adjusting to the semi-darkness, not helped by the fact he was momentarily blinded by a spotlight, as and when a reveller bopped too far to the left or right, until then their figure having shielded Gordon from its glare.

Gordon assumed the clubbers were dancing to the latest sound, though, in truth, he had no idea what the latest sound sounded like. Mr Gilmore continued to boogie and Gordon felt like an embarrassed teenager again, his father having gate-crashed the school disco. Of course, no one was taking any interest in his guardian and, it is fair to say, the angel's particular routine was no more outlandish than those of the other partygoers.

It may have been an ordinary nightclub (even if Gordon could not confirm this fact having not set foot in one for so long), but few would have used the word 'ordinary' to describe those within its walls. As Gordon's eyes began to make out more than just silhouettes and shadows, he soon concluded that these people were not the types he would have spotted queuing outside the club in his own high street on a Saturday night.

"I'm assuming this isn't a fancy-dress party?" he shouted in the direction of Mr Gilmore. The angel never heard him, or at least never responded. It has to be stated that Gordon was the type of person who found it difficult to lose his inhibitions on a dance floor. He never liked dancing. However, he felt even more awkward just standing there in his slippers. He was keen to embark on a conversation, but – because of the noise – that was proving difficult. Gordon continued to cast his eye around the room. The revellers were mostly of mature years. They appeared to be from all walks of life and eras. Each partygoer, clad in clothes so very different from the person next to him or her, danced in the way they would have done during their particular moment in history, despite the inappropriate music. No one seemed to actually hear the beat of the tune, or cared about it.

A lady in a tartan skirt, arms folded, was performing a spirited jig, while a rotund, bearded man – bells and ribbons dangling from his white trousers – was on his toes, gracefully waving a handkerchief in his outstretched hand, as though he were on a village green at a summer fete.

Elsewhere, a pair of sweethearts in elegant dress stood opposite each other, bowing and curtsying, before stepping forward, their hands meeting in the air, both then turning full circle. It could have been a routine straight out of a Jane Austen novel.

Gordon waited for Mr Gilmore to look in his direction, believing it to be the only way he would be able to attract the attention of the angel, his earlier attempt having seemingly been in vain. When their eyes did finally meet for one quick moment, Gordon popped another question.

"Where are we?" he asked, this time making no attempt to make the actual sound of the words, instead hoping the angel would be able to lip-read. Of course, their eyes had only met for an instant and Gordon again believed he had failed to gain the attention of his guardian, Mr Gilmore continuing to strut his stuff. He was surprised when the angel did give him an answer.

"Just off your high street. It's just opened," he said. "I've not been here before... Thought I'd give it a whirl."

Gordon wondered whether Mr Gilmore made a habit of frequenting nightclubs.

The angel had not needed to shout, though Gordon had not noticed that fact. As he spoke, the volume of the music appeared to drop a notch, as though they were actors in a film, the director keen to ensure viewers would be able to hear their conversation above the background noise.

"But these people," Gordon continued, "who are they exactly? I assume they're..."

Mr Gilmore nodded, still reluctant to stop dancing. "That's right, Mr Jones – dead, just like you."

Gordon sighed. The word still hurt.

"Come on, Mr Jones," Mr Gilmore chirped. "Cheer up. Let your hair down and have some fun. It is Christmas, after all."

The angel gave Gordon a friendly punch on the arm, before swivelling around full circle, almost losing his balance in the process. It was clear Mr Gilmore had no intention of bringing his routine to a halt and Gordon soon felt obliged to join in the 'fun'. He started by bending his knees slightly and clicking his fingers, though the soles of his slippers remained anchored to the floor. As we have established, Gordon did not like dancing and, needless to say, was not very good at it. Mr Gilmore peered over his glasses, which were constantly slipping from the bridge of his nose due to his own exertions; now keen to get a better look at Gordon's routine, if you could call it that. One or two of the other revellers had now stopped and were also eyeing Gordon with interest. The angel, his eyes still focused on his charge, twisted his head in the direction of an old man in a fawn-coloured toga.

"The youth of today," Mr Gilmore laughed. "They don't know how to boogie like us, do they?"

The old man in the toga was trying to mimic Gordon, his exposed knees bending to such an extent that it looked as though his spindly legs might snap at any moment. His sandal-clad feet remained motionless on the floor and it gave the impression he was exercising, rather than dancing. It has to be said, Gordon's dance was far more conservative than any other in that nightclub, though Gordon did not question why he – and only he – drew any attention. In fact, many eyes were focused on him, and more than one or two revellers were now attempting to copy his mechanical movements.

"They like to learn the latest routines," Mr Gilmore explained, himself now aping Gordon. "I can't say I've come across this one before... No, don't stop, Mr Jones."

An embarrassed Gordon had indeed come to a halt. He shook his head in bewilderment. Much to his surprise, Mr Gilmore and the other revellers did likewise. Gordon puffed out his cheeks. The revellers did as well. The self-conscious Gordon did not know where to turn and, of course, if he had done, his fellow partygoers would have done so too. He only wanted all those inquisitive eyes to focus on someone else. He nervously scratched his nose, not because he had an itch, but because his body was starting to function of its own accord. Of course, most believed that unremarkable gesture was also part of the routine.

Gordon continued to fidget, his every twitch highlighted by those around him. The more he displayed his inhibitions, the more inhibited he became. He was creating his own self-fulfilling cycle. He had to break it, and soon concluded that the only way to do that was to make bold and deliberate movements that would take the focus off those little mannerisms that revealed his insecurity. The first thing he could think of doing was removing one of his slippers and waving it in the air. He then started to balance it on his head. It worked. The daring act – it was daring for Gordon – was not questioned in any way and gave Gordon a little bit of confidence. It was comical to see revellers, clad in various types of footwear, attempting to mimic him, though it took some several moments to unbuckle their sandals or to unlace leather boots. Mr Gilmore did not attempt to remove his shoes, however.

"That's more like it," the angel grinned. "It's nice to see you having fun again."

In fact, Gordon was starting to enjoy himself. With many of the clubbers still struggling to remove their footwear, Gordon replaced his slipper and put his hands on his hips, now trying to think of the most ludicrous movements he could come up with. It was not difficult, and his fellow partygoers continued to emulate his every gesture.

"If Bill and the rest of them could see me now," he laughed. "I never thought I'd be doing this when I woke up this morning. I thought I'd be watching *Coronation Street* tonight, not dancing with an angel instead! It's madness!"

"No, it's not Madness," Mr Gilmore responded. "I think you'll find it's Robbie Williams, and it's *loving* angels instead... not *dancing*."

Gordon flashed the angel a bemused glance. Mr Gilmore merely grinned.

"I bet all these people have got some tales to tell," Gordon suggested, forcefully throwing his arm to one side, aware that his routine needed livening up. Others copied him, and it would not have been unreasonable to assume that one or two revellers almost received a black eye in the process.

"Would you like to meet some of them?" Mr Gilmore asked.

Gordon stopped abruptly. "Yes, that would be good."

The pause was interpreted as the end of the dance. The old man in the toga was the first to start clapping. Gordon realised the applause was for him and bowed in acknowledgement. Presumably, some of the partygoers did not know what a bow signified and assumed it was part of the routine, which had perhaps not come to a conclusion, after all. They started to bow and Gordon, for some strange reason, felt compelled to return another bow... and another. It was Mr Gilmore who intervened.

"This could go on forever," he groaned, clutching Gordon's arm and leading him from the dance floor, apologising profusely, as they pushed through the crowd towards the bar.

"Would you like a drink, Mr Jones?"

Gordon looked at Mr Gilmore as though he had suggested they should don fluffy red noses and blow raspberries. Somehow the thought of having a drink with an angel seemed even more ridiculous than dancing with one, though he didn't know why. He shook his head dumbly.

"No problem," Mr Gilmore smiled. "Perhaps you'd like to play a game?"

The angel nodded in the direction of two young boys. They were dressed in matching regal clothes. Gordon guessed their apparel was distinctive to the Tudor period, but – as has been stated – he was not good at history, so it was indeed merely a guess. The boys were sitting on individual stools, facing each other, one elbow rested on the bar. Both had playing cards in one outstretched hand, the cards arranged to form an arch to make it possible for the holder to view all of them at the same time, though it looked like both were fanning themselves.

"They look a bit young to be in here," Gordon pointed out.

"Age is no barrier to Death, Mr Jones," Mr Gilmore replied wistfully. "He comes to all, young or old, and no one can stop him: *Death, the only immortal who treats us all alike, whose pity and whose peace and whose refuge are for all.* I think Mark Twain said that... and Death himself may have quoted it a few times as well!"

"I just meant that they're a bit young to be in a nightclub," Gordon mused.

"Oh."

The younger of the boys started to accuse the other of cheating, and an argument ensued, which ended when the eldest threw his cards on to the bar.

"I'm not playing with you," he declared.

"Fine," the other responded, folding his arms.

"They remind me of someone," Gordon reflected. "No, apart from Veronica and Alex. I know, yes, they look like those Princes in the Tower."

"That's because they *are* those Princes in the Tower," Mr Gilmore smiled.

Gordon shook his head in astonishment. "This is incredible! I never thought I'd be rubbing shoulders with royalty. Are all the kings and queens up in heaven?"

"As I said, Death comes to us all, Mr Jones. And I'm sure Death definitely told you that! No one can escape him, not even the rich and famous."

Gordon continued to study the faces of some of the other partygoers, hoping he might recognise one or two more. "Are there any other famous people here?"

"Not sure," Mr Gilmore replied, screwing up his eyes, as though it might help his vision. "I do know John Bunyan's particularly partial to a dance."

The angel ordered a tomato juice from the barman, a man dressed in the habit of a holy man.

"Thank you, friar. Are you sure you wouldn't like a drink, Mr Jones?"

Gordon never replied. He watched, still dumbstruck, as the friar scooped a couple of cubes of ice into the angel's drink. He did not fail to notice that Mr Gilmore made no attempt to pay for his beverage and the barman never asked him to do so.

"Is there no money in heaven?" he asked tentatively.

"Money!" Mr Gilmore sighed, shaking his head. "The root of all evil! What do you think, Mr Jones?"

Gordon did not know what to think. He shook his head in bewilderment. He wondered who would actually end up paying for the drinks consumed. Would the real bar manager notice the barrel of beer had run out a bit quicker than normal come Monday morning? Of course, there were less trivial questions that Gordon needed answered. Was this a taste of heaven? Where had all these people come from? Were they even from heaven, or perhaps from hell? Were the dead permitted to wander the earth of the living? He was about to consult Mr Gilmore for some answers, but the angel was on the move again, shuffling across the edge of the dance floor, being careful not to spill his drink. Gordon set off in pursuit. He almost collided with a young man in an old-fashioned football kit, his hair greased back. He had a tray of drinks in his hands and was doing his utmost to keep it upright, the studs on his brown leather boots proving very challenging on the well-polished wooden floor. Gordon smiled, his eyes drawn to the footballer's baggy shorts that descended well below his knees.

"Didn't play for Fulham by any chance, did he?" Gordon inquired, having at last caught up with Mr Gilmore. "Some of their players move like that on *grass!*"

"I'm not sure," Mr Gilmore answered. "All I know is that he died with his boots on!"

The joke passed over Gordon.

Eventually they came to a number of tables at which sat an array of characters, most deep in conversation, the music being much quieter in this particular corner of the nightclub.

"That's better," Gordon declared. "Why's the music so loud anyway? It's enough to wake the…"

Mr Gilmore returned a playful smile. "That's right, Mr Jones. How else would people know there was a party in town?"

Gordon did not know whether to believe the angel or not. Even when he got answers to his questions, he was so often left none the wiser.

In the far corner of the room, two round tables had been pushed close together and were occupied by a large group of Elizabethans, at least a dozen men. Some of them had drinks, but most of the glasses were empty. Few could take their eyes off a bearded man who sat facing them. Gordon thought he had seen him somewhere before.

Mr Gilmore certainly knew him and made no apologies for pushing his way through, beckoning Gordon to follow, the angel losing half of the contents of his drink in the process. He held out his hand when he reached the individual who was the centre of attention. The bearded man had a pipe dangling from his lips that looked like it would slip out at any moment.

Gordon noted a 'no smoking' sign above the man's head and looked at the angel for clarification. Mr Gilmore did not respond and was already vigorously shaking the man's hand.

"Evening, Bill. You're looking well. Anne is well too, I presume."

The man nodded in response.

"I would like you to meet a friend of mine," Mr Gilmore continued. "His name's Mr Jones… He's just died."

It was hardly the most appropriate or complimentary introduction, Gordon thought. Mr Gilmore might have highlighted some achievement of his. All he could say was that Gordon was now dead.

A number of men moved their chairs back in order to allow Gordon to reach the bearded man. There was little doubt the man, even though he had not yet said anything, was the life and soul of the party, all chairs having been turned in his direction.

The man only nodded his head in acknowledgement. Gordon might have at first been forgiven for thinking he was a man of few words, though that could not, in fact, have been farther from the truth. At last he took the pipe from his mouth, blowing a ring of smoke in the air as he did so, before speaking softly. "The way to dusty death. Out, out, brief candle. Life's but a walking shadow, a poor player that struts and frets his hour upon the stage and then is heard no more."

The man took a sip from the pint of beer that one of his friends had just placed in front of him on the table; unaware some froth was now stuck to the long whiskers on his chin.

A confused Gordon looked to Mr Gilmore.

"What did he say?" Gordon whispered. "He sounds a bit like Death."

The angel giggled. "I think you will find it is Death who has quoted Mr Shakespeare on numerous occasions."

"Shakespeare?" Gordon shrieked, turning to face the bard himself. "Wow! I thought I recognised you. You were on a five-pound note once – or was it a tenner?" He started to fumble through the pockets of his trousers, but soon realised that if his wallet had been in his possession, Angel Harriet would have taken it anyway. He looked up embarrassed, but in awe. "Wow!" he repeated. "So you really are the *real* William Shakespeare?"

Shakespeare, as we should now call the bearded man, smiled. "What's in a name? That which we call a rose by any other word would smell as sweet."

"I've heard that somewhere before," Gordon stuttered. "I read lots of your books at school, you know. Some of them are quite gory, aren't they? I like those ones. I particularly like that bit in *King Lear* when they pluck out that man's eyes."

Shakespeare shook his head disapprovingly. "O, what men dare do! What men may do! What men daily do, not knowing what they do!"

Mr Gilmore and the others laughed, but Gordon only smiled politely, not knowing what he himself should do. He shifted uncomfortably. Having been the one introduced to Shakespeare, he believed it his responsibility to make conversation.

"I always found your work quite difficult to understand, to be honest," Gordon babbled. "It's a shame you never used proper English."

Shakespeare looked at Gordon in bemusement. The latter immediately regretted his comment and sought to clarify it. "What I mean is that some of the words were spelt wrong, weren't they?" He stumbled on. "Things like o'er and hast..."

The playwright looked to Mr Gilmore for an explanation. The angel tactfully changed the direction of the conversation.

"Tell Mr Shakespeare what your favourite play is, Mr Jones."

"I like *The Mousetrap*."

"I mean one that Mr Shakespeare wrote!"

"Sorry." Gordon rubbed his chin thoughtfully. "*Macbeth,* I think."

Shakespeare nodded in approval.

"That's one of the goriest, isn't it?" Gordon added.

"And one of his shortest," a wag from another table chipped in, to roars of laughter.

Gordon smiled, almost believing it was he who had been responsible for the joke, gaining confidence to continue.

"Yes, I think *Hamlet* is good too, but it does go on a bit. I like the ending, but I think some of the middle bit could have been cut out. Do you agree?"

Shakespeare put his pipe to his mouth and turned his head deliberately from Gordon.

"Cudgel thy brains no more about it, for your dull ass will not mend his pace with beating," he muttered.

Another spontaneous roar of laughter broke out from those around the table, one particularly jocular individual merrily thumping his fist against it, causing the loss of the remainder of the contents of Mr Gilmore's glass, the angel having for one moment put it down.

"What's here?" the bard continued, smiling. "The portrait of a blinking idiot."

Shakespeare looked up at Gordon. He smiled. It was a warm smile and it assured Gordon that he took no offence and meant none either.

Suddenly, one of the men produced a mobile phone from his pocket. It made no sound but was vibrating.

"It's Anne for you, Bill," he said, sliding the phone along the table. "I expect she wants to know if you're going to be late for supper again..."

There was more laughing. Shakespeare sighed. "The lady doth protest too much, methinks. Would you excuse me, Mr Jones."

The bard rose from the table, putting the mobile phone to his ear. Mr Gilmore took that as their cue to depart.

"Come on, Mr Jones. Let's see who else we can find."

"This is amazing," said Gordon, his spirits unaffected by the awkward meeting with the country's greatest scribe.

"I'd like you to meet Richard Turpin," the angel said, negotiating his way through the crowded dance floor once more. "I think you'll find you'll have much more in common with him."

"You mean Dick Turpin? The notorious highwayman?" Gordon shrieked.

"No, Richard – the plasterer from Chipping Ongar."

As a disappointed Gordon shook the hand of a man in plaster-stained overalls, he noticed that many of the clubbers on the dance floor had stopped dancing. Their heads were now turned towards the exit. That he knew it was the exit was thanks to a green neon sign informing everyone that it was indeed that. There appeared to be a disturbance of some sort. The revellers, including Mr Turpin, were now straining their eyes to make out what was causing the commotion. Mr Gilmore was standing on his toes, trying to see over the many taller figures in front of him. He resorted to jumping on the spot on two occasions, before clutching Gordon by the arm, the expression on his face having instantly changed from one of inquisitiveness to anxiety.

"What's wrong?" Gordon asked. "What is it?"

"I had a feeling this would happen," the angel replied, pushing his glasses back on to the bridge of his nose, his latest exertions having predictably dislodged them. "It's what you might call the paparazzi."

Gordon shrugged his shoulders. "Is that all?"

Two men, one with a camera, had pushed their way on to the dance floor. They turned their heads, scanning their eyes every which way in search of something or, should we say, someone. They were oblivious, or at least undaunted, by the commotion their appearance had caused.

"I expect they're here for all these famous people," Gordon whispered.

Mr Gilmore, his arm linked around Gordon's, briskly headed in a direction away from the journalists. "It's not Shakespeare they're after, Mr Jones. It's you!"

The angel sighted another illuminated 'exit' sign and began making his way towards it, forcefully pushing his way through the crowd of people between them and that particular target. It was the flashlight of a camera that stopped them in their tracks.

"Too late," Mr Gilmore sighed. "They've spotted you."

A man in a grey raincoat lifted the trilby hat from his head and pulled out the small business card that had been sitting within it, placing it in front of Gordon's stupefied face.

"*Hell and Heaven Echo*," he declared, pulling a notebook from his coat pocket. "Can I have a few words, Mr Jones?"

Gordon nodded dumbly, rubbing his eyes, the flashlight having momentarily dazzled him.

"I just want to know how you think the trial will go, Mr Jones?" the reporter continued.

"We have no comment, thank you," Mr Gilmore interrupted. "Come on, Mr Jones. Best not to say anything you might regret. We don't want to prejudice the case. Sorry, gentlemen, may I remind you of *sub judice*."

Gordon was slightly disappointed by the angel's reaction. He had never been the subject of a newspaper article. Everyone had now stopped dancing. The music had stopped too, though Gordon did not actually notice. All eyes were now upon him.

"*Mid-Heaven Advertiser*," another reporter announced, thrusting his way through the crowd and producing his press card. It was the scruffy young man Gordon had seen when leaving the court. "Are you a Christian, Mr Jones?"

Another camera flashed.

"*Heavenly Times*," a woman reporter stated. "Are you hiding some guilty secret, Mr Jones?"

Another camera flashed.

"*The Eternal Mail*. What will you do if you lose, Mr Jones?"

Another camera flashed.

"*News of the New World*. Who are you looking forward to dating in heaven... or hell, Mr Jones?"

Mr Gilmore waved his hands in the air.

"Thank you, ladies and gentlemen. That will do. We have no comment to make."

"Just tell us if he's a Christian," a voice was heard amidst the commotion. "Then we'll leave you in peace."

The angel could not resist replying on this occasion.

"Of course he is. Now will you excuse us, please."

A barrage of questions from all directions ensued, as Mr Gilmore and Gordon reconvened their trek towards the exit.

"Why is there going to be a trial if Mr Jones is a Christian?"

"What evidence has Demon Dumas got?"

"Are you confident of winning?"

"Can you remember your first kiss, Mr Jones?"

Two burly men had also arrived on the scene. One was dressed in a suit that was too small for him, enhancing his brawn, while the other wore a tartan kilt, complete with sporran. The latter was now lifting two reporters by their coat collars, one in each hand, their legs dangling in the air. The other journalists had been a bit more alert to the danger and were already making their way towards the exit.

"Let's go," Mr Gilmore said, turning to Gordon. "We'd better get out of here while the going's good. I didn't think the press would be on to our case this quickly. Still, you can't blame them. They haven't had a scoop as good as this since Angel Boris forgot how to fly."

Suddenly, the fleeing members of the media came to a halt. Something, or should we say someone, had stopped them in their tracks. A shadowy figure was now standing in front of the only exit route available to them. The pursuing bouncers, for that is what those burly men were, instantly became an irrelevance. Indeed, the tartan-clad individual holding the two reporters now eased his grip. The two unfortunate fellows fell to the ground, but quickly got to their feet, more worried about the stranger that everyone was now focused on than whether their Dictaphones and mobile phones, or indeed themselves, had come to any harm. Cameras were clicking again, but they were now trained on the new arrival. Everyone stood motionless, staring at the dark figure lurking in the shadows. One of the spotlights was now shining straight into Gordon's eyes and he could not make out the man who had stolen the limelight from him.

"Who is it?" Gordon asked, aware that Mr Gilmore had retaken his arm, his grip much tighter than before. The angel never answered.

The figure was now walking slowly towards them, revellers stepping back to give him room. The partygoers had somehow found enough space either side of them to form a wide path that would not have seemed possible to create, so packed had the dance floor been. The steps of the man made no sound. It was though he was gliding towards Gordon. Even the cameras had stopped clicking now.

The man finally passed in front of the spotlight that had been shielding his identity from Gordon; that light – his figure now blocking its glare – finally helping to illuminate him. Gordon shivered as the menacing Dumas bowed his head.

"Well, well, well," the demon purred. "If it isn't my dear Mr Jones."

Gordon edged closer to Mr Gilmore. Somehow the demon now cut a more sinister figure. Before he had been complacent and smug, but never really threatening. For the first time, Gordon feared him. There was evil in his eyes.

"Having fun, Mr Jones?" Dumas continued. "Don't stop on my account. Perhaps I can join you? Shall we dance?"

It should have been funny but it wasn't, and nobody would have dared laugh anyway.

"Come on, Mr Jones. Have you suddenly lost your sense of fun?"

He brushed Mr Gilmore aside and positioned himself within Gordon's personal space, almost because he knew it would irk him, though Gordon was not exactly irked at this particular moment, more petrified. He turned his head to avoid the demon's malevolent stare.

"Don't be scared, Mr Jones. You'll have to get used to dancing with the devil."

At this, Mr Gilmore boldly pushed his body between Gordon and the aggressor. Dumas was clearly startled by the angel's bravado. Mr Gilmore waved his hands in the air, as though he were a man attempting to banish a nuisance fly.

"That will do, Demon Dumas," he flapped. "You don't scare us. You've had your fun. Now please leave us alone."

The demon seemed amused by the angel's actions and stood back, studying him closely.

Mr Gilmore was unperturbed. "I have no idea why you are here and, quite frankly, I don't really care," the angel insisted. "You'd better have your fun now, because this whole charade is going to land you in a lot of trouble with the authorities. You know full well Mr Jones is a Christian. I can't even think what all this is about, but I know you'll regret ever bringing it to trial."

He stopped, breathless. There may have been little light, but Gordon could see the angel was red in the face.

Mr Gilmore was about to click his fingers and Gordon wondered why he had not done so to elude the press. Perhaps that had just been a bit of fun? This was no longer funny. However, Dumas had started to laugh and Mr Gilmore put his arm down.

"My dear Angel Gilmore," the demon smiled, "you're delightful, so naive. You do make me laugh when you're angry."

Dumas lifted the hat from his head and blew its feather.

He looked up sharply, meeting Gordon's eyes. On this occasion there was no time for Gordon to revert his own from that mesmerising stare. Those sparkling eyes had snared him. Only closing his own would free Gordon from their vice-like grip, but he did not dare do that.

The demon addressed Mr Gilmore, but he never took his accusing eyes off Gordon.

"You forget, Angel Gilmore, I know your subject as well as you do. You may have been one of his guardians, but I was also assigned to become his chief tempter. I have spent his entire life tempting him and he didn't even know I existed. My job was to win him for my master... and I have more than enough evidence to prove that I succeeded."

Gordon twitched. Still the demon refused to release him from his stare.

"As they say, Mr Jones, and it's very appropriate in this case, you're going down. That's right, Mr Jones. You'd better believe it... you're going down."

The demon put one hand behind his back. The other held his hat as he bowed. He knew how to play with an audience. The revellers were captivated, silent and motionless, staring blankly at the now vacant spot where Dumas had stood.

The cameras began clicking again, this time focused on Gordon's troubled face.

9

"There is no mistake; there has been no mistake; and there shall be no mistake."

Arthur Wellesley
1st Duke of Wellington

"YOU'VE GOT TO ADMIT IT'S A NICE PHOTOGRAPH," GOR-don purred, as he held a copy of the *Hell and Heaven Echo* in front of his face. "It's caught my best side." He paused and frowned. "I didn't think my ears stuck out that much, though…"

Mr Gilmore reached forward and snatched the newspaper from Gordon's hands, before flashing his charge a disapproving look over his glasses. "You don't want to be reading all that stuff, Mr Jones. Anyway, we've got things to do."

"Have we?" Gordon inquired. "I thought I didn't have to do anything. Where are we anyway?"

Gordon surveyed the room he now found himself in, rubbing the ink-stained palms of his hands on his trousers. Mr Gilmore flashed him another condemning glance, as Gordon's mother used to do when he was a boy. Gordon's eye rested upon a framed oil painting on the wall. The picture depicted a young girl leaning against a lamppost. She was crying. It was a bleak image and Gordon wondered why anyone should choose to display such a depressing painting.

"Is this *your* office?" Gordon asked. Indeed, it did not take him long to work out that they were in an office, and one that belonged to just one person, an important one at that.

Mr Gilmore shook his head.

Gordon started to poke at the inner sanctum of his ear with his finger. "I can still hear *that* music," he complained, thinking back to the nightclub. "It's odd, but I can hear it even clearer in the silence, if that makes sense?"

Mr Gilmore never responded. The angel sat opposite Gordon. A huge oak desk was between them, on which rested the angel's briefcase, its lid standing open, shielding the bulk of the angel's diminutive frame.

"I always wanted my own office," Gordon continued to waffle. "This guy must be very important. Whose office is this anyway? I presume we're allowed to be in here? Don't tell me; it's Christmas Day, no one's likely to bother us anyway, right?"

Mr Gilmore popped his head from behind the briefcase and smiled.

Gordon sighed. If someone had asked him how long he had been sitting in that particular office, as strange as it may sound, he probably would not have been able to say. He might have been sitting there for days. Of course, he assumed he had just arrived, but could not remember the moment when they had, or how they had got there. It did not occur to him to look at the date on the newspaper. That might have been the first thing any rational person would have done when the newspaper had come into their hands, but Gordon had had only eyes for the picture of himself emblazoned on its front page. He did not even read the accompanying article. Ah! *Vanitas vanitatum,* one as theatrical as Death might have quoted if he had been present. Gordon, like most of us when confronted with a picture of which we are in, was only drawn to the image of himself, the rest of its contents a mere blur. Of course, even if Gordon had looked at the date on the newspaper, it would not have helped him much. He would have noted the newspaper was dated Christmas Day and that would have confused him even more. He would have queried how the newspaper could have been printed so quickly, and that question might also have prompted him to inquire as to how it had even come to be in his hands. That point had not yet even surfaced in his mind to vex him further. Now out of sight – the angel having shoved it into his briefcase – the newspaper no longer occupied the thoughts of Gordon, seemingly much to the relief of Mr Gilmore.

"There's not much in this office, is there?" Gordon noted, reaching for the object closest to him. It was a small, framed photograph. "I wish I was that age again," he mused, studying the beaming toddler that met his eyes. "I wish I could be a child again. Life would be easier if we could live it a second time, wouldn't it, if we could use all the experience we gained from the first one?"

Mr Gilmore, as if he were a burrowing rabbit that felt the need to resurface to check there was nothing creeping up on him, again popped his head from behind the briefcase.

"Wise words, Mr Jones," he said. "Wise, indeed."

Back the head went and the 'burrowing rabbit' was gone again. The angel sporadically repeated the exercise, not necessarily because he wished to respond to any further profound remarks that came from Gordon's lips (in fact, there were no more to comment on), but to check to ensure his charge was not getting up to any mischief.

Gordon had now left his seat and was examining anything that warranted examination. Being such a bare room, the fixtures and fittings, as dull as they were, had to suffice. There was little in the way of paperwork and not even a computer, or a telephone come to that. The only sign of any stationery were a few pens positioned in a coffee mug on a shelf. Next to it was a metallic executive toy in the form of a boy holding a bucket. Gordon soon discovered that the bucket would swing if you gave it a gentle nudge. However, it also did not take him long to ascertain that the nudge had to be gentle. Needless to say, Mr Gilmore again felt the urge to poke his head from behind the briefcase when part of the stainless steel contraption – the bucket, to be precise – pinged to the floor. Gordon sheepishly retrieved the said object and attempted to replace it, but found it difficult to do so, eventually conceding defeat and choosing to nudge it behind an empty vase, one of the few other objects on the shelf. He checked to see if Mr Gilmore was watching him. He wasn't.

"What are we doing here anyway?" Gordon moaned, retaking his seat and placing his elbows on the desk, so that he could rest his chin within his cupped hands. He stared at the briefcase, Mr Gilmore now completely hidden from view; Gordon being just that bit closer to the angel. "What are you doing?" he persisted. "What's in that case?"

Mr Gilmore popped his head above the lid this time. "Nothing that will interest you, Mr Jones. I won't be long," he added, all too aware Gordon was giving a good impression of a bored schoolboy during a wet break.

"Is there anything I can help you with?" Gordon asked, moving his head in an attempt to peer around the open lid. Mr Gilmore made a point of pulling the briefcase closer to his midriff. That was not the best idea. It informed Gordon that the angel was doing his best to hide the contents from him. And, of course, that only made Gordon even more determined to find out what it was that so engrossed the angel.

"Are you planning my defence?" Gordon persevered. "Is that what you're doing in there?"

Gordon raised his head in the hope he would be able to see over the lid. At last he glimpsed a book. He was almost disappointed, believing the angel should have been using his time in a more productive manner.

"What are you reading?"

"Nothing that will interest you."

Gordon now only had eyes for that book and there was no way the angel would be allowed to carry on reading it in peace.

"Is it a good book?" Gordon probed. "I like thrillers myself. Can I have a look?"

Mr Gilmore reluctantly lifted the book from the briefcase and closed the lid. He slid it across the desktop so that it rested in front of Gordon. It finished the right way up, allowing him to easily peruse the title without having to touch the book.

"*Court Procedure and Etiquette,*" Gordon dictated. "*All you need to know.* How dull is that?"

"I knew you wouldn't be interested," said Mr Gilmore, scratching his head.

"What do you need to read that for, anyway?" Gordon asked, pushing the book back across the desk, only this time too hard, so that it fell on to the floor.

Mr Gilmore made no attempt to pick it up. "I'm just brushing up on the law, Mr Jones. Just want to make a good impression in court."

Gordon studied the angel carefully. He *now* appeared to be chewing gum.

"What are you eating?"

Mr Gilmore opened a drawer in the desk and slid a small green and silver packet across the tabletop.

"Want one?"

Gordon sighed. Not for the first time, Mr Gilmore did not look much like an angel at this particular moment.

"Mr Gilmore?" Gordon began, twiddling the packet of chewing gum within his fingers. "I don't want to sound ungrateful, but do you not think it best if someone else took on my case? There must be a few good lawyers up in heaven, you know, someone a bit more qualified. What about Perry Mason? I've heard he's good."

The angel rose from his chair and came to the other side of the desk where Gordon was sitting. He perched himself on it, his legs too short to reach the floor.

"You don't need the best lawyer," he explained. "Only the guilty need a good lawyer. You're not guilty of anything. We only need to present the facts, Mr Jones. Nothing more. Besides, I know you better than most."

Gordon looked up sorrowfully. "Do you?" He paused. "You do believe I'm a Christian, don't you, Mr Gilmore?"

"I know you are, Mr Jones... I just wish a few more did."

The angel smiled and placed his hand upon Gordon's shoulder, his dangling legs swinging backwards and forwards. "Look, if I wasn't sure you were a Christian, I still wouldn't get the best lawyer to defend you. If I wasn't sure, I'd know there was no defence anyway. We're not trying to deceive anyone – that's the job of Dumas. We only need to tell the court how it is. Please don't worry, Mr Jones. Do I look worried?"

"But you're not the one on trial!"

"Maybe not, but you forget that my reputation's on the line. If I've made a mistake – though I know I haven't – it will create quite a scene, I can assure you. That's why they've decided to bring your case to trial; to make absolutely sure there's been no mistake. What a stir it would create if an angel took a non-believer up to heaven for judgement! That's just not what's done."

Mr Gilmore jumped down from the desk and stooped to pick up his book. Gordon noticed the edges of one or two loose pieces of paper sticking out from the pages.

"What's that in there?"

"Nothing of any interest," Mr Gilmore smiled, pulling them from the book. "Just a few notes on your life."

Gordon didn't laugh. "It just looks like a mess," he responded, referring to the scribbled words on what was clearly scrap paper.

"I wouldn't go that far, Mr Jones," the angel continued to grin, now stuffing them into the breast pocket of his jacket. Gordon was oblivious to the significance of his own observation, now focusing on another loose piece of paper that had fallen from the book. He bent down to pick it up from the floor. It appeared to be a photocopy of a passport photograph, but of such poor quality, the head-and-shoulders picture was no more than a silhouette, there being no distinguishable features. Gordon only knew it was an image of a woman for the fact that the name 'Grace' was penned underneath it. He wondered who Grace might be. Was it Mr Gilmore's wife? Why would anyone keep such a poor-quality picture anyway? Strangely, Gordon did not feel the urge to pry. Instead, he attempted to pass the picture to the angel, though Mr Gilmore was not giving him his full attention and so Gordon tentatively placed it on the table next to him, believing he had come across something private that he had no right to see.

Mr Gilmore had reopened his briefcase and was now pulling out some sandwiches that were wrapped in cling film. He put them to his nose. "I hope these will be all right... Cheese and tomato," he said. "It's not my favourite, but sardines and pickle do tend to reek a bit after a few days."

He slammed the briefcase lid shut, this time checking it was secure, and sat back in his chair. The angel did not take long to discover that the chair could turn full circle. He raised his legs above the floor and – placing his outstretched hand on the desk – pushed, so that the chair revolved several times before coming to rest.

"Ready?" he inquired, rising from the chair and picking up his briefcase in one swift movement, but almost stumbling, presumably because his latest exertion had left him giddy.

Gordon watched in bewilderment. His fate seemingly lay in the hands of this man. Not for the first time, Gordon had again forgotten that Mr Gilmore was an angel.

"Ready for what?" Gordon inquired.

"Your trial, of course."

"What, *now?* What time does it start?"

"It just starts when everyone is there. You forget, Mr Jones, there is no..."

"I know," Gordon interrupted. "You don't have to tell me."

"Well? Are you ready?" Mr Gilmore peered over his glasses. "There's not much point sitting here."

Gordon reluctantly rose to his feet. "I suppose so, though I thought we might be able to go somewhere else."

"Another nightclub?"

Gordon remembered Dumas and shook his head.

"No. Let's get this over with."

Mr Gilmore smiled. "That's the spirit. Five, four, three, two..."

The angel did not get to 'one', or at least Gordon never heard him do so. Mr Gilmore's countdown had prompted his charge to close his eyes, and that had indeed probably been the angel's intention. When Gordon reopened them, he eventually formed the opinion that they were in the very same courtroom that had staged the preliminary hearing.

"I'm afraid we couldn't get the Old Bailey," Mr Gilmore explained. "It's being refurbished over Christmas."

That it may have been the same courtroom was not immediately obvious, however. Gordon and Mr Gilmore were this time sitting in the public gallery; an area that Gordon had not even realised had existed when he had stood before the archangels not so long ago. The gallery was suspended over the back of the courtroom and Gordon had not noticed it before, having not dared to turn his head on that last occasion. And, when he was exiting the courtroom and would have been facing in its direction, it had never occurred to him to look up, the departing newspaper reporter having been his sole preoccupation at the time. The gallery offered spectators an adequate, if somewhat distant, view of the court below. Gordon and Mr Gilmore were sitting in the front row; the seats behind them tiered, as though they were in a theatre waiting for the performance to begin. Gordon peered over the ledge to get a better look. There was quite a drop and he instinctively moved back. The courtroom was empty but for one or two people busy preparing the room. A woman was filling a glass decanter with water, while a man was gliding towards her, his black gown or cloak trailing behind him. Gordon immediately christened him 'Dracula'. He could not see the details on the man's face, so high was his vantage point, but he had already conjured up an image in his mind: red eyes, distinctive fangs and even a trickle of blood protruding from his lips. Of course, Gordon was so far away, he could not even pick out the man's spectacles, which might have dispelled the idea that the individual could at any moment turn into a vampire bat. Yes, they were definitely in the 'cheap' seats.

A monstrous clock dominated the wall behind the raised bench at which the archangels had previously sat. It was clearly for functional purposes and was in no way decorative. Its hands must have been the size of arms – as opposed to hands. Even from such a distance, Gordon would have been able to note the time, though he made no attempt to. The clock was positioned where the coat of arms had been and, for that reason, Gordon questioned whether this was indeed the same courtroom. The buzzing and flickering fluorescent light on the ceiling was no longer buzzing and flickering (if this was indeed the same courtroom), though Gordon had forgotten the fact it was once buzzing and flickering, and so did not add it to the arguments against this being that said same courtroom!

One other striking difference was that there was now only one 'throne' below the clock. The other two chairs (if this was indeed the same courtroom) had been removed. The solitary chair was vacant. Gordon shivered at the thought of who might soon be occupying it. Somehow one single chair looked more menacing than two or three together.

Suddenly, Gordon was distracted by a squeaking noise coming from below in the area directly underneath him, which was, of course, out of view to anyone sitting within the public gallery. The fact that the main entrance was there too meant that Gordon could not see anyone enter or exit. He looked to Mr Gilmore, in the hope he might offer an explanation for the strange sound. He didn't. The angel was engrossed in a book.

"That reminds me," Gordon inquired, wrongly assuming it to be the same book Mr Gilmore had been reading earlier, "how do I address an archangel?"

The angel lowered his book and assumed a puzzled face, clearly having not found the answer himself during his studies. Fortunately, Gordon did not wait for an answer.

"*Where Angels Fear to Tread?*" Gordon recited, his eyes drawn to the title on the cover of the book.

"Death lent it to me," Mr Gilmore replied.

"And where do they fear to tread?" Gordon inquired.

Mr Gilmore smiled. "I've no idea. That's what I'm trying to find out... not with much success, I have to add."

The squeaking sound grew louder and, as Gordon gingerly edged forward to look below, two men, both dressed in matching green boiler suits, came into view. The reason for the strange noise immediately became apparent. The squeaking was coming from the wheels of a trolley that was supporting a bulky filing cabinet, the sort you rarely see in an office these days. It was almost as though the wheels were protesting at the weight they were being forced to carry. The two men were laughing, their voices echoing off the walls, the courtroom still being devoid of many persons.

"What is that? What's in there?" Gordon asked nervously.

The angel adjusted his glasses.

"I expect that's the official record of your life," he replied. "Everyone has a file. They keep trying to persuade Angel Em to use a computer, but we've only just managed to wean her off the quill and scroll in favour of a typewriter."

They watched the men attempt to lift the filing cabinet from the trolley. It proved to be too heavy and they resorted to nudging it, an inch or two at a time, before it finally rested upright on the courtroom floor. For just one moment the men had feared it would topple on to its side.

"This will do," Gordon heard one of the men clearly say.

"I thought it had to be closer to the clerk?" the other responded.

"Then he can lift it!"

The men headed off towards the exit and were soon out of Gordon's sight once more.

Gordon shook his head in awe. "Is that really my life in there?" he questioned, nodding his head in the direction of the filing cabinet. "I didn't realise someone would be taking notes."

"Taking notes?" Mr Gilmore smiled. "Notes? That would imply some bits are missing. I don't doubt every second of your life is accounted for in there, Mr Jones. Angel Em is very thorough."

Gordon gulped and shook his head. "This is crazy. If my friends could see me now."

Instinctively, he looked to the clock, as though it might give him some clue as to what they would be doing at this particular moment. Of course, the clock told him what he already knew. It was just after 7:30pm and the hands would not move from that position – neither would his friends from theirs – however long he sat there. In fact, Gordon did not know how long he had been sitting in the public gallery, but he could sense some people were now seated behind him. He tentatively turned his head, but swiftly turned it back again. From that initial glance – and it was no more than that – he could ascertain that at least a dozen chairs were now occupied. He had not noticed the arrival of any of the occupants. Gordon wanted another look, but, because he was in the front row, he knew that in turning to face the new arrivals, he would only draw attention to himself, those behind him being in the privileged position of being able to study those in front of them without making it obvious they were doing just that. However, from the corner of his eye, Gordon could still discern a couple of individuals: a middle-aged man wearing spotty pyjamas and a woman clad in a tweed jacket and beige jodhpurs. The latter held her black riding hat in one hand and was lightly tapping a small whip on the vacant chair in front of her.

Gordon could now hear people conversing. They were talking about him; that he could have no doubt about.

"Do you think he'll win?" a man inquired.

"I don't know. He's either a Christian or he isn't..." another man replied.

Gordon felt the urge to turn around to resolve the matter, but Mr Gilmore gently put his hand upon his knee to prevent him from doing so, it clearly being a signal that it was not their place to interfere. Clearly, none of the spectators had any idea that the defendant was at this very moment sitting amongst them in the public gallery.

"There must be some evidence," another voice from behind Gordon sounded. "Dumas has got to have some proof."

"He's right," a woman added. "You don't make an accusation like that if you can't back it up."

"Maybe," another chipped in, "but then that'll mean Angel Gilmore has made a mistake. Angels don't make mistakes... do they?"

Gordon noticed Mr Gilmore twitched in response, presumably himself resisting the temptation to clarify that particular point.

"I don't know," another voice declared. "But I think this Jones chap is doomed. He's obviously a fraud."

"Or a liar."

"A charlatan."

"A fake."

"A swindler."

"A cheat."

"An impostor."

Each word caused Gordon to flinch. He assumed their accusations had become a spontaneous game in which the players were trying to come up with every relevant word found in a thesaurus.

"Humbug?" another voice, much softer, uttered.

It came from directly behind Gordon. He flinched again. On this occasion he felt as though the word had been whispered into his ear.

"Humbug?" it sounded again.

This time the speaker gently tapped Gordon on the shoulder at the same time. That was an invasion of his personal space and he believed the perpetrator had gone too far on this occasion. He turned around sharply.

"I'm no humbug!" he declared defiantly. "I'm a..."

Gordon stopped. His eyes met those of a frail pensioner, her face a maze of wrinkles. She held a brown paper bag in her hand, now virtually under his nose.

"Humbug?" she persisted, softly. "Would you like a humbug, dear? I've got some angel drops, if you'd prefer."

Mr Gilmore reached over and took a sweet from one of the two bags the woman now held aloft.

"Thank you," he beamed. "I *will*, if you don't mind. I am partial to angel drops. Do you have an orange one, they're my favourites?" He began to rummage through the bag before settling on a red one.

"Please forgive my friend here," Mr Gilmore apologised. "He's a little tetchy today. He's got a lot on his mind, that's all. No offence meant."

The woman smiled sympathetically. She had no teeth.

Gordon attempted to return an apologetic smile, but it was a half-hearted one and he quickly turned his back on the woman. Mr Gilmore followed suit, reverting his gaze to the front of the courtroom once more.

"It's all right, Mr Jones," he assured his client, patting his knee, as though he were trying to calm his pet dog. "It's going to be all right. There's no need to worry."

The angel removed the sweet from his mouth and held it up to the light, examining it closely. "I used to make these last for hours when I was a nipper," he revealed.

Gordon shifted his position. He was never the most patient person. When something had to be done, he would rather get on with it straight away.

"When's it going to start?" he moaned, rubbing his hand through his hair. "I'm sorry, but I can't stand much more of this."

Gordon could hear the old woman crunching a sweet and that only irritated him further. He never questioned how she was able to do that without any teeth; there were more important concerns on his mind at this moment.

Mr Gilmore leaned forward, resting his arms on the ledge in front of him, placing his head upon them. He sucked at his sweet with renewed vigour and one might have questioned how he had ever managed to make one sweet last even a minute. The angel may have been of advanced years – his lack of hair and the lines on his forehead evidence of that – but he often had a twinkle in his eye, if you could see it through the thick lenses of his spectacles. He had child-like mannerisms and at this very moment one could have been forgiven for thinking he was young again, an excited boy at the cinema waiting for the main picture to begin.

Gordon attempted to shut out the conversations behind him, but, in consciously trying to do so, they only became more pronounced than all the other sounds within the courtroom, such as the rustling of tin foil, as a spectator unwrapped their sandwiches, the aroma of mustard greeting Gordon's nose long before the noise reached his ears.

"It's the demon!" a voice from behind him suddenly announced, an announcement even Mr Gilmore, whose hearing capabilities would often come under question by those that met him, could not fail to catch. The proclamation alerted all to the fact that the distant figure of Dumas could now be seen below, his back to them, straightening some papers laid out on the bench in front of him. He occupied the same position he had done at the preliminary hearing.

"It must be starting soon," someone else, possibly the man in his pyjamas, suggested.

Indeed, Gordon now noticed the courtroom below was buzzing. Many more people had entered. The clerk of the court and a copy typist (or a woman that sat in front of an electronic typewriter, at any rate) were already in their seats below the raised bench at which the lone archangel would sit. Gordon was unable to pick out any details on the faces of the man and woman who sat facing him, but he was convinced it was the same clerk from the preliminary hearing, his big red nose evident at even this great distance. From his position high above, Gordon could also now discern the press bench, positioned at the side of the room, to the left of Dumas. The journalists were more identifiable by their distinctive clothes, in particular their hats and overcoats, rather than their faces, though Gordon was sure he could pick out one or two who had harassed him at the nightclub.

"I think I'd better take my seat," Mr Gilmore declared, rising to his feet. "We'll be starting soon. You needn't come until Dracula calls your name."

Gordon looked at the angel horrified.

"Don't look so alarmed," Mr Gilmore explained. "I told you before, I can't read your mind, but everyone calls him that. No doubt it was that black cloak that prompted someone to give him the job of court usher."

Mr Gilmore smiled and patted Gordon on the back.

"Now, don't worry, Mr Jones. It's going to be all right. You know that, don't you?"

The angel did not wait for an answer and headed for the door at the back of the public gallery. Within a few moments, he had returned and was again by Gordon's side, now reaching for the briefcase he had left in the aisle beside his seat. He straightened his tie, his smile one of embarrassment this time. Gordon sighed. He had been sighing quite a lot lately.

Mr Gilmore this time clicked his fingers and vanished, though why he had not done that previously, Gordon had no idea and, one might be forgiven to suggest, it is quite probable that the angel didn't either. Instantly – though Gordon did not notice at first – Mr Gilmore appeared on the same bench as Dumas, at the other end, the two immortals now both in the same positions they had occupied during the preliminary hearing. Once again, neither felt the need to greet each other.

Still Gordon found himself inadvertently listening to those behind him, most continuing to discuss his predicament.

"I wonder why anyone would pretend to be a Christian?"

"He might have believed once upon a time."

"Maybe he lost his faith? Lots do, you know."

"I don't want a bacon sandwich. Have you got any tuna?"

Gordon sat very still, sensing more people had arrived. He did not need to turn around to know that the toothless old lady was no longer the sole occupant of her row. In fact, every seat in it was filled now. Gordon found himself thinking about the moment when his name would be called. He knew that would result in him having to walk past the spectators behind him. Unlike Mr Gilmore, he would not be able to click his fingers and escape their accusing eyes. In view of that fact, he made up his mind to leave the public gallery before he was summoned. No one yet knew he was the defendant, but the moment his name was called, his identity would, of course, be revealed by the mere act of standing up. Gordon thought back to the time when he had heard his car number plate being hailed from the pulpit at church, having inadvertently left his lights on. On that occasion, he had pretended it was not his vehicle and waited a few minutes before leaving the ongoing service, in the hope most would presume he was bound for the lavatory, the announcement from the pulpit having then long been forgotten by the congregation. However, it still resulted in a little embarrassment, the absurd notion of giving his fellow parishioners the impression that he could not hold his bladder for another ten minutes causing him almost as much consternation.

Gordon slipped from his seat and made his way to the back of the public gallery, his tread purposeful but silent, the latter point explained by the fact that the steps were carpeted, his slippers perfectly suited to the terrain. As he hoped, no one looked at him, or at least he was under the impression no one had done so, Gordon having taken great pains to avoid looking at anyone himself, his head bowed as he had made his way towards the exit. One or two people were still more preoccupied with looking for a spare seat, the public gallery now almost full.

Gordon had the confidence to stop when he reached the door, knowing that the occupants of the gallery would have their backs to *him* now, and he even afforded himself one final look at the courtroom below. His view was not so good from this new vantage point, but he could still make out the bald head of Mr Gilmore, the fluorescent ceiling lights reflecting off it. Dumas was now seated, twiddling a pencil in his gloved fingers, though, of course, Gordon was unable to pick out that detail.

The courtroom had fallen silent. All those in the public gallery had brought their conversations to an end. Gordon was only able to observe backs of heads, the eyes of those heads presumably now gazing towards the action, or where the action was to take place. No one had instructed them to be quiet. It was as though they merely sensed something was about to happen below them.

Dracula was fidgeting. His eyes were planted on the door from which the archangel would emerge. Soon the vacant 'throne' would be vacant no more. Gordon wiped his sweaty hands on the sides of his trousers. In anticipation of something happening very soon, he decided to stay put, in case it might happen as he was descending the stairs in the foyer.

It could have been a game. Every eye was now centred on *that* door, the winner being the first to spot the archangel emerging from it. Gordon was physically trying not to blink, for fear he would miss the moment when it might open. Of course, the moment you make a point of trying not to blink becomes the moment you want to blink, and, due to the strain he brought upon his eyes in trying to keep them open, Gordon was eventually forced to close them for longer than it took to blink!

The man in the pyjamas started to cough. Others followed suit. Grown-up hands instinctively moved to cover up the mouths of children, almost as if they feared the cough to be contagious, though it probably had more to do with the fact that they doubted their little ones would be able to hold their silence for much longer. Gordon continued to look at *that* door. It never occurred to him that this all-powerful, divine being might just appear in his (or her) chair. He could hear the old woman sucking her sweet. Then she crunched it between her 'teeth', or whatever she used in the absence of those teeth. At that exact moment, there was a knock on the door. Many people jumped in their seats, even though their eyes had been focused on *that* door for some time, knowing full well it was to open imminently. Dracula stood to attention. "Court rise," he bellowed.

This was it. Gordon strained his eyes as the door slowly opened. At the same time, people sitting before him in the public gallery rose from their seats, blocking his view of the emerging archangel.

10

"'The time has come,' the Walrus said,
'To talk of many things:
Of shoes – and ships – and sealing wax –
Of cabbages – and kings –
And why the sea is boiling hot –
And whether pigs have wings.'"

Through the Looking-Glass and What Alice Found There
Lewis Carroll

GORDON SHOULD HAVE KNOWN BETTER THAN TO EXPECT A powerful, awe-inspiring figure to appear. Instead, a tiny spectacled pensioner, not too dissimilar to Mr Gilmore, clambered on to the 'throne'. Although the bench hid his body from the waist down, it was obvious his feet never touched the ground. With his legs unable to give him the thrust required to assume an upright position in his seat, he was forced to push his hands down on the arms of the wooden chair in order to shift his body to a point where his back was finally able to rest against something solid. When he was satisfied he was quite comfortable, he leant forward to pour himself a glass of water from the decanter standing on the bench in front of him. However, in doing so – the glass having been placed at a distance almost beyond his reach – the archangel discovered his posterior had slipped out of the position it had taken him no little effort to put it in. It meant he had to go through the whole procedure again.

Gordon was not among those to witness it for a second time. He was quickly making his way downstairs, fearing Dracula would call his name at any moment. He passed a few latecomers going in the opposite direction, but, so intent was he on getting to the foyer before his name was called, he paid no attention to them. He did not even notice a pantomime cow pass him on the stairs. If he had, he might have expressed a little sympathy for the person occupying the rear half of the costume and questioned whether he or she was doomed to spend eternity looking at the backside of the individual in front of them.

The courtroom was silent. The archangel had the full attention of everyone within its walls, his every movement under close scrutiny. He did not need to call for silence, but had found a gavel and could not resist trying it out. He tapped it lightly on the bench.

"Good evening," he muttered, straightening his tie as he did so. Only a few people responded with a mere mumble, most unsure whether the archangel wished them to reply.

"Are we ready to proceed?" the archangel inquired, leaning forward so that he could see the top of the head of the clerk of the court sitting directly below him. The young man with the big red nose sat with his back to the archangel. He turned his head, merely as a token acknowledgment, as looking directly at his superior would have involved him having to turn his entire body.

"Case number one, that of Mr Jones," the clerk stated authoritatively, examining a piece of paper, as though he needed it to inform him which case was up next. Of course, everyone *knew* which case was up next.

The archangel had removed his jacket and was now contemplating where to put it. He tried to hang it on to the back of his chair, but it proved difficult, the chair – blessed with throne-like proportions – being much wider than the average chair. The jacket slipped on to the floor out of view. The archangel made no attempt to pick it up and started to roll up the sleeves of his white shirt, finally loosening the knot in his tie and undoing his top button, as though he were preparing to chop logs.

"Will you call Mr Jones?" the clerk directed, nodding in the direction of Dracula. The usher sprang to life and began to stride towards the courtroom exit, his black cloak rising slightly in the breeze that his swift and purposeful movements had momentarily created.

Gordon, alone in the foyer, had been watching the proceedings, the door being ajar. He knew Dracula was approaching and it gave him time to seek one of the seats in the carpeted waiting area. He sat down, adopting a manner of indifference, which could not have been farther from his real state of mind at this particular moment.

"Mr Jones," the usher shouted, his head emerging from the door. "Court number one, please."

Gordon pretended to be startled. He looked up at the usher and pointed his finger towards his chest. "Who, me?" he mimed, knowing full well his time had come.

Dracula – Gordon could now clearly see that it was not the same usher from the preliminary hearing – did not want to play the game and did not respond, but stood holding the door open. He was smiling, though it was not a reassuring smile and it only succeeded in revealing a set of long, yellow teeth, his gums worn down through time. No bloodstained fangs were visible.

"Will you step this way, please, Mr Jones," he ordered impatiently, even though Gordon had already risen from his chair and was making his way towards him.

Gordon followed Dracula into the packed courtroom. He never averted his eyes from the usher's cape, which was probably just as well, as he might have stepped on it, so close was he sticking to him. He could sense heads were turning in his direction but did not dare to turn his own.

The first person that Gordon set his eyes upon, other than the usher, was Mr Gilmore. The angel was sitting in his chair and had turned his head to view his approaching client. He offered Gordon a reassuring smile. He was like a bridegroom stealing a glance at his bride as she came down the aisle. All was silent but for the pitter-patter of Gordon's slippers on the wooden floor. Strangely, the gleaming black shoes of Dracula, only occasionally visible beneath his cloak, did not seem to emit any sound, even though they looked like the sort that should.

Gordon expected to take a seat next to Mr Gilmore, but was surprised, and alarmed, to discover his destination was the dock. Dracula opened the swing door and nodded his head, indicating that he wished Gordon to enter the enclosed space.

The dock was situated just a few feet from Mr Gilmore, only the aisle between them. Inside was a chair, though Gordon did not choose to sit down. He stood upright and faced the archangel, interlocking his fingers behind his back. He could hear the clerk of the court shuffling some papers, but it was the archangel himself who spoke.

"Mr Jones, I am sure you know why you are here this evening," he said softly. "However, I must make sure you understand the allegation put forward by Demon Dumas."

Gordon flashed a glance in the direction of the demon. He could see him seated in the chair at the very far end of the long bench that was also occupied by Mr Gilmore. He was glad his guardian stood between them.

"Demon Dumas alleges that you are not a Christian, Mr Jones," the archangel continued, staring over the top of his glasses in Mr Gilmore fashion, "and that he has the right to accompany you to the gates of heaven in preparation for your meeting with the Master. To put it bluntly, Demon Dumas is convinced he will then be permitted, following your meeting with the Master, to take... to take you to *his* master. Do you understand, Mr Jones?"

Gordon nodded unconvincingly.

"To hell, Mr Jones," the brazen voice of the clerk boomed, Gordon for the first time discerning a Welsh accent. "Demon Dumas is of the opinion that you belong with his master in hell. Do you understand, Mr Jones?"

The archangel coughed, as a way of acknowledging that the clerk was correct, even if he had not intended to put it so forcefully. Gordon nodded again.

The clerk unashamedly took control. "The archangel will now ask you a simple question and you must answer it with a simple 'yes' or 'no'. Do you understand?"

Gordon nodded again.

The archangel cleared his throat.

"Mr Jones." He paused. "Are you a Christian or not a Christian?"

The clerk sighed, and the archangel looked to him, immediately realising he had not worded his question correctly. Gordon did not wait for him to do so again, however.

"A Christian, your worship," he replied confidently, turning to Mr Gilmore to check he had addressed the archangel in the proper manner. Mr Gilmore nodded to suggest he was content with the response.

"Very well, Mr Jones," the archangel continued, taking a sip from his glass of water. He stopped and looked down at some papers in front of him, unsure how to proceed.

The clerk again intervened. "A jury of twelve dead men and women will hear the facts of the case, Mr Jones, and decide upon your fate. Do you understand?"

Gordon did not feel it necessary to respond, the clerk now wiping that huge red nose with his handkerchief, even though it seemed the most inappropriate moment to do so. The handkerchief was covering his mouth as he continued, and Gordon could only just make out what he was saying. "Should the jury decide you are a Christian, you will be given your ticket to heaven and Angel Gilmore will take you to your master.

Should they decide you are not, you will be given a ticket to hell and Demon Dumas will have the right to claim you for *his* master. Do you understand, Mr Jones?"

Gordon nodded again, even though he had come to the conclusion that he had nodded once too often during the last few exchanges.

"You'd better inform him about the procedure," the archangel interrupted, gesturing to the clerk.

"Thank you for reminding me," the clerk replied, half-heartedly turning his head towards his superior, again their eyes not meeting because of the positions both occupied, which was just as well, as the archangel might have noticed the insincere smile that accompanied the acknowledgement.

The clerk refocused on Gordon. "Demon Dumas will present his evidence and any witnesses he may wish to call. You will then have the opportunity to present your case under Angel Gilmore's direction. Do you understand?"

Gordon nodded again.

There was another brief pause and the clerk was about to turn to the archangel to give instruction, when the latter seemingly remembered what had to be done next.

"Would you call the members of the jury and swear them in, please?" he directed the usher.

Dracula bowed and headed towards a side door. He opened it and disappeared.

The archangel poured himself another glass of water, the noise of the liquid clearly audible in the silence. Like Mr Gilmore, he was an individual of advanced years, but he also possessed a youthful, almost cheeky face. The few strands of hair on the top of his head needed trimming. They occasionally swayed like wheat in a field on a breezy day, at least whenever the archangel shifted his position, and not because of any draught in the courtroom, though the door behind him that he had emerged from was ajar.

The archangel had retrieved some items from under his bench: a red gown and a sentencing wig. He slipped from his chair in order to put on the gown. It was far too big for him, but he did not seem to mind. He then proceeded to place the wig on his head, flattening his few strands of 'wheat'. The wig virtually covered his entire head and ears, and if it were not for the rims of his glasses, which provided a useful resting place for the said wig, it would have covered his eyes too.

126

As the archangel was climbing back on to his chair, Dracula re-emerged, leading a single file of jurors into the courtroom. It will come as no surprise, and it didn't to Gordon, that the jurors were donned in an array of strikingly different clothes, the attire of each no bigger contrast to the person next to them. Collectively, they were a bewildering sight, almost dazzling, and Gordon found it difficult to focus on any one individual. None of the jurors looked up, resisting the temptation to snatch a glance at the man they were perhaps soon to condemn. They were ushered to the corner of the courtroom.

"When I call your name, you are to take your seat," Dracula instructed, pointing his head towards two benches, one slightly raised above the other. He held a pack of white cards in his hands and, after shuffling them, proceeded to read the name printed on the top one.

"Albert George Comyn," he announced, placing the card at the bottom of the pack.

An old man in simple clothes, the word 'rags' particularly fitting on this occasion, shuffled forward, nervously stroking his white beard as he made his way to the seat at the very far end of the front bench. Men and women followed in quick procession when they heard their name.

"Charles Alexander Hague... Countess Elizabeth Georgina Droniden... Horatio Nelson, 1st Viscount Nelson."

If you had asked Gordon to repeat the names of the first three jurors, he would not have been able to. Of course, it was a different story when it came to the fourth. When that name – so familiar to Gordon – had been called, it seemed to resonate around the courtroom. His eyes immediately sought the bearer of it, at last moving from the hair of the preceding countess, upon which they had become fixed – and not surprisingly either – that hair standing at a height of almost two feet from the top of her head. Of course, not even that incredible sight was enough to hold his gaze, and now he only had eyes for the diminutive admiral (he was smaller than Gordon thought he would be) walking within the shadow of the woman with the big hair. If he had not heard the name, he would not have even realised the great man was in his midst. Nelson was not in full uniform; far from it. He wore a baggy white shirt. The top half was unbuttoned, revealing some of his chest. It was not tucked into his white breeches either. However, one should at this point stress that the word 'white' was perhaps an exaggeration. The admiral's trousers were stained with grime and even his shirt was dominated by one enormous burgundy-coloured stain that extended from both shoulders and down his back. It was not until Nelson took his seat next to the countess that Gordon could see one arm of his shirt was not vacated.

"Rose Alice Mason... George of Shrewsbury... Mary, Queen of Scots."

Only a name of similar status would have succeeded in drawing the gaze of Gordon from the figure of Nelson. He gasped, *really* gasped this time, when he heard it. Gordon was immediately reminded of the earthly fate of yet another name so familiar to him. The stately woman, predominantly dressed in crimson-brown and black, was, of course, if you know your history, headless. To be fair, that was not strictly true. She *did* possess a head; only it was no longer attached to her neck. She held it under one of her armpits, like a footballer emerging from the tunnel would carry a ball. It has to be noted that if the head of Mary had been where it was supposed to be, she would have been a good few inches taller than Nelson and most of the other jurors. She had no problem finding her seat, the eyes in *that* head focused on the person in front of her, blinking occasionally, like any eyes on any head would do. Gordon was dumbstruck. It is safe to say his mouth had not remained open for so long since he was a child forced to stand still while his mother brushed his teeth. Of course, the appearance of the ill-fated royal did not have any similar effect on anyone else in the courtroom. She was just another juror to them.

"Eva Reinshaw... Simon, son of Meredith the miller... Cornelius Matthew George Jones..."

The rest of the names passed over Gordon. Even if Winston Churchill or Lawrence of Arabia had followed, he would have been probably still staring at the 'headless' queen. She made herself comfortable on the bench at which she sat, placing her head on the ledge in front of her, as though it were her handbag or some other inconsequential item. Gordon was mesmerised by the eyes on that severed head. They surveyed the courtroom as the eyes of the other jurors were doing at this moment, until they finally rested on Gordon himself. Only then did he avert his gaze from them.

When all the jurors were seated, Dracula approached the old man who was first to be called, handing him a card and a Bible.

"Read these words, please."

The peasant man looked up with a concerned look on his face. "Begging your pardon, squire, but I can't read."

The usher looked to the archangel for instruction. "Read it for him," the impatient clerk interrupted. "Then he can repeat it."

Dracula recited the oath; just two words at a time, clearly not of the belief the man possessed the intelligence to remember more than that.

A man in cricket whites did not experience any similar problems, nor did the countess. Nelson was next. He took the Bible in the only hand he possessed, and Dracula placed the card on top of the book. However, it kept sliding off the cover. An old woman to his left intervened and took hold of the card, lifting it to Nelson's eye. However, it was not his good eye and he was forced to tilt his head in order to read the words from the one that was in working order.

Gordon was already wondering what would happen when it came to the turn of Mary. However, she merely placed the card in front of her detached head, still positioned on the ledge. Gordon watched in wonder as the mouth of that head started to open and close, just like any mouth. Mary spoke softly, little trace of any Scottish accent in her voice.

Gordon did not pay much attention to the remaining jurors and it was the voice of the clerk that interrupted him from the trance Mary had unconsciously put him in.

"Members of the jury," the red-nosed individual started, "it is your job this evening to decide on the fate of the deceased that stands before you."

Gordon bowed his head as the eyes of the jurors, including those on Mary's severed head, immediately focused on him.

"You will come to your conclusion after hearing all the evidence," the clerk continued, "and I ask that you put any preconceived ideas and thoughts to the back of your mind, to concentrate solely on the evidence you hear in this court. Do you understand?" he added, flashing a contemptuous glance towards the press bench.

A few of the jurors nodded their heads. Mary was not one of them.

The clerk was about to continue but was interrupted by the archangel.

"You will..." The archangel paused, having to readjust his wig, it having slipped over his glasses. "You will each find a copy of the Master's book in front of you in case you need to refer to any matters of law."

"Thank you," the clerk resumed. "I was just about to get to that point," he added, another insincere smile appearing on his face.

Instinctively, a number of jurors had picked up their Bible and were flicking through the flimsy pages, including the peasant man that was unable to read.

"You will also find a pen and some paper, should you wish to make notes," the clerk rattled on. "We can provide quills if anyone would prefer," he added, noticing George of Shrewsbury had already put a biro up to his mouth and was licking the nib, clearly having never seen anything like it before.

"You will also need to appoint a foreman of the jury," the clerk ordered, "someone to speak to the court on behalf of you all."

The heads of the jurors converged somewhere towards the middle of the two benches, Mary lifting hers up above her torso, Gordon at first thinking she was about to try to reconnect it to her neck. The countess with the lofty hair eventually raised her frail hand to acknowledge that she had been appointed, some bangles on her thin wrist slipping down her arm and beyond her elbow as she did so.

The archangel turned to Gordon, this time holding on to his wig, tapping the gavel against the bench as he did so.

"I now declare this case open," he said, believing that was what he was meant to say at this particular point. Judging by the reaction of the clerk, who was muttering something to the typist close to him, it clearly wasn't.

"Mr Jones," the clerk suddenly announced, making Gordon jump. "You are he, of New Bridge Avenue, in the county of Buckinghamshire, in the country of England, in the continent of Europe, on the planet of Earth, in the galaxy of the Milky Way, in the universe of our Lord and Master?"

"I think that's me," Gordon twitched.

"And you died at 19:34.55?"

"So they keep telling me," Gordon responded, instinctively glancing towards the clock above the archangel.

"I knew it!" a voice suddenly shrieked. "I *am* right. I knew it!"

One of the jurors was on his feet and pointing at Gordon excitedly. The archangel meekly tapped his gavel in a futile attempt to silence the man donned in the clothes of an agricultural worker.

"I knew it," he repeated, waving a newspaper in the air. "I told the missus that it was you. I could see the family resemblance straight away... It's the ears, you see."

Gordon gingerly touched one of his ears. As we have already ascertained, he was now of the belief that they stuck out far too much. And he was right. They did.

"I'm not totally sure," the man continued, rubbing his weather-beaten face, "but I reckon you must be my great-great-nephew, or something like that."

Gordon was speechless.

"Don't suppose they named you after me, did they?" the man continued. "They must have talked about me – good old Cornelius... What's your Christian name, son?"

Gordon did not get time to answer.

"Silence in court!" It was the clerk, far more forceful than the archangel had been, that brought a halt to the proceedings. "I must remind you that this is a celestial court. This is not the place to renew acquaintances or to meet your ancestors. You will have plenty of time for that."

The man retook his seat. "Sorry, governor, but that might not be correct. What if he's not going to the same place as me?"

The clerk made no attempt to answer the question. "That is quite enough. Will you have this juror removed please, usher. An interest in the defendant must be declared."

The man voluntarily vacated his seat and stumbled towards Dracula. "Sorry, son," he smiled, looking to Gordon. "I should have kept quiet. You'd have got one vote at least," he added, flashing the clerk a mischievous glance.

The usher beckoned Cornelius Jones to follow him. He headed for the door, but before he reached it, the man turned and gave Gordon one final look. "I'll see you later, son," he waved. "I'll meet you for a pint in the *Angel's Inn*... if you make it, of course."

The spectators in the public gallery took the disturbance as a chance to relax and to confer over what had taken place so far. The archangel made no attempt to stop people talking. It was several moments before Dracula re-emerged with a new juror. A knight clad in full body armour appeared from the side door. No part of his skin was visible. It was as though a suit of armour – the sort you might find propped up against a wall in a stately home – was moving of its own accord. If it had been still, one might have questioned whether anyone was actually inside it. The knight was forced to sit on the end of the front bench, due to the fact that the armour made it difficult for him to bend his knees, forcing other jurors, with the help of the usher, to relocate to another seat. Now sitting, with his legs stretched out, extending into the aisle, the knight took the Bible in one hand and the card in the other. He lifted up the visor that covered his eyes, but it slipped back down and the usher eventually had to hold it open in order for him to finish reading.

"Are we ready to proceed now?" the clerk inquired sarcastically. "I presume there are no *more* Joneses among the jury?"

He nodded at Dumas and the demon rose from his seat. Gordon had almost forgotten about *him,* such an entrance the other players in the courtroom had made.

"My dear friends," Dumas began, bowing to the jury, "may I add my grateful thanks for your appearance this evening. I hope I will be able to prove to you that this case is, in fact, a simple one." He stopped and dabbed his thin moustache with a gloved finger. "I must start at the end, rather than the beginning – the end of Mr Jones's earthly existence, at any rate, as we all know that is *really* the beginning."

Gordon eyed the demon suspiciously. It was only when Dumas was looking directly at him that he felt the need to avert his eyes.

"It was while Mr Jones was in his home that Death came to him," the demon continued, now fingering his hat that was on the bench in front of him. "He had been playing charades, a modern, childish game. Death informed Mr Jones that his life had been terminated. As always at this point, I, having been the demon assigned to care for Mr Jones throughout his earthly existence, arrived to claim my master's property. You can imagine my surprise when I found my learned friend Angel Gilmore was already in the room."

Mr Gilmore muttered something under his breath, but did not interrupt.

"Not surprisingly," the demon continued, "I took issue with Angel Gilmore; he having mistakenly assumed Mr Jones was a Christian, of course."

"There's no mistake," Mr Gilmore sounded, unable to resist the temptation on this occasion. "Angels don't make…"

"Then let us see if that is so," Dumas interrupted, flashing the angel a look of contempt. "Members of the jury," the demon recommenced, his piercing eyes settling upon them, each juror under the impression he was looking directly at them, "your job is a simple one: to decide whether Mr Jones is a Christian or not. To do that, we must of course clarify what a Christian is. What is the definition of a Christian? Do you know, Mr Jones?"

Gordon was surprised a question had been aimed at him. He looked to Mr Gilmore to check if it was safe to answer. The angel shrugged his shoulders and Gordon took this to be an affirmative response.

"Well," Gordon coughed, "it's someone that believes in Jesus."

Dumas raised his eyebrows.

"Is that it? *I* also believe in your master, Mr Jones. I'm not a Christian."

"I know that," Gordon snapped. "I hadn't finished."

"My apologies, Mr Jones. Go on."

"A Christian is also someone that follows Jesus."

Dumas smiled and stared at Gordon.

"And is that what you are, Mr Jones? A follower?"

"Yes," Gordon confirmed.

"No," Dumas replied firmly. "No."

The demon freed Gordon from his stare and moved towards the filing cabinet. "No, no, no," he continued to mutter under his breath, as he opened the middle drawer, one gloved finger slowly pulling it towards him.

"And I will prove it, Mr Jones," he stated calmly, removing a red book from the open drawer.

The demon strutted towards the jury and opened the book, blowing away some imaginary dust, before raising his head, a devilish smile now on his face.

"Are you sitting comfortably?" he teased. "Then I shall begin…"

Gordon looked towards Mr Gilmore, hoping he might catch his eye. He needed one of his reassuring smiles.

11

"The past is a foreign country: they do things differently there."

The Go-Between
L.P. Hartley

"IT WAS A DARK AND STORMY NIGHT," THE THEATRICAL Dumas pronounced, pretending to be reciting the words from the red book that lay open, resting in one of his gloved hands. He looked up thoughtfully. "It was one of those nights when it is easy to imagine terrible goings-on in shadowy graveyards and dark, cobwebbed-infested cellars. One of those nights..."

"Demon Dumas!" the archangel interrupted, his wig slipping over one of the lenses of his spectacles, this time having forgotten to keep hold of it. "You may be partial to a Gothic novel, but can you just stick to the facts and leave the descriptive prose to Mary Shelley, if you don't mind."

Dumas grinned, as if he had been expecting the interruption. "I beg your pardon, but one likes to set the scene – to draw a picture," he replied politely. "May I continue?"

The archangel sighed. Dumas took that to be his cue to do so.

"Thank you. Now, where was I?"

"It was one of those nights," the clerk of the court interrupted impatiently. Dumas acknowledged the clerk with a bow, the familiar smug smile on his face.

"Yes, as I have been reminded," he continued to mock, "it was one of those nights when things went *bump;* a fouler night there had not been that year. And it was on that night that the subject before us made his entrance."

Gordon looked towards Mr Gilmore. The angel was sitting in his seat, one elbow resting against the bench. His head was slightly tilted, it being supported by the clenched fist of that one bent arm, the knuckles of his hand pressing against his cheek, so that the displaced flesh was pushed

134

almost in front of one eye. It was the position a schoolboy might occupy during double maths. For one moment Gordon thought the angel was asleep.

"It was at a hospital of no particular importance that our story begins," Dumas went on. "It was November... a Friday... the 13th, if I'm not mistaken."

The somewhat nettled archangel momentarily closed his eyes, but did not attempt to interrupt on this occasion. He knew that was exactly what the demon wanted him to do. Dumas looked almost disappointed and, aware he could not wait any longer for anyone to pass comment, reverted his eyes to the page that lay open before him. Gordon felt almost disheartened by the fact that his entire life only filled what looked to be a rather thin volume, the book no bigger or thicker than a child's Christmas annual.

"To us a child was born," Dumas announced suddenly, still holding the book well in front of his face, his other arm now neatly tucked behind his back. "I must inform you that Mr Jones weighed in at a healthy eight pounds and three ounces. He was delivered by the means of forceps, it being a somewhat problematic birth."

"Spare us the gory details, please." It was Mr Gilmore who had this time risen to the bait. "Is this all really necessary?" he added with appealing eyes, aiming them in the direction of the archangel. The higher celestial being merely shrugged his shoulders as though he were powerless to interfere.

Dumas grinned. "I would like to call my first witness," he proclaimed. "The very person who first set eyes upon Mr Jones."

Gordon assumed a puzzled look. Bizarre and perhaps insensitive as it may seem, he had not actually thought much about his late mother since his own demise. However, the idea that they might be at last reunited was soon quashed when Dumas uttered another name from his lips, a name Gordon did not take in, it being an unfamiliar one to him. As if Dumas was well aware of the fact, he repeated it. "Moira Moffett," he said. "I would like to call Mrs Moira Moffett."

Mr Gilmore turned to Gordon in the hope he might be able to shed some light on the said individual, but Gordon merely shook his head, prompting the angel to begin to rummage through the many papers in his briefcase.

The usher – few had even noticed him leave the room – reappeared with a portly individual. She wore a transparent plastic rain hat and a grey overcoat that was too big for even one of her size. She was shaking a pink umbrella, even though it did not appear to be wet. The woman was ushered to the witness box. As Dracula handed her a Bible and a card that rested on top of it, she in return gave him her umbrella, before removing her hat and coat. The usher, for fear she would pass him these items too, under the impression he was a butler, took flight, the umbrella held by the tips of two of his fingers, as though it were something offensive to the touch.

"Please read from the card, Mrs Moffett," the clerk ordered.

She obliged.

Dumas turned to face the witness. He was charm personified. "My dear Mrs Moffett, may I thank you for your attendance this evening. Please give the court your full name."

"Mrs Moira Evangeline Myrtle Josephine Moffett, née Harper-Drew."

"And could you tell me your relationship with the man standing over there, please."

He nodded in the direction of Gordon but did not feel the need to look at him.

Gordon stared at the woman, still oblivious to her identity. She returned a smile.

"I'm the midwife that delivered him," she announced proudly.

"What?" Gordon muttered under his breath.

Mr Gilmore rose from his chair. "Is this really necessary?" he asked the archangel, his arms stretched wide. "With due respect, she's hardly played a major part in my client's life."

"On the contrary, sir," the midwife responded testily. "I would say that giving him life was *quite* a major role."

Mr Gilmore smiled. "Forgive me, madam. I didn't mean that your role was unimportant, but perhaps the Master should take most of the credit for giving him life – not to mention his mother and father." A few giggles reverberated around the public gallery. "I meant no offence," Mr Gilmore continued. "I just meant that I don't see what influence you could have possibly had on my client's *character*."

The midwife looked at Dumas as if she too was bemused by her appearance in court.

"Mrs Moffett," the demon continued unperturbed. "Think back to your own lifetime, if you please. Now, first of all, do you remember Mr Jones?"

"I do. Of course, he wasn't called that then."

"How can you remember me?" Gordon protested. "You must have delivered hundreds of babies."

"Thousands," she corrected him, "but I recognise you from your ears. They stuck out even then. In fact, we joked afterwards that we should have been done with the forceps and just yanked you out by those..."

"It looks like you did!" a wag from the public gallery interrupted, his spontaneous outburst prompting raucous laughter from those seated close to him.

"Silence," the archangel ordered, though his command was expressed so meekly, the giggling did not abruptly cease, only coming to a halt naturally, as it would have done if no one had attempted to intervene.

Dumas was smiling too, though one probably did not need to highlight that point. The demon – it seemed to Gordon – was always smiling. He did not expect to see anything other than that smug grin on his face whenever he dared look at him.

"Mrs Moffett," Dumas continued, "what are your recollections of Mr Jones – your first memories of him?"

"Well, apart from his ears, he did cry a lot."

A baffled Gordon slumped to his chair, shaking his head in bewilderment. However, he rose to his feet almost immediately, fearing the clerk would rebuke him.

"He wasn't a very happy baby," the midwife explained. "He did make an awful fuss... kicking and screaming."

"Kicking?" Dumas responded. "Screaming? Thank you, Mrs Moffett. I have no further questions."

"What? Is that it?" Gordon chirped, a look of incredulity on his face. "You have got to be joking! You called a witness to tell the court that I was crying when I was born?"

"Not just crying, Mr Jones," Dumas clarified. "I think Mrs Moffett used the words 'kicking' and 'screaming'."

"This is ridiculous," Gordon wailed. The idea that the court would be examining every second of his life filled him with, not so much dread, but bemusement.

Dracula was by the side of Mrs Moffett in an instant; relieved he could discharge himself of the pink umbrella. The witness was escorted from the courtroom with the minimum of fuss.

Dumas turned his eye back to the red book, slowly and deliberately turning a page.

"This is going to take forever," Mr Gilmore protested, again appealing to the archangel, aware that his disgruntled client would also appreciate him speaking up on this matter.

"Mr Jones and Angel Gilmore do have a point, Demon Dumas," the archangel suggested. "I'm not sure that was necessary. I understand you are trying to build a picture of Mr Jones's character, but surely we can skip the first few years of life?"

"Very well," Dumas conceded. "I am happy to oblige. Let us move on a few years, if that is what you desire." He purposefully flicked through a few pages and stopped abruptly, his eye resting upon something of apparent interest. "What about the terrible twos? You were prone to tantrums, weren't you, Mr Jones?"

"What?" Gordon gasped. "I don't believe this! Every toddler has tantrums."

"Yes," the archangel intervened. "I was suggesting you moved forward more than two years!"

Dumas smiled. "I have. I was referring to when Mr Jones was... twenty-two!"

There was more laughter from the public gallery, Dumas timing the joke to perfection. Even Dracula had a smile on his face, his yellow teeth seeing the light of day once more.

"Forgive the little jest, Mr Jones," Dumas teased. "Besides, we have not come to that stage of your life just yet. You wish me to make haste, but it would be something of an injustice to miss out on your childhood, wouldn't it?"

Gordon never responded, shaking his head despairingly, as Dumas turned back a few pages.

"Take a look at this, Mr Jones."

The demon had reached for a scroll that had seemingly just appeared in his previously empty scabbard. He lifted it out as though it were a sword, then allowed it to unfurl across the courtroom floor. He deliberately stepped back to make it clear to everyone it was of a great length. "Sadly, there is not room for all of it," he added, just in case anyone was still not convinced of that fact.

"What is it?" Gordon inquired suspiciously.

"The amount of paper you used at school."

"Is that all? That's good isn't it?" Gordon suggested hopefully. "Shows I was hardworking."

"These were the lines you were ordered to write. There are 44,355 to be precise, Mr Jones. That is how many you wrote during your entire education. You could have penned a novel with that amount."

Dumas did not attempt to replace the scroll in his scabbard. He merely let go, allowing it to fall from his hand. As it did, it vanished. His glove now held a pocket watch, the type that a father might have passed on to his son in days gone by. "And you spent sixty-three hours and seven minutes in detention after the school doors were closed of a night," the demon added, holding the timepiece to his ear, almost as if he were checking to ascertain whether it was still ticking.

Gordon shook his head again, before boldly turning in the direction of Dumas. "This is farcical. I was a *child*. I wasn't the only one to mess about at school."

Dumas reverted his gaze to the red book.

"It wasn't just in school, Mr Jones. Your extracurricular activities were also interesting, to say the least. Let's have a look at some of your hobbies, shall we?"

Dumas put his gloved finger on the open page and moved it down what was presumably a list. He made an appropriate noise or gesture when he came to something that he believed to be incriminating.

"What's it say?" Gordon asked anxiously. "I just remember spending most of my time at the park – and I liked drawing when I was young. I used to draw a lot. That's not a sin, is it?"

"You're right, you did like art, Mr Jones – and the park." Dumas hesitated and grinned, as though he had spotted something of particular interest. "In fact, you combined both activities, didn't you? You certainly enjoyed decorating the play equipment with indelible markers. I would hardly call it art, though, just a few squiggles. I've got some pictures of your work in here, Mr Jones. Would you like to see them? I'm sure the jury would."

Gordon bowed his head.

"You liked sport as well," Dumas went on. "Games that involved throwing things and running were particularly appealing."

"Yes, I wasn't too bad at cricket."

"Cricket? Oh no, I'm talking about throwing stones at greenhouses and then legging it as fast as you can."

Again Gordon bowed his head.

Dumas was in the process of trying to remove something from a pocket in his tunic, the sash that ran diagonally across his chest inconveniently lying across the opening. The fact he did not make the object appear in an instant, as he seemed to have the power to do, suggested he wanted Gordon to witness him in the act of retrieving it. He had to wait for Gordon to lift his head and, until he did so, his fingers fumbled in search of the opening of the pocket, the demon pretending his gloves had suddenly become a hindrance to him. There was little doubt he was teasing Gordon, and only when he was sure the latter was now watching intently, fearful of what Dumas might produce, did the demon conclude his charade, finally satisfied the curiosity of all in the courtroom had been aroused.

The object was small and round, and when it came into view, few were able to immediately discern what it was. Dumas threw it towards Gordon who instinctively lifted his hand to catch it. He failed to do so.

"And you said you were *good* at cricket?" Dumas quipped.

The tiny object rolled across the wooden courtroom floor and came to rest close to Dracula.

"It's a strawberry bonbon!" Gordon smiled. "I haven't had one of those for ages. They were my favourites."

Dumas was blowing the tips of his gloves in a bid to rid them of some grains of sugar that the sweet had relinquished during his little act.

"Can you remember where you used to get them from?" the demon inquired.

"I can," Gordon replied. "The shop was on the corner of my road. It's not there anymore. I loved penny sweets. I bet they don't cost a penny now, though."

"I'm surprised you remember how much they cost, Mr Jones. You see, you didn't wait to save up your pennies, did you? It was far more convenient to fill your pockets whenever you wished – and easy too. Poor old Mr Manning did not have the best of eyesight... and he was very slow on his feet."

"All right," Gordon responded, holding his hand up. "You don't need to tell me all this. I know it's wrong to steal, but that's all I ever pinched. Everyone used to do it. It was just a bit of harmless fun."

Dumas turned another page in the book and Gordon noticed him doing so.

"You don't have to bother," he said. "I know you'll find a few more things in there that I'm not particularly proud of, but I was young and I didn't do anything that bad. It's not the same as mugging old ladies, is it? I wasn't the worse child in town."

"That's quite right," Mr Gilmore interrupted, rising from his chair. "Boys will be boys. I know it's not my time to speak, but I don't suppose Demon Dumas is going to inform the jury that Mr Jones also went to church from an early age."

"Did he really?" Dumas asked, pretending he had no idea of the fact. "That is interesting."

"Yes," the angel continued. "Not many children of his age would have been seen dead in a church, yet Mr Jones went almost every week."

Dumas turned a couple of pages in the red book, pretending to be searching for the relevant part in Gordon's life. "You are right, Angel Gilmore. He did attend Sunday school, didn't he? His parents had to drag him there kicking and screaming, of course." The demon paused. "*Still* kicking and screaming, Mr Jones?" he added looking up, a smirk clearly visible on his face.

"But the important thing is that he didn't stop going to church," the angel continued. "He continued to do so throughout his life."

"Yes, I know," Dumas sneered. "We shall examine his habits a little bit later."

"Can I say something?" Gordon offered. The archangel looked to the demon for permission to give permission. Dumas offered no complaint, inviting Gordon to proceed, his invitation being in the form of a bow.

"I know I've done things I'm not proud of," Gordon explained. "And I've no doubt you'll find things in that book that will paint an even blacker picture of me. I know I was no angel, like you lot," he added, looking to the archangel, "but it's irrelevant, isn't it? That's all in the past. It doesn't matter now."

"It doesn't?" Dumas inquired.

"No. All that was before I became a Christian."

Dumas smiled. He had been waiting for Gordon to say words to that effect.

"Hallelujah!" he pronounced. The archangel was not impressed by his use of language, but remained silent.

"You're right, Mr Jones," Dumas nodded, dramatically ripping some pages from the red book and allowing them to slip to the floor. "We don't need these. All that was before you became a Christian, wasn't it? The slate was wiped clean when you confessed all those misdemeanours before your master, all those little sins; that's what you believe, isn't it?"

"And that is true," Mr Gilmore interrupted, this time remaining seated, as at that moment he was in the process of blowing his nose.

"That's right," Gordon reiterated. "It's wrong to judge me on my past. When I became a Christian, my past became an irrelevance. That's what Jesus died on the cross for... my sins. He paid my debt."

Gordon looked to Mr Gilmore and this time received the reassuring smile he had earlier been searching for. It gave him even more confidence to continue.

"When I gave my life to God, I became a new person. I was reborn. That's what it says in the Bible, doesn't it? We have to be reborn."

Dumas clapped his hands, slowly and deliberately. His condescending act had the desired effect and stopped Gordon in his tracks.

"Bravo!" Dumas mocked. "Bravo, Mr Jones! What words of wisdom. I am almost prompted to drop my case." He stopped, tapping the red book with his gloved fingers, now a meditative expression on his face, one he was clearly faking. "The only problem is, Mr Jones, I can't find any evidence in here of your *second* birth."

"Pardon?"

"You said you were reborn."

"That's right, when I became a Christian."

"Of course, we know all about your natural birth, thanks to Mrs Moffett, but I can't find much in here about your second one."

"I've told you, it's when I became a Christian – the 12th of February." Gordon hesitated. "Oh, what year was it?"

Dumas shook his head. "You're like a king or queen now, Mr Jones," he bowed, as if to emphasise his point. "You've not got one, but *two* birthdays. Of course, you never forget your first birthday, but the other one passes by every year without a mere thought, doesn't it?"

Gordon shrugged his shoulders.

"Being born again," Dumas mused. "It's a curious expression, isn't it? Non-Christians laugh at the idea and you can't blame them. Maybe it's because of their reaction that Christians don't like to use the phrase much either and, need I say, rarely pay any attention to it."

The demon stopped and deliberately shook his head. He was no longer smiling. He had an ominous expression on his face. His tone was no longer frivolous and that gave Gordon new cause for concern. Gordon preferred it when the demon was at his most mocking. He almost wished that smug smile would return to his face, anything but the threatening demeanour he had now assumed.

"Don't you understand, Mr Jones?" Dumas expounded, staring accusingly at the defendant. "To a Christian, the second birth should be more important than the first one. That's the one you should have been celebrating every year. You don't have much to do with your natural birth; the likes of Mrs Moffett had more of a hand in that than you. But your second birth – that was *your* choice. You chose to be born again. You decided that the old self must die – to make way for something new."

"It did," Gordon protested, unconvincingly.

"Did it? Do you remember the commitment you made as a spotty teenager, the night you became a Christian? Or should I ask whether you understood what that commitment involved?"

"Of course I did," Gordon snapped, his response clearly that of one riled and, it has to be said, of one not themself convinced by their own defence. "And I'm still committed," he pleaded with added fervour, almost in an attempt to assure himself. "I went to church before I became a Christian and I carried on going. And I still go to this day. In fact, I went this morning."

"So nothing has changed?" Dumas inquired.

"No. Nothing," Gordon insisted. "Although I don't think I'll be going to church this Sunday."

"Nothing has changed," Dumas repeated. Just in case the jury had not caught them the first time, he repeated the words again, only a lot louder and slower on this occasion: "Nothing has changed."

Mr Gilmore rose to his feet. He knew more than anyone where this was leading.

"Mr Jones himself has changed, of course," the angel attempted to clarify. "And the court will see *that* change when you get a bit further into *that* book. As with any birth, the new arrival has to grow. It takes time for their character to form."

Dumas moved towards Mr Gilmore. His immaculate boots made no sound on the wooden floor. He again shook his head. His face remained grave. Gordon didn't like it. He would rather see that smug smile – anything but this.

When he was opposite the angel, Dumas – the red book having been placed under an armpit – put the palms of his hands on the bench that was between them, leaning forward, so that he was at the same height as his foe, their heads now a mere foot apart. Mr Gilmore, defiantly, did not attempt to avert his gaze from those looming eyes.

"Change?" Dumas bellowed. "You think your client *changed?*"

He paused for effect and then stood upright, turning abruptly to face the jury. He slammed the red book shut, it now being back in his hands. Nelson was among those to flinch.

"Do you still not understand, you foolish people?" the demon sounded. "Have you all missed the point?"

He headed towards Gordon and, when he reached him, placed his gloved hand on the ledge of the dock. He did not look at him, his head still turned in the direction of the jury, though Gordon still felt the need to bow his head.

"You think I was the fool for wanting to bring up the past," Dumas continued, "to examine those years before Mr Jones became a Christian, but I wanted to do so for one purpose – and one purpose alone." Dumas paused again. "To prove to you just how little Mr Jones changed."

The courtroom fell silent. The curtain had fallen to bring an end to Act One. Dumas sauntered back to his seat. *That* smug smile had returned to his face.

12

*"Ay, in the very temple of Delight
Veil'd Melancholy has her sovran shrine."*

Ode on Melancholy
John Keats

A YOUNG MAN WEARING A BLUE BOILER SUIT HAD EMERGED from the side door of the courtroom. He was carrying a cardboard box. However, at first glance one might have been forgiven for thinking he was hugging it. That the box was of a substantial weight was not in doubt, but it was its bulk that prevented the man from keeping pace with the usher. The man was only just able to wrap his arms around the box so that the fingertips of both hands met on its exposed side. The bottom of the box banged against his thighs with each step and he had to stretch his neck in order to rest his chin on top of it, that being imperative in order to be able to see where he was going. Dracula, striding towards the bench at which Dumas and Mr Gilmore were seated, his trailing cape, as ever, a few inches off the ground due to the current of air his haste had momentarily created, was one of those individuals that are seemingly incapable of doing anything slowly. He seemed almost irritated by the fact that the man had difficulty in keeping up with him.

Another man, older, decked out in biblical robes, his feet clad in sandals, staff in hand, followed the man in the boiler suit. Dracula stood back when they reached Dumas, nodding his head to inform the man in the boiler suit to place the box on the bench in front of the demon. Of course, the man did not get there immediately, and for a split second the usher did not think he would get there at all, at one point instinctively stretching out a hand for fear the box was slipping from the grasp of the carrier. One has to stress it was merely a hand, no more than a token gesture, for that hand would have done very little to have prevented the box from falling to the floor if it had indeed been on its way there.

The man in the boiler suit, having fulfilled his task, stood back and puffed out his cheeks one final time, on this occasion as a sign of his relief. It was the old man at the rear who took up a position next to the box, leaning forward on his staff. He was, in fact, the most striking of the new arrivals, a white moustache and beard failing to hide a labyrinth of lines on his face. His hair, also strikingly white, reached down to his shoulders. It was almost dazzling. Of course, all eyes were not on him – but on the box. It was a box no different from any box that might contain a newly purchased electrical item or household appliance, but no one in that courtroom believed it contained anything as uninteresting as that.

A seemingly contagious cough had struck those in the public gallery. People were using the natural break in the proceedings to clear their throats and blow their noses. Mr Gilmore was doing the same. Gordon, if he had not been so preoccupied by the box, or should we say its contents, whatever they might be, might have questioned whether you could still catch a cold in heaven.

Some members of the jury were conversing, though only to the person next to them. They spoke without turning their heads, for fear they might miss the moment when the box was opened. Mary, Queen of Scots had lifted her severed head from the ledge, it now resting within her folded arms, presumably because the new position offered a better vantage point. Nelson had removed a mini-telescope from a pocket in his trousers and had put it to his good eye. Needless to say, he was searching for any sign on the box that might reveal what lay inside it. However, the only words on the box would have probably confused him even more: "*Made in Taiwan / fragile / handle with care.*" Indeed, it should be stressed again, it was just an ordinary box, at least ordinary to someone from an era in which cardboard boxes *were* ordinary.

The old man with the white hair remained standing, a few feet from the box. He did not seem embarrassed to be doing so. He adopted the stance of one who was used to standing beside that box. Dumas was also now standing, both hands placed on top of the side that was exposed to the ceiling, his fingers lightly tapping it, a thoughtful expression on his face. The demon did not acknowledge the old man beside him. Like everyone else in the courtroom, he only had eyes for the box, though unlike most in the courtroom, he knew exactly what was inside it.

At last Dumas broke the silence.

"Contrary to what you might all be thinking," he began, "that February evening when Mr Jones became a Christian – and I use the term loosely – was not a bad one for me."

Most were surprised by his introduction, assuming he would start by revealing the contents of the box. Of course, that was what the demon assumed everyone would be expecting him to do.

Dumas brushed past the old man and moved to the centre of the courtroom, taking up his favourite position on the main 'stage' just in front of the clerk of the court. He had left the red book on the bench and was now holding his hat.

"People think my master is beyond reproach when someone gives their life to your master," he continued. "It isn't so. There might be a party in heaven, but my master is not so stupid as to think the battle is over. On the contrary, it has only just begun. Many a man has dipped his finger in the honey."

"A little more than a finger," Mr Gilmore whispered under his breath. Dumas heard him.

"A hand or an arm, it makes no difference, Angel Gilmore," he responded. "You know only too well that it often doesn't stay there. Hundreds, thousands, millions," Dumas continued, raising his voice the bigger the number got, "dare I say *billions,* over the years, have dipped their finger in the honey, only to eventually decide they don't like the taste, after all."

Mr Gilmore folded his arms.

"So," Dumas resumed, "as I said, it did not unduly worry me when Mr Jones supposedly gave his life to your master as a teenager all those years ago."

"Objection!" Mr Gilmore interrupted. "The demon has no right to use the word 'supposedly'. The members of the jury should be under no doubt that Mr Jones *did* give his life to the Master that night. *That* fact is not in dispute."

Dumas smiled. "My apologies, Angel Gilmore. You are, as always, quite correct. I do not contest the fact that he did utter words to that effect, to become a follower of your master, so, technically, I must concede that you are right. Let us indeed say that Mr Jones became a Christian, whatever that might mean in his case."

The angel was about to protest again but received a subtle shake of the head from the archangel as a reminder it was not his time to speak.

Dumas tapped his hat against his chin. "Let us look at the night of the 12th of February... what year was it now?" he mocked, pretending he was as forgetful as Gordon. "Anyway, it was an *unforgettable* night, one full of emotion. Mr Jones was at a Christian youth event. It went something like this: a trendy Christian band – four good-looking individuals, I might add – whipped everyone up into a frenzy and then told them all about Jesus."

Dumas clearly did not like to say the name, but felt it was necessary to do so on this occasion. He almost spat the word out. "You were on quite a high, Mr Jones, weren't you?" He paused and turned to the jury. "It was a *legal* high, I should clarify, before my learned friend Angel Gilmore has palpitations."

The angel did not look amused.

"Yes," Dumas went on, "Mr Jones was merely high on life. The music was great. He had his friends around him and he felt good about things – the perfect night to become a Christian. Yes, Mr Jones?" Dumas paused and blew the plume on his hat. "And he *did* become a Christian – supposedly," the demon added.

Mr Gilmore frowned but did not rise to the bait this time.

"And that is about it," Dumas continued. "Mr Jones confessed his sins and the trumpets in heaven sounded. Is that right, Mr Jones? Is that what happened that night?"

Gordon shifted uneasily. "I suppose so, but there was a bit more to it than that."

"Tell us about it," Dumas invited, strutting towards the bench and retaking his seat. "I'm sure the jury would prefer it to come from your own lips."

Gordon cleared his throat and started to address the court. He deliberately focused on the least outrageously attired juror he could find – a postman. He did his utmost to prevent his eye wandering towards the severed head of Mary.

"It was an amazing night," Gordon stuttered. "For several weeks I had had this feeling deep inside that I needed to make a proper commitment. Yes, I'd been going to church, but I admit I'd been going to church because I'd always been going to church. The bandleader challenged us to make that commitment. I did, there and then. I knew I needed a personal relationship with Jesus. I didn't really have that before. Bill and Clare were with me. I asked Jesus into my life and then they prayed for me, and... I suppose that's when I became a Christian, if you like."

He turned his head towards the archangel, as though he wanted clarification that he had spoken well, even though he was himself pleasantly surprised by the manner in which he had delivered his testimony. The archangel returned a heartening smile.

"You haven't mentioned that warm, fuzzy feeling inside?" Dumas inquired, slowly rising from his chair. "Did you not get it, Mr Jones?"

"Pardon?"

"When you *became* a Christian? Lots of Christians speak of it, don't they?"

"Objection!" It was Mr Gilmore again. "The warm, fuzzy feeling inside is irrelevant. Some get it and some don't," the angel attempted to explain.

"But did *you* get it, Mr Jones?" Dumas persevered. "Did you feel any different when you prayed that prayer? Did you feel like it made a difference?"

Gordon hesitated. "I think so... I don't know... I can't remember."

"You can't remember?"

"Objection!" Mr Gilmore stood up this time and looked appealingly towards the archangel. "The important thing is that my client *made* a commitment. Demon Dumas is well aware that the conversion moment is very different for every person. Some people are more emotional than others. Just because you don't experience that warm, fuzzy feeling inside does not mean your commitment is not genuine."

The archangel nodded at Mr Gilmore. "Thank you. You have made your point – and made it well."

Dumas was unperturbed by the interruption.

"I only wanted to ascertain if Mr Jones had ever himself felt that warm, fuzzy feeling inside," the demon continued. "You see, as you say, some Christians never experience it. The conversion moment can be a bit of an anticlimax. They say the prayer and then... well, not a lot happens. There is no shooting star, or bolt of lightning, or – at the very least – that warm, fuzzy feeling inside."

Mr Gilmore was out of his seat again. "You miss the point, Demon Dumas. I don't want to devalue the importance or significance of the conversion moment, but that's not what it's all about. One has to look at the greater picture. It's about what happens afterwards that matters – how that conversion affects the individual."

Dumas nodded in agreement.

"Yes, you're right, Angel Gilmore," he said. "How is the individual affected by it? Does the individual *change* because of it? It's that word again – *change*."

Dumas made his way ominously towards the dock. "I have a question for you, Mr Jones," he stated, his face having adopted a pondering expression. "Are you the sort of person that breaks promises?"

"I don't think so."

"Are you sure?"

"I'm not great at keeping New Year resolutions, but who is?" Gordon offered. "Anyway, what does it matter if I only manage to make it until January the 5th before eating chocolate again? You're not going to tell me that eating chocolate's a sin, are you?"

Dumas smiled. "Mr Jones," he continued, turning his back on Gordon, "on that night you became a Christian, can you remember making any promises?"

"Of course I can," Gordon sighed. "I see what you're getting at now. Yes, I asked God to forgive my sins and *promised* to follow him – to live my life his way. That's the promise you're talking about, isn't it?"

"And let me assure the court," Dumas announced, turning to face the jurors, "I can categorically confirm that Mr Jones *did* keep that promise."

It was not the response Gordon was expecting. He looked at Dumas suspiciously.

"Yes," Dumas went on, placing his hat upon the bench and picking up the red book. "There was a change – initially. Mr Jones *did* live the way his master wanted him to." He turned a page and examined its contents. "Indeed, I must congratulate you, Mr Jones, on what was a very good first week after your rebirth. Your master would have been proud of you."

The demon turned another page. Gordon was waiting for the 'but', but – if you excuse the pun – it never came… not yet anyway.

"As I said," Dumas reiterated, "I was not concerned when Mr Jones made his commitment or even during those early days afterwards. I tend to sit back and let my charges enjoy the moment. I have no need to intervene at this point. I know my day will come. As easy as it is for a man to dip his finger in the honey, it is just as easy for him to take it out again."

Dumas made his way towards the jury. He stopped when he reached the front bench and ran a gloved finger along the ledge, as though he were looking for dust.

"Who dare tell sweethearts caught up in a whirlwind of romance that the washing-up still has to be done when the sun rises?" the demon dreamily put forward. "Let them have their moment. And let the new Christian have theirs. Drunk on emotion, most make their promises to their new master without any thought. They will follow him forever – there's no going back to their old ways now, they insist. That night is the first night of the rest of their lives."

"Give us a break!" Mr Gilmore muttered under his breath.

Dumas ignored the angel. "Of course, the new Christian, like new lovers, eventually has to sober up. For some, the hangover is instant, though, more often than not, as in the case of Mr Jones, it takes a few weeks to kick in. But it does in the end. The romance eventually fades amidst the necessary habits and chores of everyday life. Yes, even Christians still have to go to work; yes, even Christians still have to clean the toilet; yes, even Christians still have to iron their socks."

Dumas was now grinning profusely. "I have reclaimed many a soul by the dawn of the next day, but I can wait if it takes a little longer. I know it won't be long before the honeymoon is over."

"But I didn't give up," Gordon protested. "I kept going to church."

"I know, Mr Jones," Dumas responded, turning sharply to face Gordon. "In a way, that made it even easier for me. I didn't have to do anything in your case. You just slipped back into your old ways, your old habits. You didn't even notice that you had stepped back on to my escalator."

"Your what?" Gordon challenged.

"Think not of an escalator in a department store that so obviously goes up and down, but think of those flat ones at an airport that take you from check-in to the departure lounge. Of course, mine is much slower and sometimes you are not even aware it's moving. Yes, Mr Jones, you were not even aware you were on it. You drifted away from your master without even noticing you were doing so."

"That's rubbish," Gordon insisted. "That's not true. I never stopped worshipping... or praying... *or* reading my Bible."

"But you did all that *before* you became a Christian, didn't you? You were going through the motions before you made that promise to follow your master. You've admitted that, haven't you? And, a few weeks after you became a Christian – it might have been months or years, it doesn't matter to me – you slipped back into your old ways. Your prayers and worship were no more than habits, things Christians were supposed to do. You might have been washing-up or mopping the bathroom floor. You were going through the motions *again.*"

Gordon bowed his head. If he was under the impression that was the end of the demon's rant, he was wrong. He had merely paused.

"As I said, I didn't need to do much to win you back," Dumas insisted. "Sometimes I have to intervene in more dramatic ways, bring a certain calamity to the life of my subject, something that will shake their faith. I was happy to let you carry on as you were. To be honest, there were a couple of times when I thought I might have to step in. You did occasionally have an obscure feeling that you were going through the motions again. That might have been problematic for me, but you soon dispelled the notion, instead of bucking up your ideas and stepping off my escalator. As I said, you made no attempt to get off it, Mr Jones... because you didn't even know you were *on* it."

Gordon shook his head.

Dumas studied him closely. "I put it to you, Mr Jones, that your conversion – on that February night – meant very little to you in the end."

Gordon was about to protest, but Dumas lifted his hand to prevent him from doing so.

"As you told us," the demon went on, "you couldn't even remember whether you experienced a warm, fuzzy feeling inside."

"Not that again," Gordon groaned.

Dumas smiled. "Sadly for you, Mr Jones, you didn't even have a supernatural experience to cling to. The earth didn't shake for you on that night. You didn't feel any different afterwards and that can be a major problem as the months go on. You soon doubted whether anything of much importance ever happened on that night, after all."

Mr Gilmore was about to rise from his seat, but never got the chance. In one swift movement, Dumas had reached for a cylindrical scroll from his previously empty scabbard, like a gunfighter pulling out the gun in his holster.

"Did you read the small print when you signed the contract, Mr Jones?" the demon inquired, fingering the scroll that was neatly held in place by a red ribbon.

"Contract?" Gordon queried.

"When you signed on the dotted line – when you supposedly became a Christian."

The demon untied the ribbon and unfurled the scroll, one hand holding the top of the page and the other the bottom in order to cast his eye upon its contents.

"Don't tell me you never read the small print, Mr Jones?" he added with mock surprise, letting the scroll snap back into a roll and replacing it in his scabbard. "Did you really understand the commitment you made on that February evening?"

"Yes," Gordon replied, steadying himself. "I've told you already: to follow Jesus – and I did do that. I tried."

It was Dumas's turn to shake his head.

"The problem is," the demon continued, "is that Christians are too quick to commit to the cause in order to claim the free gift – eternal salvation. They like that part of the bargain, but it is a bargain, and they should be aware of that. It isn't *really* free. You have to give something in return."

Gordon looked puzzled. "Do I?"

"Yes – your life."

Gordon flashed an uneasy glance in the direction of Mr Gilmore. The angel was nodding in agreement with the demon.

"Were you not aware of that fact, Mr Jones?" the demon asked. "I can't believe that. In fact, you yourself even told the court that you gave your life to your master – when you were reborn. And that is what you have to do. You must lose your life in order to gain an everlasting one, not necessarily lose your life in a physical sense, but when you become a Christian you agree to give your life to your master – live it the way he wants you to. And that's easy at first, when you are still on your honeymoon, on top of the mountain, but your master even took his disciples down from there. It is in the valley of monotony – the everyday – where he wants you to live for him. And that is what you promised to do – on that February night – to live for him, Mr Jones. Do you not remember?"

Gordon nodded unconvincingly.

"And that is why we are here tonight," Dumas stated. "We are here because you have not kept your side of the bargain. You have broken the contract, Mr Jones," Dumas insisted, tapping the scroll in his scabbard.

"That's not true. I've done my best. I tried to do what God wanted me to do."

Dumas shook his head again.

"No, Mr Jones. Let me put it like this." The demon turned his back on Gordon and gazed upwards, in the direction of the public gallery. "In promising to follow your new master, you accepted that you now had to go *his* way. You had a new vision... new instructions to follow. Do you agree?

"Yes."

"And that meant doing what he wanted you to do, yes?"

"Yes."

"He's the boss now and you take orders from him, yes?"

"Yes."

Dumas swivelled around abruptly and stared menacingly at Gordon.

"And yet you have broken almost every rule in his book?"

"Have I? What rules?"

The demon received the response he wanted and expected, but faked a look of astonishment.

"What rules?" Dumas repeated. "*These* rules!"

The demon pointed to the cardboard box. It was the signal for the man in the blue boiler suit to open it. He moved forward, removing a pair of scissors from his overalls as he did so. When he reached the box, he pierced the tape that secured the lid, running the point of the scissors along the middle of it, just like Gordon used to do with his fingernail on the foil that covered the two sticks of his favourite chocolate bar.

Once more, all eyes settled on the box. The man in the boiler suit plunged both arms in and carefully started to remove the contents. The old man watched intently and, just before the load emerged, moved forward and took it from the man in the boiler suit, having first rested his staff against the bench. In transferring the load from one pair of hands to another, the men had shuffled closer together and their turned backs now shielded the box and its contents from the view of Gordon. Some members of the jury had a better view and one or two gasped in amazement.

"I told you so," a voice exclaimed.

"It's smaller than I thought it would be," another added.

"What is it?" a third person inquired.

Nelson had put his telescope to his eye again.

It was several moments before Gordon could see the object for himself. To be precise, it was two objects and the old man now held both, one in each hand. He turned to face the jury. At the same time, Dumas bellowed, "Thou shalt have no other gods before me... Thou shalt not..."

The demon recited them all, every one of which was only too familiar to Gordon. Dumas never paused for breath and had no need to read the faint words carved on the stone tablets that the old man now held for all to view. He knew them by heart. When he finished, the exercise taking almost no time at all, such was the speed and faultlessness of his delivery, he stared at Gordon menacingly.

"Do *these* rules ring a bell?"

"Of course they do," Gordon replied. "Everyone knows the Ten Commandments. You should have said that in the first place. I know them off by heart."

"No doubt they became a little too familiar to you, Mr Jones."

Gordon never heard the last comment. "Is that really *them* – the originals?" he asked in awe.

"I think you will find the originals were broken by a certain individual," Dumas sneered, flashing an accusing glance towards the old man. "This is the second version, Mr Jones, but the words are the same."

Gordon stared at the stone tablets. Being a bit shortsighted, he could not read the words for himself and assumed they would be in another language anyway, though he wasn't sure which one. The tablets were of a great weight and yet the old man held them with ease. They were propped upright, the base of each in the open palms of both of his hands, their backs leaning against his arms, the tops resting against his shoulders. He was clearly used to displaying them in this fashion.

"Shall we go through some of them?" Dumas inquired, with the sole intention of doing just that. He rolled his eyes down the list, five commands on each tablet. "Let's start with the big one, shall we? Thou shalt not kill."

"What?" Gordon protested, faking a laugh. "Don't be ridiculous. I've never killed anyone. I've never hurt a soul in my life."

Gordon continued to shake his head. He knew he had nothing to worry about on this occasion. He sat down. "I wouldn't hurt a fly," he muttered under his breath.

Dumas smiled. "It's funny you should say that, Mr Jones."

Gordon remained seated but lifted his head. He should have known better than to think that the demon would not respond to his seemingly innocuous comment.

Dumas clicked his fingers and six men clad in black entered the courtroom bearing a coffin on their shoulders. Their methodical steps were in unison. Gordon shivered at the very sight of the object they carried. He flashed Mr Gilmore a confused glance, but it was in vain. The angel was in his seat, frantically rummaging through his papers, and he did not look up. Gordon wanted to assure his guardian that he had *not* somehow missed the moment when Gordon had plunged a knife into his boss one Monday morning, but thought better of it.

The coffin was gently lowered to the ground and the pallbearers waited for further orders, their heads bowed. Gordon fidgeted in his seat. He knew he had physically never harmed anyone, but he still feared what might be inside.

Dumas nodded and two of the pallbearers gently lifted the lid of the coffin. Gordon was no longer seated. In fact, he was now on his toes, leaning over the dock to get a better view. He did not need to. He had no difficulty making out the contents.

"Insects?" he cried. "What sort of a joke is this?"

Dumas walked to the coffin and knelt beside it. He cupped his gloved hand, dipping it into the mass of dead creatures, letting an assortment of wasps, flies and spiders slip through his fingers back into the coffin. He repeated the process, fingering the invertebrates and as though they were gold coins in a treasure chest. He sensed Gordon had relaxed.

"What's the matter, Mr Jones? They're *just* insects, that's what you're thinking, aren't you?"

"Well, yes, I am."

"They are still your master's creatures. All attentively and lovingly created by his hand... and all wantonly destroyed in yours."

"What?"

"This is the sum total of your destruction throughout your life on earth. I suppose you thought it a bit of harmless fun to swat that nuisance fly with your newspaper, or to deliberately place your size-ten boot on that little ant that was merely going about its business on your patio."

"This is madness. Everyone does it – they're a nuisance. In fact," Gordon suggested boldly, "I'm not even sure why God created them. You can hardly call it murder. Didn't God give us dominion over all other living creatures? We eat animals, don't we?"

"Would you like a bluebottle?" Dumas responded smugly, lifting one between two fingers, licking his lips as he did so.

Gordon grimaced. "Of course not. Look, this is madness and you know it."

"Interesting, though," Dumas continued unperturbed, "your wanton destruction of your master's living creatures, be it as small or insignificant as you deem it to be, does perhaps highlight your lack of respect for his creation."

"All right," Gordon conceded, raising his hands in symbolic submission. "I know I should have been a bit more respectful, but it's hardly the crime of the century, is it? If that's my only crime..."

Dumas brought Gordon to a halt through the click of his fingers. Gordon still thought it remarkable that the demon could make a sound even when wearing leather gloves. As the six men departed with the coffin on their shoulders, another man in black entered pushing a wheelbarrow. It was full of stationery.

"Now what?" Gordon groaned. "Am I going to be vilified for chewing the end off my pencil? Oh, and I did have a habit of snapping rulers in two... and a reputation for mercilessly tearing pieces of paper in half, of course!"

Gordon smiled at his own sarcasm. Dumas did not respond.

"Thou shalt not steal," he said calmly.

"No, no, no," Gordon replied, shaking his head defiantly. "You've got that wrong. That was all *before* I became a Christian. I was a young boy when I took those sweets. I've never stolen anything else."

Dumas was sifting through heaps of white copier paper that filled the wheelbarrow, occasionally spotting a pack of pens or a notebook. He lifted up a stapler in order to highlight the diversity of the contents, only pausing when he was sure the jurors had seen almost everything.

"All this didn't come from a shop," he continued. "You wouldn't have had the nerve, Mr Jones. You took all this from the stationery cupboard at work over seven years, all for use at home."

"Is that it?" a disinterested Gordon sounded. "It's not exactly stealing, is it?"

"Isn't it?

"No. Everyone does it."

Gordon stopped. He realised he had said those words before.

The wheelbarrow was pushed away. Dumas reverted his eyes to the stone tablets that the old man was still holding. The man showed no sign that he may be flagging or that he may have felt the need to put them down to give his arms a rest. He never even adjusted his position.

"Shall we have another one, Mr Jones?" the demon asked. "Perhaps you would like to choose one?"

Gordon remained silent.

"I'll choose another then," Dumas suggested. "Thou shalt have no other gods before me."

"Oh, come on," Gordon challenged, more than a hint of sarcasm in his voice. "Did you spot me doing a rain dance, or bowing to that ornamental Buddha statue in my garden?"

Gordon was faking a laugh and only stopped when he suddenly noticed the demon had donned a white football shirt. It had been placed over his tunic. Of course, Gordon never saw him do so. The demon now cut a ridiculous figure, his curly locks running down the back of the polyester shirt. He was grinning profusely. He gave a twirl, pushing away his dangling hair, so that Gordon was able to read the name emblazoned on the back of the shirt. It read '*Dumas*'. The numbers '*666*' were printed underneath it.

Gordon shook his head in bewilderment.

"Man has worshipped something since the beginning of time," Dumas mused. "Be it the sun or a simple wooden figure carved by his own hands. You see, man was created to worship. If he doesn't worship his creator, then he will turn to something else to worship: money... a film star... a football team." He paused. "You had at least eleven idols, didn't you, Mr Jones?" the demon announced, kissing the badge on the shirt. "Your particular team was very important to you, wasn't it?"

"What's wrong with that?"

"Nothing... unless it becomes more important than your master, when it becomes your chief focus, when it gets in the way of him."

Gordon blinked and the football shirt vanished, the demon's tunic and crimson sash visible once more.

Dumas went on. "Because people no longer prostrate themselves in front of statues, most think idolatry is something that belongs to another time. But the person today has more idols than their pagan ancestors ever had – they're just different. In fact, the temptation for idolatry now is stronger than ever. There are more distractions, you see. And, of course, football was not your only idol, was it?"

Dumas had picked up the red book again. He was running his finger down a page.

"Do you know how many hours you spent watching TV, Mr Jones?" he inquired, looking up, shaking his head, a sham expression of astonishment on his face. "It says here... no, surely, that must be a misprint?" He paused. "Then there's your car – not to mention the latest model that you've been saving up for. That's why you've *religiously* been doing overtime at work, isn't it? There's nothing wrong with all these pursuits, Mr Jones, unless they get in the way of your relationship with your master, of course. Did they? Did you put these things first... before your master?"

Gordon remained silent. He knew Dumas did not need him to answer.

"Of course," the demon elaborated, "it was my job to ensure that you never realised you had idols. I had to persuade you that your obsessions for football, TV and cars – to name just a few – were harmless. If you had realised something had got in the way of your Christianity, you might have tried to remove it." He halted suddenly. "Of course, there is only one true idol in your life, isn't there, Mr Jones?"

Dumas shook his head again, as though he had already anticipated Gordon's answer.

"No," the demon revealed, "your one true idol is *not* your master – it's yourself. You worship yourself, don't you? Most humans do, of course. You made and based all your decisions on how you were feeling, or how they would make you feel. It was all about you, wasn't it, Mr Jones? That's what was really important in your life – yourself?"

Dumas turned his eyes back to the stone tablets.

"Thou shalt not covet thy neighbour's Porsche," he grinned.

"What?"

"Of course, we can substitute Porsche for a number of other things... swimming pool... five-bedroom penthouse... career..."

"Oh, come on," Gordon argued. "I'm no different to anyone else. I'm not the only one to cover... or whatever it is. Everyone sometimes wishes they had what their neighbour has."

"That's right, Mr Jones – keep up with the Joneses. We all want to keep up with the Joneses, don't we? Even the Joneses do!"

"It's human nature, isn't it?" Gordon persevered. "We all want the best things for ourselves and sometimes try to get them. Everyone does it..." He stopped. At first he thought Dumas was going to repeat the words, but he had no need to.

Mr Gilmore was still sitting in his seat, now wiping his glasses with his handkerchief.

"I could go on forever," Dumas continued, reverting his eyes to the stone tablets. "But I think one more should suffice. The jury is getting the picture, I think."

He rolled his eyes down the list. He pretended to be deciding on which one to choose, but it was obvious even to Gordon that he had already made his mind up and was ready to launch his next attack. At last he grinned, as though his eyes had inadvertently fallen on one that he had forgotten.

"Thou shalt not commit adultery," he said slowly.

Gordon raised his head and met the demon's mischievous eyes. He gulped, though, of course, he had already feared that Dumas was going to choose *that* one.

13

"How do I love thee? Let me count the ways."

Sonnets from the Portuguese
Elizabeth Barrett Browning

"WHAT ARE YOU TALKING ABOUT?" AN EMBARRASSED GORdon protested. "What do you mean I looked at her *lustfully?*"

Dumas smiled. He did not need to answer. He knew Gordon and everyone else in the courtroom knew *exactly* what he meant.

"It's hardly committing adultery, is it?" the crimson-faced Gordon continued to stutter. "I'm not even married... and she was just a very pretty girl. I bet every single male on the planet looked at her... well, you know... *lustfully,* as you put it. It's not exactly the same as... well, you know... Oh, this is ridiculous!"

Mr Gilmore was wiping his brow with his handkerchief as he rose.

"Objection!" he pronounced, already on his feet before he had said the word, his face flushed. One could have been forgiven for thinking it was *his* private life under scrutiny. "Is this fair on Mr Jones?" he pleaded. "It's a delicate subject. Can I request that this particular chapter in his life be heard in-camera?"

The archangel looked to the clerk of the court, not because he could not make a decision for himself, but for the fact he did not understand the request. The clerk, as though he had eyes in the back of his head, immediately came to his assistance. "In private," he answered the archangel, making no attempt to turn his head, seemingly as unimpressed by Mr Gilmore's demonstration of his recently acquired knowledge of legal terminology as he was of the archangel's lack of it. "Mr Gilmore is simply asking for the press and public to be excluded from this part of the trial," the clerk explained.

"No need to be embarrassed on our account, Mr Jones," a wag from the public gallery sniggered.

The archangel sought his gavel, though by the time he had found it, the object hidden underneath some papers sprawled out in front of him, there was no need for him to use it.

It was Dumas who intervened.

"Bless my soul!" the demon chirped. "It was not my intention to put everyone into a dither," he lied. "Please accept my apologies. Indeed, I think I have made my point and I will spare Mr Jones (and Angel Gilmore) further embarrassment and move on. If the subject is a taboo one – and I understand there are many from eras that might consider it so – I am happy to move on to something else. My list is a long one."

Mr Gilmore retook his seat. Dumas reverted his eyes to the stone tablets, the customary smirk having returned to his face. Still the old man with the white hair stood upright and showed no signs of fatigue.

"I thought you said that commandment was going to be the last one?" the sharp-witted Gordon observed, flashing the demon a hopeful glance.

"My apologies," Dumas replied. "You are right, of course, Mr Jones. I did say 'one more', didn't I? Forgive me. Maybe I'm beginning to enjoy myself a little bit too much."

The word 'beginning' was not totally accurate. It seemed to Gordon that he had been having fun at his expense from the start.

"Anyway," Gordon added, "the other rules don't really apply, do they? I don't even know what a couple of them mean."

Dumas was stimulated by the comment and tilted his head. It was his way of inviting Gordon to elaborate.

"Well," Gordon obliged, "remember the Sabbath, that's one of them, isn't it?" he said, screwing up his eyes in the vain hope some of the chipped characters on the stone tablets would become legible to him. "I mean, that's a bit outdated now," he went on. "Even Christians accept it's all right to work on a Sunday... and most go shopping after church," he added, shaking his head disapprovingly. "I must stress that I don't – not unless it's an emergency."

Dumas attacked. "An emergency, Mr Jones? You mean if you run out of milk?"

"What I'm trying to say is that I keep Sundays special. I don't go to a car boot sale or the shopping mall. I go to church, you know that, so you can't accuse *me* of not remembering the Sabbath."

"Yes," Dumas nodded. "I know that you go to church in the morning... and then watch TV for the rest of the day."

"And there's nothing wrong with that," Gordon defended.

"We have not mentioned Father Time yet, have we?" Dumas pondered. "Time. It's the one thing many Christians really do not want to give up in their walk with their master. Our time is precious... too precious to give up for anyone. Am I right, Mr Jones?"

Gordon hesitated. "I suppose so," he admitted. "I didn't have much of it. I worked five days a week... sometimes six."

"Six? Wasn't that your choice? Didn't you do overtime to get a bit of extra money – when you wanted something for yourself? The point is that you obediently gave up time for your boss and accepted that without any problem, so long as the rest of it was yours to do as you please, yes?"

"I suppose so."

"And you spent that time on yourself, didn't you?"

"What do you mean?"

"I mean you gave very little of it away... to others... to your master."

"I went to church every Sunday morning. I gave him my time then."

"Is that it?"

"Well... I didn't have much of it... I was busy," Gordon dithered.

"Demon Dumas!" Mr Gilmore interrupted, leaping to the defence of his client. "My master is not some sort of tyrant. He knows his children need time to rest – to do as they please – that is why he set aside a day from the others, be that day a Sunday or a Saturday... or even if their Sabbath is an hour or two in the evening. There's nothing wrong with watching *EastEnders* on a Sunday afternoon. I'm quite partial to it myself."

"Forgive me if I'm wrong, Angel Gilmore," Dumas took over. "I thought that the point of keeping one day apart from the rest was so that people could forget about the everyday – all the necessary chores of life – and focus on their master, yes? Didn't your client watch TV every day? What I'm trying to say is that, in the case of Mr Jones, once he had got home from church (and even that was just a weekly habit), Sunday was just like any other day to him. Of course, I have to take some credit for that: helping to make each day like the next so that the week becomes a blur. It's a useful ploy: one that prevents the likes of Mr Jones forgetting to devote even *one* day to their master. And as for being too busy, Mr Jones..."

"But I *was* busy. I barely had a minute to spare."

"Me again, I think," Dumas grinned. "I just helped convince you that you had no time. Like the rest, you busied yourself with often meaningless pursuits. Most of the time you were busy doing nothing of any importance. You were like a spinning top, whizzing round and round at great speed, but going nowhere in particular."

Dumas dabbed his moustache. "The busier you are, or think you are, the more difficult it becomes to spend time with your master, and that, as Mr Gilmore would agree, is the only thing of real lasting worth. Yes, you made yourself so busy, became so entrenched in your daily habits, that you made it almost impossible for your master to use you for anything else. Time, Mr Jones – it's so precious. Tick-tock. Tick-tock. Tick-tock."

Dumas stopped and made a point of staring at the clock above the archangel.

"And it is time to move on," he taunted. "No time to lose."

Of course, the final comment was symbolic, the words deliberately chosen, though Gordon did not comprehend their relevance.

"Do we have to?" Gordon suggested, nodding in the direction of the stone tablets. "Is there any point going on with this? Look, you've had your fun and we've already established that I'm no Jack the Ripper. As I was saying, a lot of those rules are not exactly relevant now, are they?" he added, running his eye down the list of commandments. "You have to admit that some are a bit past their sell-by date."

"Past their sell-by date?" Dumas inquired.

The demon was not the only one to take issue with the seemingly inoffensive observation. The old man with the white hair frowned, the first indication he had emotions. Even some members of the jury shook their heads disapprovingly, Mary, Queen of Scots not among them, one should add.

"I just mean that they come from a different time," Gordon stumbled on. "They're not all really appropriate today, are they? The world is a different place. Besides, even those living in Old Testament times broke them. In fact, what was the point of the Ten Commandments? Why did God give his people rules if he knew full well that no one would obey them?"

Dumas looked to Mr Gilmore. "Would you like to explain?"

The angel stood up. "Perhaps man needed to find out for himself how hopeless he is," Mr Gilmore said, a sympathetic smile on his face. "Yes, he failed miserably to stick to the rules – and will continue to do so. That should have left him in no doubt that he is unable to reach the standard his master set. He cannot get there by his own means… and must rely on the grace of the creator of the universe himself."

Gordon looked confused.

Mr Gilmore went on. "There was a reason why your creator sent his son to earth as a human. It was to show the world that a man *could* live a perfect life; that it was possible to live by the rules. That is how he wanted us to live. And, even though he knows that no one has lived (or ever will live) up to the life that his son lived on earth, he still wants his children to at least try to do that – to try to live by the rules. Do you understand?"

"I suppose so," Gordon replied. "But I still think the Ten Commandments are a bit outdated, with due respect," he this time added, flashing a glance towards the old man who was clearly making a deliberate effort not to show any further emotion. "And didn't Jesus modify the rules himself?" Gordon continued. "When he came to earth? Didn't he come up with a new commandment? One greater than the others... or something like that?"

Mr Gilmore took to his seat. "I think Mr Jones is confusing the new commandment with the greatest commandment," he clarified.

Gordon nodded. "See! It's confusing, isn't it? No wonder I might have broken one or two of them!"

The flippant remark did not go down well. Mr Gilmore turned his head towards his charge and frowned. Gordon's apology was immediate, delivered via regretful eyes.

"Of course," the angel went on, "as I'm sure my client knows only too well, the new commandment is the same as the second greatest commandment – to love one another."

Gordon smiled sheepishly.

Dumas shook his head. "It's so confusing, isn't it, Mr Jones?" the demon mocked. "Love your God and love your neighbour. Those are the greatest commandments. Of course, you'd be a fool to believe the new ones make the old ones redundant. Don't you see, Mr Jones, you automatically comply with the new ones if you obey the old ones?"

Dumas paused. "Your master didn't *modify* the rules, as you put it. That would suggest he moved the goalposts, *changed* the rules. The old commandments are not *past their sell-by date,* but as relevant today as they were back then. They are merely encapsulated in the new ones. Indeed, when your master was asked what the greatest commandment was, he took it as a chance to explain his rules in the simplest of terms, so that even imbeciles like you, Mr Jones, could have no doubt how he wanted you to live your life."

Dumas stopped and stared at Gordon. "Still confused? Oh, Mr Jones, can it be so difficult? How simple can it be put? Number one: love the Lord your God with all your heart and with all your soul and with all your mind. Number two: love your neighbour as yourself. If you can't get your head around ten commandments, what about just two, Mr Jones – the two *greatest* commandments?"

"There you are, then!" Gordon stated. "Perhaps you should be concentrating on those two?"

Dumas smiled. "Don't worry, Mr Jones. That is *exactly* what I intend to do."

The demon turned to the old man holding the stone tablets, the first time he had acknowledged his presence. It was the signal that he had served his purpose. With the assistance of the man in the blue boiler suit, the stone tablets were carefully returned to the cardboard box. Gordon wondered what the fate of the Ark of the Covenant had been, but did not feel now was the time to inquire.

The old man with the white hair retrieved his staff and followed the man in the blue boiler suit out of the courtroom. Dumas waited for the side door to close before taking to the 'stage' again. He did not resume his 'act' until he was sure all eyes were again fixed upon him. He repeated the words once more: "Love the Lord your God with all your heart and with all your soul and with all your mind." Gordon twitched as he did so.

"*Did* you love your master with all your heart and soul and mind, Mr Jones?" the demon asked.

Gordon felt compelled to nod, the intended affirmative response from his lips having, for some reason, not been entirely audible.

Dumas shook his head, his gloved fingers twiddling the locks of his hair. "I don't think so, Mr Jones," he said bluntly. "Love is a word used far too often in your times. We demons might have had to go to great pains to trivialise the word if you humans had not done it for us. Do you *really* know what love is?"

A line from the lyrics of a popular song flashed into Gordon's mind, and the thought almost brought a smile to his face; one should stress the word 'almost'.

"With all your heart... and soul... and mind," Dumas repeated methodically. "I put the question to you again, Mr Jones, did you love your master with all your heart and soul and mind?"

Gordon was about to speak when Dumas raised his gloved hand. "No need to answer it again, Mr Jones. Let me put another question to you, an easier one to answer, I think. Do you love music?"

Gordon eyed the demon suspiciously, believing it to be a trick of some sort.

"Come, Mr Jones. It's a simple question. Do you love music?" Dumas repeated.

"Yes."

"Would you like to hear some now?"

"I suppose so."

Dumas clicked his fingers and a lone trumpet sounded, followed by a drum and then a violin. Musicians from every era and walk of life entered the courtroom in single file. They were all playing different tunes. The discordant notes that came forth from the various instruments should have resulted in an unbearable cacophony, but instead the effect was uplifting and inspiring. Gordon found that he had the ability to hear every tune. When he focused on a certain individual he could only hear the tune they played and all the others were shut out of his mind. He could pick and choose, only needing to shift his eyes to whatever instrument he chose to hear. It was like a living jukebox. There was every type of music and some of the people were singing – reciting a song that Gordon had enjoyed during his life. Every song or piece of music he had treasured on earth was being sung or played simultaneously in that courtroom.

Dumas was moving his arm rapidly, mimicking the conductor of an orchestra. All of a sudden, he clapped his hands and the music ceased. "Thank you. Thank you," he said, still clapping. "That will be all for now, thank you."

Gordon was disappointed. For just one moment he had been lost in the music, overwhelmed by it, in a comforting sort of way.

The singers and musicians exited from the door they had emerged from, the usher closing it tight when the last individual had departed. It took several moments to clear the courtroom; the last song Gordon had heard still resonating in his ears.

"I noticed you were tapping your foot a lot, Mr Jones," Dumas announced suddenly.

Gordon nodded dumbly, not questioning how the demon had come to that conclusion, the lower half of his body being, of course, out of view, submerged in the dock.

"What if I were?" Gordon inquired, adopting a defensive stance. "There's nothing wrong with tapping my foot to the beat of the music, is there? You're not going to tell me there's a commandment against that, are you? Thou shalt not sing and dance!"

A puritan among the jury muttered something under his breath, loud enough for most to hear, if not comprehend. Dumas ignored him, leaning one arm on the bench, studying Gordon with intent.

"It is safe to say you love music, Mr Jones," the demon stated. "And, of course, you love your master, don't you?" He halted. "Funny then that you *still* could not bring yourself to worship him."

"What do you mean?" Gordon asked, a combination of irritability and confusion in his voice.

"You Christians are not very good at worshipping, are you?" Dumas explained. "You certainly lack imagination when it comes to worshipping your master; a few songs on a Sunday morning are about all most can muster. In fact, most Christians are stupid enough to think that worship is nothing more than singing another song or hymn in church. Having a time of worship to them signifies the moment when the church organist or worship band reach for their instruments. Is that you, Mr Jones? I think it is."

Gordon remained silent.

"It's those that aren't very musical – who don't like singing – that I feel sorry for," Dumas went on. "They have to sing song after song in church, simply because no one has the imagination to come up with alternative ways to worship. Still, you were lucky – you've always liked music and singing... and yet..." The demon paused, scratching his forehead, "and yet, you still couldn't get to grips with that either."

"What do you mean?" Gordon protested. "I sang all the songs, even the old-fashioned hymns with all those strange words... and I loved *Amazing Grace* – that's my favourite."

"You call that worship?" Dumas snapped. "You might have been singing the latest number one hit most of the time. Your mind was focused on everything else but your master if I remember correctly."

"All right," Gordon admitted, "I don't suppose I'm the only one who gets distracted now and again. It's difficult to concentrate sometimes. I've always found worship difficult... I mean, the time when we sing songs."

"And yet I ask myself the question, why?" Dumas returned. "*Why* should you find worship difficult, even worship through a popular medium like music, something you so enjoy? Let me answer the question for you, Mr Jones."

Gordon did not respond. There was no point. He merely shrugged his shoulders.

"I put it to you simply that you do *not* love the Lord your God with all your heart and soul and mind," Dumas suggested. "That is why your worship was half-hearted. You have to love someone to truly worship them and learning to love your master more and more was what it was all about, what you should have been setting your sights on, Mr Jones. Instead of spinning around doing nothing of lasting importance, the day you became a follower of this master of yours, you finally had a purpose in life. As your master himself announced, the first and greatest commandment was to love the Lord your God with all your heart and with all your soul and with all your mind. Did you do that, Mr Jones? No."

"It wasn't always easy," Gordon pleaded. "Sometimes God felt a bit distant. I didn't always feel like God was there when I was worshipping him. Sometimes I didn't always feel like singing. I didn't always get anything from it."

"You didn't get anything from it? What did you expect to get from it?"

"I don't know."

"It was not supposed to be about *you*, Mr Jones. For once it was about someone else and not yourself. It was not important that you never got anything out of it, as you say. The whole idea was to please your master – to make *him* smile. Did you know your master smiled? That should have been your main aim in your life: to make him smile."

"I know," a glum Gordon admitted.

"You Christians are all the same," Dumas continued. "You really don't understand what worship is all about, do you? You miss the point of it. Even when you're singing all your silly songs of adoration, you're still thinking about yourselves, is that not right, Mr Jones?"

"No."

"It is, Mr Jones. Am I not right when I say you became disheartened and even irritated by the fact you did not get that warm, fuzzy feeling inside when you sang your songs?"

"Oh no! Not that again," Gordon wailed.

"You were even jealous when you saw others with their eyes closed and hands held in the air. To you, that was a sign that they had really connected. But you didn't feel the same, did you, Mr Jones?"

"It was not through want of trying," Gordon insisted passionately. "I wanted to experience what they did. Honestly I did."

"That is the problem, Mr Jones. You were looking for an experience. You were looking to get something for yourself out of it. Let me remind you, worship is supposed to be about the person you are worshipping!"

Gordon bowed his head, as Dumas twisted the knife.

"And because you didn't get that warm, fuzzy feeling inside when you sang your songs, you started to convince yourself the whole act of worship (or in your case merely singing hymns) was a waste of time. And once that thought had entered your head (probably put there by yours truly, I should add) it was not long before you were going through the motions again, like you did before you supposedly became a Christian. You're a fool, Mr Jones," Dumas added, the last word uttered with menace in his voice. "Even I can see your master deliberately denies some of his followers the ability to feel close to him at times. He doesn't want you to depend on your feelings. It is faith, not feelings and emotions, which matter more to him. You say your master felt distant at times? How much better would it have been if you had still, despite your own feelings, carried on worshipping him? He wanted you to rely on his promises, not your emotions. Any friendship based purely on emotions has no foundation. Do you not see that, Mr Jones?"

Dumas paused and deliberately shook his head. Even Mr Gilmore was nodding in agreement.

"If you didn't feel like singing," Dumas carried on, "you could have worshipped him in other ways. As I said, worship is not all about music. Of course, I should not even need to say that your whole life was supposed to have been lived as an act of worship to your master. Everything you did should have brought him pleasure. Don't you see, there are infinite ways to express adoration and love for someone? Worship comes in all shapes and forms. You don't necessarily need a song to convey your feelings; you can just express them in the simplest ways... through your actions, thoughts and speech. Yes, you could have just talked to your master a little bit more often, Mr Jones."

"Prayer!" Gordon groaned, just like the surgeon had done not so very long ago. "I thought we would be getting on to that soon."

Dumas relaxed, the smile returning to his face.

"You Christians make such a mess of it," he said. "Let me assure you, Mr Jones, we demons were spitting *flames* when you humans – many years ago – finally woke up to the fact that you could talk to your master directly and not have to go through a third party to do so. It made it so easy for you, far more convenient than having to visit a stranger in a box and then confessing your sins to *him.* You had your own hotline to the creator of the universe himself. And yet..." He sighed as though he were sorry. "And yet, this simple way to draw closer to your master has become for many the hardest thing to do."

"I pray," Gordon insisted. "You know that I do."

"Yes, but only usually when you are in need of something."

"There is nothing wrong in asking for things," Mr Gilmore interrupted. "The Master wants his children to come to him for all their needs."

Dumas chuckled. "And your client certainly did so – when he wanted something for himself."

"I prayed for others too," Gordon protested.

"There is praying and praying, Mr Jones."

"Pardon?"

"I have heard you pray one or two prayers that came from the heart, but most of the time you were just going through the motions... again. It is only when you have been desperate, at times of great need, that you have really prayed like you meant it. It is amazing how focused you are when you want something, I mean *really* want something."

Mr Gilmore rose from his seat and looked to the archangel for permission to speak, though he never waited for a response. "It is, of course, no coincidence that our most sincere prayers are said in times of great need," the angel explained. "Indeed, the Master himself will use a big problem to get his children to come closer. He wants nothing more than for them to call upon him for help."

"Thank you, Mr Gilmore," Dumas responded patronisingly. "You are quite right, but I think your master wants his children to call on him a little bit more often – and not just on Sundays or when they need a favour."

Dumas looked to Gordon. "Do you know that your master knows what you're going to ask him for... even before the words leave your lips?"

Gordon shrugged his shoulders. "If that's so... why do we need to pray? And, if he knows what's going to happen in the future, will my prayers even make a difference?"

As soon as he had uttered the question, Gordon regretted it. He realised this was not the time for a theological debate.

Dumas was grinning profusely. "Predestination! I love it when Christians get on to that subject! But you miss the point, Mr Jones. You see, asking your master for things is not the point of prayer. It is to get to know him better. Unless you converse with someone, you'll never get to know that person. You can't have much of a relationship with someone if you don't communicate."

Gordon sighed. "Sometimes it's easy to forget to pray. We all lead busy lives."

Dumas was quick to pounce. "Forget? Too busy? Could you not spare just a few minutes – even while the adverts were on?" he added, a smirk on his face. "Sometimes you would go *days* without praying, Mr Jones. Prayer should come as naturally as breathing, in that you are not even conscious of the fact you are doing it. You should be so in tune with your master – in every waking hour – that he is constantly the preoccupation of your mind. You shouldn't have to make a conscious effort to talk to him, to only communicate when you have closed your bedroom door and dropped to your knees."

"There was just so much going on in my life," Gordon continued to moan. "How could I think of him every minute of the day?"

"Yes, I know. I found it easy to distract you, of course: to remind you of that TV programme that was just about to start, or the fact that that cream bun in the fridge was *still* in the fridge, or the fact that that shelf still needed to be put up. It says something that you even put DIY – which you loathed – before talking to your master. Does that suggest you love the Lord your God with all your heart and soul and mind?"

Gordon shook his head. "I found prayer difficult, I have to admit."

"Like you found worship, or should I say, singing all those silly songs."

"I suppose so," Gordon shrugged. "Besides, you said yourself that you were responsible for making my mind wander."

"I had to at first, as I say," Dumas admitted, "when you were praying on a regular basis, but it wasn't long before you started to think your prayers were as ineffective as your 'happy-clappy' songs. You even started to wonder if you were talking to the ceiling, some days. Of course, you soon put that idea out of your head, *fortunately* for me. You see, you might have tried to do something about it if you had *really* believed that to be the case. No, you were happy to go on as you were; still unaware you were on my escalator."

"Not that again," Gordon whined.

"Did you really believe your prayers would be answered?" Dumas asked. "Or can I put it like this: did you even really *want* your prayers to be answered?"

"What? Of course I did."

"Did you? Maybe the ones that affected you, when you were really in need of help, but what about all those others, when you read the names off a list? Did it really matter if they were answered or not? Once those names had dropped off the prayer list at church, they soon slipped from your mind. I suggest you never even found out if some prayers had ever been answered, because you became convinced you could not change things anyway. Deep down, you believed your prayers were pointless. And if, by chance, you found out that your prayers *had* been answered, it was easy to convince yourself it was fate, and not your intervention, that had led to that conclusion. As I said, soon I no longer needed to even distract you from your prayers. You had all but given up dropping to your knees in the first place. Am I not right, Mr Jones?"

Gordon looked to Mr Gilmore in the hope that the angel might come to his intervention. He remained silent.

"I told you, I just found praying difficult," Gordon sighed.

"No one said it was going to be easy," Dumas replied.

"Yes, you did – you said it should come as naturally as breathing."

Dumas smiled. "It should, but you still have to work at it."

"I don't understand. That's a contradiction. We don't work at breathing."

"Think of when you start a new job," the demon attempted to explain. "At first that job seems difficult and you need to make a conscious effort to get the work done, to think over every step. But then, over time – for some it's longer than others – the job becomes second nature to you. You can now do it without even thinking about what you're doing. But you are still working, and working hard, only now you don't always know you're doing it."

Gordon still looked doubtful. Dumas went on. "Yes, prayer is hard work, don't doubt it. At first you have to labour at it – and the work of the labourer is not always pleasant. It takes time to really tune in with your master; to get to that state of mind where you are not conscious of the fact you are even praying."

Dumas paused. "Prayer is not a battle, Mr Jones – it's *the* battle. Of all my tasks, my most important is trying to stop humans communicating with their master. And when I don't succeed, I have lost that battle. You wondered if your prayers could change things. Yes. Believe it! Even we demons know its power. It gets results – maybe not the results you always desire, but then you're not standing in the shoes of your master. You can't see the bigger picture. I'm just glad – in your case – it was *I* that won the battle."

Dumas had a look of satisfaction on his face. "You see, every time you did not pray for someone, Mr Jones... that someone was the poorer for it," he added.

The demon took a longer pause in order for everyone in the courtroom to digest his final comment. Gordon lowered his head.

"Let us move on," Dumas stated after a few moments, reaching for the red book that had been left on the bench. "As we are beginning to see, Mr Jones, your relationship with your master did not exactly blossom. You virtually gave up singing your silly songs... and even talking to him. Is that how someone in love treats the object of their affection? If a husband and wife treated each other like that, the relationship would be over."

There was a cough from among the jurors. It had come from Nelson and was clearly deliberate. "I beg your pardon," the admiral whispered. "It's just that I knew of a marriage like that."

There were one or two giggles from the public gallery. Such was the reputation of the man that had made the comment, most clearly knew what he was referring to.

Mr Gilmore sprang to his feet.

"Let me remind the court that you always hurt the one you love," the angel pointed out, this time not looking to either the archangel or Dumas for permission to speak. "Demon Dumas cannot say that Mr Jones did not love his master. He said himself that prayer was not easy. It takes time to build a relationship – to be really in tune with someone. You have to learn to trust them first."

"Trust!" Dumas bellowed excitedly. "Yes, I was getting to that. Thank you, Angel Gilmore. I could not have had a better cue."

The demon stared at Gordon. "Did you *trust* your master, Mr Jones? Did you?"

"Yes," Gordon announced boldly.

"Catch, Mr Jones!"

Dumas had hurled a tiny object towards the dock. This time Gordon caught it. He slowly unclasped his fingers to reveal what now lay in the palm of his hand, but it took him several seconds before he found the courage to look at it.

14

"Little Lamb, who made thee?
Dost thou know who made thee?"

The Lamb
William Blake

"IT'S MY LUCKY CORNISH PIXIE!" GORDON EXCLAIMED.

Mr Gilmore sighed, as his client playfully fingered the plastic figure.

"A bit louder, please, Mr Jones," Dumas demanded. "Please tell the court exactly what you're holding in your hand."

Gordon looked up. "It's my lucky Cornish pixie key ring," he whispered, his face flushed, his initial joy at being reunited with something that he clearly held in affection quickly subsiding.

"A bit louder, please, Mr Jones," Dumas repeated.

"I said it was my lucky Cornish pixie," Gordon snapped.

"Thank you," the demon responded, turning to the red book and pretending to search for a particular page. "Of course, this object was acquired long before Mr Jones became a Christian... and it was discarded as soon as he did. Is that right, Mr Jones?"

Gordon remained silent.

"Oh!" Dumas cried in mock surprise, slapping his forehead with his hand, as though he were an actor in a Victorian melodrama. "You're quite right; I forgot, you kept it in your coat pocket, didn't you?"

"But it was attached to my car keys. That's what key rings are for."

"And yet you could not do without it, could you? Did you really believe it would bring you good luck?"

"No."

"And yet on a certain day when you were due to go for an interview, you became quite distressed when you lost it. You searched high and low. And, when you found it, you were ready to call for the fattened calf to celebrate."

Mr Gilmore rose.

"This is ridiculous," the angel said, shaking his head. "There's probably a simple explanation. He's already told you that his car keys were attached to it. Did it not occur to you that he would have needed those keys in order to get to *that* interview?"

"Not if he was going by bus," Dumas grinned.

"This is madness," Gordon interposed. "So what if I was fond of a little key ring? I'd had it a long time. It reminded me of a childhood holiday, that's all. I didn't *really* believe it would bring me luck."

Dumas smiled. "You were just hedging your bets, weren't you, Mr Jones? Just a bit of extra insurance – just in case your master couldn't deliver on that particular day."

Gordon bowed his head. The demon noticed him fingering the pixie.

"Keep it," he offered. "Put it in your pocket. You might need a bit of luck!"

Mr Gilmore frowned.

"Scorpio, weren't you, Mr Jones?" Dumas continued, now holding an open newspaper in his hands. He turned the pages and stopped when he reached the one he had been seeking. "It says here you are going to meet a tall, dark stranger..." The demon lifted his head, a thoughtful expression on his face. "I expect that was Death," he smiled.

Gordon shook his head. "This is nonsense. What's wrong with reading your horoscope now and again? It's just a bit of harmless fun. I didn't take it seriously. I didn't believe in all that rubbish."

"Didn't you?" Dumas inquired, feigning another look of surprise. "And yet you read your horoscope in the paper every day, without fail."

"It was just a habit."

The demon paused. "It's funny that you managed to keep old habits but couldn't successfully adopt new ones... like reading your Bible."

Gordon bowed his head again. He had been waiting for this subject to come up and had not been looking forward to it.

"I have your Bible here, Mr Jones," Dumas announced, waving the book in the air, until Gordon had raised his head. The demon pretended to blow some dust off the leather cover. The archangel sighed.

"You had a lot of books on your bookshelves at home, Mr Jones," Dumas continued. "I had difficulty finding this amongst all the biographies and thrillers. Anyone would think you liked reading."

"I did."

"Just not this particular book," Dumas suggested, opening the Bible as though he were examining it for the first time. "Was it not exciting enough for you, Mr Jones? Surely that's not the reason why you never read it? I mean, it's got more in it than the average novel: murder, adultery, espionage, skulduggery... you'll even find some of my associates in it."

"I know I should have read it a bit more than I did," Gordon admitted. "I just didn't seem to find the time..."

Gordon stopped, but it was too late.

"Ah! That word again," Dumas pounced. "Yes, it would have been difficult to find the time. You had other things to read, didn't you? Your newspaper, for starters." The demon reverted his eyes to the red book. "If I'm not mistaken, in an average week, you spent two hours and thirty-two minutes reading your newspaper. Would you like to know how much time you spent reading your Bible?"

Gordon scoffed. "I'm sure you're going to tell me."

"Not me, Mr Jones, but someone far more qualified than I."

Dumas smiled and nodded to the usher. "I would like to call my next witness... Sir Isaac Newton."

Dracula was gone before the demon had said the name. He returned with an old man of dishevelled appearance. It looked like he had just got out of bed, and Gordon wondered whether the crumpled white blouse and grey trousers he wore were indeed his nightwear.

His modest clothes were not what drew attention, however. It was the flashes of red visible through the clasped fingers of one hand that did. The half-hidden object Newton held was circular, no bigger than a cricket ball, and it could have easily been mistaken for one.

Newton was led to the witness box. As he was being sworn in, a man in a yellow boiler suit positioned a blackboard in the centre of the courtroom. It was no more than three feet in height and stood on legs, the sort of blackboard you might find in a playroom.

"Sir Isaac," Dumas started, nodding to the witness. "I would like to thank you for your appearance this evening. If you would be so good, could you please tell the court how much time Mr Jones spent reading his Bible in the last year of his earthly life."

Newton left the witness box and moved to the blackboard, dropping to his knees. Gordon was still trying to identify the red object he held in his hand, as the famous mathematician picked up a piece of white chalk with his free one and started to hurriedly scribble some numbers, occasionally using the frilly sleeve of his blouse to rub one out. Within a few moments, he put the chalk down and turned to face the demon, as if he was being timed and wanted the stopwatch to be stopped at that very moment.

"Well?" Dumas inquired.

Newton cleared his throat. "Mr Jones read his Bible for an average of 24.643845 seconds a day," he said, rising to his feet.

"Thank you, sir," Dumas nodded. "I have no further questions."

Newton returned a graceful bow and followed Dracula towards the side door. As he did so, he lifted the mystery red object to his mouth and took a bite from it. Of course, Gordon should have realised it was an apple. The man in the yellow boiler suit, the blackboard now folded flat under his arm, brought up the rear.

"Interesting," Dumas reflected. "What did Sir Isaac conclude? I think he said twenty-five seconds, if we are generous and round it up to the nearest second? Twenty-five seconds, Mr Jones. That's how long you spent reading your Bible every day this year."

Gordon sighed. "It's been a…"

"Busy year?" Dumas suggested.

Gordon did not attempt to respond.

"Of course," the demon continued, "to be fair to you, this year was a particularly poor one as far as reading your Bible goes. It was not like that in the early days, was it? In fact, you managed to read it every day for the first few weeks after you supposedly became a Christian, didn't you?"

The demon paused and stared at Gordon. "Of course, it didn't take me too long to wean you off your spiritual milk."

"My what?"

"Your spiritual milk, Mr Jones. Every newborn needs milk to help them grow, don't they? Born-again Christians are no different."

The demon lifted Gordon's Bible into the air and held it aloft as he spoke.

"Mr Jones, this book was your nourishment. You should have been hungry for it, getting fat on it. You should have been salivating in anticipation every time you picked it up." He stopped and shook his head. "You yourself admitted to the court that your master sometimes felt distant. Is it any wonder? You didn't talk to him and you didn't find out what he had to say to *you*. Did you really expect to get closer to him by feasting on his word for less than half a minute a day?"

"I know," Gordon confessed. "I should have read it more."

Dumas lowered the Bible and started to flick through the pages once more.

"It's a big book, isn't it?" he said patronisingly. "Even more pages than that instruction manual for your computer. That reminds me, did you know that you only utilised about three per cent of what your home computer is capable of, Mr Jones?"

"What?"

"Yes, you haven't a clue what it can do, have you? Do you know why?"

"No."

"Because you skipped reading *that* instruction manual. You started to read it, of course, but only did so to help you get going. Then you went your own way, figured the rest out for yourself. That's fine, but you never discovered what your computer was really capable of. Once or twice, you dipped into the manual when you had a problem to solve, but that was it. Most of the pages have never even been turned."

Gordon considered informing Dumas that manuals had long gone, but realised now was not the time to educate him on the benefits of help screens, search engines or even the internet, come to that.

Dumas stroked his moustache. "Your Bible is supposed to be your instruction manual on living. When you supposedly became a Christian, you promised to follow your master, to do his will. How do you think you can do that without finding out exactly what he wants you to do? Why did your master feel distant? I put it to you, it was because you didn't give him the chance to talk to you. This book is his word, the answer to all your questions. It should have been the benchmark for everything in your life. It is the ultimate guidebook and yet you have not even read it all. How can you say you live your life by it if you don't even know what's *in* it?"

"Did you say read it *all?* You mean cover to cover?" Gordon remonstrated. "That would have taken a lifetime!"

Dumas reached for his pocket and retrieved a calculator. "Your particular version of the Bible has 727,969 words, Mr Jones," the demon pointed out as he tapped some buttons. Of course, Gordon was not convinced he was genuinely pressing the correct ones, particularly as it would have required considerable dexterity to do so when wearing leather gloves.

"You manage an average 4,486 words of your paperback every day on the train," Dumas went on. "If you had started reading your Bible on the first day of January, not including weekends or your annual holiday entitlement – and I'll even knock off the days you were sick – you would have read it by the middle of September," he concluded, looking up. "I can recall Sir Isaac if you would like verification?"

"That won't be necessary," the archangel sounded.

"The point is, Mr Jones," Dumas summed up, "it wouldn't have taken a lifetime. In fact, you could have read it over and over again even during the modest number of years you were allocated on earth. I can work out exactly how many times, if you wish?"

"I know I should have read it more," Gordon acknowledged, a remorseful expression on his face. "I've already told you that. I just found it difficult."

"Like singing your silly songs… and prayer," Dumas reminded him.

"Yes, if you like, but we all know it's not easy being a Christian, is it?"

"That's right," Dumas nodded. "You do indeed need help. And where do you get that help and guidance from, Mr Jones? In here," he pronounced, holding the Bible aloft once more. "In here, Mr Jones. That's why you need to *read* it."

"I know," Gordon continued to whine. "And I did read it regularly once upon a time. I don't know why I stopped."

Dumas sighed. "To be fair to you, Mr Jones, as I said, I should take the credit for that."

Gordon let out another groan. "I thought you might."

"That's right," Dumas explained. "Just another old trick in the book. I just made you feel guilty."

"Pardon?"

"Quiet times, that's what you Christians call them, don't you?"

"Sorry?"

"The part of the day when you're supposed to be quiet before your master – when you read your Bible and come before him in structured prayer. Of course, new converts always struggle with the idea. You're encouraged to set aside some time for your master – every day, am I not right?"

"And I did… at first," Gordon regretfully added.

"You're not unusual," Dumas went on. "These quiet times can last for a few days, a week, a month, it doesn't really matter, but the day will come when you miss one. Of course, that's usually down to me as well. At first you think you've committed a cardinal sin: you've failed to spend time with your master. Needless to say, people around you will assure you it doesn't matter."

"It doesn't," Mr Gilmore intervened. "God is not some mad despot, I've told you. He doesn't want his children to spend time with him out of duty."

The demon shook his head. "That's what most Christians would say, but it does matter. It's foolhardy to think it doesn't. Once you think it's all right to miss one day, you're not so crestfallen when you miss another... and another. You get to the point when it almost becomes acceptable to go a whole week without reading your Bible. But, of course, eventually the feeling of guilt surfaces: all that your master has done for you, and yet you cannot give him even five minutes in a day. And you become demoralised, start beating yourself up for not being able to reach the high standards demanded of you. Of course, when you reach that point, it's not long before you give up totally. You conclude that if you can't reach those heights, there's not much point trying to do so. You're just wasting your time – precious time. Is that not right, Mr Jones? Is that why your Bible sits on the shelf at home gathering dust?"

"It doesn't," Gordon protested. "I *still* read it. I might not have read it as much as I should, but I still read it – occasionally."

"Of course," Dumas continued, "it is one thing to read the Bible but another to actually feed on it. Even when you did dip into it, I was not unduly concerned, Mr Jones. In fact, I've been known to read it as well. As I have mentioned, many of my associates are in it and, I have to admit, it's a rip-roaring read. You see, even a non-Christian can tell you that Noah built an ark or that Moses parted the Red Sea. There are some foolish enough to believe the Bible is fiction, of course, but even those that consider it to be factual are just as foolish if they believe it to be only a mere history book. Even we demons know it is more than that. It is like no other book. It is alive. Used in the proper manner, it is life-transforming. To be honest, Mr Jones..." Dumas moved towards the dock and whispered, "...my master is scared stiff of it."

Gordon looked at the demon in surprise. He knew he was not joking.

"And I should have been shaking in my boots when that book was in your hands, Mr Jones," Dumas continued, turning his back on Gordon and heading towards the clerk of the court, "but I wasn't. I knew you were wasting your time reading it, even if it wasn't *much* of your time."

"What do you mean, I was *wasting* my time?"

Dumas turned sharply to face Gordon.

182

"Because unless you really take in what you are reading and act on it, unless it succeeds in changing your life and the lives of others, you might as well be reading that biography or thriller. In your case, Mr Jones, you just read a few chapters and then forgot about it. You're not meant to just read it. You must understand what your master is trying to say through it – and then put it into practice. I can never recall you meditating."

"What? I'm not into all that yoga stuff."

Dumas smiled. "Meditation is not some mystical paranormal activity. It's about chewing your food, over and over again, before swallowing it. In your case, reading the Bible was no different to how you ate a doughnut. You would wolf it down so quickly you would not even taste it. You weren't even able to recall what filling was in it." Dumas paused. "When it comes to taking nourishment from your Bible, you were starving, Mr Jones... starving to death. Fancy a doughnut?"

At first Gordon thought the demon was going to produce one.

"Love the Lord your God with all your heart and soul and mind," Dumas continued. "That was what you were told to do, but you have to trust him first. You never trusted your master."

"I did."

Dumas shook his head. "You cannot really trust someone until you get to know them, and you never got to know your master because you never read his word."

The demon suddenly clicked his fingers: "I call my next witness... Death."

Dracula was clearly not expecting the sudden change in direction. He jumped in his seat.

Fearing he was uncharacteristically slow off the mark, he seemingly attempted to make amends by heading towards the main exit with even greater haste than normal. He opened the door and his head momentarily disappeared from view, but all could still hear his distant voice echoing around the foyer: "Mr Death. Court one, please."

His announcement appeared to be in vain. There was no response and there was no one in the foyer, even if that was only apparent to Dracula. He turned to face the archangel. "He doesn't seem to be here, your worship."

The archangel frowned and looked to Dumas for a response.

"Will you call him again, please," the demon instructed. "He has been informed that his presence is required, but you know what he's like. You've all met him, of course."

The usher sighed and tried again. This time more than his head left the courtroom and he closed the door behind him. He was still in the foyer when Death himself appeared in the witness box. Of course, no one had noticed the moment he had done so.

"*And come he slow or come he fast, it is but Death who comes at last,*" Death recited theatrically. "My dear Sir Walter Scott said that of me, I do believe."

It was the voice that reassured Gordon it was indeed Death that now stood in the witness box. Otherwise he would not have known it was he. Death was now dressed in dazzling white. He had a yellow flower in the buttonhole of his suit jacket. Other than that, everything of his personal attire was white and – as white is no bigger contrast to black – the present appearance of Death could have been no bigger contrast to when Gordon first set eyes on him in his living room.

Dumas had noticed that Gordon was confused.

"Yes, it *is* dear Death, Mr Jones," he clarified. "Is something bothering you?"

"He's changed his clothes."

"No. He hasn't."

"Yes, he has. He was in black – he looked so dark and gloomy before."

"I am the door to eternity, Mr Jones," Death interrupted. "There is nothing bleak about me."

"That is right," Dumas added. "You only perceived Death to be something dark and uninviting when he came to you – and that is the image you had throughout your life. The reality is much different."

The usher returned to the courtroom and closed the door behind him. He looked to the archangel. "He's still not..." He stopped, finally aware of a presence in the witness box.

"I think you were looking for me," the new witness declared. "I *am* Death."

"You can say that again," the usher snapped. "I've been calling you for ages."

Death sighed. As we know, it was not the first time he had been the subject of that joke and he knew it would not be the last.

"Mr Death," Dumas began, "do you remember the deceased who stands before us this evening?"

"I do," Death replied. "I don't forget a face, even though I come across many, and, of course, one cannot forget those ears – it's not me that has the ears of an ass!" he added, a mischievous grin appearing. Gordon tutted in response.

"Good evening, Mr Jones," Death bowed. "I don't suppose you will forget me in a hurry... either."

Death was not required to take the oath, presumably being beyond such things, though Gordon never noticed that fact.

"Mr Death," Dumas continued. "I would like you to recall the very first moment you called upon Mr Jones."

"I can do that."

"I have just one question. Was Mr Jones pleased to meet you?"

Death smiled, bending his head towards the yellow flower in his buttonhole. He dreamily closed his eyes and took a long sniff.

"That is perhaps not a word I would use," he said sadly. "Mr Jones was much like everyone else. People are shocked and confused when I appear in their midst and, of course, they don't usually believe me when I tell them who I am. I can't recall anything different in the case of Mr Jones."

"*La mort ne surprend point le sage; il est toujours prêt à partir.*"

The words had come from the lips of Dumas. Death nodded his head in appreciation and obligingly translated them: "*Death never takes the wise man by surprise; he is always ready to go...* Jean de La Fontaine."

The demon shook his head thoughtfully. "So Mr Jones was... shocked and confused when you came to him?"

Mr Gilmore rose from his seat. "There is nothing unusual about that. Death himself said that most people react in the same way."

"Even Christians?" Dumas asked, turning to the angel, an expression of fake astonishment now on his face.

"Yes, *even* Christians," a defiant Mr Gilmore replied. "There's no shame in that. It's a natural reaction. Of course people are going to be shocked and confused. The act of dying is a mystery to the human being. They have no experience of it. Nobody has died and lived to tell the tale – I mean to tell it on earth."

Dumas turned to Death. "Sorry, I do have another question for you." He paused. "Did Mr Jones mention heaven at all?"

Death shook his head. "I don't think so. In fact, he asked me where he was going."

Dumas turned sharply to Gordon who had already bowed his head.

"Did you fear death, Mr Jones?" the demon asked after a longer pause.

Gordon looked up at Death.

"No, I don't mean *him*," the demon intervened. "I mean the act of dying. When you were alive... did you fear to die?"

Gordon hesitated. "I suppose so, if I'm honest," he admitted.

"But you believed your master had gifted you with eternal life? You believed you were going to heaven, didn't you?"

Gordon fidgeted. "Yes, of course I did," he said unconvincingly. "It's just that I enjoyed life on earth too. I'm no different to anyone else – I didn't want to leave it. And, of course, I was initially shocked when I was told that I had. Perhaps I shouldn't have been, but we all just assume we've got years left, don't we? So yes, in answer to your question," Gordon continued defiantly, "I probably was still a bit afraid of dying – making that great leap into the unknown."

Dumas paused. "The unknown? I thought you said you believed you were going to heaven, Mr Jones?"

Mr Gilmore rose again. "Demon Dumas is clearly putting words into my client's mouth," he said, looking towards the archangel for assistance.

"It was your client that said the word first," Dumas smirked.

"All right, twisting his words to your gain," the angel muttered, as he retook his seat. "I know what you're up to. It isn't fair."

"Look," Gordon intervened, "what I meant by 'unknown' is that we have no idea what heaven is like, do we? It's a mystery to all humans, until we get there. And I'm still none the wiser now," he added, casting his eye around the assortment of figures in the courtroom. "I still don't understand what this dying business is all about. Yes, I'm still confused and – if I'm honest – I still think I'm going to wake up and discover this has all been a dream."

The demon perched himself on the bench and looked at Gordon.

"Do you know why even Christians fear death, Mr Jones?" he asked, again with no intention of letting Gordon answer. "It is because they become too attached to the world that they know. Life on earth – for those in the Western world, I must stress – is comfortable and cosy. And even Christians forget that they are like a wisp of smoke. Yes, they too are not on their little green and blue planet for long; a drop in the ocean when you compare it to eternity, though, to be more accurate, it is not even a mere drop. Let me remind you, this life is only the dress rehearsal for the great production that goes on forever. You see, even Christians forget to focus on the main event."

Dumas slipped off the bench and strutted towards the jury, his head titled back, his hat in one hand. He did not address anyone in particular. "Of course, the likes of Angel Gilmore should take some of the blame," the demon added nonchalantly.

"What?" Gordon uttered. "What did *he* do?"

"The problem with having angels to look after you is that you become too cosseted while on earth – too protected. Thanks to Angel Gilmore and his friends, you didn't have many near-death experiences. You didn't have to think about death that often."

Mr Gilmore shook his head, clearly not of the opinion some of his work had been a hindrance to his charge.

"Yes," Dumas continued. "You didn't even like to think about death, Mr Jones."

"Of course I didn't."

"But you should have. You convinced yourself, with my help, that even thinking about death was morbid, but it was to your detriment that you didn't remind yourself that you were mortal and that one day your life on earth would be over. As I said, earth is only meant to be your temporary home. You shouldn't make yourself too comfortable there. Your true home is with your master, whoever that master may be. Yes, Mr Jones, you should have spent your time on earth preparing for eternity. If you had done so, you would have lived your life as your master had intended you to."

Dumas did not let up. "You see, when you live thinking about the eternal, nothing much on earth really matters. All that you think is important pales into insignificance. Believe me, within the first few seconds of standing in heaven (if you were going there, of course) you would have wondered why you paid so much importance to your life on earth. And, needless to say, if you had trusted your master, you would not have feared leaving it. You would have realised that our friend Death is merely the gate to eternity and nothing to resist or fear. Indeed, isn't death supposed to be the triumphant completion of your sanctification, Mr Jones, very much necessary, all part of your master's plan?"

The demon stared at the motionless Gordon, who was now trying to work out the meaning of the word 'sanctification'.

"Death said you were shocked and confused, Mr Jones. Why?" Dumas persisted. "I can understand you might have been shocked and confused initially – when Death first appeared – but surely those thoughts would have eventually given way to more positive emotions, if you trusted your master, of course? Yes, if you really trusted your master, why were you not celebrating? Death did not report you jumping for joy once you had got over the initial shock. There was never any singing or dancing... No, the trumpets were silent." The demon took a breath. "Come to that, Death didn't even report a measly smile on your face. Why were you not trembling uncontrollably or giggling in excitement at the very thought that you would soon be kneeling before his throne? Yes, his throne. Why not, Mr Jones... why not?"

Dumas again did not wait for an answer. "Were your actions and emotions those of someone who *really* trusted their master? No. You didn't trust your master. How could you? You've never really got to know him properly, have you? You can't trust someone until you know them and you can't get to know them until you listen to what they have to say."

Dumas lifted his arm, dramatically stretching it as far above his head as he could reach. In his clenched fist was Gordon's Bible.

"You didn't find out what your master had to say, did you?" he went on, raising his voice. "This book was your guide to eternity. It would have shown you how to prepare for it – shown you the road to follow. But you didn't take that road, did you? No. So I put it to you again, did you *really* believe you were bound for heaven, Mr Jones?" He halted for effect. "Or had you just been hedging your bets?"

Gordon had again bowed his head, this time even before the demon had finished speaking. He was unconscious of the fact that his fingers were still twiddling the Cornish pixie within his pocket.

15

"If a man will begin with certainties, he shall end in doubts; but if he will be content to begin with doubts, he shall end in certainties."

The Advancement of Learning
Francis Bacon

YOU COULD NOT BLAME GORDON FOR INITIALLY FAILING to hear the scratching sound coming from the far corner of the courtroom. Only now – in the silence – did it become audible to him. For this reason, he would not have been able to tell you when the noise had started. Sensing that Dumas had returned to his seat, Gordon raised his head and immediately located the source of the sound. A man was sitting on a three-legged stool, though Gordon was not aware of that fact, due to the head of the individual being all that was visible to him. And – it should be stated – even that head was not always in view, only occasionally popping up from behind an upright slab of stone that shielded the rest of the man's body. A white bed sheet was spread out on the floor next to him. Upon it lay an assortment of tools; chisels to be precise. It was clear he also had one in his hand at this particular moment, though Gordon could not see it, only hear it tapping and chipping at the stone. Mr Gilmore blew his nose. The eyes of Gordon instinctively left the stonemason – for that was the present occupation of the man – and rested on the angel, who had now risen from his seat.

"I must thank you for giving me this opportunity to address the jury," Mr Gilmore nodded to the archangel. "I know it is not my time to speak, but I think it is important that I am allowed to respond to what the court has just heard – while it is all still fresh in our minds."

Dumas was leaning back in his chair, his hat in his hand. "Be my guest," he waved nonchalantly. "It makes no difference to me, Angel Gilmore. You may think me arrogant, but there is very little you can do or say that will hinder my case."

The angel felt obliged to thank his adversary, though it was merely via a nugatory nod of the head. He started to fumble through some papers in his briefcase, which was positioned on the bench in front of him, the open lid screening the contents from those that sat opposite, including the clerk of the court who was eyeing him with suspicion. For one moment Gordon wondered whether Mr Gilmore was trying to secretly unravel the cling film on his sandwiches, but at last he produced a number of sheets of paper of varying sizes and closed the briefcase lid. Gordon was able to read the top sheet, due to the fact there was only one word on it and it filled most of the page. In capital letters, scribbled with a purple felt tip pen, was the name 'Grace'. That name again. It was underlined and a question mark succeeded it, persuading Gordon that Grace was probably not the wife of Mr Gilmore, after all. Gordon was still wondering who Grace might be when the angel consigned that particular sheet to the bottom of the pile.

"I would like to make an admission on behalf of my client," Mr Gilmore announced, lifting up his head. "It may come as a surprise to some, but I think it is important that members of the jury are made aware of it before we go any further."

Some of the jurors fidgeted in their seats, in anticipation of some crucial piece of evidence that would require their full attention. The knight in armour, with the assistance of the person next to him, attempted to shift his body back into an upright position; that is to say, one in which his back and the tops of his legs formed an angle of ninety degrees, he having slipped down his chair so much that it was now almost double that.

Mr Gilmore adjusted his spectacles. "Faith," he stated, peering over the lenses. "Demon Dumas alluded to the matter of faith. I would like to bring that subject up now, if I may, as I feel it has a lot to do with how my client lived his life. It might explain much."

He paused and turned to Gordon. "And so I now have a question for *you*, Mr Jones."

Gordon was not expecting his guardian to involve him. He returned a startled look.

"Don't worry, Mr Jones, it's a simple question," Mr Gilmore continued. "But it requires an honest answer. The court needs to hear the truth."

Gordon nodded.

"Would you say you had a *strong* faith?" the angel asked.

Gordon hesitated. He did not know what Mr Gilmore wanted him to say.

The angel sensed that fact. "Be honest, Mr Jones," he added. "I asked for an honest answer – the truth, the whole truth and nothing but the truth. Did you have a strong faith?"

Gordon coughed. "No," he said sorrowfully. "I had a lot of doubts."

There was no reaction. None of the jurors gasped. In fact, no one seemed very shocked. Gordon was more surprised by the fact that his revelation had been received with apparent indifference.

"Thank you for your honesty, Mr Jones," Mr Gilmore replied, taking his seat again.

Gordon looked at his guardian in bemusement. Why had he sat down? Was that it?

Dumas was not so naive. The demon rose from his chair and started to clap.

"Very clever, Angel Gilmore," he mocked. "However, you'd perhaps better explain to the jury the point you were trying to make – in case they're as deficient in the brain department as your client seems to be."

Mr Gilmore remained in his seat but looked towards the still perplexed Gordon. "It's not a bad thing to have some doubts, Mr Jones, that's all," he said softly.

Gordon nodded in response, but the gormless expression on his face suggested he did not understand.

Dumas took over. "Let *me* explain, Mr Jones. Angel Gilmore is trying to suggest a reason why you found it difficult to follow your master. He is of the opinion it was because of your doubts and not your laziness. He reckons your lack of faith is the reason why you found it difficult to sing those silly songs... to pray... to read your Bible, etcetera, etcetera... in short, the reason why you never trusted him enough to live your life for him."

Mr Gilmore got to his feet. He paused, before deliberately turning to look at the jury, a wistful look in his eyes. "I ask this," the angel began, "can any Christian, hand on heart, claim that he or she has *never* sometimes questioned if their God is real? Don't be alarmed, Mr Jones," he added, swivelling around to face the dock, "it's not blasphemy. Your master knows the weaknesses of man and he knew from the very beginning that people would find it difficult to believe in him. Do not think it was a coincidence that even one of the disciples was a great doubter. They were ordinary men – just like you, Mr Jones – and that was the point. The Master deliberately chose ordinary men to follow him. He didn't want superheroes. Yes, even Thomas, the greatest of doubters, was chosen. Why? To teach *ordinary* men – even those with doubts – that they are also called. He wants people to come to him, complete with all their human frailties, and to *learn* to trust him."

Dumas had turned his head. He was pretending not to be listening, running the plume on his hat through his gloved fingers. The angel cleared his throat and adjusted his glasses once more.

"I'm not saying that Mr Jones never had any faith – he did. But there is a place for doubt in the mind of a Christian too."

Gordon looked at the angel, an expression of perplexity on his face.

"Doubt is not necessarily a problem," Mr Gilmore continued. "In fact, it may surprise you to learn it is a necessity. Doubt is essential to the existence of human faith, you see. Who said that? If Death were here now, I'm sure he'd know."

Gordon looked at the empty witness box. He had not seen Death arrive and he had not seen him go.

"To have faith, you need doubt," Mr Gilmore attempted to explain. "You cannot have one without the other. Faith is not possible without doubt. Of course, the Master wants us to have faith, but it doesn't always at first come in abundance. You have to learn to trust him – and then your faith will grow."

Gordon sighed. "It's not easy trusting in something when you're not always sure it's there. If only he had revealed himself." He stopped. He thought of the surgeon again and shamefully bowed his head. No one needed to remind Gordon of the cross.

Mr Gilmore offered Gordon a reassuring smile. "Yes, the Master could sit on a cloud all day in sight of everyone, but then there would be no need to have any faith. You would be able to see him. True, your worship would be a lot sincerer, but he does not want his children to be like robots, forced to love him. You cannot force someone to love you."

"But I found it so difficult to believe in him some days," Gordon poured out. "I wanted to believe, I really did."

"If something is easy to believe in, there is no need to have faith," Mr Gilmore smiled.

"But why do we need faith?" Gordon asked, a hint of desperation in his voice.

The angel left his seat and moved to the dock, placing his hand upon the door.

"May I?" Mr Gilmore asked, turning to the archangel.

The archangel nodded.

"Step out of the dock, Mr Jones," Mr Gilmore ordered, opening the door. Gordon flashed a glance towards the clerk of the court before proceeding.

"Now turn your back on me, Mr Jones," the angel went on. "And lean back. Don't worry... I'm going to catch you."

Gordon hesitated. He looked at Mr Gilmore doubtfully. He was a lot smaller than Gordon.

"Trust me," Mr Gilmore smiled. Gordon reluctantly turned his back, but try as he might, he could not let himself fall into the angel's arms. Just before he got to the point of no return he straightened his arched back and stood upright.

"I can't do it," he apologised.

"You've got to trust me, Mr Jones," the angel insisted, holding his hands out, his palms turned to the ceiling. "The first time is always the most difficult. One more try, Mr Jones – now trust me."

At last Gordon closed his eyes and finally let himself fall into the arms of the angel. Mr Gilmore caught him – just. Dumas started to clap. "Bravo, Mr Jones," he sneered.

Mr Gilmore requested Gordon to repeat the process.

"Of course," the angel puffed, "once you have done it once, a few times, you know full well you are in safe hands. You start to trust the person catching you. That is what all Christians must do – learn to trust their master."

The exercise was repeated and Mr Gilmore would have done so a third time. It was the demon that intervened.

"Spare us, Angel Gilmore, please. I think the court gets the message."

Dracula was now standing beside the dock and held the door open, as if he believed Gordon might not return there.

Mr Gilmore walked back to his seat, using his handkerchief to clean his glasses. He was red in the face and Gordon wondered if he could have *managed* a third time.

"Of course," Mr Gilmore continued, "you need faith that the person will catch you in the first place. You have to have faith in them. That is why faith is so important – because faith leads to trust. In putting your faith in someone, you learn to trust that person. You'll start to rely on them and not on yourself. And that is what the Master wants more than anything: for you to be dependent on *him.*"

Gordon sighed. "I know what you're saying, but isn't it a Catch-22 situation? We need faith to trust in God, but we only grow in faith when we start to trust him?"

Mr Gilmore smiled, replacing his glasses. "I'm not saying it's easy – even the disciples struggled to believe."

"And they had Jesus by their side!" Gordon complained. "We don't even have that." He stopped, the protestations of the surgeon flashing into his mind once more.

Mr Gilmore paused. "To trust in someone when you are struggling to believe, when they appear to be distant, a long way from your side, that indeed requires faith. *Blessed are those who have not seen and yet have believed,*" the angel added. "Blessed indeed."

Mr Gilmore walked towards the jury. A television was standing on a small table just in front of their bench.

"Let me assure you, there is nothing mystical about faith," the angel explained, resting his hand on the top of the television. "All humans have faith in something. Few understand how a TV works, but few doubt it will not work when they switch it on. Why? Because they have switched it on many times before and it has always worked. However, if someone had shown them a TV for the first time and told them what it does – they would probably laugh in their face."

He stopped and pressed a button on the television. Some jurors – those of a pre-electrical era – were startled when it flickered into life, assuming it had been merely an odd piece of furniture. Mr Gilmore turned the television off. "Of course," he went on, "if I turn it on a second time, they will not only believe it will do the same again... but expect it to."

The angel obliged and the likes of Nelson sat mesmerised, their eyes once more rooted to the moving pictures on the screen, a scene from *It's a Wonderful Life.*

"Forgive me," the angel said, as he turned the television off for a final time, "but this bit always makes me cry."

A man in an orange boiler suit seemingly appeared from nowhere to remove the television, much to the annoyance of the captivated jurors. The angel moved towards the dock and turned his back on Gordon.

"It is not a contradiction to say a believer can lack faith. '*I do believe – help me overcome my unbelief.*' Our master was confronted by those very words while on earth. Yes, a believer can still have doubts. People are under the misapprehension that you either believe or you don't, but

194

it's not always as black and white as that. Christians are at different levels of faith – otherwise they'd all be performing miracles."

Mr Gilmore was in full flow and reluctant to stop, fearing the demon might interrupt him at any moment.

"There is a limit to the faith of every person," he went on, "but it is that person – and not the Master – who controls that limit. In order to go beyond that limit, they have to learn to trust him. And when they start to do that, they will soon discover that he does not let them down. And, of course, the more faithful he appears to the person putting their trust in him... the more they will be inclined to trust him in future. It is self-fulfilling."

Mr Gilmore turned to face Gordon. He smiled sympathetically.

"No, Mr Jones, do not think that your doubts meant that you were not really a Christian," the angel assured him. "Demon Dumas would like the jury to believe that but, on the contrary, confronting doubts can highlight sincerity in a Christian. It can reveal that you are not just going through the motions. A simple and accepting faith is not necessarily a strong one, you see. Many Christians are spoon-fed and never ask any questions, but the more you question, the more you are seeking your master in a far deeper way. It shows you care and want to get even closer to him. You shouldn't sweep doubts under the carpet or refrain from debating those dodgy theological issues, but confront them head on. Tell the Master about your fears and doubts. He already knows what is on your heart and you cannot hide from him."

Dumas had had enough. He rose to his feet.

"That is all very interesting, Angel Gilmore," he scoffed. "If it applied to your client, of course."

"What do you mean?" the angel replied, agitated by the fact he had more to say and had been prevented from doing so.

"Please take your seat, Angel Gilmore. It's my turn now."

The angel reluctantly obeyed.

"I fully concur with what you are saying," Dumas nodded thoughtfully. "It is perhaps only natural to have doubts... especially when I'm putting them into your head. But Mr Jones did not make any attempt to overcome his. He didn't ask questions, as you say. He didn't confront his doubts and come to his master for help. As you said, he was simply going through the motions."

"I didn't say that," Mr Gilmore started to rise, looking towards the archangel. "He's twisting things again."

The archangel was pouring himself a glass of water, his other hand on his wig to prevent it slipping over his glasses.

"I think you had better let Demon Dumas continue now, Angel Gilmore," he suggested. "You have had a good run for your money."

Mr Gilmore reluctantly sat down and folded his arms.

Dumas left his seat and came to the centre of the courtroom. "Humans are forever going through the motions, aren't they, Mr Jones? And you are exceptional at it. You like an easy ride, don't you? That's why my escalator is so appealing."

Gordon tutted. Not that again.

"You were never one for rocking the boat," the demon continued. "No, you never asked questions. As we have seen, you hardly ever spoke to your master or turned to his word for the answers, at any rate. Yes, you went to church every Sunday, but you never did so with the intention of enlightening your mind. It might have helped if you had questioned what you were even doing at church in the first place. You might as well have been washing your car (that's really what you would rather have been doing) or tucked up in bed like most of your neighbours. Church was just something you happened to do on a Sunday morning. You had been doing it all your life and there was no reason to stop doing it. Yes, Angel Gilmore, doubts can be positive," Dumas added, flashing a glance towards his foe, "but in the case of Mr Jones, I don't doubt – if you excuse the pun – that his lack of any faith is beyond reasonable doubt. There was no faith – only doubts."

Dumas paused, and Gordon once more became aware of the stonemason still tapping away.

"Did you ever really believe in your master, Mr Jones?" the demon probed.

"Of course I did," Gordon replied, his attention averted from the tapping.

"No, I mean *really* believe," Dumas continued. "Did you *really* believe your master was with you? You've already admitted you didn't always feel close to him. Perhaps you didn't really believe he was *ever* there at all?"

Gordon looked to Mr Gilmore, but the angel remained seated.

"What about the time when your mother became seriously ill? Was he there then?" Dumas inquired.

Gordon momentarily closed his eyes. The expression on his face told the jury that the demon had touched a raw spot.

"You prayed for her, didn't you?" Dumas added, now metaphorically starting to pick at the scab. "And it was one of those prayers that really came from the heart, wasn't it? You prayed like you had never prayed before or ever prayed again. You wanted her to live more than anything, didn't you? Yes, that was some prayer. Did it work?"

Gordon never replied.

"No," Dumas answered for him. "She died, didn't she?"

Mr Gilmore was on his feet. The archangel put a finger to his lips to prevent him from speaking on this occasion and the angel reluctantly retook his seat.

"Yes, she died, didn't she, Mr Jones?" the demon went on, shaking his head. "Why? You never understood why, did you? Why did your master let her die? Why didn't he answer your prayer? Why? You asked that question for days after she died. In fact, let's be honest, Mr Jones, you've been asking it ever since, haven't you?"

Gordon sighed, wiping a solitary tear that had started to fall from his eye.

Dumas moved towards the dock.

"You never spoke to your master for months after that, Mr Jones. Why? Did you blame him? Were you bitter because he didn't answer your prayer?"

"No. That's not how it was."

"It would have been better if it had been," Dumas insisted.

Gordon looked up for an explanation.

"Yes, Mr Jones," the demon continued. "It would have been better if you had had it out with your master – asked some questions and released your anger. He's big enough to take it. Instead, you stopped talking to him completely. You started to convince yourself (or I did) that your master had not let her die, but that it had happened because your master wasn't even there in the first place. No one was there. Yes, your doubts resurfaced. How could a God of love allow that to happen? You humans can never get your heads around that one, can you? Ask a non-believer why they don't believe in God and most will say it is because there is too much suffering in the world. Yes, if there was a living and loving God, why – why, oh, why – does he allow all this suffering?"

Gordon bowed his head.

Mr Gilmore was itching to speak, but Dumas was in full flow now.

"Surely you don't think that Christians are immune from suffering, do you, Mr Jones? Sadly, you have to go through the same trials and tribulations as everyone else. Why, though? Have you ever asked yourself why that should be? Why doesn't your master spare you? He could, couldn't he?"

Gordon looked up, unsettled by the idea.

Dumas sauntered back towards the centre of the courtroom. He had succeeded in putting more doubts into the mind of Gordon.

The demon sensed that Mr Gilmore was about to intervene.

"Don't bother, Angel Gilmore," he said, wagging his finger. "I'll explain." The demon paused. "It's like this, Mr Jones... your master doesn't always *want* to spare you."

"What?"

"Things often happen when you least expect them to, don't they? There you are, going along quite nicely, when a bolt out of the blue suddenly hits you. Your life is turned upside down in one moment... like the time you were made redundant. You loved that job. Why did your master let that happen?"

Dumas stopped. A muffled drilling sound was audible and the demon was making sure everyone could hear the noise. After a few moments, he removed an alarm clock from under his sash. It was one of those old-fashioned types that had to be wound up, and the harsh ring became louder and more penetrating as he held it aloft.

"Wake up, Mr Jones!" the demon yelled theatrically, turning abruptly to see if Gordon had reacted. "Wake up!"

Gordon had instinctively stood to attention.

"I don't mean now," Dumas smiled, pushing down a button on the clock to bring the noise to an abrupt halt. "Did you not hear the alarm bells when you were alive? Your master had to give you a wake-up call on numerous occasions, you see. He wanted nothing more than to be in charge of your life, but he would never force himself upon you. And so, when you ignored him and went your own way, he had to try something to get you to come back to him – to get you to remember he was there."

"I don't understand."

"Mr Jones, when all was well, your master had to sit in the shadows. You didn't need him, or you thought you didn't. Could it be possible that it was he who sent that bolt out of the blue or (if you don't think he could be that cruel) at the very least used it to remind you he was there? Sometimes it might have been just a gentle nudge, but sometimes he had to shout or set the alarm bells ringing in order for you to hear him. Don't you see, when you are in the pit of despair, that is when you call upon him for help, is it not? Yes, could it not be that he used your times of ordeal in an attempt to get you to come back to him – to lean on him and not rely on yourself? Did he just want to make you aware of the fact that you were drifting away on my escalator? Wake up! Wake up! But you merely hit the snooze button and went back to sleep."

Gordon shook his head. "I didn't. I did come back to him. I did call out to him, like he wanted me to, but it didn't do my mother much good, did it? He didn't answer my prayers."

Dumas exaggerated a sigh.

"Not in the way you wanted him to. You didn't get what you wanted and so you were off again. You didn't stick with him. When the days are dark, when there seems to be no explanation, it's so much easier to believe that your master doesn't exist than to trust him. Will you stand by your master when there doesn't appear to be an answer? No. Not in your case, Mr Jones. O ye of little faith."

Dumas paused and turned his back on Gordon, running his fingers through the locks of his hair.

"Don't look so glum, Mr Jones. You're not the only one. Many more before you have failed as well. You forget that I've spent your entire life trying to get you to step on to my escalator – and keep you there." Dumas chuckled to himself. "It's not all your fault, Mr Jones," he added. "I'm just good at my job, you see... and, of course, I have many weapons in my armoury."

For one moment Gordon thought he was going to remove a sword from under his sash.

"Temptation," the demon stated. "That's my chief weapon. You cannot resist it, can you? Of course, you tried to at first, but secretly you didn't really want to break all those bad habits, did you? After falling flat on your face countless times, you eventually stopped picking yourself up. Instead of being even more determined not to yield to temptation next time, I merely convinced you that you were fighting a losing battle. It was a battle you couldn't win and so why even bother trying to fight it?"

Mr Gilmore was shaking his head. Dumas noticed the fact.

"You disagree on something, Angel Gilmore?"

The angel nodded.

"Temptation in itself is not his greatest weapon, Mr Jones – deception is," the angel explained, rising to his feet. "You see, it's possible to resist temptation when you know you're being tempted, but not so easy when you don't."

Gordon looked confused.

"Yes, he's clever," Mr Gilmore went on. "Most of the time he tricked you into thinking temptation was not even a problem in your life. Yes, he had to be a bit subtler in your case. You see, if you had been an alcoholic or into pornography – if there had been an obvious problem in your walk with your master – you might have taken steps to sort it out. You were not even aware he was tempting you most of the time. And you often only realised (not that you always did) that you had failed the test when it was too late: after you had been gossiping or criticising members of your church; you know what I mean, all those habits that you often don't even think are particularly harmful. You can't stop sinning if you don't even know you're committing a sin. And, of course, if you started to have an inkling that you were maybe doing something that was wrong, Dumas would convince you otherwise – fill your head with the same old lies. You know the ones: it doesn't really matter; I'm not hurting anyone; everyone does it. Yes, deception – that's his greatest weapon," the angel added, retaking his seat.

Dumas bowed to his foe, pleased by the fact his talents were seemingly 'appreciated'. "Yes, as I said, Mr Jones, I'm good at my job," he smirked.

Gordon looked to Mr Gilmore. "It's not fair. How are we supposed to live a good life with him deceiving us, as you put it?"

"Come, Mr Jones," Dumas intervened. "You shouldn't look at temptation as an annoyance but take it as a compliment. You must have been doing something right – at least in the early days... I've no need to tempt those already on my escalator, do I?"

Gordon was not convinced. He looked up towards the archangel.

"Why?" he pleaded. "What I don't understand is why God lets him get away with it? I thought God had defeated the enemy? Why did he let Dumas tempt me – to get at me like this?" he added, flashing the demon a look of disdain.

The archangel returned a sympathetic smile. However, it was Mr Gilmore who spoke.

"He *has* defeated him, make no mistake," the angel insisted. "Think of it like this, Mr Jones," he went on, nodding in the direction of Dumas. "*His* master may think that he is the true ruler of this world, but he and his demons are really like little yapping dogs. Trust me, their bark is worse than their bite."

Dumas was not amused by the comparison and, ironically, responded with what almost resembled a snarl.

"You don't have to be scared of him," the angel explained. "He's on a leash, you see. Demons like Dumas can only operate within the boundaries set by the true master of this world and, more importantly, the next. Yes, my master could prevent Demon Dumas *getting* at you (or should I really say 'barking' at you), but the truth is that my master actually uses him for his *own* purposes."

Dumas shook his head in disagreement but did not intervene. Gordon looked puzzled.

"You see," Mr Gilmore continued, rising to his feet again, "Demon Dumas is under the false impression that he is advancing *his* master's purposes when he tempts you – but really he is actually advancing the purposes of *mine*. When he 'gets at you' – as you put it – he is only ever permitted to go as far as the purposes of my master allow. Should the Master feel that Demon Dumas's dealings with you do not further his own purposes, he will simply not allow it to happen in the first place. Do you understand?"

"Sort of."

"Yes," the angel continued, "everything that happens in life serves a purpose – even the things composed or generated by the likes of Demon Dumas. My master will use it all to help build the character of his children. Yes, if you like, to test them. You can't be faithful to your master until you have been tempted to be unfaithful to him. Each time you resisted temptation, reacted in a positive way, you would have grown closer to your master."

Dumas had no intention of letting the angel have the final say on the matter. "Of course," the demon retaliated, "I myself am happy to let your master think that my interferences are helping to build the characters of *his* children. How foolish! In reality, most merely fail the test and – instead of getting closer to your master – only come closer to mine... just like you did, Mr Jones."

Gordon shook his head.

"Yes," Dumas went on, "I agree that everything in life is a test – to see how you react. Of course, I need not tell the court how *you* approached the rapids, Mr Jones."

Gordon looked up.

Dumas smiled. "Needless to say," the demon continued, "the river runs smooth most of the time, but everyone has to negotiate the rapids at some point. Do they cause you to capsize or are you the canoeist that revels in them – determined to push clean through rather than be pushed off course? Yes, what matters is how you approach and deal with the trials of life. It should not matter whether the waters are calm or not – the Christian should know the peace of his master in both. Did you, Mr Jones? Did the trials and tribulations of life push you closer to your master... or mine?"

Gordon could still hear the tapping from the stonemason and it was becoming an irritation to him. The noise was getting inside his head. *Tap. Tap. Tap.* It went on and seemed to be getting louder.

"You've never been very patient, have you, Mr Jones?" Dumas persisted. "You want things *now* and are not prepared to work for them. No one said trying to live the way your master wanted you to live was going to be easy. It takes time – years and years – but that is why you were given years and years. You had a lifetime. And this life of yours was meant to be all about preparing you for the next one – the one that goes on forever... the one that really matters. Let me remind you: there is only one thing you take with you to eternity and that is your character. You had a lifetime to improve it."

Gordon did not respond. He knew the demon was right.

Dumas grinned. "You are the Peter Pan of Christianity, Mr Jones. The boy who never grew up."

"What?"

"You may have grown up physically, but spiritually you're still in nappies. A baby is fed; no physical effort on the part of the baby is required. Your second birth, the day you supposedly gave your life to your master, is not the same. You don't grow naturally. This time your development requires effort on your part. You have to feed *yourself.* Physical growth cannot be stopped, but spiritual growth must be started and then worked at, otherwise you will remain a mere child in the faith. That is you, Mr Jones."

Dumas stopped and sighed. He stared at Gordon, studying him closely.

"I can't imagine you in a frilly pinafore with a feather duster in your hand, Mr Jones." The demon smiled, perhaps an indication he was doing just that.

"What do you mean?" Gordon quizzed.

"It's like this," Dumas explained. "In return for eternal life, you were supposed to give up this mortal one; to become a servant of your master.

Of course, your master doesn't force people to serve him. They have to voluntarily surrender to him themselves... but you did, didn't you, when you signed on the dotted line?" he added, tapping the cylindrical scroll that had again seemingly just appeared in his previously empty scabbard. "I know Christians keen to save souls tend not to dwell on the small print – and we've already seen that you never read it. However, I would have thought that they would have at least *told* you about your new role as a servant?"

Gordon remained silent.

"Yes," Dumas went on, "that doesn't sound so appealing, does it? It's not chic being a servant. Did you serve him, Mr Jones? Of course, it goes without saying that if you really loved your master you would have served him without question. You would have done all that you could to make him happy."

The demon shook his head and lifted up the red book that had been lying open on the bench.

"*Love the Lord your God with all your heart and with all your soul and with all your mind,*" he said slowly. "Did you, Mr Jones? Did you love him with all your heart and soul and mind? Sadly, we have little evidence to suggest that you did."

Dumas turned a page of the red book and stared at it before raising his head.

"Can you remember what else your master commanded of you, Mr Jones? Love him with all your heart and soul and mind. What else?"

"And love your neighbour," Gordon whispered.

Dumas smiled. "That's right. *As I have loved you, so you must love one another.* Yes, let's see if you did any better with the second part of the deal, shall we, Mr Jones? Did you love your neighbour?"

The smirking demon made his way to his seat.

Tap. Tap. Tap. The stonemason worked on.

16

"Lost, yesterday, somewhere between sunrise and sunset, two golden hours, each set with sixty diamond minutes. No reward is offered, for they are gone for ever."

Lost, Two Golden Hours
Horace Mann

"COURT RISE."

The archangel had left the courtroom for a brief period and was now returning to his seat. He was wiping his mouth with his handkerchief, but anyone close to him would have noticed that he had missed the smudge of jam on his cheek.

Not everyone had heard the usher utter his command and, as a result, some people had not got to their feet. The archangel did not notice. As he hauled himself on to his chair and replaced his wig, he only had eyes for dozens of men and women, boys and girls, who had started to file into the courtroom during his absence. More and more were still coming through the door that Dracula held open. The line of people grew longer and one line soon became two. Still more and more entered, forcing those already in the courtroom to budge up even further, some individuals pressing against the benches. One man managed to knock some papers from the desk of the copy typist with his trailing overcoat, though in the confusion no one seemed to notice or care.

The anxious clerk of the court stood up and attempted to converse with the archangel. The latter, unable to hear him due to much chattering and shuffling of feet, was forced to lean forward in a bid to ascertain what was going on, his chest almost flat against the bench. It looked like he might fall at any moment. It did not help that he had to use one hand to hold on to his wig, for fear it might slip down and land on the head of the clerk. It was certainly not a very dignified position for an archangel to be in.

Few of the new arrivals raised their voice above a whisper, but the general commotion caused by so many fidgeting bodies made it difficult for anyone to be heard, and the archangel felt it was a good moment to bang his gavel in a bid to re-establish order.

"Demon Dumas!" he called out, shifting his body into an upright position again. "What is the meaning of this commotion? My clerk informs me that this is your doing."

The demon stood to attention and bowed.

"It is my next witness," he smiled. "I took the liberty of calling them during your absence to save some time."

"You say *them?*" the archangel inquired suspiciously, casting an eye on the now packed courtroom floor. "Exactly how many are you calling?"

"I believe there are still several hundred in the court foyer," Dumas responded. "And there are still more outside. Sadly, there won't be room for *all* of them."

Gordon could no longer hear the stonemason at work and once again forgot his presence, not surprising since he was also now out of sight, a number of witnesses crowded around his work, more due to necessity than curiosity. One woman had the nerve to place her handbag on the top of the work of art, though the stonemason remained focused and continued tapping away, even if few were now aware of the fact he was doing so.

Like everyone else, Gordon was studying the witnesses with intent. He was looking for a familiar face among them. He convinced himself that he had set eyes on at least one or two before, but was certainly of the opinion that he did not know any of them personally. What was perhaps odd – odd for this particular court case – was that all of the witnesses were in contemporary dress, a fact that Gordon had initially failed to notice. Most were clad in jeans and jumpers. A minority wore clothes that gave away their profession: nurses, policemen and fire officers in full uniform. Many of the children present were in their pyjamas or dressing gowns. Some of the adults were wrapped in bath robes, their hair still wet, while a handful of more unfortunate individuals only had bath towels to protect their modesty, steam coming from the uncovered parts of their skin, their bath-time presumably having been rudely interrupted by a celestial summons.

Gordon found himself drawn to an individual dressed as Santa Claus. For one moment he wondered whether he was the genuine article.

The usher was frantically trying to bring some order to the situation, but only succeeded in getting lost in the crowd himself. The main floor of the courtroom was now full and there was nowhere for anyone to budge. It was also impossible to close the courtroom door, meaning that a couple of people remained stranded in the doorway, halfway in the also packed foyer and halfway in the courtroom itself.

Mr Gilmore attempted to look to Gordon for an explanation, but too many people stood between him and the dock in which his client was standing. The diminutive angel briefly raised himself on to the tips of his toes, but it had no effect. He was still unable to see over the heads of those forced to stand in the aisle that separated him from Gordon. In a desperate attempt to communicate with his charge, he took the rather unusual step of standing on his chair, but stood down almost immediately when he heard a cough. He thought it was the archangel reprimanding him, but it was, in fact, Dumas. The demon had ceremoniously cleared his throat in order to signal that he was ready to proceed. He rarely spoke from his bench, preferring to strut his stuff on the open space in front of the clerk. However, his witnesses now occupied that space and he found himself hemmed in between his chair and table.

It took a few moments to establish silence or at least to reach a level of noise that was acceptable to the demon. He now had the attention of his witnesses, but he could not stop them coughing and sneezing. One even had the audacity to choose this moment to blow their nose. A baby was still wailing, despite its mother's attempts to pacify the child.

Dumas glanced down at the red book that lay open on the bench in front of him, before raising his head, his final deliberate act being a signal to all that he was about to begin.

"Please accept my humble apologies for the disturbance," the demon started, offering another condescending bow. "It is for the benefit of Mr Jones that I call so many witnesses. The more there are, the more chance he has, you see."

Of course, Gordon couldn't see (figuratively) at this particular moment. He had no idea what the demon was up to. He couldn't see (physically) much either. He could just about view Dumas at the far end of the bench that he shared with Mr Gilmore. Gordon was the sort of person that liked his own space and his main concern at this particular moment was the fact that one witness was so close to him, he could smell his breath. He quickly ascertained that the man had been eating pickled onions. He wondered why people insisted on eating pickled onions at Christmas and seemingly at no other time of the year.

"Who would like to take the oath first?" the demon grinned mischievously. The clerk stood up and turned to the archangel. The latter puffed out his cheeks and then blew out the air.

"May I suggest they take the oath collectively?" the clerk offered. It was no surprise the relieved archangel agreed wholeheartedly to the proposal.

The usher took several minutes to force his way through the crowd to reach the witness box, which was, ironically, empty. He retrieved the Bible and card. "Would you repeat these words after me," he bellowed, addressing the crowd before him.

And for one surreal moment, Dracula became the 'conductor' of a 'choir'. He threw out a sentence and then, when it was time for his 'singers' to repeat the line, mimed it again, his hand waving an imaginary baton in a bid to get them to respond in unison. However, more than one or two were too slow off the mark. Perhaps they lacked inches and their view of the 'conductor' had been blocked, but the resultant chant (one could scarcely call it a song) from the hundreds of witnesses was almost inaudible. The sound reverberated around the courtroom walls and it made Gordon shudder.

The archangel signalled to the usher that the procedure was satisfactory. "You had better begin, Demon Dumas, and it better be worth it," he added under his breath.

Dumas nodded in response and launched himself on to the bench via his chair. The act was so swift and graceful, the archangel did not have a chance to intervene, as unlikely as that would have been anyway. He merely removed his glasses and rubbed his weary eyes. It looked like the novelty of presiding over a trial was wearing off somewhat.

"My friends," Dumas started, "I must firstly thank you for your attendance this evening, on what is, of course, a very special day for you *Christians*. It is a time when you like to celebrate your master's birthday... watching television, I do believe."

"Or playing charades," Gordon muttered under his breath. An elderly lady had also responded to the demon, by way of a tut. Dumas held aloft his hat and stared at the perpetrator, finding no problem in picking her out from the crowd. "And rest assured, madam, you will not miss one second of that *Coronation Street* double bill," he smiled.

The woman murmured something in reply, but Dumas pretended not to hear her. He waved his hat towards the jury but addressed the hordes of people below him. "I do not think it is necessary for the jurors to know each of you by name, but your addresses are indeed of relevance. If you would be so good, please tell the court your postcode."

There was no 'conductor' to assist the witnesses on this occasion. Dracula did not feel obliged to aid them. It meant the six letters and numbers were again muttered more in tandem than unison, though Gordon could have repeated every one in the order that they were delivered. He knew instantly that every witness standing before him shared his own postcode.

Dumas continued, pacing the bench he was standing on, going as far as the briefcase of Mr Gilmore that rested on the tabletop. "Residents of South Buckinghamshire, I have only one question to put to you."

The archangel looked relieved.

"It is this," Dumas went on, turning to go back the other way, his tunic almost fluttering in the face of Mr Gilmore, so sharp was his turn. "Firstly, I ask you to look at this man who stands before you..." He paused and the witnesses shuffled their positions in order to focus on Gordon, though some were not able to set eyes upon the defendant due to being a few inches smaller than those around them and so tightly packed. Gordon sensed he was blushing. It was unnerving to have so many eyes focused on him.

"Tell me," Dumas ordered, stopping abruptly, "is this man that stands before you a Christian?"

There were one or two muffled responses. Most people remained silent.

"What do you mean?" one witness shouted. "Whether he went to church or not?"

"How are we supposed to know?" another sounded. "I've never met him before."

Dumas folded his arms, content with the fact he had got the response he was looking for. He turned to face Gordon.

"What are you looking at me like that for?" Gordon twitched, looking up at the demon, an even more imposing figure now that he had the added height of the bench he was standing upon. "How are they supposed to know whether I'm a Christian or not? I don't even know these people."

"But they are *your* neighbours, Mr Jones," Dumas responded quickly. "These are the people you were supposed to love."

"What? Don't be ridiculous," Gordon exclaimed. "I'm sure they're very nice people, but how can I love them? I've told you, I don't even know them."

"Yes, you do, Mr Jones," a man clad in a blue dressing gown chirped up. "I work in the mini-supermarket opposite the cemetery. You get your paper from me, some days."

Gordon squinted. "Well, yes," he admitted, "your face does look a bit familiar."

"And I live opposite you, Mr Jones," a frail lady close to where Gordon was standing whispered. "I see you every day reversing your car out of the drive."

"Do you?" Gordon responded tersely. "Can't say I recognise you... Sorry."

"I don't get out much these days," the woman replied. "It's not easy for me, you see, not since I had my hip operation."

Dumas shook his head. "Oh dear, Mr Jones. If just one person could tell me that you were a Christian, your troubles would be over. We can bring an end to this trial and hang out the bunting. We will have the evidence required to prove that you indeed do belong to your master."

He stopped and addressed the crowd below him, waving his hat theatrically in the air as he spoke. "I repeat, for the sake of Mr Jones here; I repeat, does anyone know if this man is a Christian?"

There was silence. A few people shook their heads. Others merely returned expressions of confusion or indifference.

"Thank you," Dumas bowed. "That will be all. You can return to your television sets none the wiser to this little charade. Au revoir, my friends, and I won't spoil the surprise, madam," Dumas grinned, focusing on the woman who had interrupted him with a tut, "only it's not a happy ending!"

The witnesses started to head for the door from which they had entered, though 'headed' was not really the right word. All they really managed to do was to turn to face it. It would take some time for the backlog to clear. Dumas looked to the archangel and smiled.

"If you would permit me?" The demon did not wait for an answer and clicked his fingers. The witnesses collectively disappeared in a flash and all was quiet again. The archangel frowned.

The athletic Dumas jumped to the floor, this time without the aid of his chair. He made no noise when his boots hit the ground.

"Well, Mr Jones?" he inquired, placing his hat on the table. "Have you anything to say?"

"That wasn't fair," Gordon protested. "What you failed to point out to the jury is that the church I attend is a few miles from my house, so none of the congregation live close to me. The point I'm trying to make is that we don't share the same postcode. One of the members at my church would have been able to tell you I was a Christian if they had been here."

"You mean one of your friends?"

"Yes, if you like. None of those people that were here a minute ago knew me, not intimately at any rate. Now if you were to ask someone that knew me well..."

Dumas smiled and looked to the usher. "I call Stuart Attwood," he announced.

Gordon instantly looked to Mr Gilmore and nodded. At last the defendant recognised a name. "It's all right. I used to work with him," Gordon whispered across the aisle to his guardian. The angel smiled tentatively.

Dracula led a middle-aged man into the witness box. The man never looked at Gordon. He was in awe of his surroundings and could not stop fidgeting as he took the oath. Gordon had hoped to make eye contact with his friend, but the apprehensive Mr Attwood never gave him the chance and refrained from trying to steal even a glance at the defendant.

Dumas left his bench and walked to the witness box, Mr Attwood watching him attentively. The demon stopped and placed the palms of his gloved hands on the ledge of the dock, leaning forward so that his head was a mere foot away from the eyes of the very average-looking individual that stood before him.

"Please give the court your full name and address, Mr Attwood."

"Stuart George Attwood, 34 Grove Terrace."

"Thank you," Dumas sniffed, at last retreating a little from the personal space of the intimidated Mr Attwood. However, the witness still never dared take his eyes off the demon.

"Do you know this man that stands before you?" Dumas asked him.

Instinctively, Mr Attwood knew where Gordon was positioned. His eyes fixed on his associate within an instant, now relieved he had been given permission to avert them from the demon. However, he was just as

210

quick to revert them back, fearing in some way that something would happen to him if he didn't. "I do," he coughed nervously.

Gordon snapped. "Well, of course he does! You know full well that he does. We worked in the same office for seven years! My desk was opposite his. Isn't that right, Stu?"

The witness returned a sheepish smile, but never turned his head towards Gordon.

Dumas turned his back on Mr Attwood as he addressed him.

"I have only one question for you, Mr Attwood. Do you know if Mr Jones is a Christian?"

Gordon stared at his friend. Mr Gilmore had looked disinterested, but now pushed up his glasses in anticipation of the answer.

Mr Attwood looked almost disappointed by the question. He clearly believed it to be a trivial one. The demon might have just asked him if he enjoyed playing chess or preferred his chips with or without vinegar. He looked nonplussed. He shook his head, but his answer contrasted that particular gesture. "Yes. He probably is."

Mr Gilmore had not expected that reply. He looked up at the archangel, who also seemed surprised. Gordon smiled.

Dumas remained cool. "You say 'probably'? Why do you say 'probably'? Can you not say for sure? Please concentrate, Mr Attwood; it is a very serious question."

The witness straightened his body, but there was still a look of confusion etched on his face.

"What evidence do you have to back up your answer, Mr Attwood?" Dumas persisted. "Why would you say that Mr Jones is *probably* a Christian? Please, it is important."

There was a brief moment of silence. Clearly, Mr Attwood wanted to give the right answer, though was not sure what that might be.

"Well, I know Jonesy went to church," he concluded.

Gordon was beaming. He wanted to attract the attention of Mr Gilmore. He genuinely believed that this was a pivotal moment in his trial. It was swinging his way, at last. However, the angel did not respond, pretending not to notice that Gordon was staring at him. Mr Gilmore was studying the witness intently and his facial expression was one of apprehension. He certainly did not portray a figure about to uncork the Champagne bottles. Failing to gain the attention of his guardian, Gordon turned to view the jurors, hoping to catch one of them perhaps making a note of this seemingly important moment. No one did.

"He went to church?" Dumas reiterated. "You say that Mr Jones went to church. Of course, he has been doing that practically all his life, even before he supposedly became a Christian. You may not be aware, Mr Attwood, but the court has already established that fact. Do you have any other evidence?"

Mr Attwood shook his head. "Not really."

"So the only evidence that you can put forward is that you know for a fact that Mr Jones was a churchgoer?"

"I suppose so."

"Did he talk about his church much?"

"Occasionally. One or two times, enough that I knew he went to church every Sunday morning."

"Did he ever mention..." Dumas hesitated, clearly reluctant to complete the sentence. "Did he ever mention... Jesus?"

"Jesus?"

"Jesus Christ," Dumas repeated, more boldly this time, almost as though it had become easier to say now that he had said it once.

"I don't think so," Mr Attwood replied.

"Thank you, Mr Attwood. That will be all. I am much obliged."

The usher opened the door of the witness box and led the confused Mr Attwood out of the courtroom. He did not attempt to acknowledge Gordon. It would have been in vain anyway. Gordon had his head bowed and did not see his friend disappear, his jubilation now having quickly turned to shame. Mr Gilmore was pressing his hand against his forehead, clearly agitated.

"Why didn't you talk about Jesus, Mr Jones?" Dumas turned to the defendant.

Gordon lifted his head but remained silent.

"Let me answer the question for you, Mr Jones. Can I be as bold as to say that you were embarrassed by your master? It's not very cool to talk about Jesus, is it? You had no problem talking about church, lots of people with no or little faith go to church, but it's a different story when it comes to talking about your relationship with Jesus. You can talk about church to your heart's content, those endless jumble sales and charity coffee mornings, but, whatever you do, Mr Jones, don't say the 'J' word!"

Gordon was motionless. No one said anything.

Dumas continued. "Did you not know you were given a mission, Mr Jones? Once you had received the good news of your salvation, it was up to you to spread the message. If you knew the cure for cancer, would you not share it with others? If you saw a man drowning, would you not offer your hand to pull him from the water? If you knew there was a bomb on a plane, would you not tell someone?"

Still Gordon remained silent.

The demon went on. "Did you not believe that people were destined for eternal damnation unless they turned to... let's call him, in case I cause you some embarrassment, JC, shall we?" He stopped and stared at Gordon. "Jesus. Jesus. Jesus!" Dumas chanted. "To Christians, that should be the most beautiful word in the world. I find it strange that you should have found it so difficult to say on earth."

Dumas paused for effect. He knew no one would dare interrupt him at this point. There was nothing more he wanted than for the jury to digest the last few moments.

"Did you see that thriller on the TV last night, Mr Jones?"

Gordon looked up. The tone in the voice of the demon had switched from solemnity to joviality in an instant. "The one about the man who loses his memory and..."

"Oh, that one!" Gordon interrupted. "It's my favourite."

"I know," Dumas replied. "Perhaps you would like to tell the jury about it."

Gordon did. He wasted no time in relaying the plot. He barely paused for breath. Mr Gilmore took off his glasses and shook his head. There was nothing he could do. At last Gordon stopped, aware that the accusing eyes of the demon were upon him, his arms now folded.

"Sorry," Gordon said. "I get a bit carried away sometimes."

"Especially when you really love something," Dumas continued. "You like nothing better than talking about the things you love, don't you, Mr Jones? Shall we talk about another film or Fulham? You could talk about football until the cows come home. Or what about that new sports model in the car showroom? Or perhaps..." The demon stopped. He knew he did not need any further examples. "Why didn't you talk about Jesus, Mr Jones? Did you not love him too? Did you not have the same passion for him? Did you not want to share what he has done for you with others? Why were you not standing on the rooftops shouting out how much Jesus loves you? You had seven years to talk to Mr Attwood about Jesus."

Suddenly the demon threw a Bible towards Gordon to gasps from the public gallery. It landed on the floor in front of the dock, open at one of the Gospels. "*Go into all the world and preach the good news,* Mr Jones. You can read it for yourself. I'm sure you're familiar with the passage."

Gordon made no attempt to look at the Bible. He shook his head despairingly, before turning pleadingly towards the archangel.

"I just found it difficult. I'm no missionary," he said meekly. "I could never go abroad – too many creepy crawlies for starters. I can't stand anything like that. I suppose that explains why I got rid of so many of them," he added, referring to the coffin-load that Dumas had earlier produced. "I'm sorry, but I'm a home-loving sort of person. I could never go to Africa."

"Go to Africa?" Dumas mused. "My dear, Mr Jones, you didn't even go into Buckinghamshire!"

Gordon sighed. "I didn't know what to say to people. I haven't got the gift, you see. I'm no preacher."

"You only had to talk to them. You have no problem talking about that latest film or football match. You were supposed to be a witness for your master, that's all. It wasn't your job to convert people."

"It wasn't?"

"No. He only asked you to be a witness for him. All you had to do was lead them to your master. He does the rest. You were not even expected to argue his case or prove his existence, just to talk about what he has done for you, to share your story."

Gordon groaned. "You mean my testimony, like when I became a Christian. But my testimony is not the most exciting; you know that already. I wasn't some hoodlum who gave up dealing with drugs. You know that there was not exactly a bolt of lightning or anything like that when I became a Christian. Who wants to listen to my testimony?"

"You're a fool, Mr Jones," Dumas responded. "Testimonies like yours are even more important. Your story may not be jaw-dropping, but then, few are. Don't you see, there are millions just like you who live ordinary lives that would find it easier to relate to someone just like them? As inspiring a tale of a mass murderer turning from his wicked ways is... it is hardly relevant to the average man on the street."

Gordon knew he could not argue, but he remained on the defensive. "All right, I understand what you're saying, but you can't just bring the subject up. All those neighbours you had here would have run a mile if I had started talking to them about Jesus. Most people do. Be honest."

Dumas deliberately shook his head. "You didn't even need to talk about your master if you didn't want to. You only had to be a witness."

"What do you mean?"

"*Preach the gospel – and use words if necessary.* I think that famous quotation was pinned up on the missionary board at your church."

Mr Gilmore was nodding his head in agreement.

"Don't you understand, Mr Jones?" Dumas continued. "People should have seen that you were a Christian – a servant."

"Not that again."

"I see that word still irks you, Mr Jones. Don't you get it? In heaven – if that was where you were destined to go – you would have served your master forever, but you were supposed to serve him on earth too."

"I did," Gordon responded doubtfully.

"Did you? It's not a popular job, of course. Who leaves school with the desire to become a servant? Everyone wants to be the one in charge. All through your working life you focused on the next rung of your career ladder, Mr Jones, to get higher and higher, but your CV will be of no importance in eternity. Your master will not measure your greatness on whether you made it to the boardroom or not. He doesn't care about your status or earthly achievements, only your service. Did you serve him? All he wants to know is what you did for others. You may not have a gift for preaching, Mr Jones, but no skill is required to sweep the hall after church or clean the toilet."

"I *did* do things like that."

"Once or twice, I have to admit… and rest assured the vicar noticed. Of course, you made sure of that. You were not so obliging when there was merely an audience of one – your master. That is who you should have been trying to impress." He stopped. "Were you a witness through your service, Mr Jones? No. You never became a servant. The only one you served was yourself. If you had stopped worrying about your own needs, you might have seen those all around you." Dumas paused again. "Love your neighbour as yourself? Of course you didn't, Mr Jones. You would have had to love your master to have done that. Your aim in life should have been to please your creator and nothing pleases him more than when someone does something good for another. If you have no desire to serve your master in this way, to show love to your neighbours, one has to question if that master is at the centre of your life. You cannot be a non-serving Christian, you see. That is a contradiction."

Dumas stopped. Suddenly he produced a bundle of bank notes from, presumably, a hidden pocket within his tunic.

"Do you know that there are 86,400 seconds in one day, Mr Jones? Did you know that?" He never waited for an answer. "If you had been given £86,400, what would you have done with it?" he asked, waving the bundle of notes in front of his face.

Gordon shook his head. "I don't know."

"I would like to think that you would have given some of it to those in need."

"Yes, I would have done that. I'm not mean. I tithed and I gave money to charity. That's not one of my faults. You can't have a go at me for that. Yes, I would have given lots of it away – if I had had that sort of money."

Dumas smiled. "I don't doubt you, Mr Jones, but that would have been easy if you had so much of it. Of course, you're right, you didn't have that sort of money, though you did have 86,400 seconds in every day. How many of those 86,400 did you give away? As I have said, time is more precious than money. That would have been the greatest sacrifice you could have made – giving away your time. Yes, how many seconds did you sacrifice for your master and his people?"

Gordon bowed his head. He did not need to answer.

Dumas shook his head. "Of course, how Christians can use that word 'sacrifice', I do not know. How can you talk of making sacrifices to the son of God?" he mused.

The demon lifted his hat from the table and placed it on his head, as though it was to make it clear to everyone that he was coming to a conclusion.

"This jury has to decide whether you are a Christian, Mr Jones," he declared. "How do they do that? They must decide whether you believed or not. And the evidence is found in your actions. It is what you *do* – or don't do – that reveals what you *really* believe."

The demon turned to face the jury as he said the last word of the sentence. All twelve sat motionless. In fact, they had barely moved for several minutes, transfixed by all that had gone on in front of them.

In the ensuing silence, Gordon could hear the stonemason again. *Tap. Tap. Tap.*

Dumas noticed the fact.

"Shall I tell you what he's doing, Mr Jones, in case you haven't already guessed? He is inscribing an epitaph on your tombstone."

Gordon raised his eyebrows. The stonemason did not look up and continued with his work.

"What do you think will be your epitaph, Mr Jones?" Dumas asked. "*Well done, good and faithful servant,* may I suggest?" He paused. "Lots of people have fun writing their own epitaph when they're still alive. Some even go as far as to insist on it being inscribed on their tombstone. It's usually something pretty flattering, of course. You rarely find the truth carved in stone."

Gordon remained silent as the demon again looked towards the jury.

"I put it to this court that you did not love your master or his people, Mr Jones. The only person you *really* loved was yourself. When you supposedly became a Christian, your mission in life should have become a simple one. It was to serve your master and his people. You never served either. You carried on serving yourself. That is not the mission of a Christian. And so I ask again, Mr Jones, is there any evidence to prove you were a Christian?" Dumas smiled. "I hope, for your sake, that Angel Gilmore can find some."

The demon turned his eyes to the open red book that was still lying on the bench. He picked it up and closed it, caressing the spine with a gloved finger.

"I have taken the liberty of writing your epitaph, Mr Jones," he said, walking towards the filing cabinet.

The stonemason had put down his hammer and chisel, and now stood beside his work, admiring it like an artist would study his finished painting.

The demon grinned. He leaned against the filing cabinet and looked towards the tombstone. "Here lies Mr Jones... mission accomplished. No, sorry, that's not right, is it?" he mocked. "Here lies Mr Jones... mission *unaccomplished.*" He opened the filing cabinet and placed the red book within it. With the tip of his gloved finger he gently pushed the open drawer and it slammed shut.

17

"Wandering between two worlds, one dead,
The other powerless to be born."

Stanzas from the Grande Chartreuse
Matthew Arnold

GORDON SHUDDERED. HE SLUMPED TO HIS CHAIR AND bowed his head. The noise of the filing cabinet drawer slamming shut was still reverberating around his ears. No one spoke and Gordon sensed they were all waiting for him to look up. He had no desire to do so but knew he could not remain in this position for much longer. Slowly, he lifted his head, expecting to set eyes on the smug smile of Dumas. It was therefore something of a surprise when the first thing he saw were the coloured lights of a Christmas tree – the Christmas tree in his living room, to be precise. He was back home. He was even sitting in his favourite armchair. Was it all a dream? No. The magenta-coloured fairy light was not flickering. All was still. His silhouetted friends remained where he had left them, rooted to the spot, none betraying the possibility that they might have slipped away and only readopted their absurd poses when they had seen their housemate returning. No, this was no game. Gordon did not take long to establish that fact, though he still felt the need to glance at the carriage clock on the mantelpiece. In the dim light, he could just about make out where the hands of the timepiece were positioned, and established – if he needed any confirmation – that it was still 7:34pm.

Gordon did not at first notice Mr Gilmore, but he sensed something moving in the corner of his eye and he turned his head to see the angel emerging from the hallway. He had a white envelope in his hand.

"It's for you," the angel said, handing it over to Gordon. "It was on your doormat."

Gordon rose from his chair and started to open the envelope. Incredible as it may seem, that became his focus and the question as to why he was now back in the living room of his home was momentarily put to the back of his mind.

"Strange," he mused. "Someone must have put it through the letterbox this evening, when we were playing charades, but we usually hear the letterbox. It makes such a noise."

He removed the Christmas card. The picture on the front was of a crib: the baby Jesus within, a lone star in the sky illuminating the child's face. Gordon did not look at the image, too intent on discovering the identity of the card's sender. He hurriedly opened it. The message inside, scrawled in a ballpoint pen, was a simple one, wishing Gordon a merry Christmas and signed with "much love". However, the name of the sender was not legible, their signature seemingly written in haste. Gordon could only make out that the name began with a 'G'.

"That's weird," Gordon continued to reflect, examining the empty envelope in case it contained a clue to the identity of the sender. "I've no idea who it's from. As you've discovered, I don't know many of my neighbours – and none whose name begins with a 'G'."

Mr Gilmore peered over Gordon's shoulder.

"Didn't send *yourself* a card, did you?" he quipped. "People do resort to that, you know."

"Very funny. Anyway, why would someone only post it tonight? It's Christmas Day. It's a bit late now, isn't it? Christmas is over."

"They could have saved the card for next year?" the angel suggested, aware of the fact that the thrifty Gordon had been known to recycle Christmas cards in the past. Gordon shrugged his shoulders and placed the card on the mantelpiece, knocking another on to the floor as he did so. He instantly picked it up and made room for both. Mr Gilmore had moved to the dining table and placed his briefcase upon it. He opened the lid and started to shuffle some papers within.

The actions of the angel reminded Gordon that he had a more pressing mystery on his mind.

"Why are we back here?" he queried, watching Mr Gilmore continue to fumble through the contents of his briefcase. "Has the trial finished? I didn't expect to come home again."

"No, it hasn't finished," the angel answered. "Dumas has had his say, that's all. Now it's our turn."

"What do you mean?"

Mr Gilmore looked up. "It's our chance to prove to the jury that you are indeed a Christian, Mr Jones."

"Oh," Gordon exclaimed. "That's good, then, isn't it?"

The angel did not reply. He was now casting his eye around the room.

"What are you looking for?" Gordon asked.

"Evidence."

"What evidence?"

"Any evidence that will help to prove that you are a Christian, Mr Jones."

Gordon looked around and shook his head, an expression of bewilderment on his face, not that anything should have surprised him now.

"Why me?" he sighed, slumping into his armchair. "I cannot have been the only Christian to have messed up their life. Why did Dumas pick on me? It's not fair."

Gordon stopped and stared at Mr Gilmore. The angel was now on his knees. He had opened a cupboard and was rummaging through a box.

"Mr Gilmore?" Gordon coughed nervously. "Can I ask you a question?"

"Of course," the angel replied without looking up.

"I just want to know if you think we're going to win this case. Do we have a chance?"

Gordon did not wait for an answer, but continued to reflect. "I know I'm a Christian, but Dumas is right, isn't he? I *have* made a mess of it all. I didn't serve God or his people. I only really thought about myself."

Mr Gilmore stopped what he was doing and turned on his knees to face Gordon. He smiled, his glasses slipping down the bridge of his nose. That smile was the reassurance Gordon needed. It was not one of sympathy or pity, but hope.

Gordon shook his head. "I still don't understand. A moment ago, when I found myself back here, I thought it had all been a dream. Is it, Mr Gilmore? Is it a dream? Am I still dreaming? Am I going to wake up and get the chance to redeem my ways, like Ebenezer Scrooge? Is the point of all this to get me to mend my ways – to give me a second chance? Is it a dream, Mr Gilmore? Is it?"

The angel did not look at Gordon. He had returned to the contents of the box in the cupboard.

Gordon continued to ponder his fate. "Yes, what if this is some sort of vision? Maybe God is doing all this to teach me a lesson, to get me to buck up my ideas? It worked for Scrooge. That would explain everything. What would be the point of my trial, if not? If I'm already assured a place in heaven, if you say that I am – and that is what God has promised me, after all – why all this? It would all be a waste of time if it wasn't to teach me a lesson. I must still have some time left on earth. Yes, it is a dream, isn't it? I am going to wake up soon and get a chance to do better. Am I right, Mr Gilmore?"

The angel closed the cupboard door and sprang to his feet in an instant, belying his many years.

He looked at Gordon closely.

"Do you have any salt and vinegar crisps?" he inquired, looking to a half-empty bowl. "I'm not so fond of cheese and onion."

Gordon sighed.

Mr Gilmore did not attempt to look for any replacement nourishment and Gordon, if he had been a little sharper, would have realised that the angel was merely attempting to evade his question.

Gordon shook his head sorrowfully.

"Oh, cheer up, Mr Jones," the angel chirped. "It's our turn to put Dumas in his place now. It's going to be all right, you'll see. The trumpets will soon be sounding to welcome you home."

"Trumpets?" Gordon reflected. "Will they really be playing? For me; for someone who has spent his entire life putting himself first?"

Gordon got up from his chair and moved towards Bill. He stared into his face. "I wish I could talk to them one final time. I've got so much to tell them. I think people thought I was a bit boring, but have I got a story to tell now!" He moved to Alex and readjusted the black and white scarf around his neck. "I wish I could warn you all – let you all know that it *really* is real, that there is a heaven. I'm not saying I didn't believe it was true," Gordon added, momentarily turning towards his guardian, "but somehow when you're on earth, you don't think much about it… you don't grasp it totally. Oh, why don't we *really* believe? Why did I waste my time running about like a headless chicken? Everything that I thought was important on earth means nothing now. Why didn't I just serve him?"

Gordon concluded his soliloquy with a shake of his head.

Mr Gilmore was now standing facing Gordon. He had his hands in his pockets and was listening intently. He smiled and nodded in agreement, before turning to a china vase on the mantelpiece. He gingerly upturned it, expecting something to fall out. He was disappointed when nothing did.

"What exactly are you looking for?" Gordon inquired.

"Evidence, Mr Jones, I've told you. I'm looking for evidence."

"But what sort of evidence?"

"I don't know exactly, but anything that might help your case. Where's your Bible?"

"It's on the shelf – but I thought Dumas had it."

Mr Gilmore lifted Gordon's Bible from the bookcase. Gordon did not seek an explanation as to how it had come to be back in its original place. The angel looked like he was about to blow the dust from it.

"Don't!" Gordon intervened. "It wasn't funny the first time."

"What about some Bible study notes, prayer lists, anything like that?" the angel suggested, his voice betraying a growing sense of urgency.

Gordon shook his head. "I've got a Graham Kendrick worship CD somewhere. Will that help?"

Mr Gilmore grinned.

"Your fish!" he exclaimed suddenly. "I forgot about that. Where's your fish?"

"It's over there," Gordon nodded in the direction of Blubber. "I just hope he'll go to a good home. They'd better not flush him down the toilet," he added, remembering the coffin full of insects that Dumas had produced.

"Not that fish," Mr Gilmore returned, sifting through some drawers. "I'm sure you put it in here. I must have made a note of it somewhere." The angel flashed a glance towards the mess of papers on the table next to his briefcase and decided he would have more joy continuing his search than referring to his notes.

"Why would I keep a fish in a drawer?" a confused Gordon queried.

"Not a real fish," Mr Gilmore sighed. "The symbol of a Christian – that little metallic badge that clipped on to your shirt. I distinctly remember you wearing one in your early days."

"Oh! I haven't seen that for years."

"Shame," Mr Gilmore reflected. "It would have been good if you'd been wearing it when you died."

Gordon returned a look of dismay. "Displaying a fish on your shirt is no proof you're a Christian," he pointed out. "I thought you'd be the first to say that, Mr Gilmore. Lots of non-Christians wear crosses around their necks."

"I know, Mr Jones. It's just that wearing that fish is proof that you were not embarrassed by revealing you were a Christian, or, if you were, you were at least willing to endure the embarrassment for your master.

That is the point of those fish – or is the correct word fishes – I never know? It is for people to inquire as to why you are wearing a fish. The fact you were happy for them to do so shows that you *did* – despite what Dumas implied – want to tell others about Jesus. What's this?"

Mr Gilmore held up a piece of paper with a list of names on it. "Is *this* a prayer list?"

"Sort of – it's a Fulham team sheet," a smirking Gordon replied.

The angel smiled. "I'm glad you've chirped up a bit, Mr Jones – not lost your sense of humour."

The angel pulled a chair from under the dining table and proceeded to stand upon it. He was still too short to reach the top row of the bookcase and had to squint to read the spines of the books.

"You don't have many books on theology, do you?" he concluded with disappointment.

"Veronica has a few on *sociology,* if that's any help?" Gordon responded playfully.

Mr Gilmore jumped from the chair. "Oh well, the physical evidence is not so important, of course," he said. The angel retrieved a pen and a notebook from his briefcase. "It's people that matter most," he continued. "Now, is there anyone that I should know about?"

"What do you mean?"

"Witnesses," Mr Gilmore explained. "It's time to sort out who will speak on your behalf. I know the obvious ones: your housemates and your friends at church, but is there anyone else I should know about, someone not so obvious? It would be good if a non-Christian could speak on your behalf."

Gordon stroked his chin. "There's Stuart Attwood…"

Mr Gilmore frowned and handed Gordon the notebook and pen. "Now, write down some names of some non-Christians – anyone that you might have spoken to about your faith. You can probably omit Stuart Attwood," he added with a hint of sarcasm in his voice.

Gordon sat down at the table and started to write, as Mr Gilmore dipped his head back into his open briefcase. After a few moments, Gordon gingerly pushed the notebook along the table towards the angel. Mr Gilmore popped his head from around the lid and peered at the list over his glasses. His face did not betray his feelings.

"What's the matter?" Gordon asked.

"Is that it?"

"Yes."

The angel sighed and tore the sheet of paper from the notebook. He crushed it into a ball and tossed it over his shoulder. It fell just short of the wastepaper basket. Gordon got up and walked towards it. When he was sure the angel was not watching, he picked it up and placed it into the bin. Mr Gilmore had his back to Gordon and so his charge did not see him smiling.

Gordon returned to the table and tried to sneak a look at some of the pieces of paper that Mr Gilmore had now spread out upon it. Most were filled with writing that was barely legible, the handwriting making it almost impossible for Gordon to secretly read any of the contents without revealing the fact that he was doing just that. However, the angel was looking intently at a sheet with just one word upon it and Gordon could not fail to notice it. The word was 'Grace' and it was followed by a question mark.

"For once and for all, who's Grace?" Gordon inquired. "I keep seeing that name – you had it on another piece of paper in court."

Mr Gilmore underlined the name with a pencil and lifted his head thoughtfully.

"I was going to ask *you* that, Mr Jones. Do you know anyone called Grace?"

"No. I don't think so."

"Strange," Mr Gilmore replied, shaking his head. "That name keeps coming back to me. I just have some vague feeling that you *do* know someone called Grace and that she may be able to help us."

Gordon shook his head. "No. I definitely don't know anyone of that name."

The angel started to bundle his papers into his briefcase, not attempting to put them in any order. "Not to worry," he said. "Perhaps I've mixed it up with someone else."

Gordon looked at the mess and could only agree, Mr Gilmore now attempting to shut the lid of the briefcase, the protruding papers at first preventing him from doing so.

"Where are we going?" Gordon asked, sensing that the angel had concluded his business.

"Upstairs. I haven't seen your room yet. You don't mind, do you?"

Gordon shook his head. "Be my guest."

He followed the angel up the stairs. Gordon felt a pang of sorrow when he entered his room. It already felt a long time since he had seen it.

Mr Gilmore did not take long to look around. It was the tidiest room in the house.

"That will do," the angel concluded. "There's not much of interest here. Now, I've just got to prepare the summonses for your witnesses. I can leave you here, can't I?"

Gordon shrugged his shoulders. "I suppose so. How long are you going to be? I don't like staying in the house on my own. It's creepy. I think I'll stay in my room – I don't like seeing my friends in that state."

Gordon sat on his bed and began to tug at a loose piece of thread on his duvet cover. "Mr Gilmore?" he hesitated. "Would it be possible to…" He looked up at the angel with teasing eyes, like a child that wanted another sweet but didn't want to ask for one. He was secretly hoping that Mr Gilmore already knew what the question was going to be and that he would duly answer it. The angel remained silent and Gordon was forced to continue. "Remember that time when we went into the future, for my wake?" he stuttered. "Can we do that again – while I'm waiting? There's so much I'd like to see."

He did not expect his wish to be granted. The angel smiled. "I don't suppose it will do any harm. In the meantime, try to come up with some more names of anyone that might be able to help you – and do try to recall if you know someone called Grace."

"I've told you I definitely don't," Gordon insisted, closing his eyes in anticipation of his journey to some futuristic world.

The angel clicked his fingers and disappeared. Gordon opened his eyes. He was somewhat disappointed to find himself still in his bedroom. He was in no doubt it was his room, but not as he knew it. There were one or two additions. The first thing he noticed was a different football calendar on the wall above his computer. The page for December was on display, but it was not the same picture he had seen when he woke up this morning. Indeed, it was not the same calendar. He had not seen it before and he could not even recognise the kit his favourite team was wearing. The players in the picture were decked out in the appropriate colours, but there were subtle changes on the shirts that they wore. He did not even recognise one of the players in the action shot.

The perplexed Gordon sat on his bed and stroked the duvet cover. *That* definitely belonged to him. He had had it for years and it looked like it too. Was this the future? He glanced at the calendar again. Of course, *that* would reveal the year! Gordon shot up and turned the page over so that the cover was now displayed. Yes, as he thought, it was next year's calendar. It was indeed the future – but just one year on. He had hoped to go a little bit further forward in time and was more than disappointed, to say the least. It did, however, bring him some comfort, Gordon concluding the fact that none of his friends had had the heart to move into his room following his demise, even though it was the largest bedroom in the house. Someone had even put up a new Fulham calendar in his honour.

Suddenly Gordon became aware of voices from downstairs. He got up and tiptoed out of his room, slowly descending the stairs that were so familiar to him. He would normally hurtle down them, at least two at a time, but not now. He still felt strangely lost in his own home, as though he did not belong there. And, of course, he didn't – not anymore at least. The voices became louder and now recognisable. It was his old housemates – there was no doubt about that. He stood at the closed door of the living room and hesitated before he placed his fingers around the doorknob. He was trembling as he entered. What if they could see him? Would he definitely be invisible to them this time? He wished Mr Gilmore were by his side.

The scene that greeted Gordon was not too different from what he had been expecting. Clare and Veronica were sitting on the sofa, Alex lying at their feet on the carpet, his head resting against their shins. They were all watching television. Only Bill was absent.

There was discarded Christmas wrapping paper everywhere. Gordon almost felt the urge to pick it up. The Christmas tree lights were on and Gordon looked for the magenta-coloured fairy light. It was *still* flickering. No one had fixed it.

Of course, no one noticed Gordon enter, but he still stood motionless, fearing that any movement would make his housemates aware of his presence. He did not move from the door of the living room, preferring to keep his distance, just in case he had to make a quick exit. Of course, he need not have been concerned. He could have sung *Merry Christmas* at the top of his voice and no one would have stirred. Gordon was no longer part of this world, a point emphasised by his now vacant armchair. At least no one was sitting in it. That would not have felt right. It was *his* chair, not that he doubted that his friends did put it to use now and again. He did not expect them to keep it as a shrine to him, like they had seemingly done with his bedroom, but it would have been weird to see someone else sitting in his chair, especially on Christmas Day.

"It doesn't seem like a year, does it?" Veronica mused, sipping a glass of wine. The adverts had come on the television and Alex reached for the remote control, pressing the mute button. "I said we should have gone somewhere else this year," Veronica continued. "It's a bit strange without him being here."

"Don't be silly, Veronica," Alex replied, turning his neck to look up at her, affectionately placing his hand upon her knee. "He would not have wanted anything else. There's no need to be morbid. Life goes on. He would say the same if he were here now and one of us was gone. Yes, life goes on."

Gordon found the courage to move to his armchair, though he still did so with caution, not that his slippers would have made any noise on the carpet. He stood behind it and gingerly placed his hand on one of the arms, stroking the velvet material. His housemates fell silent and – now that there was no sound coming from the television – Gordon could hear that somebody was in the kitchen. The individual was whistling a tune. Of course, it must be Bill. Gordon had forgotten about Bill.

"It was such a weird night, wasn't it," Clare reconvened the conversation, finding the silence even more uncomfortable. "I suppose it was quite fitting he should go while playing charades. He always loved that game."

Gordon shook his head. Whatever had given her that impression? He wanted to tell her that he hated it and saw no good reason to ever take part in such a worthless pursuit. Of course, he wouldn't have to ever again.

"The weirdest thing was you wearing Gordon's Fulham scarf, Alex," Clare continued. "Do you remember? No one noticed until much later that night."

"I still don't know to this day how I came to be wearing it," Alex conceded, touching the customary blue and white scarf around his neck. "I tell you, though, I wouldn't be seen dead ever wearing it again!"

Alex was aware that it was perhaps not the most appropriate sentence to utter at a moment like this, but all felt the need to chuckle.

"It was the wine," Veronica insisted. "You must have drunk too much wine. Oh, and don't you remember that we also couldn't explain those wine stains on the carpet?"

"That's right," Clare took over. "No one owned up to doing it... and then there was that plate of chicken – that was even weirder. Where did that come from? *He* must have cooked it, but I don't remember him doing so. It's funny the things you remember and the things you don't."

"I wonder where he is now?" Veronica put forward. "Do you think he's watching us from somewhere?"

Gordon smiled ruefully.

"I bet he's the life and soul of the party up there. He always liked to party," Alex grinned.

Gordon shook his head again. He hated parties. It seemed his friends had forgotten a lot about him in a year.

"We should play charades," Veronica suggested, "in his honour. He would like that – just in case he's watching from up there."

Gordon longed to jump in front of the television and offer his protestations. Anything but charades!

Suddenly there was a sound of colliding plates from the kitchen. Bill must be washing up. Gordon had to almost whisper the words to convince his brain that this was possible. Bill never washed up, you see. Gordon smiled, pleased that his best friend had presumably turned over a new leaf in his absence. Of course, now that Gordon was not there, someone else would *have* to have taken a bit more responsibility for the housework. He wondered who vacuumed the carpet these days. He bent down and ran his fingers through it. No one, it would seem.

Gordon was about to head towards the kitchen in search of Bill when Mr Gilmore returned.

"Ah, here you are, Mr Jones," the angel smiled, puffing a little. "I've been looking for you. I thought you said you would be staying upstairs?" he added, a hint of annoyance in his voice. He looked towards Gordon's housemates. The adverts had concluded and all eyes were once again on the television.

"What's that tune?" Mr Gilmore asked, turning his good ear towards the sound coming from the kitchen. He was referring to the whistling that accompanied the colliding of plates.

"*Amazing Grace,* I think," Gordon responded. "That's my favourite hymn. I always used to sing it when I was washing up. I bet Bill has got that from me. Good old Bill! Maybe he's whistling it in my honour. That would certainly be more appropriate than playing charades!"

Gordon was about to head for the kitchen, but the angel stopped him.

"Sorry, Mr Jones. It's time to go now."

"Is it? All right."

He looked to his friends. They had turned off the television and were now unpacking a board game. He was pleased that they had dismissed the idea of playing charades 'in his honour'. Gordon felt a sudden chill, the thought of Dumas and the trial suddenly re-entering his mind. He wondered whether he would see his housemates again. Would he be coming back to his house after the trial? No, probably not. This was the last time he would see it. Gordon cut a melancholy figure, his eyes now wistfully focused on the flickering magenta-coloured fairy light.

"Are you ready?" Mr Gilmore inquired, a sympathetic smile on his face.

"I want to be the dog!" Veronica shouted suddenly, attempting to wrestle a tiny figure from the clasped hand of Alex. "You know I'm always the dog. You're trying to wind me up. You can be the iron!"

Veronica attempted in vain to unclasp the fingers of the much stronger Alex, the two now locked in friendly combat on the sofa, as Clare started to shuffle the cards. Gordon sighed. "Life goes on," he whispered sorrowfully. "Life goes on."

18

"For the growing good of the world is partly dependent on unhistoric acts; and that things are not so ill with you and me as they might have been, is half owing to the number who lived faithfully a hidden life, and rest in unvisited tombs."

Middlemarch
George Eliot

DUMAS WAS THE FIRST TO NOTICE THAT GORDON HAD reappeared in the dock. The demon acknowledged him with a bow. Gordon shuddered and averted his eyes from him. The clerk was standing beside his desk, blowing his nose, but the archangel was not in his chair and was nowhere to be seen, his wig resting on the back of the vacant 'throne'. His absence explained the noise. People in the public gallery, thankful for another break in the proceedings, were talking among themselves, and their individual conversations collectively resonated throughout the courtroom, the din enough to engulf the sound made by the stonemason who had reconvened his work. *Tap. Tap. Tap.* Gordon only became aware of the noise again when he spotted the man out of the corner of his eye, or at least his moving elbows from behind the tombstone. The words of Dumas – *'mission unaccomplished'* – immediately came to his mind and he gulped. He looked to Mr Gilmore and remembered *that* reassuring smile that had brought him comfort back in his living room. Yes, there *was* still hope. Perhaps even now the stonemason was engraving a more flattering epitaph.

One or two court officials, including the usher, had strayed from their chairs and were engaged in idle chat, but otherwise the courtroom was the same as when Gordon had left it. The huge hands on the clock above the archangel's chair informed all that it was still just after half past seven.

Mr Gilmore approached the dock in order to converse with Gordon.

"Are you all right, Mr Jones?" he asked, another reassuring smile on his face.

"I think so. Did you manage to get hold of my witnesses?"

Mr Gilmore hesitated, the smile disappearing.

"What's wrong?" Gordon inquired.

"I'm afraid I couldn't find any non-Christians, not any that will help your case," the angel admitted.

"Is that a problem?" Gordon asked.

Mr Gilmore shook his head. "No, nothing to worry about," he replied, the warm smile returning to his face. "Of course, it would have been helpful if I had found a few. You see, I can call your vicar and all the other church members, but that's what the court will be expecting me to do. No one doubts that they will put in a good word for you, but it doesn't have the same impact as a non-Christian doing so. I just wanted to find one person – one soul that would prove to the court that you're a Christian."

"And you couldn't find *one*," a doleful Gordon responded, shaking his head. "What a mess I made of it all."

The angel placed his hand upon Gordon's shoulder. "What about you, Mr Jones? Have you come up with any further names? It's not too late, you know."

Gordon shook his head.

"What about Grace?" the angel persisted. "Are you sure you don't know someone called Grace?"

"No. I've told you," Gordon replied testily. "I don't know anyone called Grace."

Mr Gilmore took off his glasses and shook his head. "I don't understand it. I first wrote that name down a long time ago. I don't know why. I just felt it was important at the time – I just thought it might come in handy one day. Now I can't remember why I wrote it down. There must have been some reason."

Gordon sighed. The angel's forgetfulness did not fill him with confidence.

"So have I got *any* witnesses?" Gordon queried. "Will anyone be putting in a good word for me?"

"Of course, Mr Jones. O ye of little faith," Mr Gilmore added, nodding his head towards a bundle of papers that he held under his armpit. "There's enough evidence here," he said, a sheet slipping to the floor, the angel oblivious to the fact. "Are you hungry?" he continued. "I've got a sandwich in my pocket if you are."

Gordon pictured the same ones that the angel had wrapped up a long time ago or what seemed to be a long time ago. He politely declined.

"Should be starting again soon," Mr Gilmore pointed out, nodding in the direction of the press bench, a mouthful of sandwich now hindering his speech, not that that seemed to bother the diminutive angel. "The reporters are back, pencils and quills at the ready," he continued to babble. "Dumas is not going to like the front page tomorrow."

His attempts to reassure Gordon were wasted on this occasion. His charge was no longer listening to his small talk. He was staring at the courtroom clock, but he was not really looking at it; his body and head just happened to be facing in that direction. Gordon was whistling a tune, though no sound actually came from his lips. He was blowing out the notes, to be precise. Mr Gilmore had not noticed.

Suddenly Gordon froze. "Grace," he whispered, before lightly tapping his clenched fist on the dock. "Grace," he repeated. "Of course, *that's* it!"

Mr Gilmore almost spat out the contents of his mouth, but managed to gulp the food down before replying excitedly. "You remember a Grace?"

"No," Gordon turned to the angel. "I've told you, I don't know any Grace, but it's the hymn, you see?"

"Pardon?"

Gordon smiled. "Hearing Bill whistling the tune in the kitchen reminded me. The words just came back into my head. That's what it's all about, isn't it? It's grace that will save me – amazing grace. Grace is not a person... but the grace of God."

Gordon started to whistle the tune again, this time louder. The clerk of the court looked up and raised his eyebrows, his handkerchief still dabbing that huge nose.

"Thanks, Bill," Gordon smiled. "And you too, of course, Lord," he added, looking up, his grin widening.

Mr Gilmore did not attempt to stop Gordon, encouraged by the fact that the spirits of his client were on the rise.

"I've been a fool," Gordon said, shaking his head in disbelief. "You've been wasting your time looking for someone called Grace, Mr Gilmore. It's grace, you see. Not a person, but the *grace* of God. That's what Christianity is all about, isn't it? It's by grace that we are saved, and by nothing else. Otherwise none of us would be good enough to get to heaven. That's what I believe. I've just got to tell the court that, just like I told those people sitting next to me in the waiting room – the tennis player, the surgeon... and Angel Harriet said it too."

Mr Gilmore looked confused.

"I told them it was not about good deeds," Gordon continued to gush, "but the grace of God. And it's true. I just have to remind the jury of that fact. No one can condemn me... all because of the grace of God."

Gordon reconvened whistling the tune of his favourite hymn. He paused and then mimed the opening line: "*Amazing grace, how sweet the sound, that saved a wretch like me.*" He looked to the angel beside him. "I know I've not lived as I ought to have done, but I am *still* saved. From the moment I became a Christian, I was saved, and nothing will change that. That's the grace of God, isn't it?"

Mr Gilmore smiled. "Yes, you are right, Mr Jones. That is the grace of God," he added in wonder. The angel stopped. "You're right, of course, Mr Jones... but... but I still can't get *that* name out of my head."

"But it's *not* a name," Gordon persisted, almost annoyed by the fact that the angel had seemingly not experienced the same enlightenment. "It's just..."

"Court rise."

The usher uttered the command again as the archangel re-emerged from his personal door. Mr Gilmore – and others farther away from their seats – hurried back into position, all startled by the sudden reappearance of the celestial being, who seemed to be in such a hurry himself, he did not even notice the wig on his chair, shuffling himself on to his 'throne' (he was getting adept at that particular manoeuvre now) without placing it on his head.

"Mr Jones," he coughed, "it is now time for you to have *your* say. It is the moment when you get the chance to put your case. Do you understand?" Gordon nodded and straightened himself. He was still smiling and the archangel noticed the fact, though continued unperturbed. "Under the direction of Angel Gilmore, you will be able to call witnesses to speak on your behalf. Is that clear?"

"It is."

"Good. When you are ready, Angel Gilmore."

The archangel nodded to the junior angel and began to pour himself a glass of water as Mr Gilmore proceeded to rifle through his briefcase. He dumped some more papers on the bench in front of him and started to sort through them. He had still not noticed that one sheet lay at the foot of the dock beside Gordon, and Dracula – seemingly of the opinion that the angel was looking for that particular piece of paper – took it upon himself to retrieve it, placing it on the very edge of the bench at which Mr Gilmore sat. The angel did not even notice. A conceited Dumas was smiling, muttering something under his breath.

At last Mr Gilmore grabbed a piece of paper – not the one that had been gathered from the floor – and rose to his feet. "I would like to call my first witness…"

He stopped and looked at the sheet within his hand, lowering his glasses and screwing up his eyes in order to read the name. He lifted his head and looked to the archangel. "Sorry, I think this might be my shopping list."

There was laughter and Gordon sighed. He did not notice that his guardian was also smiling and, if he had seen that controlled smile, he may not have risen to his feet so quickly, an act that took many by surprise, though not Mr Gilmore.

"I would like to speak," Gordon said, addressing the archangel boldly. The latter looked to Mr Gilmore for clarification. Gordon also turned to his guardian. "Please, Mr Gilmore, I've got something important to say."

Mr Gilmore sat down and smiled. Anyone might have been forgiven for thinking that the angel had been waiting for Gordon's intervention.

"Thank you," Gordon nodded. "Please do not think I do not appreciate what you are doing for me, Mr Gilmore, and I don't want you to think that I've no faith in you. On the contrary, I would like to publicly thank you for all your assistance throughout my life," Gordon went on, "even if I was not aware of it." He paused and reverted his eyes to the archangel. "But it's time for me to stand up and be counted. What I'm trying to say, your worship, is that we… we don't have any witnesses. We won't be calling any."

Some gasps from the public gallery followed. Some of the jurors shook their heads in astonishment. The severed head of Mary almost rolled off the ledge it had been resting on. Only Mr Gilmore seemed unsurprised, which would have surprised Gordon if he had been looking at him.

"No witnesses?" the archangel attempted to clarify, looking down at the clerk of the court in order to ascertain whether that was permitted.

"Are you sure you don't want to call any witnesses? Do you understand what you are saying, Mr Jones?"

The archangel, having gained no response from his clerk, turned to Mr Gilmore. "Is this right, Angel Gilmore? You won't be calling any witnesses?"

The angel looked to Gordon and offered one of his reassuring smiles.

"That is right," he said.

Gordon returned a smile; buoyed by the fact his guardian had faith in him. Of course, he had always had faith in him.

"You see," Gordon started, finding the confidence to look at Dumas, "Demon Dumas is right. There isn't much evidence to prove that I'm a Christian. I won't waste your time pretending there is. We could call the vicar at my church to speak on my behalf, but I have to admit, I don't think even he will be able to say a huge amount in my favour, other than that I helped out at the odd jumble sale."

Mr Gilmore rose to his feet. "Can I just interrupt at this moment," he apologised. "I think it is important for the jury to know that we do have *some* evidence," he insisted, lifting up some of his many pieces of paper, before retaking his seat.

Gordon smiled. "Yes, there might be some evidence, but I'm the first to admit that it probably wouldn't convict me if Christianity were a crime. I'm weary. I've had enough of playing charades." Gordon paused. "You see, I no longer have the desire to try to convince this jury of my godliness, for want of a better word. No matter what verdict you pass, I know that I can't fool God. He knows everything about my life, and I know I will ultimately have to stand before him and explain why I was such a failure as a Christian. At the end of the day, I don't care who takes me to meet him: Demon Dumas or Mr Gilmore. It is God that I will have to give an account of my life to. He will be my judge and jury... with respect," Gordon added, nodding in the direction of the archangel. "I have no evidence to prove that I'm a Christian, nothing tangible" – Gordon knew lawyers often used that word, even if he was unsure of its exact meaning – "I can't claim to have done very much at all with my life since becoming a Christian and it would be wrong of me to try to convince you otherwise. Yes, Dumas is right. I didn't become a servant. I didn't serve God and I didn't serve his people."

Dumas remained seated. There was no expression on his face. Even the smug smile was absent now.

No one uttered a word. The only sound now audible was from the stonemason, still tapping at the tombstone, though Gordon was no longer irritated by the sound and, it has to be said, at this particular moment, did not even notice it.

"I don't know if this is all a dream," Gordon continued, glancing at the assortment of characters that filled the courtroom, "but if it is, and I wake up and get a second chance, I hope I will live the rest of my life differently." He paused. "Of course, I'm no longer so gullible to suggest that I would succeed in doing so. It's all too easy to lose sight of heaven in the blur of everyday life – I'm evidence of that – but I'm sure I'm not the only Christian guilty of living for themselves and not for others."

Gordon had a hand in his pocket and felt the Cornish pixie within. He lifted it out and shook his head, before deliberately letting it slip from his hand on to the floor. "I know I messed things up, but God knew that I would. He still loves me. Yes, he still loves me. And it is by his grace that I know that I can stand before him free from sin. That's not down to me, or what I did – or didn't do – but because of his grace, because he sent his son to die for me. I know that when I stand before him – despite all my failings – he will not reject me and I will be pure in his eyes."

Gordon looked to Mr Gilmore. "That's it really. I don't have much else to say. I just thank God that he loves me no matter what. I just thank him for his grace."

It was Dumas who spoke first, rising to his feet. He was clapping.

"Well said, Mr Jones," he mocked. "I'm sure you have tugged a few heartstrings among the jury. Of course, it's all a bit too late now, isn't it? The problem I have, you see, is that we still have no evidence to prove you really believed in what you have just told the court. Yes, you put it so eloquently, but – when you were alive – did you really believe that? We have no evidence that you did."

"And you have no evidence to prove that he didn't," Mr Gilmore interrupted.

Dumas ignored the angel. "A faith without action is useless, you see," the demon continued. "And, as there was little or no action in your case, Mr Jones, we can only assume that your faith is useless... utterly useless. How then can it possibly save you?"

"It is not useless," Mr Gilmore answered for his client. "Mr Jones rightly reminded you that it is not about how many good deeds he performed, but about grace. It is by the grace of his master – and not through any actions of his own – that he has a place in heaven reserved for him, and no one – I repeat, no one – can deny the believer that."

The archangel did not attempt to intervene, content to let the two adversaries slug it out. He sat motionless. He merely listened, absorbed in the moment. The same could be said of everyone in that courtroom.

"Do you still not get it?" Dumas persisted. "We still don't have any evidence to prove that you were *really* a believer, Mr Jones. There were no actions and so one has to question whether there was a faith at all. I mean, a *real* faith." Dumas turned to the jury. "Mr Jones admitted himself that there was no evidence to prove that he was a Christian. He did nothing to suggest he was a servant of God. Why? Because he didn't really know this God, he didn't really believe in him. There is no proof that this man is really a Christian and – as we all know the rules – he therefore belongs to me. That is all I ever wished to accomplish from this charade, as you call it: to claim what rightfully belongs to my master."

Mr Gilmore was about to protest, but Dumas had not finished.

"Evidence!" the demon roared, thumping his fist uncharacteristically on the table before him. "Show me one scrap of evidence to prove Mr Jones is a Christian. Show me just one thing – one measly Christian act of kindness that he carried out. Is that too much to ask?"

Mr Gilmore started to shuffle through his papers.

"Evidence!" Dumas repeated. "There is *no* evidence."

"There is."

The response did not come from Mr Gilmore on this occasion, or from Gordon. The two words were whispered, and had come from afar, from the public gallery to be precise. They should not have been audible to anyone on that courtroom floor, but for a celestial being – the archangel to be specific – they were piercing, and he did not fail to hear them. Every single person in the courtroom could have been speaking, but he would have still heard those words.

"Who said that?" he questioned tenderly, looking towards the upper reaches of the courtroom. A woman in the public gallery slowly rose to her feet. "It was me," she admitted. Her voice was soft and, from the few words she had so far spoken, one would have immediately assumed she was of a gentle disposition, someone who did not normally seek to be the centre of attention. However, she was not embarrassed by the fact she had interrupted the proceedings and that all eyes were now upon her. She stood upright. Dumas had turned in his chair to face her. He looked agitated. Mr Gilmore had also turned full circle, his head now tilted, his chin pointing upwards, as he screwed up his eyes in a bid to focus on the ordinary-looking member of the public that had brought a sudden and unexpected halt to the trial. His eyes were not good enough to pick out her features and he remained oblivious to her identity, as was Gordon, it has to be said.

The archangel did not reprimand the woman for her interruption. Some might have said that he had been expecting it. "Have you something to say?" he asked kindly. "Please. It is important you speak up if you have something to share with us."

"I do."

The archangel nodded to the usher and Dracula left the courtroom via the main door. He needed to ascend the foyer stairs in order to reach the public gallery, but within a ridiculously short space of time he had done so and was soon escorting the woman towards the witness box. Gordon studied her closely as she placed her hand on the Bible and read from the card. She was wearing a pink dressing gown, one that had seen better days. She did not appear to be of a great age – possibly not much older than Gordon – but the wrinkles on her face were so profound, anyone might have been forgiven for thinking the stonemason had formed them with his chisel. She wore no make-up and her black hair, interspersed with streaks of grey, was stringy, as though a comb had not touched it in weeks. Despite her somewhat dishevelled appearance, she held her head high and adopted a dignified posture.

No one asked the woman to begin, but she felt obliged to do so. She continued to speak softly, no louder than a whisper.

"I'm sorry for the interruption, but I had to speak up," she said. "I've been following the trial ever since I saw Mr Jones's picture in the paper. I recognised him, you see. I never forgot his face, even though he was a lot younger when I met him."

Gordon looked at Mr Gilmore for an explanation, but the angel did not take his eyes off the unexpected witness.

"I don't really know where to start," the woman coughed. "I'm not used to this sort of thing."

"Take your time," the archangel reassured her. "Just tell us what you know about Mr Jones."

She nodded and took a breath before beginning. "I died a long time ago now; it's been many years, though I haven't been counting. You know how you lose track of time here."

The archangel returned a grin.

"I suppose I should start with my marriage," she continued. "I got married when I was very young – too young, if I'm honest. We had problems almost immediately. My husband started to drink and he became very violent. He was an alcoholic." She paused. "Don't get me wrong, I still loved him; it was the drink, you see. I knew it wasn't really him when he hit me." There was a longer pause this time. "He died unexpectedly... drank himself to death. Everyone said I was lucky to be rid of him, but I was devastated. I just fell apart. I refused all the help offered me and turned my back on my friends and family. I shunned all company, preferring to wallow in my own self-pity. I don't know to this day how I got myself in such a mess."

The woman was not looking at anyone as she spoke, her head bowed, but her words were still clear and audible, so silent was the courtroom.

"I started to drink," she went on, "even though I had seen it destroy my husband. Very soon I found myself hanging out with what most would call the dregs of society, if you like, people I would never have dreamed of hanging out with. I took drugs on a couple of occasions too. There's more – a lot more, I'm afraid – but it isn't pretty and I will spare you the gory details."

The woman momentarily raised her head. Still there was no sound in the courtroom. Even the stonemason had downed his tools, though no one was aware of that fact.

"I was depressed, you see, when I decided to do... *it,*" the woman resumed, struggling to complete the sentence. "I had been depressed before, but I soon found out what *real* depression was. I always used to think people that took their own lives were fools. There must be something worth living for? How could life be so bad that you want to end everything? Well, I reached that stage myself – don't ask me how. I had a jar of sleeping tablets in my coat pocket. I had been collecting them over a period of a few weeks, so it was not a spur-of-the-moment decision."

The woman now directed her eyes into the void. They were not focused on anything. If they had been lined up in the direction of one particular person, she still would not have been aware of that individual at this moment.

"I was not a religious person," she continued solemnly. "I never went to church in all my life; only for a wedding or a funeral, that's all. I didn't have anything against the church, but I was indifferent to it. Anyway, I prayed that morning when I woke up. I don't know why or who to. In

239

my desperation, I closed my eyes and just called out to someone. If there was a God, I asked him to help me. I pleaded with him. I can remember the words now as if I had said them yesterday. I just asked for one little sign that would persuade me that life was still worth living. There was nothing."

The woman turned to face Gordon. "There was no earthquake, nothing," she said. "I opened my eyes and saw the peeling paint on the walls of my bedroom. I can remember screaming to God... but there was still nothing."

Gordon found himself bowing his head in a bid to avert his eyes from the woman, as though he felt in some way responsible for increasing her shame by continuing to look at her. In response, she turned her head from him, taking a ragged tissue from her pocket and wiping one eye with it.

"Anyway," the woman went on, "my mind was made up, though I didn't want to do it at home; I don't know why. You would have thought I would have been past caring about things like that. I went to a park and sat on a bench. I don't know how long I had been sitting there. I had my hand inside my pocket, resting on the jar of tablets. I was crying, but no one stopped. They all just walked on by. I just remember thinking that these people had no idea what I was about to do. Would they have stopped if they did? No one even looked at me. Mr Jones didn't either when he came along."

Gordon's heart missed a beat when he heard his name. He was so entranced by the story, foolishly he had not been expecting to be part of it.

"Yes," the woman continued, "he walked past at first, like the rest of them, his head down, and he would have probably been the last person I saw before removing that jar from my pocket. I even remember taking a firmer grip of it at that moment."

The woman again looked to Gordon, this time studying him closely, though she conveyed only a feeling of warmth and he did not feel uneasy, his own eyes on this occasion remaining fixed upon her.

"Yes," she said, "you *stopped,* Mr Jones; you did stop... in the end. You stopped and turned around. You didn't come to me immediately but stood there for a couple of moments. I could sense you from the corner of my eye, even through the tears, be you a mere blur. And then you came. Do you remember?"

Gordon looked to Mr Gilmore and shook his head dumbly.

"You were very nervous," the woman smiled. "You didn't sit down beside me. You just asked if I was OK, that's all. I nodded, even though I had tears rolling down my cheeks, my hand still on the jar of tablets hidden inside my pocket. You hesitated, not sure what to do, and then asked if there was anything you could do to help. I shook my head and you hesitated again, before you went on your way, like the rest of them."

Dumas tutted, making sure everyone could hear him.

The archangel flashed the demon an accusing glance. "Carry on," he informed the woman, knowing only too well that the story had not come to an end.

"Well," she continued, "Mr Jones – of course, I never knew his name until now – started to go on his way, but he hadn't gone far when he stopped again. He stood there for what must have been no more than ten seconds and... he prayed for me."

Gordon felt numb. He still could not even remember the woman. He had a vague recollection of a figure crying on a park bench, but it was a long time ago, and he could not recall praying for her. He felt almost embarrassed that the incident was of no significance to him.

"Of course," she elaborated, "I didn't realise he was praying, not until I heard him utter the word 'amen' at the end of it, louder than he intended," she added, a brief smile appearing on her face. "I knew he didn't want me to know that he was praying for me. It wasn't a condescending act... he didn't pray in my face... and I never even heard any words of the prayer itself, but it hit me like a bolt of lightning. I remember trembling. You see, no one had ever prayed for me before. As I said, I never believed in God, but here was a complete stranger taking time out – if only a few seconds – for me. And I don't suppose to this day that Mr Jones knew just what an impact that prayer had on me... or my life."

Mr Gilmore was trying to suppress the grin that had spontaneously appeared on his face, for fear he was being insensitive to the woman, her story being one of much sorrow.

"I can't say that I went home and gave my life to God, or anything like that," the woman admitted, "and I can't pretend that things changed much at first – I soon put that prayer to the back of my mind – but *that* jar... yes, that jar remained in my coat pocket and I forgot about it."

The woman looked to the archangel, sensing that she may have overrun her allotted time. "Shall I go on?" she asked.

The archangel smiled. "Yes," he said. "You must."

"I didn't know at the time that I was pregnant," the woman obliged. "I found out a few weeks later. To my shame, I didn't know who the father was." She paused. "But that is when I started to rebuild my life. I had to, for the sake of my unborn child. I had a reason to live now. I even started to read the Bible. I met a Christian at the health centre that I attended, you see."

"Praise be!" Dumas mocked, prompting another look of disdain from the archangel.

The woman ignored the demon. She may not have even heard him. He was no figure of fear to her, as he was to many witnesses, merely an irrelevance.

"I'm not saying I understood everything I read," the woman continued, "but I didn't feel alone anymore."

Dumas tutted again. No one heard him this time.

"I gave birth to a healthy girl," the woman smiled. "I got my life back on track for her sake. She *became* my life." The woman paused. "To my shame, I cannot say I rushed to church to thank God for what he had done for me. I didn't even feel the inclination to pick up a Bible again... and I didn't... not until many years later."

The woman had not finished her story and the smile soon disappeared as she braced herself to relate something even more painful.

"My daughter was almost ten when my world came crashing down on me again," she reflected. "I didn't even feel ill at the time. It was just a routine check-up, but within a couple of weeks I was given the news everyone dreads. I had just a few months to live. I cried out to God again. I shouted at him. How could he do this? Why me? After all that I had been through. I had got my life back in order and here he was striking me down again. I had a reason to live now and yet I was not going to be able to do so. How cruel can he be? Perhaps there *wasn't* a God, after all?"

The woman turned to the archangel, the smile reappearing on her face – a look of wonder in her eyes – as though only she and he shared a great secret.

"Of course," the woman continued, "I can see now that it was all part of *his* plan. I became a Christian a week before my death. It was not the dying that I feared, but leaving my daughter. I won't lie to you and say those final days were easy, but I was at peace – for the first time in my life, I can honestly say that I was at peace."

The woman momentarily closed her eyes and let out a sigh – one of relief and contentment. It was obvious to all that she had concluded her testimony. Gordon pushed away a single tear that had fallen unnoticed and was now resting on his cheek.

"What happened to your daughter?" the archangel inquired. The wise would have known that he already knew the answer and that he had merely asked the question for the benefit of everyone else.

The woman smiled with pride and looked up to the public gallery.

"She's up there."

A young woman wearing the uniform of a nurse abruptly looked down at her lap in a futile bid to hide her embarrassment, as heads turned in her direction.

"Now we are reunited," her mother continued. "She only came home a few months ago. She became a nurse and worked for a Christian charity in Mozambique. She didn't have a long life, she didn't even live to be twenty – she was killed after being hit by a car on the way to the health centre – but she did more in a few years than many do in a lifetime. She spent her working life holding the hands of dying children. She gave hope to so many before she left the earth. She was only a slip of a thing, but she was a courageous and inspirational woman. She was amazing. Everyone that met her thought she was amazing."

The woman, tears clearly visible in her eyes, stopped and looked at Gordon. "I've been up in the public gallery listening to what has been said about your life, Mr Jones. I made a mess of mine too, so I know I cannot judge you. But let me say this: Mr Dumas asked if there was any evidence to prove you are a Christian. Well, there it is. You may argue it wasn't much that you did for me on that cold December day, but it was something. You can't do everything, but you can do something. And you did, Mr Jones... You did."

She looked at the stonemason. "Maybe that should be your epitaph, Mr Jones. You did something."

Mr Gilmore had reached for his handkerchief and was blowing his nose. Dumas remained silent. The archangel was smiling. It was the warmest, most heartfelt smile you will ever see.

"Thank you," the archangel said to the woman. "Thank you."

The woman was about to leave the witness box, the usher holding the door open for her.

"Hold on," the clerk interrupted, scratching *that* nose of his. "Before you go, if you don't mind, I didn't catch your name. We need it for the records."

"Alice Kirby," the woman replied. "My name's Alice Kirby."

"And your daughter?"

The woman looked up towards the public gallery. She smiled.

"That's my amazing…"

Mr Gilmore had already whispered the name.

"…Grace," the proud mother continued, her eyes gleaming. "That's my amazing Grace."

19

"And grace will lead me home."

Amazing Grace
John Newton

GORDON GLANCED AT HIS WATCH. AS SOON AS HE DID, HE knew it was a futile act. The hands of the timepiece, just like those of the huge clock on the wall above what was once again the now empty chair of the archangel, remained in the same position. It was still just after half past seven, as he knew it would always be. Dumas was the only one to notice Gordon rebuke himself for his forgetfulness. The demon was leaning back in his chair, his legs stretched out upon the bench in front of him. "Old habits die hard, Mr Jones," he smirked, just loud enough for Gordon to hear. Of course, Gordon knew that the demon was alluding to his daily failings as a Christian, rather than his tendency to look at his watch more than was necessary.

Mr Gilmore was beside Gordon, leaning against the dock, reading the front page of a newspaper. Gordon glanced at the banner headline: *Jury retires to consider verdict.* Strangely, he no longer had any desire to read the accompanying article and wondered why his guardian angel was now doing so, Mr Gilmore having once chided Gordon for his unhealthy interest in the reflections of the press.

The appearance of Grace and the testimony of her mother had filled Gordon with renewed hope, but now that both were out of sight again, he felt the need for more reassurance.

"It's been about ten minutes," Gordon turned to Mr Gilmore, nodding at his watch. "That's a long time for the jury to be out, isn't it?" he added, almost consulting his watch again as he did so.

Mr Gilmore folded the newspaper and tucked it under his armpit, before placing his hand upon Gordon's shoulder. He smiled. "I'm proud of you, Mr Jones."

"Are you?"

"Yes," the angel continued. "And I can only apologise for the fact that I forgot who Grace was. I *knew* that there was someone called Grace."

Gordon groaned. "You're not still harping on about that, are you?" He stopped. "Sorry, I didn't mean that as a joke... harps and angels, and all that," he added, feeling the need to explain himself. Mr Gilmore felt obliged to respond with a grin. "Anyway," Gordon continued, "what I mean is that it wouldn't have mattered if Grace and her mother had come forward or not, would it? It was just one incident in my life – an isolated incident, it seems. What difference does it make? It's about the grace of God – fortunately for me. It's not about what I did or didn't do. I'm saved by the grace of God."

A breathless Gordon stopped and looked at his guardian, almost for clarification.

Mr Gilmore sighed. He peered over his glasses and stared Gordon in the eye. This was his way of informing his charge that he had something important to say.

"You are right, Mr Jones, I know," he started. "But sometimes I wonder if it would be better if it wasn't just about the grace of God. What if it was also about what you did on earth? What if the amount of good deeds you performed on earth *did* matter? Imagine what it would be like if you had to perform a certain number of good acts in order to secure your place in heaven?"

Gordon returned a look of confusion – some might even say it was a look of concern. Mr Gilmore noticed it and chuckled.

"Don't worry," the angel assured him. "It isn't about good deeds, but if it was – and you lived each day knowing it was – don't you think Christians would try a bit harder for their master?"

Mr Gilmore paused. He was now gazing at the archangel's vacant chair. "The word 'do-gooder' has become a bit of a joke," he mused. "Of course, non-believers sometimes use it to describe a Christian; wrongly assuming that the good people go to heaven and the bad ones go to hell. Christians spend a lot of time explaining to them that where you spend eternity is not dependent on how good a person you are, but all about the grace of God. That is correct, of course, but some Christians – because of that grace – become almost complacent and start to think they don't need to do anything."

"So they *don't* do anything," Gordon interrupted. "Like me."

Mr Gilmore smiled. "You should want to be a 'do-gooder', not to earn salvation – you can't – but because you want to make your master smile. And nothing makes him happier than when his children are doing good deeds for others. No, you don't *have* to do anything, but the Master *wants* you to do something. He will not force you to serve him, but, if you love him, you should want to please him. At the end of the day, you should want him to be proud of you because of what you did for him on earth. '*Well done, good and faithful servant.*' Those are the words you should long to hear when you finally stand before his throne."

Gordon bowed his head. "I don't think God will be saying that to me."

He looked towards Dumas. The demon was twiddling a pencil within his gloved fingers. Even now, there was still an air of arrogance about him.

"He's right, isn't he?" Gordon sighed. "Dumas is right. How can I stand before God in glory? I didn't serve God... because I didn't love him, I mean *really* love him, did I? And I certainly never loved my neighbour. I only loved myself. Dumas is right – there's so little evidence to prove that I loved anyone."

"Love..." Mr Gilmore pondered. "Most people do not know what love is. You might not believe it, Mr Jones, but I was a romantic at heart."

Gordon looked down at the suited angel, noticing a tomato stain on his white shirt collar. Yes, he did find it difficult to believe.

"And yet," Mr Gilmore continued, "so much rubbish has been said about love, you'd never believe it. Forget love at first sight and all that nonsense. Love does not come naturally. You don't just love someone. You have to make an effort to love them – you have to learn to love them. It takes time and hard work. Love is not a bunch of roses, or a box of chocolates... Love is giving up your time, your money, your energy, your comforts. It's about putting someone else before yourself."

"And that's not easy, is it?" Gordon lamented.

"No. It's not. It's not even easy when you like a person, or in the case of your master, when they have done something for you. Needless to say, it's even more difficult when a person seems unlovable – that obnoxious know-it-all at work, or the geek at church who is a constant source of irritation... you know, the people that everyone tries to avoid..."

Mr Gilmore smiled, noticing Gordon nodding his head. "Yes, it's a bit easier to love the popular guy," the angel added, "but you also have to learn to love those that irk you... those that offend you... and, dare I say it, even those that may persecute you."

"How?" Gordon argued. "How do you love people like that? If I didn't even truly love my master – after all he did for me – how do you love those sort of people?"

The angel returned a sympathetic smile. "The only way to do that is to go against human instinct and spend time with them," he said. "You can't grow to love someone unless you make an effort to get to know that person. Of course, you can still carry out acts of love without loving a person," he added. "And you did, Mr Jones – when you prayed for the mother of Grace Kirby."

"But that's about all I did do," Gordon tutted. "It was an isolated incident and all I did was give up half a minute. Grace gave up her life!"

Mr Gilmore nodded. "She gave up what is most precious to anyone – time. Of all the sacrifices you must make in order to learn to love, time is the greatest. Dumas is right on that count. It's the most valuable gift you can give to someone, Mr Jones. You can make more money, but you can't add a second to your life. You have a set amount of time on earth and it's precious."

Mr Gilmore looked to Gordon, attempting to re-establish eye contact, his charge gazing at the ceiling. "Do you know what Dumas was trying to do throughout this trial?"

Gordon glanced at the demon. "No," he replied, shaking his head. "Not really."

The angel paused. "Dumas doesn't know what goes on in every individual heart. I don't either. No one knows how much you *really* loved your master. Only the master himself has that privilege. No, all Dumas – or myself for that matter – could do was to look for any evidence that your heart was affected by the love for your master. Yes, you are saved by grace and not by good deeds, but good deeds are the only proof we have that you've been saved; faith without action is useless, after all. Do you understand, Mr Jones? What was important in your life can be measured by how much time you devoted to it."

Gordon shook his head. "That doesn't sound good," he said sorrowfully. "I didn't spend a lot of time for God, did I? Dumas established that. My number one priority was myself – not God or his people. If you're saying that you only have my actions to go by, you don't have a lot of evidence to prove I'm a Christian... Dumas is right."

"But we have *some* evidence," the angel insisted. "You are correct, of course, it wouldn't have mattered if Grace or her mother had come forward, but their appearance showed the jury that there was at least some evidence to prove that your master was in your heart. As Death might say, it showed that you did carry out – in the words of one William Wordsworth – those *little, nameless, unremembered acts of kindness and of love.* And that is what your master wanted you to do. We are not all called to go to Africa like Grace, but we are called to do something, and sometimes the most important service is the service that no one notices. Many are willing to do great things for the Master, but there are *little* things that need to be done as well – those 'unremembered acts' that sometimes only *he* notices. What you did for Grace's mother was nothing as far as you were concerned – you didn't even remember it – but your kindness meant everything to her and it had a huge consequence. I'm not saying there will be thousands of people in heaven because of what you did on earth, Mr Jones, but if there is just one... just one... then what a wonderful legacy that would be."

Mr Gilmore paused for breath. "Your master loves you just as you are, Mr Jones – for all your faults. You may not have always served him the way he commanded, but he still loves you and you *will* – because of his grace – still stand before him in glory." Mr Gilmore stopped and smiled: "*Tis grace hath brought me safe thus far, and grace will lead me home.*"

Gordon bowed his head, not for the first time. He now had tears in his eyes. He felt a sudden feeling of being overwhelmed, no longer in control of his emotions, but it was not in a negative sense. In fact, it was a liberating feeling and he felt as though he had been touched inside by something magical.

Mr Gilmore stared at the still bowing Gordon.

"Mr Jones," he said softly, "let me assure you that your place in heaven was never in doubt. Your master does not break a promise. And at his feet your sanctification will be complete. You will finally understand what it is all about. You will really know what love is. You will worship him, not out of duty, but because you want to. Your worship will be spontaneous and sincere. You will want to serve him like you've never served him before."

Gordon looked up. "*Weak is the effort of my heart, and cold my warmest thought; but when I see thee as thou art, I'll praise thee as I ought.*" He stopped and smiled. "That's not *Amazing Grace,* but another hymn, I think."

"I know," Mr Gilmore smiled. "That's my favourite."

The angel took Gordon's hand and squeezed it softly. Gordon could have been forgiven for thinking it was the *Master* himself doing so.

"Court rise."

It was almost as if the archangel had been listening to the conversation between Gordon and Mr Gilmore. He could not have re-entered the courtroom at a more opportune moment. People rose to their feet and Mr Gilmore went back to his seat. He made a point of flashing Gordon one final smile. If you had tried to describe that smile, you would have had difficulty choosing just one adjective to do so. In that smile was love, compassion, gentleness, understanding and reassurance. Gordon pushed away the tears in his eyes with the palms of his hands and nodded to his guardian, intent on expressing his gratitude one final time.

The stone-faced jurors re-entered. Gordon did not notice them. He no longer felt the need to look into their eyes in an attempt to see if their expressions revealed his fate. No, he knew his fate now – and there were no longer any doubts in his mind.

The archangel banged his gavel. He had no need to, of course. All eyes were now upon him, just as they had been the moment he had first appeared at the beginning of the trial. He placed the gavel down gently and looked towards the jurors. They had all – with the exception of the fidgeting knight in armour – settled back into their seats.

"Members of the jury," the archangel started, "have you come to a decision?"

The countess stood and cleared her throat. "We have, your worship." Her voice was firm and officious. The archangel looked at Gordon. "Please stand, Mr Jones."

Gordon was already standing. He had barely used his seat during the whole trial. He straightened himself and stared at the archangel, as though it were he that was responsible for his fate.

The archangel reached for his wig and placed it on his head, before turning towards the countess, who was still standing. The only sound came from the stonemason tapping away, but few heard his toiling now. All that was missing from this particular moment was a drum roll.

"Madam," the archangel declared, "in the verdict of the jury," he went on, glancing down at a piece of paper in front of him, "do you find

Mr…" He stopped and put his finger on the name before reading it. "Do you find Mr William Brian Jones to be a Christian?"

The countess did not get the chance to answer. It was Gordon himself who interrupted the proceedings.

"William?" he questioned in a high-pitched tone that made a few people jump. "Did you call me *William?*"

The archangel peered over his glasses towards Gordon and then reverted his eyes towards the piece of paper in front of him.

"Yes. Is there a problem?" he inquired.

"Yes," Mr Gilmore intervened, rising to his feet. "There is a problem. My client's name is Gordon."

"That's right," Gordon went on. "I think you might be getting confused with my housemate, Bill."

The pencil in Dumas's hand snapped. It was followed by the sound of a heavy metal object rolling across the wooden floor. The stonemason had dropped his chisel.

No one said anything. They did not need to. Of course, for one moment, or maybe two or three, no one knew *what* to say. The phrase 'stunned silence' is probably overused in everyday conversation, but there was nothing as suitable to describe this particular moment, and editors would have probably forgiven their reporters for penning the cliché in their copy.

"Is there something wrong?" Gordon asked dumbly. He looked at a number of the blank faces in the courtroom. Mr Gilmore was rubbing his eyes vigorously, his spectacles now resting on his lap. Dumas was leaning back in his chair and had covered his entire face with his hat, his legs once more outstretched on the table in front of him.

"Oh no!" Gordon continued. "You've got the wrong man, haven't you? I shouldn't be here. It should be… it should be *Bill.*"

The clerk of the court was frantically examining his papers. He knew that he would not find a solution within them, but it appeared that he did not know what else to do. No one did. Dumas had now removed his hat and was laughing, a scoffing guffaw, clearly a deliberate act to help highlight the incompetence of those around him.

"So that wasn't Bill whistling *Amazing Grace* in the kitchen," Gordon stuttered. "That was me! And that explains why Bill wasn't at my wake. It wasn't *him* upstairs in my room – that was also *me!* And that's why I didn't recognise half of the people there. It wasn't *my* funeral… It was *his!*"

Gordon looked pleadingly towards the archangel. "I shouldn't be here, should I? I should still be…"

Gordon never had the chance to finish his sentence. A subtle click of the fingers was all it took to silence him… to root him to the spot… to ensure he did not move another inch or say another syllable in that courtroom. Gordon now stood motionless in the dock, just like his friends back home. He too now cut a ridiculous figure, one arm bent at the elbow, a finger raised towards the ceiling, a look of astonishment on his face. Needless to say, from the moment the archangel clicked his fingers, Gordon was not aware of anything in that courtroom. It meant he did not witness the arrival of Death. All eyes were now focused on that said individual – accusing eyes, one should add. Death stood in the middle of the courtroom, a solitary figure. He looked up to the archangel and shrugged his shoulders. "What can I say?" he pleaded. Most were expecting him to quote some renowned literary work. He didn't.

"I don't suppose anything that I say will help much?" Death suggested with appealing eyes.

Still the archangel remained silent. There was no need to converse. Only Dumas showed any sign of animation. He was now slowly and deliberately clapping his hands, the smirk on his face growing ever wider.

"It was an easy mistake to make," Death continued. "There are just so many Joneses. In fact, I went to another Jones in the street at first. All right, I accept that there might be two Joneses in the same road, but two Joneses in the same *room?* They were not even related. What are the chances of that? It was Buckinghamshire… not Llanelli!" He glanced at the now frozen figure of Gordon in the dock. "I just assumed it was the one looking so ill. In fact, he looked awful. And, of course, he later confirmed his name was Jones. I didn't think to check it was *the* Jones. Anyone would have presumed he was the one."

Death stopped. He had been waiting for someone to interrupt him. No one had obliged. The archangel stared at him blankly. His wig had slipped over one of his eyes, but he made no attempt to readjust it. Death turned to Mr Gilmore and Dumas for a response.

"Anyone could have made the mistake," he insisted. "I'm entitled to one now and again, aren't I? It doesn't happen often. In fact, this is the first one in more than 342 earth years. Please, someone say something."

The archangel picked up his gavel and tapped it once against the bench. It was not a heavy blow. It was almost half-hearted, but everyone heard it, so silent was the courtroom now. He looked at the statuesque figure of Gordon in the dock. "I withdraw the case of Mr Jones... *Gordon* Jones," he said deliberately.

The archangel took off his wig and folded it neatly, gently placing it on the bench in front of him. He got up from his chair, allowing his red robe to slip from his back on to the floor. He never noticed that very few people had responded to the usher's plea for them to rise from their seats. The archangel made his way to the door and calmly opened it. His back was to the courtroom and nobody saw the grin on his face. If they had, they might have suggested this little, unassuming celestial being had known all along that it was Gordon Jones – and not Bill – that stood in the dock before him.

As the door closed behind the archangel, Death smiled and lifted his arms, so that his palms were turned towards the ceiling. "What can I say, my friends," he announced, a fake expression of remorse on his face. "I could say 'sorry', but – as Elton John remarked – *sorry seems to be the hardest word.*"

No one laughed. It should have been funny, but few were actually listening. Mr Gilmore was stuffing his papers back into his briefcase. Dumas was fiddling with the broken pencil in his gloved hands, examining it as though it was an act more important than conversing with the 'fool' that stood before him.

"No harm done," Death said softly, more to reassure himself than to convince anyone else. "No harm done."

When he realised no one was going to converse with him, Death sighed and clapped his hands. In a blink of an eye, he was back in the living room of Gordon's house. Gordon was there too. This time Gordon was in his armchair, curled up in the position that Death had found him in when he had first set eyes upon him. Of course, Gordon was now as still as his frozen friends, oblivious to all that was going on around him. Someone else was moving now. It was Bill. Death stood beside him.

"What's going on?" Bill inquired suspiciously, looking at the uninvited guest. "Who are you? How did you get in?"

"I am Death."

Bill shook his head and repeated his question, louder this time. "I SAID, WHO ARE..."

"Please!" Death pleaded, moving his hand towards Bill's mouth. "I'm not in the mood to go through all that again."

"What's going on?" Bill protested, becoming increasingly agitated. "What's happened to *them?*" he continued, turning towards his motionless friends. "Alex? Gordon? Why aren't they moving?"

Death looked at his clipboard and cleared his throat.

"I am sorry to inform you that your life on planet earth was terminated exactly 37.7 seconds ago."

"What?"

"And everyone calls *me* deaf," the visitor quipped. "I said that your life was terminated... I'm trying to tell you that you are dead, Mr Jones; as dead as a doornail, as the great Charles Dickens once remarked... dead... dead... dead." He stopped. "Sorry, that was probably a little bit insensitive, but I'm not in the best of moods."

Bill was shaking his head. "Dead?"

"That's right, Mr Jones. I'm sorry." Death paused and moved his head closer to Bill's, as though he was going to reveal a secret. "You *are* Mr Jones – Mr William Brian Jones – aren't you?" he whispered.

Bill nodded. "How do you know my name?"

"It's a name that will be etched on my memory for a long time to come, Mr Jones... believe me."

Bill moved in turn to each of his friends and looked into their eyes. He knew none of them was about to start laughing. It was clear that this was no game and he immediately comprehended the fact that he would not be able to rouse them from their current state. He stumbled towards the dining table and noticed the plate of chicken legs that Mr Gilmore had brought back from Gordon's wake – though, of course, it was, as we now know, in fact... *Bill's* wake. He shook his head, still in a state of bemusement. He knew the plate had not been there when he had started to act out his charade, but his mind was a whirl of thoughts, and that particular conundrum was soon replaced by another – one probably more pressing.

Bill did not notice the moment when Mr Gilmore arrived on the scene. The angel nodded at Death and peered over his glasses into his face, a glint in his eye.

"I see you have caught up with the right Mr Jones this time," he said with a grin. "This is *the* Mr Jones, isn't it?"

"Very funny," Death replied, folding his arms in defiance.

"And who are *you?*" Bill piped up, looking down at Mr Gilmore. "And how did you both get in? What's going on... I mean *really* going on? I can't be dead. I'm too young."

Death shook his head, feigning pity. "I'm sorry, Mr Jones. That's how it goes, I'm afraid."

"But I was feeling fine. There must be some mistake."

Mr Gilmore glanced at Death who offered a sheepish smile in return.

"Are you sure I'm dead?" Bill persevered. "You're sure you haven't got the wrong man? His name is Jones as well," he added, nodding at Gordon. "And he looked terrible tonight!"

Mr Gilmore turned and smiled at the lifeless Gordon, a figure of peace, curled up, now oblivious to what was going on around him. "Sweet dreams, Mr Jones," he whispered. "Sweet dreams, Mr *Gordon* Jones."

The angel then turned to Bill and smiled sympathetically.

"I'm sorry, Mr Jones. It's true. There's no mistake. Angels don't make mistakes," he added, flashing Death another playful grin.

"An angel?" an exasperated Bill questioned. "Did you say you were an angel?" He ran his eye down Mr Gilmore's suit and smiled. "Where are your wings?" he teased.

Mr Gilmore put his hands up. "I'll explain one day, Mr Jones, but, please, it's been a long day – even for one in eternity – and I think we should get going."

"Where to?"

Mr Gilmore grinned. "Where do you think, Mr Jones? I'm an angel, aren't I?"

"Heaven!" Bill exclaimed.

Mr Gilmore smiled again. "Perhaps you'd like to say cheerio to your friends."

Bill looked at Alex and began to finger the black and white scarf around his neck, a look of bemusement on his face. Then he turned to Gordon. He was the only one of the party whose eyes were closed. "Trust Gordon to fall asleep the moment I pop my clogs!" Bill muttered, shaking his head. "Poor old Gordon. He always misses the excitement."

Mr Gilmore took hold of Bill's arm.

"Are you ready, Mr Jones?"

Bill tentatively looked down at the hand now gripping his arm. He shook his head, still unable to fully comprehend the situation he now found himself in.

"Are we going straight away... right now?" he inquired. "How are we getting there?"

Mr Gilmore did not reply, but returned a warm smile. He looked at Death and nodded, and then raised his free arm, about to click his fingers.

"Hey! Hold on a minute."

It was a familiar voice. The angel recognised it immediately.

"And where do you think you're going with him, my dear Angel Gilmore?" Dumas sneered. "I think you'll find *this* one belongs to me," the demon added.

The angel relaxed his grip on Bill's arm. He sighed and closed his eyes, failing to notice the smug smile on the demon's face.

"Well?" Dumas persisted. "Have you any evidence to prove he belongs to you?"

A weary Mr Gilmore opened his eyes and looked pleadingly at Bill. "You don't happen to know anyone called Grace, do you?"

About the Author

Paul Wreyford started to write *What Happened After Mr Jones Died* 'a long time ago' but put it on hold 'too many times' to concentrate on his career as a newspaper journalist.

He is also the author of many non-fiction books, which reflect his love of Britain, history and literature.

Paul now lives with his wife and two children on the beautiful North Cornwall coast. When not writing books, he is busy penning sermons in his role as a lay preacher on the local Methodist circuit.

Other Christian Fiction Recommended by the Publisher

I, Messiah

Donald Southey

ISBN 978-1-907509-09-4

www.onwardsandupwards.org/i-messiah

A robot advanced enough to be aware of its own existence begins to ask questions about moral choices, as well as the origins and meaning of life. When the robot begins to suggest that religion is not illogical, its owner becomes concerned that there must be a fault in its software. Soon what started as a mere curiosity turns into an unexpected movement that spreads throughout the machine population.

The Lost Journey Homeward

Eve Bonham

ISBN 978-1-910197-57-8

www.onwardsandupwards.org/the-lost-journey-homeward

"The past three years seemed hollow and heartless, a reckless waste of her time and talents. She closed her mind to the image of home where life had been simple and love had existed, knowing she had lost the key to it. She could never go back."

"He was driving too fast, to put miles between him and all he loved, to get so far that he could not change his mind and they could not follow. The torrents of rainwater would wash out his tracks and, if he was lucky, eliminate all traces of his past."

A brother and sister – living in different countries – find their lives spiralling out of control. They are looking for love but finding heartache. Their journeys are different, but will they find the one who is waiting for them?

Available from all good bookshops.